ROBBI RENEE

SUMMER'S ECHO

Published by
BLACK ODYSSEY MEDIA

www.blackodyssey.net
Email: info@blackodyssey.net

This book is a work of fiction. Any references to events, real people, or real places are used fictitiously. Other names, characters, places, and events are products of the author's imagination, and any resemblance to actual events or places or persons, living or dead, is entirely coincidental.

SUMMER'S ECHO. Copyright © 2025 by ROBBI RENEE

Library of Congress Control Number: 2025902594

First Trade Paperback Printing: August 2025
ISBN: 978-1-957950-83-9
ISBN: 978-1-957950-84-6 (e-book)

Cover Design by Navi' Robins

To the extent that the image or images on the cover of this book depict a person or persons, such person or persons are merely models and are not intended to portray any character in the book.

All rights reserved. Black Odyssey Media, LLC | Dallas, TX.

This book or parts thereof may not be reproduced in any form, stored in a retrieval system, or transmitted in any form by any means—electronic, mechanical, photocopy, recording, or otherwise—without prior written permission of the publisher, excepting brief quotes or tags used in reviews, interviews, or complimentary promotion, and as permissible by United States of America copyright law.

10 9 8 7 6 5 4 3 2 1

Manufactured in the United States of America

Distributed by Kensington Publishing Corp.

The authorized representative in the EU for product safety and compliance is eucomply OU, Parnu mnt 139b-14, Apt 123
Tallinn, Berline 11317, hello@eucomplianceprtner.com

Dear Reader,

I want to thank you immensely for supporting Black Odyssey Media and our ongoing efforts to spotlight the diverse narratives of blossoming and seasoned storytellers. With every manuscript we acquire, we believe that it took talent, discipline, and remarkable courage to construct that story, flesh out those characters, and prepare it for the world. Debut or seasoned, our authors are the real heroes and heroines in *OUR* story. For them, we are eternally grateful.

Whether you are new to Robbi Renee or Black Odyssey Media, we hope that you are here to stay. Our goal is to make a lasting impact in the publishing landscape, one step at a time and one book at a time. As always, we welcome your feedback and kindly ask that you leave a review. For upcoming releases, announcements, submission guidelines, etc., please be sure to visit our website at www.blackodyssey.net or scan the QR code below. And remember, no matter where you are in your journey, the best of both worlds begins now!

Joyfully,

Shawanda "N'Tyse" Williams
Founder/Publisher

AUTHOR'S NOTE

I can't tell you how excited I am to finally share *Summer's Echo* with you! This story has been living in my heart for so long, and bringing it to life has been an emotional and deeply fulfilling journey.

At its core, *Summer's Echo* is a friends-to-lovers story—the kind that sneaks up on you, wrapping you in warmth and familiarity before you even realize it's happening. Summer and Echo's story is about finding your way back, about second chances, about the people who feel like home, no matter how much time has passed.

This book is for those who believe in slow dances under the stars, inside jokes that never get old, the kind of love that isn't just passionate but patient. This love story is simple, yet complicated; sweet, yet deeply romantic; and undeniably irresistible.

I hope you fall in love with Summer and Echo the way I did. Thank you for taking this journey with me and for believing in love stories that feel like fate.

Written with Love,
Robbi Renee

CHAPTER ONE

**Summer
October 2019**

MY CHILDHOOD CHURCH, Holy Trinity, carried whispers of memories in its aged, sacred walls. The countless Sundays I'd spent singing in the choir, watching my grandmother serve on the usher board and my mother work as the church secretary filled my heart with so much joy today. The stained-glass windows etched with biblical scenes casted a colorful pattern of light throughout the sanctuary. Today, it was classic yet romantically decorated for the wedding of my dreams. Guests would be greeted with a grand floral arch, large arrangements of roses, and pictures of the bride and groom scattered throughout the vestibule. Vividly brilliant ruby-red and blush roses beautifully arranged in towering brass vases and ten-arm candelabras framing the altar exuded the perfect ember for an early evening wedding. The stunning ten-foot columns cascading with greenery and sparkling string lights was the focal point where the bride and groom would stand in just a few hours.

My fiancé, Deshawn, and two hundred of our closest family and friends had packed the cathedral waiting for me to saunter down the matching sapphire aisle runner adorned with our initials, S&D, written in a fancy script. The nerves, anticipation, and months of planning to become Mrs. Deshawn Micah Towns were finally over. The wedding was absolutely beautiful. Or at least I contemplated that it was, since I—the bride—wasn't in attendance. That October day was perfect for a fall wedding, but just not perfect enough for me to marry Deshawn.

My eyes were clouded with tears as I drove down the familiar winding road then pulled my SUV into the mostly empty parking lot of Camp Summit Quest. Sliding the gear into park, I shook my head, dropping it to the steering wheel, stunned by the fact that my wedding was supposed to start in exactly ten minutes, and I was nowhere to be found.

Gazing down at the gorgeous handmade wedding invitation, I read the words: *You are cordially invited to the wedding ceremony of Summer Sierra Knight and Deshawn Micah Towns on October 26, 2019, at 5 o'clock in the evening.* Yet here I was, sitting in my truck in a place I had frequented from the time I was ten years old until I was a teenager, pondering, *Summer, what the hell are you doing, girl?*

I peered in the rearview mirror and was disappointed in the reflection staring back at me. Puffy, red eyes slightly concealed by dark-rimmed glasses. Shoulder-length, wavy sewn-in hair I'd stressed over for months before the wedding was pulled into a messy bun. I looked *exactly* like what I was going through.

The white sweatshirt with *Bride* bedazzled across the front and matching joggers clung to my curves—a far cry from the Casablanca Bridal gown I'd said yes to a few months ago. The white A-line silhouette wedding gown embellished with delicately beaded lace appliques and Swarovski crystals should be draped over my body right now. The dress was stunning...perfect even. I giggled to myself, considering the *ooh*s and *aah*s I'd anticipated from my wedding guests at the first sight of me walking down the aisle. I would've been a beguiling bride, but…

"Not today. Maybe one day, but not today," I whispered, my throat tight as the afternoon sun glared through the car window. The constant blaring of my cell phone heightened my misery. Mama, Raqi, Trinity, Brooke. Everybody was calling me, worried, searching for the runaway bride.

Early this morning, the sun had poured through my bedroom window, brightening every corner, but I was already awake to greet it. I couldn't sleep… Actually, sleep had eluded me for weeks, leaving me restless and lost in my thoughts. My phone had buzzed constantly on the nightstand, each text message delivering well wishes for the big day. I'd let out a quiet sigh, wishing I shared in the merriment. *Melancholy* was the best way to describe my mood.

Trying to cling to normalcy, I'd brewed my coffee and read my daily devotion just as I always did. I was on autopilot, dressing and packing my bag with calculated movements. Walking to my car, I'd waved at my neighbor across the street just like any other day. I halted when she'd happily muttered, "See you in a few hours, the future Mrs. Towns." I'd flashed her a closed-mouth fake smile.

Sliding into my car, nervous anxiety clawed at my core, sharp and relentless. I was supposed to be nervous, right? Because it wasn't just any other day—it was my wedding day. I pulled out of my driveway and stopped at the red light heading out of my subdivision. My phone chimed again with a special tone—Deshawn's tone.

Shawn: Good morning, babe. You up? Is that attitude any better?

I'd stared at the message, my thumb hovering over the keyboard, the frustration from last night still lingering like a dull ache behind my ribs. Instead of actually listening when I'd told him how I was feeling—my worries, my fears, the uncertainty sitting like a stone in my chest, he'd dismissed it all as me just having an attitude. Like I was being dramatic. Like my feelings didn't matter. I rolled my eyes and tapped out the bare minimum response.

Me: 👍

That was petty of me, but right now, I didn't care. A few seconds later, his reply popped up.

Shawn: Good. I'll see you soon.

No *I love you.* No *Are you okay?* Not even a hint of concern about why I might have felt off in the first place. Not even, *I can't wait to see you at the altar.* Just *Good.* Our wedding was in just a few hours. This should've been the time where I felt excited, giddy, and in love, but instead, all I felt was a growing knot in my stomach. And I couldn't tell if it was just pre-wedding nerves…or something deeper.

I stared blankly, replaying our simple exchange in my mind, stuck in the moment until the sharp honk of a horn behind me jolted me back to reality. I blinked, shaking off the haze, and pressed the gas, making a left out of my neighborhood onto the main street. The plan was simple: Head across town for my early morning wedding day hair appointment, stick to my schedule, keep the day moving forward. That was the plan. But somewhere along the way, my SUV veered in the opposite direction. I wasn't even sure when I made the choice—or if it was ever really a choice at all.

The voice of Koryn Hawthorne spilled through the speakers, her soulful melody a quiet guide as I drove directionless in thought but instinctively following a road I knew by heart. Her words about falling, about grace, about God loving us even when we stumbled cut straight through me. My hands tightened on the wheel as tears pooled in my eyes. The lyrics didn't just touch me. They pierced with fear and a peculiar sense of freedom. And I wasn't sure which one scared me more.

My phone rang, shattering the moment and bringing me back to reality. Glancing at the clock, I saw it was three-ten—ten minutes past when I was supposed to arrive at the church. A wave of nausea rolled through me as a storm of nerves raged in my gut. Every second that passed was another reminder of what I was about to do—*or not do*. I couldn't get dolled up for him, couldn't fake the joy or force the smiles. I couldn't walk down that aisle pretending that our relationship was something that it was not. A hallow pain stretched through me as I whispered the truth aloud to no one but myself.

"I can't marry him."

Ignoring the constant phone calls, I stepped out of my SUV, checking the surroundings. I seamlessly navigated through the overgrown brush to get to my favorite spot at Camp Summit Quest. The pathway was hidden, tucked just beyond a curtain of overgrown oak trees. Most people would pass it by without a second glance, but not me. It had been my sanctuary every summer as a kid—a place where I could let my imagination run free. But today, it was my escape. My solace from the noise of the world, the pressure of expectations. It was deep into the campgrounds, not frequented by many on a cool fall day. The old hollowed tree near the end of the path came into view. It hadn't changed much— moss covered and weathered but still sturdy, and the keeper of so many of my secrets. It offered the ideal place to think, to breathe, to mourn what I'd left behind. Who was I kidding? This was a place for me to hide.

I treaded through the tangled brush until I reached the hidden hilltop—a secret haven overlooking a man-made creek. With every step, my heart sagged a little more, burdened by the thoughts I carried. I inhaled deeply, and without meaning to, the corners of my mouth curved into something resembling a smile.

The air up here always smelled like clean, fresh linen and sweet blossoms, lightening my burden, if only for a moment. I dusted off the stump, taking in my surroundings, gazing at the old tree as if it might remember me after all these years. It held pieces of my younger self, sacred stories that disappeared with the whisper of the wind.

A subtle breeze threaded through the trees, causing dry, brittle leaves to crackle. My eyes darted around as if someone could find me in the quiet cocoon of the park. Only one person in my life knew this spot was my secret hideaway, and he lived a thousand miles away, so there was no real threat of being found. I got what I wanted; to be alone with this excruciating pang in my chest. The kind of pain, I imagined, that only came from making a choice I knew would change everything.

5:32 p.m.
The resounding ringing from the phone startled me. My heart plummeted to my feet at the sight of his name on the screen. "Shit. Shawn," I whispered, releasing the phone from my grasp as if it was suddenly boiling hot. Waiting for the call to go to voicemail, I immediately pressed the message icon to see if he'd left one.

He did. *"Baby, where are you? Are you okay? What the fuck, Summer? How could you do this to me?"*

"I'm sorry," I whispered into the stillness, the words catching in my throat. "I'm so sorry." I kept repeating the words over and over, like I was rehearsing for the inevitable conversation with my fiancé. Deshawn and I had so much to talk about, and we would—soon. But not now. Not today.

"I can't marry him," I cried, sharing my secrets again with the wind. My voice trembled, barely louder than a whisper. The words felt like a boulder weighing heavy on my chest every time I said them, as if saying them aloud made the situation more real. Images of the day I'd left behind at the church flooded my mind—

my family and friends, the elegantly decorated reception hall, my stunning bridesmaids, and most vivid of all, my loving parents.

"My parents," I yelped, the realization riddling me like bullets. "Teresa Knight is going to kill me." The thought of my parents' reaction—my mother's disappointment—brought a fresh wave of thunderous sobs. The tears spilled freely, blurring my vision, clouding my lenses just enough for the beauty around me to dissolve into nothing.

"They are going to be so upset," I mumbled through hiccupping breaths, attempting to quell the tears. All of the time and money they'd spent—gone, just like that. Frustration bubbled up inside me, and I yanked the glasses from my face, tossing them onto a small pile of leaves. What the hell was I even doing here? Alone. On my damn wedding day.

"Stupid, stupid, stupid," I fussed at only myself.

My brown eyes throbbed, swollen and red from crying. Without my glasses, everything was a blurry mess—a perfect reflection of my own fucked-up emotions. I buried my face in my hands, the burden of my choices pressing down on me with unbearable intensity. The tears didn't stop, and the pain in my chest felt endless, but beneath the sorrow and guilt, I knew that I'd made the right decision. As if sent by the heavens, a divine kaleidoscope-colored creature—a butterfly—fluttered down and landed softly beside me. It lingered there, delicate and unassuming, as if sensing I needed a friend. I let a faint smile slip through, grateful for its quiet companionship.

My gaze shifted to my phone, its screen glowing with another call from Deshawn. His name flashed a few more times, and with deep sighs, I declined the call…again, and then again. The silence settled around me, brooding but oddly comforting as if the butterfly's graceful stillness had absorbed some of my pain.

6:07 p.m.

I shook my head, the thought nagging at me: The happy couple should've been man and wife by now. A painful tightness settled in my lungs as I pictured Deshawn standing at the altar in his custom-fit white-and-black striped tuxedo jacket, looking every bit as striking as I knew he would. There was no denying it: Deshawn Towns was fine.

The first time I'd laid eyes on him at a day party in Atlanta during SpelHouse homecoming, I'd literally drooled, mouth hanging open like a fool. His rugged jawline, framed by a slight shadow stubble, added to his allure when he'd flashed me that devastating smile. He was beautiful in a way that made my pulse quicken. Thick and brown-sugar sweet, Deshawn stood six feet tall with broad shoulders and a commanding build wrapped in flawless dark chocolate skin. Delicious, rock-hard, slightly bowed legs pleasantly filled every pair of pants like they were made just for his body. His bold, deep-set, slanted eyes, a shade so deep they nearly mirrored the color of his skin, seemed to hold the best-kept secrets. His low-cut, wavy Caesar always looked fresh from the barbershop. And what can I say about his lips? Soft, full, with an easy curve that triggered my senses into overdrive. But his arms were my favorite. Goodness gracious, those damn arms were sculpted pieces of art. The intricately designed half-sleeve tattoo accentuated the crushingly powerful perfection. That muthafucker was sexy as hell with an air of mystery that had hooked me from the start.

The relationship felt like a whirlwind at first. After that first night in Atlanta, Shawn seamlessly became a fixture in my life. Weekly phone calls quickly turned into daily check-ins, and casual lunch meetings during the week became quiet weekend dinners. He wasn't much of a romantic, but I found comfort in the simplicity of being around him. On unpredictable, high-stress days, I discovered a deep craving for the steadiness he provided—

the basics felt like a refuge. There were no dramatic highs or lows, no surprises, just easy predictability. For Shawn, romance was working dinners in his office or reorganizing his Excel budget spreadsheet while encouraging me to do the same.

After a long-time corporate career as an advertising executive, I'd recently become an entrepreneur, starting my own creative design firm, and Deshawn was an attorney in the general counsel's office of a large company. When we were not gallivanting to galas or striving to be a power couple professionally, we enjoyed traveling and exploring our mutual love for food and wine. He'd never been married, no children, loved his mama, and did I say fine as hell? The kind of man most women dreamed about. On paper, he was perfect—*we* were picture perfect. But no matter how flawless he seemed, he wasn't my dream. He was *never* my dream. And that was something I couldn't continue to sweep under the rug.

I let out a harsh exhale through puffy lips, tears burning hot against my skin. My mind swarmed with relentless and overwhelming memories of the man I'd nearly vowed my life to, each one a tangled mix of joy and pain. The good, the bad—each moment played out in my mind like a never-ending reel, refusing to let me find an iota of peace.

"Heffa, you didn't show up for your wedding… Ain't no peace for you for the foreseeable future," I muttered to myself, my voice thick with frustration and self-loathing. But as I sat there, raw and shaken, the question burned inside me: Had I just walked away from my future or saved myself from the inevitable? The truth hurt, but it was *my* truth—*my* cross to bear.

7:13 p.m.

Daylight savings was upon us, and the days were slipping away faster than I could catch them. It was already starting to get dark earlier, and the park was no exception. The overhead lamps scattered along the walking trails and parking lot flickered to life, casting a soft glow over the green expanse. The cool breeze brushed against my skin, sharper now than before—chillier than I was prepared for because I had no plan. I had no place to go. My parents would welcome me home, but I wasn't ready for their questions and disappointing stares. I'm sure my condo was the first place everyone had looked, and Deshawn's apartment—basically my apartment since I stayed there so much lately—was definitely not an option.

"I could probably go to Hailee's," I thought aloud. But even as the words left my lips, I knew that would be a *no*, too. Hailee Burns, one of my best friends since middle school, would just call our other friends, Brooke Thompson and Trinity Clay, if they weren't already at her house—and soon, all three of my best friends would be crowded around me, filling my cup like they always did. They wouldn't judge me, I knew that much, but I wasn't in the mood for their reassurances or advice. I needed silence, space to just…think…breathe. I owed everyone an explanation. My family. My friends. And most importantly, Deshawn. But at this moment, the only truth I knew for sure was the one that had been circling my mind like a mantra: *I can't marry him.*

With a final burst of fiery orange, the sun dipped below the horizon, leaving the inky sky. My gaze swept across the picturesque scene, watching nightfall cover the rolling greens like a blanket. The darkness swallowed the distance like the lingering anguish eating me alive. The bushes shook unexpectedly, a quick and frantic rustle that sent a jolt through me. Clutching my chest, my heart raced as I spun around, bracing for the worst. But when I looked, nothing was there. I let out a shaky sigh of relief, forcing myself to reposition and refocus on my current dilemma: Where on earth was I going to go tonight? Checking my phone again, I scrolled through a list of nearby hotels. My fingers trembled from exhaustion and the autumn chill. The heaviness of my decision depleted me. I was drained, both mentally and physically. Sleep was what I needed right now. Tomorrow would be the reckoning, demanding much more from me than I could fathom tonight.

The rustling started again, faint initially, but I ignored it this time, assuming it was just the cool wind stirring the leaves like before. Tired, my body slumped forward, the tension in my shoulders pulling me down as I pressed my palms into my forehead. The sound grew nearer. I pinched the crease between my eyes to quell the merciless pounding beating like a drum.

"Sunshine."

Surprisingly, I didn't startle at the familiar sound behind me. I didn't need to turn around to recognize that voice—the smooth baritone timbre that lived in my dreams, pleasantly haunting me with its unmistakable familiarity.

"What's good, baby girl? Are you okay?" the voice uttered, hitting me like a wave, crashing over my senses with a combination of recognition and relief. The air was cool, but a warmth coursed through my veins. It was as if time stood still for a moment. My breath caught in my throat, and my eyelids fluttered shut. He lived there. I could see his smile when I closed my eyes. Was this real? Was he here, or was my exhausted mind playing tricks on me?

"E, what are you doing here?"

My expression felt composed, but my breastbone rose and fell in rapid succession, shallow breaths betraying the calm I tried to maintain. The years between us slowly unraveled in my head. With each labored, ragged breath, the memories tumbled over the next like a song stuck on repeat. I was frozen at the mere whisper of my name. The name he gave me. The name reserved only for him. I was never *Summer* to him, but instead his *Sunshine*, his *Sun*, and him? He was mine—*Summer's Echo*.

CHAPTER TWO

Echo
October 2019

I STARED AT Summer, taking in the sight of her red tear-stained eyes, puffy cheeks, and swollen lips. It broke something inside me. But then, there was that smile—the faint curve at the corner of her mouth. That familiar, bittersweet smile sent a chill down my spine, awakening memories I desperately wanted to bury, but they resurrected every time I saw her face—shit, heard the mention of her name. She was here, in the flesh. After years of minimal contact, punctuated by social media stalking and distant updates through friends, I saw her again for the first time last year at a mutual friend's wedding reception. Her boyfriend—now fiancé—had been glued to her side, a quiet confirmation that the closeness we once shared had long since faded. But here we were. Time had passed, lives had changed, but for just a second, this felt like an old, familiar rhythm. But in reality, nothing was the same. So yeah, Summer's question was valid. What the hell was I doing here?

When I boarded a red-eye flight to St. Louis last night, I couldn't believe I was going through with this. Attending Summer Knight's wedding was exactly what I swore I wouldn't—shit, I couldn't—do. The thought of witnessing her promise forever to another man…take another man's last name felt like a slow death. And yet, this morning, I stood in my childhood bedroom knotting a tie and rehearsing how I'd sit in the church and pretend like my world wasn't ripping at the seams.

"This is bullshit. Why am I torturing myself?" I'd mumbled, tugging the tie tighter than necessary. Since I was seventeen years old, she'd been mine. My best friend, my confidant, my homie. But life—and the life-altering mistake that changed everything had reshaped us—twisted our paths in ways I never saw coming. The distance between us had grown jagged and unyielding, so vast that now she was about to become somebody else's wife.

"You look nice," my sister, Sadie, had whispered from the doorway. I smiled, extending my arms to receive her hug. When I'd arrived last night, the house was quiet. My parents were in Chicago visiting a sick relative, and I didn't realize Sadie was home. She was the youngest of the Abara family, still living at home while attending college.

"My Sadie. How are you, baby sister?" I'd crooned, excited to see her after almost six months. I lived in Los Angeles, so my trips home were few and far between because my siblings preferred to visit me in the City of Angels.

"I'm good. Surprised to see you here," she'd said, stepping into my open arms. "I thought you weren't coming." She'd raised her eyebrows in question, though her expression showed no genuine shock.

I'd shrugged, forcing a chuckle. "I guess I enjoy torturing myself."

"Maybe it's for the best," she'd said softly. "Seeing her take this step may push you to do the same—to find your one true love."

I stood almost a foot taller than my sister, so I'd peered down at her still wrapped in my arms as she gazed up at me. My dark brown eyes locked on her pretty hazel ones, mirroring our mother's. My stare was heavy and filled with angst, but I'd smiled then kissed the top of her head. "I already found my one true love,"

I'd said, my voice steady and laced with quiet conviction. "One summer in 2004."

Echo
That One Summer in 2004

I wanted to make a good first impression at Camp Summit Quest, so I made sure my jean shorts were ironed to perfection and my yellow Polo shirt was crisp. My hair was freshly tapered under the Chicago Bears hat, and I was ready—at least on the outside. Two months ago, my father had announced that he'd accepted a professorship at Washington University in St. Louis. I wasn't just upset—I was pissed. We'd moved three times since I'd started sixth grade, and Chicago was the first place I'd actually called home. I'd been there since freshman year of high school, and the thought of moving the summer before my senior year? Ridiculous.

We'd been in St. Louis for nearly a month, and I was already missing everything about the Windy City—my school, my neighborhood, and most of all, my friends. When we'd first moved to Chicago, I'd told myself I wouldn't bother making new friends since I figured we'd move again in a year anyway. But after a year, my dad got promoted, my parents bought a house, and for once, I thought we'd finally settle down.

Our old neighborhood was packed with younger kids, so my siblings made friends in no time. It wasn't until I discovered the neighborhood basketball court that I found my people. That's where I met my best friend, Marlo Hill. He and a bunch of other guys were always talking about this sleepaway camp called Camp Wildwood Adventures. I thought it sounded a bit childish at first—what teenager still goes to camp? To my surprise, a lot of them did. So, for the past three summers, I'd headed to Camp Wildwood with my friends.

Now, though, I was missing out on our last summer before senior year. I tried begging my dad to let me go back one more time, but he just gave me the look—a blank narrowed-eyed glare. The look that told me to shut up while I was ahead. Camp Wildwood sat on the edge of Milwaukee, just over an hour from our home in Chicago. But for my father, the nearly six-hour drive from St. Louis was out of the question. So here I was, stuck with Camp Summit Quest in the hill country of Missouri instead. Supposedly, it's like Wildwood, but somehow, I had a hard time believing it would measure up.

One thing's for sure, Camp Wildwood Adventures and Camp Summit Quest weren't your typical get-rid-of-the-kids-for-the-summer camps. They were competitive, focused on prepping us for college and the real world. Leadership workshops, team-building exercises, the works were the foundation of the experience. And we had a ton of fun, too.

As we pulled off the highway, we were greeted by the Camp Summit Quest sign carved into a big wooden fixture. The long, narrow road ahead led us to a vibrant, nature-filled retreat. The camp was nestled in a picturesque lakeside setting surrounded by towering trees. It seriously looked like something straight out of a postcard. I nodded. I had to admit, I was low-key impressed.

"Echo, this may be better than Camp Wildwood," my mother said in her thick Nigerian accent. The joy in her tone was evident.

I nodded, unsure if I agreed with her, but muttered, "Yeah, mum," not wanting to get into it. As we got closer, I started noticing the hustle and bustle of the first day—campers everywhere, and more importantly, the fine girls in their khaki shorts and light blue t-shirts. Their uniforms fit their curves like a glove, and I couldn't help but perk up.

Dad pulled our SUV into a parking space in front of the information area. I slowly climbed out of the car, stretching my long legs. I'd shot up four inches over the past year, rounding out at six-foot-two. Glancing around, I took a deep breath, trying to psych myself up for this new adventure.

"You'll find your way," my father said, rounding the truck to join me on the passenger side. He was always a man of few words.

I nodded. Making new friends wasn't my concern—I was used to being the new kid on the block—but I missed my crew from Wildwood. I missed the pranks, hazing the incoming counselors, and sneaking away to the senior counselors' swim party. There was something about those summers I wasn't ready to let go of.

Glancing around, I digested the space. Large trees surrounded the campgrounds, their branches swaying gently in the light summer breeze. Wooden-frame buildings were sporadically placed throughout. In the center of what appeared to be the campers' lodging area was a grassy clearing lined with picnic tables under a pavilion, a slide, and old wooden swings. It looked more like a park instead of a camp. Squinting against the sun, I caught sight of a young woman hurrying toward us, her pace brisk and purposeful.

"Hello, and welcome to Camp Summit Quest. We sometimes shorten it to Camp Quest," the petite, fair-skinned woman exclaimed, her voice practically dripping with cheer as she pumped my parents' hands like she was trying to win a contest. "I'm Marissa, Camp Quest class of 2000 and the dean of counselors," she added with exaggerated pride before turning her overly enthusiastic gaze on me. "And you are?" Her chipper tone made me wince internally.

I arched a brow, barely suppressing an eye roll. *Dean of counselors...okay.* Clearing my throat, I replied, "Echo. Echo Abara." My tone was measured, contrasting her sugary enthusiasm.

"Welcome, Echo Abara." She chuckled. "We're excited to have you here from Wildwood." Her vibrancy didn't falter for a second, and I forced a polite smile in response.

My artificial smile melted into something genuine as my eyes locked on a gorgeous girl who seemed to light up the space around her without even realizing it. Her caramel skin glowed under the sunlight, and her curves stopped me in my tracks. A delicate floral scent lingered in the air as she walked by, teasing my senses and leaving me completely dumbstruck. I couldn't help but notice how her denim jumper fit her just right, hugging her in all the perfect ways without looking overly tight like so many of the other girls who passed by. Her straight hair swayed with every step, bouncing lightly as she turned to flash me a fake smile. But even that small gesture hit me like a jolt, leaving me standing there wondering who she was.

"Summer, I expect you to be in uniform before the welcome event," Marissa called over her shoulder, the chipper tone a bit sterner.

"I'm going to change now, Marissa," the pretty girl sang, rolling her eyes with a playful smirk.

Summer, I thought. Yeah, that name fit her perfectly. Bright, warm, and impossible to ignore.

Marissa turned her focus back to me. "Alright, Echo, say your goodbyes, and I'll take you to your lodge," she said, pressing her clipboard to her chest.

Her voice snapped me out of my daze because I was still focused on Summer. Marissa stared at me, her eyes silently signaling for me to hurry up.

I hugged my mother tightly, then turned to my little sister, Sadie, who had cried nonstop until my parents finally let her tag along for the ride. At just eight years old, she had no problem making it clear that I was, hands-down, her favorite person. Squatting to her level, I planted a soft kiss on her forehead, and she immediately threw her arms around my shoulders, holding on like she never wanted to let go.

"Write to me, okay?" I said, my voice gentle.

"Okay. I promise," she whined, her tone thick with reluctance, as though even the thought of me leaving was too much for her to take.

Standing, I shook my dad's hand. He nodded, and I nodded back. That was all we needed—no hugs, just a nod of respect and understanding. Obi Abara wasn't exactly the emotional type, but I knew what that nod meant. It said everything he didn't have to. With one last glance at my family, I turned and followed Marissa, ready—or at least as ready as I could be—for whatever this new chapter at Camp Summit Quest had in store.

The counselors' lodge was way better than the setup at Camp Wildwood. This place felt more like a cool apartment—four people to a room, a shared bathroom, and an open living area where we could just chill. When Marissa introduced me to my roommates—Maxell, Kyle, and Bryant—I immediately felt at ease. They were a lot like me: into rap music, especially Jay-Z; crazy about sports, specifically basketball; and always had an eye for pretty girls. It didn't take long to feel like I could vibe with them.

Marissa let us know that we had about fifteen minutes to meet in the common area, so I headed to my room. On the bottom bunk, I saw an envelope with my name written on it, two pairs of khaki shorts, and a few camp shirts neatly folded. I quickly changed and caught up with my new roommates, falling into step with them as we made our way out. Whatever was coming next, I hoped I was ready.

The outdoor auditorium buzzed with energy, filled with counselors fitted in matching camp gear. Up front, several senior counselors took turns speaking, reviewing the rules and procedures for the summer. My attention, however, wandered as my gaze darted around the space, taking in the scene. Counselors laughed and hugged, catching up like old friends—most of them probably hadn't seen each other since last summer.

And then there was me. Definitely the new guy. Curious glances and subtle whispers of *Who's he? Where's he from?* floated in my direction. I brushed off the questioning stares, determined not to let them bother me—at least, until I saw her. *Summer.*

She was sitting a few rows over, eyeing me as another girl leaned close, whispering something in her ear. Summer's reaction was typical for a girl—she rolled her eyes dramatically—and I couldn't help myself. I laughed loud enough for her to notice. For the briefest second, our eyes locked, and something about her made all my worries about being the new kid fade into the background. I walked with my roommates as they introduced me to a few of the other guys. We'd just finished reviewing the schedule and getting our camper group assignments, so everyone was hanging around, waiting for the next set of instructions. I exchanged daps with a couple of the guys, starting to feel a little more at ease. But just as I was settling in, I heard Marissa call my name.

"Echo, can you come here for a second?" Marissa asked, waving me over from the front of the space.

Since I was into drawing and graphic design, I was assigned to co-lead the Quest Creative Crew. Marissa described it as the group for campers who lived and breathed creativity, finding expression through every form of art imaginable. I was excited to sketch by the lake and build unique fixtures from materials we'd gather from the woods. Art was like breathing for me, and I was ready to help these kids craft their next masterpiece.

"Hey, Marissa," I said, huffing as I jogged over after crossing the quad.

She shot me an awkward look and then turned toward *her.* Summer was so damn pretty. Her shoulder-length hair was now pulled into a high ponytail, showing off her silky skin, sprinkled with the cutest freckles at the peaks of her cheeks. She had doelike, dark brown eyes framed by clear glasses, and when the sun hit them just right, a hint of hazel was revealed. Even under the t-shirt and khaki shorts, Summer was thick.

"Summer, this is Echo. He's here from St. Louis, and it's his first year at Camp Quest as a senior counselor. I expect you to show him the ropes," Marissa instructed.

I grinned with my hand extended to greet her, but to my surprise, Summer frowned. "Show him the ropes?" she repeated, clearly not happy. "What do you mean?" She didn't even try to erase the scowl from her pretty face.

"Every year, you say that you need help with the Creative Crew, and Echo's your guy. He started a computer art class thingy or something like that at his last camp," Marissa said, continuing her introduction as if my résumé needed more padding.

"It was actually a computer-aided drafting class," I corrected, unable to hide the big, proud grin spreading across my face. "I taught campers how to draw objects on the computer using a software program."

Summer's sharp gaze snapped from me to Marissa, her expression shifting faster than I could process. "Yeah, okay, that's cool and all," she said, her tone laced with impatience, "but I thought Trinity was helping me this year." She narrowed her eyes slightly.

"Trinity is on swimmer duty this year," Marissa shot back. "Now, Summer Knight, meet Echo Abara. I trust that you two will work together to make this summer unforgettable for your campers," she said, nodded firmly, then walked away.

Summer's grimace was growing, and it was starting to piss me off. She didn't even know me, yet she looked at me like I'd stolen her iPod or something. "I pretty much already have the activities scheduled for the campers, so..." her voice trailed off, and she shrugged. "I guess you can just follow my lead."

A soft snicker slipped through my lips. "Nah, Summer Moon... That's not how this works."

She rolled her eyes so hard it was a wonder they didn't get stuck. Her arms folded tight across her chest, begging my pardon. "My name is Summer. Not Summer Moon, not Sunny Day, not Midsummer's Night Dream, or any other stupid joke you can come up with about my name. Trust me, I've heard it all. If you can't refer to me as such, then I suggest you find another assignment," she shot back, not backing down.

And honestly...I loved that shit.

I stepped closer, towering over her petite frame. Biting the corner of my lip, amusement flickered across my face. I was already looking forward to fucking with her all summer long. Leaning down, I whispered, "I wasn't joking about your name, just pointing out how bright you shine...like the sun."

I heard her breath hitch as she swallowed hard, pushing her glasses farther up on her nose. Her fan of curly lashes fluttered while she blinked rapidly. "Now, Summer, I'm ready to follow your lead. Show me the way."

CHAPTER THREE

Summer
October 2019

ECHO HONOR ABARA was my best friend—shit, my best-kept secret. I willed my paralyzed limbs to steadily turn, to face the voice that had pranced in my memories for far too long. My glasses were still smeared with dried tears, distorting the image before me, but I didn't need clarity to recognize him. The stretch of his long, lean frame was forever embossed into my psyche, a silhouette that time could never erase.

But it wasn't his body that had me captivated. It was the quiet intensity of his eyes. Echo watched me in silence, his gaze soft yet piercing—the kind of look that had always unnerved me. Even as a teenager, he possessed a subtle forcefulness. His unspoken power provided him the ability to see past all my defenses and straight into my soul. Echo wasn't just looking at me, he was reading me, peeling back every layer without uttering a single word. Somehow, he left me feeling both vulnerable and safe all at once.

His velvet pools followed my slight movements with a calm and deliberate focus. Words were unnecessary. The silence between us was louder than any conversation we could have aloud—harboring secrets and speaking truths that language could never fully capture. I shook my head, attempting to dispel the image of him that felt both surreal and all too real. It had to be a dream, a beautiful hallucination. There was no way Echo Abara was standing here, at Camp Quest, at our spot.

How did he find me? How did he know I'd come here? The questions swirled, unanswered, in the back of my mind.

"Echo," I stammered, his name sticking in my throat. "Wha– What's good? What are you doing here?" I stood frozen, realizing this, in fact, wasn't a dream. My best friend, the one person who knew my heart better than anyone, was standing before me—a real flesh-and-blood human. It had been about year—twelve long, agonizing months since I'd last seen him.

Echo paused, tilting his head slightly, his narrowed eyes searching mine, always able to decipher my unspoken words. "Everybody's looking for you, Sun," he said softly, the words laced with compassion.

I swallowed hard, nodding. "But you…you knew where to find me." The realization sent a flush of warmth to my cheeks. "How did you know I'd come here?" I blinked rapidly, trying my best to see him clearly through foggy glasses and the haze clouding my thoughts.

"It didn't take long to figure it out. This has always been your hideaway—our spot. Your safe place." Echo chuckled, a low, soothing sound that tugged at my heart. "For weeks during that one perfect summer, this place was our solace. Then it became our Saturday getaway when our parents drove us crazy during senior year." His voice carried a warmth that made the memories feel close enough to touch. "So, I couldn't think of any other place you would want to be…under the circumstances," he added, his tone gentle, cautious.

With hesitant steps, Echo closed the distance between us, his hands buried deep in the pockets of his suit pants. It was as if he was anchoring himself against the pull we both seemed to feel, a gravity neither of us could name.

"Summer, are you okay?" he asked, concern etching every handsome line on his face. His voice was steady, but the crease in his brow revealed a deeper worry. "I'm…everyone is worried about you."

I nodded, but didn't answer his question. I couldn't—not yet. "Did anybody follow you, E? Did you tell anyone I was here?" My words spilled out shaky as I glanced over his shoulder, scanning the trail, expecting an angry procession of family members.

"Nah. Come on now," he said, shaking his head. "You know I wouldn't do that to you. Your parents' spot is basically Find Summer headquarters. I snuck away once I realized where you'd be."

Echo moved closer to me, unsure of my state, but his steps betrayed his uncertainty. He carefully studied my face, searching, almost pleading, for any clues of what was circling through my head. When he finally reached me, he gently cupped my chin, his touch featherlight but purposeful. His thumb grazed my cheek, nearly drawing the truth straight from my soul like a sorcerer. It was a gesture so familiar—so much like the Echo I remembered—that I nearly broke under its spell.

"Sun," he said, his voice cracking just a little, "you need to call your parents, or I can call them for you. They're worried sick. Can I tell them you're okay—just let them know you're safe?"

Unshed tears welled up as I buried my face in the palms of my hands. The mention of my parents sent a sharp ache through my chest. It started subtly, like a faint buzzing under my skin, but within seconds, the sensation grew louder. The soft whimpering I tried to contain escaped my lips; the sobs tore through the silence, loud and unsettling. My heart pounded violently, slamming against my ribs, the rhythm erratic and out of control. It was happening. The magnitude of my situation finally shattered the fragile calm I'd been clinging to all day, releasing a wave of panic that erupted deep within me. Unable to speak, I leaned into the warmth of his hands, letting them cradle the heaviness of my despair.

Through the chaos, his quiet, comforting voice whispered calmly, "Breathe. Just breathe, Sunshine." Following his lead, finally, I nodded, giving him permission to make the phone call. Echo tilted his head slightly, his expression softening as he reached for his phone. I watched as he dialed, my heart heavy but grateful, knowing that for a moment, I didn't have to carry this alone.

When I'd made the decision to basically run away this morning, I didn't pause to consider my parents: their worry, their heartbreak, the gnawing fear as the minutes ticked by, and their daughter—their baby girl—was nowhere to be found. Making my parents proud had always been my life's mission, but in this moment, I was certain I had failed. The weight of Oliver and Teresa's disappointment pressed heavily on my heart. My chest tightened as guilt clawed at me, but Echo's calm presence kept me grounded. I studied his face, trying to piece together what he was doing here while hearing the heartbreak in my mother's raspy tone. Immediately, I felt myself shrink, retreating into the self-conscious little girl I thought I'd left behind.

Summer
That One Summer in 2004

It was a sweltering hot Saturday morning in June, the kind where the heat clung to your skin even before you've stepped outside. Our eighties ranch-style home sat on a cul-de-sac in a quaint mostly Black neighborhood. The cinnamon-colored brick with chestnut-brown shutters was shaded by the mature oak tree in the front yard where little pig-tailed girls jumped double Dutch and sweat-laced boys tossed a basketball in a makeshift hoop.

I groaned as the sun peeked through my window, its unwelcomed warmth dragging me from the bed I had no desire to leave. Regret hit me like a ton of bricks. Why had I stayed out so late at the midnight drive-in with my friends watching *Training Day*? Then again, Denzel Washington was worth every minute. Still, I was paying the price today as I wrestled with my sluggish body.

Lifting the blinds, I rolled my eyes. Sure, the neighborhood kids were cute, but their boisterous cackles creeping through my window were getting on my last nerve. With a sigh, I rolled out of bed, catching a blurry glimpse of my reflection in the dresser mirror. I slid on my glasses to get a closer look. Time for my daily round of self-criticism. I stood there with my hair wrapped in a satin scarf, wearing an old New Edition t-shirt and yellow panties. Carefully, I unraveled the scarf from my head, finger-combing my relaxed hair, allowing it to fall loose around my face, brushing my shoulders. I loved the new auburn-brown hue that complemented my smooth caramel skin and coffee-colored eyes perfectly. For a moment, I smiled wide, admiring my dimples, which pierced the centers of my cheeks.

But, as usual, I studied the things that I hated. Okay, maybe *hate* was a strong word, but I focused on the things I strongly disliked—my glasses, large breasts, the slight jiggle in my stomach and hips, which seemed too grown for a girl still trying to figure herself out. The pretty smile that I loved faded, and I sighed. Why was it always so much easier to see the flaws?

Just as I spiraled down the endless road of negativity, my mother's voice echoed in my mind. *"You are beautiful, special, and worthy,"* she would always say in the steady and reassuring tone that I needed. I whispered the mantra to myself: *"I am beautiful, special, and worthy."* I repeated the words over and over, reassurance washing over me until the bad thoughts faded, disappearing just as fast as they'd come.

Besides, I had bigger and better things to focus on today. I was heading back to Camp Quest, the sleepaway camp in Brighton

Falls where I'd spent every summer since middle school. For the last three summers, I'd been a counselor there—it was my escape, my happy place. I'd just wrapped up my junior year of high school with a strong grade point average, and I couldn't wait for all the class of 2005 shenanigans my upcoming senior year would bring. But first, there was one more summer at Camp Quest—a summer that already felt like it was going to be something unforgettable. I could just feel it.

The rapid knocking at my bedroom door broke me from my haze. I slipped into a pair of shorts before yelling, "Come in."

"Rise and shine." My daddy's boisterous guffaw filled my tiny yellow bedroom. I rolled my eyes but couldn't prevent the smile creeping up my cheeks. My daddy was my dude. I admired our matching reflections in the mirror.

"Good morning, Daddy," I said.

"Give me some love," he requested. I kissed his cheek and fell into the hug I looked forward to every morning.

"You're getting paid the big bucks this summer, huh? You can pay some rent," he teased.

I shook my head. "Daddy, you're so silly. Every penny is going toward a car, so I will not be paying any rent, sir. Y'all still have to feed me until I'm at least twenty-one," I said, nudging him playfully.

Although I thought my dad was the corniest guy ever, I secretly couldn't wait for his cheesy jokes and that big, booming laugh. It was like clockwork: He'd crack some goofy joke, and I'd dramatically sigh with all the irritation I could muster, but deep down, I loved every minute. On those days when I felt like my light was dimming, I craved the sound of his voice. Oliver Knight had a way of making me feel like I was the brightest star in the room, even when I didn't believe it myself. And today was one of those days. I always looked forward to summer camp, but this year was different. This would be my last hoorah at Camp Quest, and the thought of it being over was bittersweet.

"One step at time, one day at a time, Summer. Enjoy it. Don't worry about what might happen—focus on today. Okay?" my dad whispered, somehow knowing exactly what was going on in my head. I nodded, and he gently lifted my chin. This man—my daddy—he was everything to me. His face held that familiar tenderness that gave me a sense of safety and certainty, like nothing could go wrong as long as he was around. But it was the pride in his voice when he talked to me… It was like taking a breath of fresh air, instantly bringing me back to life, just when I needed it most.

"Hey, my sassy girl! Are you ready?" *Mama.* While daddy was my dude, my mama? She was my favorite girl, hands down. She was truly one-of-a-kind; there was not another like her. She was what some would call a redbone with her smooth milky skin, short coal-black hair, and high cheekbones dusted with freckles. She had a curvy yet petite frame that I would've killed to inherit. We were the same height, but her bold and feisty energy made her seem ten feet tall. While safety resided in my daddy's tone, my mama's voice was something different. It was a mix of humility, conviction, and straight-up confidence. Every time she uttered *Summer Sierra*, it was like she was convincing me that I could take on the world, as long as I committed my heart and mind to it. Teresa Knight was truly my muse. My parents were standing in my room gazing at me as if I was getting prepared to go off to war. They did this every year.

"Get a move on, Summer Sierra, so we won't be late." Mama's somber voice matched the same bittersweet emotion that lingered on her pretty face. Being the mother of four—three girls and one boy—Mama was often emotional about everything—birthdays, graduations, first kisses, and anything else related to "her babies", especially her girls, as she lovingly called the three of us.

I was the youngest, the last one still living at home. My brother, Oliver Jr.—OJ—was the oldest—ten years my senior, practically a second father at times. At least that's what he'd say. Then there was my sister, Annette, six years ahead of me, the perfect blend of responsible and nurturing. And finally, Raquel—Raqi to everyone who knew her—just four years older. Where I was sassy, she was saucy. OJ and Annette were long gone, married and busy managing their own homes. For a long time, it was just Raqi and me, but just a few weeks ago, she'd graduated from college and was now packing for her move to Chicago for her first big job. One by one, my siblings all left, carving out lives of their own, leaving me behind in the quiet that used to feel full.

My mother swore she wasn't planning on having any more children, but she always says she was pleasantly surprised when I arrived, bright and early, on the first day of summer—hence, my name. But lately, Mama's emotions seemed to stretch far beyond Raqi's upcoming move to Chicago or me turning seventeen in a few weeks and heading off for my last summer camp experience. It wasn't just sadness or nostalgia; it was pride—a deep, quiet pride that settled over her whenever she looked at me, like she was holding on to every moment before everything changed.

My mother had become a mom at just seventeen, giving birth to my brother. Her plans for college, travel, and a career were put on pause. When she and my dad married, those plans were postponed indefinitely, as Annette and Raqi came along soon after. Granny never let her forget it. *"You better get a handle on those girls before they become fast tails and have a house full of li'l babies,"* she would fuss, her words sharp but laced with that old-school worry only Granny could deliver. It wasn't hard to imagine Mama brushing it off with a casual wave, her patience with Granny far exceeding anything I could ever muster. Still, I imagined those words must have stung, no matter how often she heard them. Mama had sacrificed so much—her dreams, her freedom, her youth. And yet, even when Granny taunted her, she never wavered. She always made it clear her family was worth every sacrifice. Maybe Mama's emotions weren't just about me, but about her. About the girl she used to be, the dreams she once carried at seventeen. Maybe, when she looked at me, she wasn't just seeing her teenage daughter, she was seeing a version of herself, one still brimming with the hopes she had to let go of.

I often wondered if she was anything like me at seventeen. Did she walk with the same outward confidence, yet inward self-consciousness, convincing herself she had it all figured out? Did she laugh a little too loud, speak a little too boldly, just to cover up the quiet doubts creeping beneath the surface? Did she stare at her reflection, adjusting her posture, tilting her chin higher—not because she felt unshakable, but because she needed to believe she was? Most people wouldn't believe it, but under all that sass and swagger, I was an unsure little girl, always second-guessing myself.

Of course, I could light up a room, cracking jokes and commanding attention with my wit and charm, but inside…I was a storm of shy, awkward feelings. Classic Gemini shit—one side of me was sugary sweet and the other a sharp-tongued, no-nonsense chick who could cut someone down with just a few words. Even though my insecurities were fading, I still often felt uneasy about the voluptuousness of my body, mainly because of the kind of attention it drew. I was groped by the nasty little boys on the playground for having breasts and a booty and stared at inappropriately by grown men. When I got to middle school, some girls my age craved that kind of attention; they chased after it. But I wanted nothing to do with it. I'd hide under shirts two sizes too big and baggy jeans, even wrapping my breasts with Ace bandages to make them look smaller. It got to the point where my parents wondered if I even liked boys.

Our house had walls as thin as paper, so one night, I heard my mother praying. *"Please, Jesus, let this girl like boys. Lord, I don't know what I'd do."* Her whispered prayers made me laugh because I could visualize her dramatic self, collapsing to her knees in that tiny bathroom that doubled as her prayer closet, one hand pressed on her black vinyl gold-foil–printed Holy Bible and the other raised toward the heavens. On the other hand, it worried me because if my own mother had these doubts, what did others think? That might have been the very time I realized how much I cared about other people's opinions, maybe more than I cared about my own.

Sure, I thought I was cute in the face and was mostly confident and self-assured, but deep down, I was always questioning myself. Does this dress fit? Are my legs too big? Can people see my fat rolls? Admittedly, I was jealous of my sisters and honestly my mama, too, because they all had cute little perfect bodies. *Where did I come from? Why didn't God give me the tiny waist and perky perfect little breasts?* Probably because He knew my ass would be one of the fast-tail girls my granny spoke about.

After breakfast, I hopped in the shower and got dressed, knowing we had to hit the road soon. Daddy had already loaded his truck, and I was certain he was pacing outside, waiting for me with his usual patience.

"Summer Sierra, let's go," my mother shouted.

Blowing myself a kiss in the mirror for that extra boost of confidence, I was ready! I strolled into the living room where my mom and sister were lounging on the couch. To my surprise, Daddy was in the kitchen—not outside—but still quietly grumbling about us running late. My mom, Raqi, and I all laughed knowing how serious Daddy was about time. If we were even a minute off schedule, he'd have a mini fit.

"You ready, shuga?" he asked, taking a sip from his coffee cup.

I nodded. We finally hopped into the car and headed toward Camp Quest. The familiar narrow road stretched before us, winding its way off the highway and into the trees, the same path we'd taken every summer for years. But this time, it felt different. The closer we got, the stronger the feeling grew—this was going to be the kind of summer where anything felt possible.

CHAPTER FOUR

**Summer
October 2019**

ECHO CALLED MY parents, dialing the same phone number etched in his memory. My Daddy answered almost instantly, his voice tight with worry as Echo patiently fielded his anxious questions. But even as he spoke, Echo's focus never disconnected from me; silent but heavy with meaning, a language only I could understand.

"Yes, sir. I found her, and she's okay," Echo said, his tone composed. "She said she's not ready to come home right now, but she wanted you to know that she's safe." He paused, nodding as if agreeing with whatever my mother was shouting on the other end of the line. "Ms. Teresa, calm down," he said. "I promise I'll take care of her. Yes, ma'am. You have my word." He bobbed his head. "Okay. Bye."

Echo ended the call, slipping his phone into his pocket, his gaze never leaving mine. As much as I wanted to look away, I couldn't. He was unreadable, yet a steady anchor that rooted me in a moment filled with both chaos and calm. His words, *I'll take care her*, played over and over in my head like the melody of my favorite song. We were kids the last time he vowed to take care of me, but the earnest bass of his voice erased any doubts. I didn't need to question him, wouldn't ask if he still meant it. I knew Echo would always keep his promises, especially the ones left unspoken.

"Thank you," I said.

"You're welcome," he replied.

I swallowed hard. "I know my mama is pissed, and Daddy is just…disappointed," I said, my voice shaking as the words tumbled out. It felt like disgrace and shame were gripping me by the throat, tightening their hold with every syllable.

"Nah," Echo said, his brow creasing slightly as he shook his head. "They're just concerned. You know there's nothing you could ever do to truly disappoint them. They love you, Sun. I'm sure they know you have your reasons."

His reassurance settled over me, softening the storm of guilt swirling in my chest. But as much as I wanted to believe him, the weight of my parents' expectations felt like a shadow I couldn't escape. *I'm sure they know you have your reasons.* I heard his words, fully comprehended what he said, but intentionally ignored them. Confronting my reasons meant unearthing a truth I wasn't ready to face. Instead, I shifted the conversation in another direction.

"You look nice, E," I said, forcing a sparse grin, a sparkle of light softening my misty eyes.

He shook his head, dragging his teeth over his bottom lip, the knowing expression said it all—he saw right through my act. He wasn't fooled by my deflection, but he let it slide without question. "Well," he began, his voice low with a slight tinge of humor, "my best friend was supposed to be getting married a few hours ago, but…" He paused, then shrugged lightly. "Change of plans, I guess."

Silence stretched between us as I turned the thought over in my mind. *Yeah, change of plans.*

Then I turned away, drawn once more to the gentle flow of the creek. Snatching the glasses from my face, I swiped my cheeks, but the tears wouldn't stop. They kept spilling down my face—hot and relentless. I tugged on the bottom of my t-shirt, attempting to clean my glasses again, but it was useless. A new wave of weeping brewed in my chest, threatening to break free.

"I didn't think you were coming," I said, my voice thick, a knotted tangle of sadness and anger. "You said you couldn't…you didn't want to watch me get married, remember?" An invisible thread pulled between us, tight and heavy with the weight of our unresolved encounter from a year ago, which had caused yet another rift in our relationship, lingering like a dark cloud.

Echo turned toward me with his hands stuffed in his pockets, his features soft, carrying something I couldn't quite name—something mature, familiar, and an undeniable trace of adoration. He shrugged, the motion almost dismissive, as if brushing off the gravity of my words. "Change of plans, I guess," he muttered again, a small smirk playing on the corner of his lips. Finally, he eased down beside me on the old tree stump where we'd spent so many nights together—nights that felt eerily like this one.

Echo
July 2019
A Few Months Earlier

I nudged a few unpacked boxes out of the way as I stepped into my condo, shaking my head at the mess that still surrounded me. When I'd decided to buy a place, I hadn't factored in the endless hours it would take to unpack, organize, and decorate.

Maybe I can get Kemi to help me, I thought.

My sister, Yekemi, had an impeccable eye for design. She'd moved to Los Angeles a year ago, and while I liked to think it was to be near me, I knew her real motive—advancing her career in beauty and fashion.

Tossing the mail and my keys on the counter, my steps slowed as I made my way farther into the two-story open-concept condo to admire the view from the floor-to-ceiling windows overlooking the bustling city. The warm hues of the July sun setting reflected off the glass, and without thinking, I let out a contented breath. I'd called LA home for the past eight years and thought it was about time to plant some roots here. There was a time that I thought my situation would be temporary and I would return to the Midwest. I always considered Chicago home, so maybe I'd return there one day. Maybe return to *her*. But that was no longer my fantasy or reality. I was never going back.

To my surprise, my parents had settled in St. Louis for good. My dad received tenure at his university, and my mom launched a small catering business once my youngest sister, Sadie, was in high school. The house I grew up in became their forever home, a rarity for a family that had moved as much as we had.

I often wondered about Summer after we parted ways before college. She headed to Atlanta, and I stayed in St. Louis. I didn't want to intrude on her new life, and truthfully, I needed time to adjust to my own. I threw myself into my studies, graduating with degrees in art and English from Washington University before diving straight into an MBA program. It was hard as hell, but over the years, I'd learned to tuck the memories of Summer away in the farthest corners of my mind. They were locked there, only to be uncovered when I allowed myself the luxury of reminiscing.

When I first moved to LA, I landed an internship at NBC Universal, which was a fancy way of saying I was an errand boy. Despite my degrees from one of the most prestigious universities in the country, I was scraping by, making barely a thousand dollars a month. Thankfully, my education was covered due to my dad's tenure benefits, so that thousand dollars was just enough to secure a closet-sized room in an apartment I shared with three other people—one of whom was my ex, Kourtni Lang. It wasn't glamorous, but it was a start.

Over time, I worked my way up the ranks to become a senior graphic designer, working on popular studio films, television shows, and even a few independent passion projects that were gaining recognition. I poured my heart and soul into my work, thriving in a competitive, cut-throat industry and flourishing within the company for years. But recently, I'd felt compelled to step out on faith, hope, and everything in between to start my own business.

The Black creative community in LA was small, close-knit, and deeply inspiring. Over the years, I'd made many lifelong friendships and invaluable connections that motivated the decision to take a leap. Of course, having a father who was a stickler about saving and investing didn't hurt either. Once I moved beyond living on ramen noodles, he practically demanded that I set aside a fixed amount of money monthly. He took those savings and invested them on my behalf, creating a solid safety net if my entrepreneurial dream did not go as planned.

It had been a hell of a long week, so a glass of cognac was more than necessary. I laughed at the lone glass, plate, fork, knife, and spoon sitting in the sink—a clear sign that I'd barely settled into my new place after two weeks. I hadn't had time to breathe, let alone unpack. Taking a sip of the Angel's Envy neat, I let the warmth settle my nerves. My attention shifted to the pile of mail transferred to my new address cluttering the already cluttered counter. I shook my head, never understanding why I received so much mail when ninety percent of my life was managed online.

I sifted through endless sales ads, credit card offers, and outright junk until a shiny ivory envelope with an embossed seal caught my eye. The ornate letters *S* and *D* pressed into the wax seemed to sparkle under the kitchen light. It was addressed to me, with a PO Box in St. Louis listed as the return address. A familiar unease settled in my chest as I turned it over in my hands. Taking another sip of the smooth brown liquor, I prepared myself, knowing that I'd need a little liquid courage to confront whatever was inside the envelope. I pulled out the stool at the kitchen island and plopped down, running a finger beneath the intricate seal. The card I pulled out matched the same iridescent sheen of the envelope. The meticulously inked handwritten calligraphy was elegant, but despite its beauty, the message it carried was downright ugly.

You are cordially invited to the wedding ceremony of Summer Sierra Knight and Deshawn Micah Towns.

"I don't want this bullshit," I barked, then balled up the paper and hurled it against the wall. Anger simmered in my core, threatening to boil over. No, it wasn't just anger, it was something sharper. Rage. Shit, more like hurt. A hurt I hadn't experienced since the last time I'd seen Summer Knight. "Why the hell would she send this to me?" I muttered, my voice barely above a whisper, thick with frustration.

Exhaling deeply to simmer my angst, I was fixed on the crumpled paper on the floor. I shook my head, torn between walking away from it and picking it up to destroy it further. I started to sip my drink but instead, drained it in one long, burning gulp. My first instinct was to call her, to demand answers. Ask her why she thought I'd want to see this shit. But it had been about a year since our last conversation, and that encounter wasn't unpleasant, but it definitely didn't rekindle our friendship.

Picking up my phone, my thumb hovered over her name—*Sunshine*—the word stared back, mocking me. I needed clarity, but it wouldn't come from her, so instead, I dialed the one person who would keep it one hundred with me, no filter. The one person who'd seen me through all the highs and lows with Summer. The line rang twice before a familiar voice greeted me.

"Yo," Maxell said.

Since meeting at camp all those years ago, Max and I had become more like brothers than friends. He'd been my sounding board through every twist and turn with Summer—and Kourtni, for that matter. If anyone could understand how seeing the announcement of Summer's wedding hit me like a sucker punch, it was him.

"I got mail today," I said, not bothering with small talk.

"Oh yeah," Maxell replied, his tone a mix of interest and expectation. I was pretty damn sure he'd received the same invitation.

"Yeah," I muttered, rubbing the bridge of my nose like I could knead the frustration out of my skull. "Why the hell would she send me this shit?"

Max *tsk*ed knowingly, the kind of sound that came from someone who was about to tell you the whole truth and nothing but the truth. "I don't know, man. Maybe because no matter where y'all are in life, she still needs your support. She's always had your support."

I shook my head, the weight of the words pressing on my chest. "Not this time. I can't do it, Max. I can't watch that."

"Why not?" he shot back, calm but unwavering. "If I remember correctly, she gave you a chance to tell her what you wanted. Asked you straight up, but you—"

"Man, don't start. I don't need a damn recap," I snapped, harsher than I intended.

Max wasn't fazed though. "So let me ask again: If you're not planning to tell her how you feel, what's stopping you from showing up to watch her be happy? What's the problem, E?"

The silence between us grew heavy, like it was daring me to fill it with the truth I didn't want to face. This felt like a death—a kind of loss that was hard to explain, but impossible to ignore—a quiet grief I knew would linger for the rest of my life.

"Happy…" I muttered, almost to myself. "You think she's happy with that nigga?"

Max's pause told me he was considering his words carefully. "I don't know, but she's marrying that nigga, E. That tells me something."

"Tells you what?" I asked, irritation simmering beneath the surface. I wanted the truth, but damn if I was ready to hear it.

"That Summer is ready," Max said plainly. "All her friends are getting married, having babies, building lives. What did you think her next step would be?" He fell silent, leaving me to stew in the immensity of his words. I opened my mouth to argue, but nothing came out. I just sat there, suffocating in the truth. "Remember when I told you that you were going to fuck around and let her find her peace in someone else?" Max said, cutting through the quiet like a knife.

"And you think that's him? Deshawn?" I practically spat the name, incredulous and annoyed.

"I didn't say that. He might not be the right dude, but he's Mister Right Now." His words were an uppercut to the gut. A fucking TKO. *Mister Right Now.* The thought of Summer settling for someone who wasn't her forever felt like a betrayal—to both of us. "So, what are you wearing to the wedding?" Max teased, grating on my nerves like nails on a chalkboard.

"Man, fuck you," I snapped, but he barely seemed fazed, his smug satisfaction growing with every second at my expense.

"Relax, E. I'm just saying, if you're gonna show up, at least make sure you're looking better than the groom." I shook my head, pacing the room as his words sank in. I couldn't decide what was worse, walking into that wedding, watching her walk down the aisle toward someone else, or not showing up for Summer when she might need me most.

Summer
July 2019
A Few Months Earlier

The July humidity clung to me like a second skin, and the damp heat seemed to slow down my every movement. By the time I made it to the post office, my neatly styled twist-out had transformed into a full-blown afro, courtesy of the morning rain in one hundred degrees of relentless summer. Exhaustion had wrapped itself around me after a day that started at seven and showed no signs of slowing down.

The morning had kicked off with a visit to my gynecologist, and then to get the tatas checked during my annual mammogram—both necessary evils in my ever-growing list of adult responsibilities. Normally, I'd be working from the comfort of home, but this week, I was onsite with a client. Between appointments, Deshawn and I managed a quick lunch meeting with the wedding photographer, and now I was making one final stop at the post office before collapsing at home. Deshawn had mentioned stopping by later, and I silently prayed he'd bring dinner. My energy reserves were long depleted.

The wedding RSVPs had been flooding in, and with each one, my anxiety about the cost of this increasingly extravagant event mounted. My parents insisted on footing the bill despite our offers to cover it ourselves. What started as a simple celebration had spiraled into a full-blown spectacle. I'd fallen into the wedding rabbit hole, becoming intrigued by every fluff and frill available, even becoming a bit of a bridezilla when I couldn't get my way. With roughly ninety days before the wedding, I couldn't add another flower spray, drape of satin, or light feature.

Strutting into the post office in my fitted purple slacks and sleek black blouse, I felt every bit the poised bride-to-be I'd become. I'd decided to have the RSVP cards returned to a PO Box since Deshawn and I spent most of our time bouncing between our separate places. Shortly before meeting him, I'd purchased a townhouse in Midtown—close enough to the city to stay connected but far enough to enjoy some peace. Deshawn, on the other hand, preferred the fast pace of his downtown apartment, just minutes from his office.

Despite the wedding rapidly approaching, we hadn't finalized where we'd live as husband and wife. I loved my townhouse and the balance it brought to my life, but Shawn thrived on the hustle and bustle, often dismissing my hints about settling into a quieter lifestyle.

"We're too young for the white picket fence right now," he'd say, waving off the idea of suburban bliss.

What he didn't seem to realize—or maybe didn't want to acknowledge—was that I was ready for that life, a yard with a picket fence, a belly full of baby, and maybe even a dog. I didn't just want it; I craved it. But in Shawn's world, that future seemed distant, as though it was something to strive for years down the line. For me, it was right there, waiting. Maybe after the wedding he could see it the way I did.

I unlocked the PO Box, pulling out a hefty stack of envelopes. Each one marked another step closer to the big day. A tinge of anxiety prickled beneath my skin as I shoved as many as I could into my tote bag, already picturing a glass of wine to get me through a night sorting through them alone. As I locked the box and turned to leave, a few envelopes slipped from my grasp and scattered across the floor. I bent to retrieve them, but one immediately caught my attention.

2814 West Angelos Blvd., Los Angeles, CA 90011

I froze. My breath hitched as recognition hit me like a tidal wave. *Echo.* Of all the invitations sent, he was the only one in LA.

Clutching the envelope to my chest, I scanned the post office, suddenly feeling like I held the world's most dangerous secret. My heart pounded as I dashed to my car, slamming the door shut before tossing the tote onto the passenger seat. I caught a glimpse of my reflection in the rearview mirror, my wide eyes and trembling lips betraying the storm within. *Breathe, Summer. Just breathe.*

For a moment, I simply sat there, staring at nothing and contemplating everything. I hadn't planned to send Echo an invitation. My friends had begged me not to. But deep down, I needed him to know. I needed him to see that this was real. That I wanted him there. That some foolish, desperate part of me hoped he'd come. But would he? My hands shook as I carefully slid my finger under the seal. The edges of the envelope felt sharp against my skin, matching the tension curling in my stomach. I pulled out the RSVP card, my heart slamming against my ribcage as I read the words scribbled in his familiar handwriting.

Congratulations, Sunshine, but I can't. I stared at the words. My lips trembled, and I pressed them together, trying to hold back the wave of emotion threatening to overtake me. But it was no use. The tears came anyway.

CHAPTER FIVE

Summer
October 2019

THE BURST OF wind gushing through the trees disrupted our heartbreaking recollections. Still perched at the tree, I felt him draw me in closer to quell the chill from the wind. Echo gently brushed a finger down the bridge of my nose. He calmly wrapped his arm around my shoulders, instantly comforting me without needing to be asked. We both let out a quiet, shared sigh. This felt good—recognizable, like home. His tender touch and the genuine concern in his embrace stirred something deep inside me, and before I knew it, another sudden, uncontrollable cry escaped my lips, startling away the butterfly that had accompanied me earlier.

Time slowed for just a second, the years of our friendship steadily played in my head like the slow build of Whitney Houston's "I Will Always Love You." Stillness, reticence, refusal to acquiesce—all the feelings and behaviors that prevented a breakthrough in this, what I called twisted friendship between Echo and me. The white noise created by the steady flow of the creek intertwined with Echo's clean, yet spicy scent, leaving me in a daze when he tugged at my waist. His embrace encouraged me to resume seeking respite in the comfort of him.

While he was familiar, his caress was different. Echo's grown man vibe was a far cry from the lanky frame I'd met as a naïve teenager. Who knew that over a decade later, I would be a runaway bride, cuddled in the arms of my best friend at our secret spot, reminiscing about our twisted friendship?

"Sun," he began, shaking me from my daze, "I wouldn't have forgiven myself if I weren't here for you. Honestly, I didn't make the decision to come until a few days ago. But our friendship..." He paused, choosing his words carefully, "it's stronger than any of the issues we've had. I had to be here."

I let myself sink into the pool of memories that only my best friend could stir. Each moment we'd shared felt alive, rippling through me like a soft current.

"I'll always show up for you, Summer. No matter what. Don't ever forget that, okay?" He tenderly pinched my nose, the familiar touch stirring something deep in me. Instinctively, I scrunched my face, just like I always had when we were flirtatious kids—when everything was simple and we thought we had all the time in the world.

I nodded. "I've never forgotten, E. Never," I whispered, the words carrying all the weight of the years and everything left unsaid. The summer breeze stilled as if nature was holding its breath. But for the first time, the silence between us wasn't uncomfortable. A cold, yet soothing finger swiped up and down my forearm as we listened to the gentle rustle of the leaves. Chuckling, I said, "E, do you remember that first week of camp?" I angled my head in his direction, but he stayed fixed on the stillness. I could almost see the distant memory flickering across his mind.

"Shit, how could I forget that stank-ass attitude of yours? Just mean for no reason. I think you enjoyed giving me a hard time." He shot me a teasing grin.

"You loved it when I gave you a hard time." I elbowed him amusedly. "You were just as bad as me—constantly making jokes, calling me spoiled, pushing your finger into my glasses, calling me every name but my birth name. You, sir, were the one who drove me crazy."

Echo nuzzled closer to me, wrapping me in his suit jacket to keep me warm. "Nah, man. We just had a funny way of building our friendship. And I thought you were kinda cute." He winked, and my face betrayed me with a telltale flush.

Summer
That One Summer in 2004

The first week of camp was always pure chaos. The kind you'd expect with almost two hundred campers—most of them barely teenagers—and a swarm of junior counselors trying to keep things together. Camper accidents were pretty much guaranteed. Not to mention the homesickness that hit like clockwork during the first few days away from their families. It always took a solid five or six days for things to settle down. But now that the schedule hiccups were resolved and everyone was falling into a normal routine, I could focus on my group, the Creative Crew. These kids had a spark, skilled in just about everything creative—from drama to drawing to writing and even fashion design, they could do it all.

I was far from an artist myself, but I loved creative writing. It was like a secret escape, a place where my thoughts flowed freely. Building a whole world of characters and poetry in my sketchbook was like a magic. I could lose myself in it for hours. And being here with kids who understood that feeling? It's everything. Today, David, one of my favorite returning campers, had his turn to share what he was most excited for this summer.

"I'm most excited about…" he started, his pubescent voice squeaking as he tapped his chin like he was in deep thought. Then his cute baby face split into a goofy grin, braces gleaming. "The girls. I'm excited about the girls." The room erupted in laughter. I couldn't help but laugh, too, caught up in the moment.

A deep, vibrating hum came from the doorway; the sound definitely didn't come from one of the kids. It carried a borderline grown-man quality, immediately drawing the attention of the campers...and me. It was him—Echo Abara. He'd only been here a week, but he walked around like he owned the place. His skinny arms and legs, just starting to show hints of muscle, were wrapped in rich brown skin that was smoother than any boy's I'd ever seen. With an easy swagger, he approached me with unshaken confidence. He was always nibbling or licking his thick bottom lip, and the girls ate it up.

Does he think he's LL Cool J or something? I rolled my eyes, refusing to be just another counselor going weak in the knees for him.

They were always talking about the new boy, giggling and swooning every chance they got. It made me sick. Sure, he was cute. And tall. And nice. And...ridiculously appealing. *Ugh.* But he was still a boy—a cocky, self-assured boy who seemed to know exactly the effect he had on people...on me. That alone was enough to annoy me.

"Oh, so she does smile," he said, teasing me while he handed out snacks to the class.

I narrowed my eyes, crossing my arms over my chest in defiance. "Yes, I smile when there's something to smile about," I shot back, my voice sharp as I fought to keep the blush from my cheeks.

He stepped right up to me, so close that I could see the onyx rings encircling his cocoa- brown irises that seemed to absorb the warmth of the sunlight beaming through the windows. I couldn't lie to myself or anyone else; Echo was fine, but annoying as hell. For the past week, he'd been coming up with a new nickname for me almost every day: Summertime, Sunny Day, Sunlight—the list just kept getting longer. But once he found out my full name was Summer Knight, it was over.

"Midsummer Night's Dream, what are we doing today?" he teased, that signature arrogance dripping from his tone. I loved and hated his cockiness at the same time. I bit the inside of my cheek, determine not to let even a hint of intrigue grace my lips.

"And what kind of name is Echo...*oh, oh,*" I repeated, drawing out the last part, making fun of him for a change.

He tapped the tip of my nose, and my face immediately scrunched, pushing his hand away. "That's cute. I see what you did there," he said, clearly amused. Then his expression changed, shifting to a soft yet serious look. "You know what, Summertime? I think we're gonna be good friends."

The sincerity in his tone caught me off guard, but I shook my head anyway. "Never...*er...er,*" I repeated dramatically, tossing my head back in a fit of giggles. I couldn't help it, the banter between us was too much fun. "Come on, you've gotta admit, that was pretty funny, right?" I asked, still breathless.

"Nah." He groaned, but the deepening flush on his cheeks told a different story, and before long, we were both cracking up.

The energy eventually gave way to a few seconds of somewhat awkward silence. I shifted my focus everywhere but on him, suddenly hyperaware of the space between us. Finally, he broke the quiet. "So, what's on the schedule today? I'm following your lead, remember?" he said, his tone casual but sprinkled with just enough playfulness to send a spark of happiness through me. I had a feeling that maybe Echo was right. Maybe we were going to be friends.

Echo did just what he said...followed my lead. I walked him around the art room, identifying the supplies, showing him pictures from last year and my project ideas for this year. He hung on to my every word. For once, the smug goofiness was momentarily set aside. He looked completely serious, paying close attention and even throwing in some solid ideas of his own.

I couldn't help but wonder if I'd misjudged him. Beneath all the jokes, the silliness, and that undeniable charisma, there seemed to be something more—a smart, artistic, and genuinely intelligent guy. Maybe his first impression wasn't his best impression. Or maybe, just maybe, I was being too serious. *It's summer, Summer. Let your hair down,* I told myself. *Maybe he's just the kind of guy who knows how to have fun.*

By the time the group finished the first part of their project, we were covered in dirt and glue. We'd spent the afternoon collecting leaves, flowers, and other elements found around the campgrounds during our hike. When we returned to the art room, we glued the items on to a canvas to create a messy masterpiece collage. We'd be adding to the canvas all week, and I was already exhausted but couldn't wait to see the final product. As we cleaned up, Echo was sweeping up stray leaves off the floor while I wiped down the tables.

"So, Summer Sun," he began with yet another nickname, "where are you from?"

Normally, I'd bark out a smart remark, but instead, I decided to humor him. "St. Louis. You?"

"Everywhere," he replied, shaking his head, "but I live in St. Louis now."

"Now?" I asked, arching a brow as I tucked away the last box of glue sticks. "So, where were you before?"

"Chicago," he said, still sweeping.

"Chicago Chicago or the *saditty suburbs*?" I teased, carefully enunciating my last words for effect.

He froze mid-sweep and shot me a look so sharp you'd think I'd insulted his mama. "Chicago Chicago," he blurted, adding an unmistakable firmness to his tone. "Southside, you know what I'm saying." His voice dropped a little, the bass almost daring me to challenge him. "What do you know about Chicago anyway?" His gaze locked on mine.

"My daddy," I shot back.

He shrugged confusedly. "Okay…your daddy what?"

"He's from Chicago…Southside, too. The ghetto," I said, lowering my voice dramatically.

He leaned against the desk, his tongue idly running over that damn lip again, while we allowed the silence to brush over us like a soft, well-worn blanket. We were the only two people in the room, but right then, it felt like we were the only people left in the world.

"*Um*, why did y'all move to St. Louis?" I asked, feeling a bit of nervous energy creep into my voice.

He jerked, almost as if I'd broken him from a trance, his eyes refocusing on me. "My dad got a new job at the university," Echo responded, hanging the broom on a hook.

"*Um*, which one? There's more than one, ya know," I teased.

"My bad," he said. "Washington University. He's a professor. Mathematics."

"Oh, so he's smart smart," I joked.

Echo snickered, nodding. "Yeah, I guess you can say that. What about your parents?" he asked, curiosity brightening his face as he hopped on top of the desk.

"My dad retired from the Navy, and now he owns an auto repair shop and fixes up old cars. My mom is an office manager at a real estate office."

For a second, I felt a little embarrassed. His dad was a college professor, and mine hadn't even gone to college. But I shrugged it off. My parents worked hard, and my brother and sisters and I never lacked anything.

"That's pretty cool," Echo said, and to my surprise, he seemed like he meant it.

I nodded. We wandered around the room for a minute, neither of us really wanting to end this question-and-answer session. "What about your mom?" I asked after a moment.

He shook his head, a faint shadow passing over his expression. "She doesn't really work anymore. We moved so much, it was hard for her to keep a job." His voice was quiet, edged with something unspoken.

I nodded, offering a small understanding nod, sensing it was best to let it go.

"What do you think of St. Louis so far?" I asked.

He shrugged, glancing down at his Carolina-blue-and-white Jordans. "I haven't seen much of it yet. We only moved about a month ago, and my room is barely unpacked," he said.

His voice was missing its usual edge of confidence, replaced by something subdued—resignation, maybe. I sensed he wasn't thrilled about the move, but he was trying to play it cool. I didn't miss the quiet frustration, though.

"That's gotta be tough. Leaving your friends, your school... your senior year," I said, my voice rising with each word as I imagined myself in his place.

He let out a long breath, his mind clearly drifting to some faraway place. "Yeah, man, don't remind me." Echo's tone was low, almost resigned, then he shrugged, trying to brush it off. "It is what it is, though." But the way his voice trailed off told me it wasn't as simple as that. I found myself just watching him—this boy who had left behind his whole life to start over... again. He tried to wear a mask of indifference, but I saw something else—a quiet, reluctant strength that tugged at my heartstrings.

In that moment, I wanted to be his friend. I wanted to show him that St. Louis could be more than just another stop on his journey—that maybe, one day, he could find a reason to love it, a reason to call it home.

CHAPTER SIX

Echo
That One Summer in 2004

ANOTHER COUPLE OF weeks with Summer and I working together with the Creative Crew, she'd finally eased up a little and let me take the lead during class a few times. It felt good to do what I loved, especially since we had the right software now. I'd been itching to start teaching the computer drafting class, and it was worth the wait. I couldn't help but wonder what kind of donors Camp Quest had on their side because each kid had their own tablet to create their projects. That kind of luxury would've never been available at my old camp.

Even Summer seemed excited to learn some of the techniques I was teaching the campers, which was a miracle in itself. It felt like we'd fallen into a comfortable rhythm. Every morning, we had breakfast with the same group of counselors before walking to the art room together. By lunchtime, the vibe was the same—easy, like we'd been doing this forever. Like clockwork, I'd casually toss out a flirty line or two, just to watch her eyes roll in that way only she could, or she'd hit me with her best hard-to-get mean girl act. And then there were those damn dimples, caving in despite her effort to play tough. I knew she secretly loved our playtime. I know I did.

We ended every class the same way to—our game of questions. Each round pulled us closer without either of us wanting to admit it.

After class today, we walked our campers to the quad where ice cream was being served. Instead of hanging with the other counselors, we took a walk, drifting toward one of the wooden swings near the lodges. We sat side by side, swaying while she enjoyed an ice cream sandwich, while I ate a Drumstick.

"What high school are you going to?" She hit me with a question that I quickly realized was a rite of passage for every St. Louis native meeting someone new.

Apparently, around here, that question was more than just small talk. Summer explained that it was code—the quickest way to figure out who you knew, what part of town you were from, how smart you might be, and, depending on the school, even how much money your parents probably made. It was like a secret handshake, and I was just starting to catch on.

"I'm going to Carter Prep Academy," I answered.

Summer perked up just a bit, a trace of surprise brightening her features. "Oh, so you're smart smart like your daddy!" she teased as she sat crisscrossed legs, casually running her tongue around the edge of the ice cream sandwich.

I tossed my head back, caught up in the charm of her quick wit. "Why you say that? What school do you go to?" I asked as if I was familiar with any high schools in St. Louis.

"Riverdale. A *public* school. Carter Prep is, like, the best and most expensive private school in the city," she said, switching to an exaggerated snooty tone. "Most of their students go off to the Harvards of the world."

I shook my head. "Well, I mean, I am smart, but Harvard ain't for me."

Summer arched a perplexed eyebrow, her expression twisting in offense, like I'd insulted Mariah Carey, her favorite singer. "It's

Harvard. You talk like it's some kind of trade school or something," she said, her whole face now furrowed as she studied me.

"Nah, no diss," I replied quickly, shaking my head. "My father would love for me to go to an Ivy League, but I've dreamed of being a Morehouse man since I was six years old." My posture straightened a bit, proud just saying it. Her head snapped in my direction, her pretty face a mix of shock and surprise. I was confused by her reaction. "What? What's wrong with Morehouse?" I asked, tossing my hands up.

She shook her head quickly, that auburn-brown ponytail of hers swaying as she pushed her glasses back up on her nose. "Nothing. Nothing at all," she said, her tone softer now. "Actually, Spelman's been my dream since I was like ten."

A small smile curved the corner of my lips. The kind that didn't come often, a rare feeling—one of those this feels-like-fate moments. We were only teenagers, but something about her felt timeless, like she could be my forever. For a brief second, the image of me and Summer being a SpelHouse connection played vividly in my mind, as if it was already written.

I stepped closer, leaning casually against the table beside her. "See, Sunshine, our friendship was meant to be," I teased, winking as I reached out to press the tip of her button nose with my finger.

She swatted my hand away. "Echo, stop," she whined, but the protest lacked any real bite. A comfortable hush fell between us, the kind that needed no words. Both of us sat there, steadily becoming comfortable in the silence, losing in a moment of possibilities—Morehouse for me, Spelman for her, and a future that suddenly didn't feel so far away.

"Sunshine, huh?" she said, interrupting my musings, her voice questioning. "That's a new one." I nodded, trying to keep my cool as she smiled, a soft, shy curve of her lips. "I like it," she admitted quietly. Her words caught me off guard, and for what felt like a lifetime, I just stared at her, stunned. She'd completely thrown me off my game, so much so that, for once, I didn't have a comeback ready.

Finally, I cleared my throat, breaking the silence. "Alright, man, I gotta bounce. Thanks for your help today, by the way. Turns out you know more about computers than I thought you would."

She rolled her eyes dramatically. I swore those big, brown things were going to get stuck someday. "Whatever. I'm smart, too, smarty pants," she shot back, playfully sticking out her tongue.

I gave her a lingering glance before turning to head toward my lodge, but after only a few steps, I hesitated. I caught her just as she bent to pick up the ice cream wrapper from the ground, my attention snagged on her again. I lingered a second too long, tracing the curves of her figure, drawn to the effortless way she moved. Summer's body was…thick. Like grown-woman thick. Like that girl on Tyra Banks' modeling show that my sister watched. I think her name was Toccara. The judges called her plus-sized for the runway, but I just called her fine. That was my Sunshine, and no matter how much I tried, I couldn't deny how intrigued I was.

She lifted her head suddenly, catching me in the act. *Busted.* A knowing, yet coy smile spread across her pretty face, and I froze for a moment. Mine faltered, my cheeks burned like a horny li'l boy who couldn't keep his cool around a pretty girl. Regaining my composure, I found my swag again. "Come on, Sunshine. I'll walk you to your room."

She didn't say a word, just gave a little nod as she caught up to me. Her lodge was just a few steps away, so it didn't take long for me to watch her disappear through the door before turning in the opposite direction. Instead of heading to my room, I circled around the building, passing by her bedroom window. Just before I was completely out of sight, I tapped on the glass to get her attention and stuck out my tongue—payback for earlier. Summer shook her head before tossing up her middle finger without missing a beat. I clutched my chest in mock offense, and just like that, we were laughing, two little kids wrapped up in our own silliness until she was gone from view. Even after I walked away, I couldn't shake the stupid heat creeping up my neck, the blush lingering long after I should've moved on.

"Hey, Mum," I said into the phone, leaning back in the chair. We couldn't have mobile phones at camp, so we had to make calls from the lobby of the main building.

"Echo," my mother cooed, making me smile instantly. "We miss you, especially Didi."

"I miss you guys, too."

"You haven't called in a bit," she added, her voice tinged with curiosity. "Things must be good."

I nodded though she couldn't see me. "Yes, ma'am. It's…cool."

"Cool, huh?" she mocked me before continuing. "Have you made any new friends?"

"A few," I admitted. "A lot of counselors are from St. Louis, so that's cool, and one guy goes to my new school, so…" My voice faded as I tried to figure out how to explain the mix of comfort and unfamiliarity.

My mother took a deep breath, a sound so full of relief that I could almost feel her body relaxing through the phone. While my dad taught me to be a man—practice strength and discipline—my mum? She taught me something just as important, to be a gentleman—how to care and not be afraid to show it. So, my happiness was important to her, maybe more than it mattered to me. "I'm glad you're having a good time."

In the background, there was a sudden burst of commotion, followed by familiar chaotic shouting. I let out a snort, knowing without a doubt it was my rowdy siblings. "Is that Echo, mum?" someone yelled.

"I wanna talk first," Sadie's voice chimed in, clear and demanding as always.

"One at a time," my mum fussed. For the next fifteen minutes, I was passed around like a toy, catching up with my family. Then there was a soft knock on the window in front of me. I lifted my head and saw *her*.

She stood there looking so innocent and devious at the same time as the last of the evening sun sparkled behind her. The counselors were finished for the day since the campers were watching a movie at the outdoor auditorium. Summer held up a paper bag with what I was hoping was food, a blanket, and an old boom box. I cocked my head in disbelief, immediately recognizing it was my boom box. I shook my head, unable to stop the grin from forming on my face because I knew exactly what this meant. She wanted to go to our hideaway. In just a few weeks, it had become our thing—sneaking off after dark when the campers were asleep and the counselors were distracted, probably off doing God only knows what. Our little nook tucked away near a man-made stream felt like another world, one where time didn't exist and everything was simple. It was our escape.

"Mum, I gotta go," I said hurriedly, cutting off the chaos on the other end of the line. "I love you, too." Hanging up the phone, I jogged to catch up to Summer before she could disappear into the trees. "Sunshine, hold up."

"I was about to leave you," she said, turning to face me while she walked backward.

"Leave *me*?" I said, pointing a finger to my chest for effect. "After going in my room to steal my radio?"

"You mean the radio you left in *my room* the other night?" she countered, one brow lifted in challenge.

"Oh, right." I'd forgotten I left it in there after our late-night Uno game with our friends. "Well, still sounds like theft to me," I said, shrugging. The sound of the stream grew louder as we walked side by side, the soft crunch of leaves and twigs under our feet. I took her hand, steadying her as we navigated some rough terrain, moving deeper into the trees. Their overgrown branches and weathered trunks forged a trail through the thick grove, shielding our hideaway from the rest of the world.

Nestled at the tip of the campsite, a towering oak tree with aged branches boldly stood, reaching toward the sky. Ancient, it looked like it held secrets of campers from years past. We'd stumbled on this spot a few weeks ago during one of our treasure hunts with the Creative Crew. To most, this part of the camp was unremarkable, rarely frequented because to the blind eye, there's nothing to see. But for me and Summer, it held purpose and beauty and magic. The tree's trunk was wide and weathered, with a hollowed-out nook that seemed to be carved by the hands of time. The opening was just wide enough for the two of us—our sanctuary. While the space felt like a secret chamber just for us, the etchings of initials, dates, and tiny hearts carved into the bark were reminders that this place had been others' secret long ago.

A hedge of wild ferns and moss-covered stones shielded us from the world but didn't conceal the beauty of the rolling green pastures and breathtaking views that stretched across the campgrounds. Summer spread out the blanket and sat cross-legged just as she'd done every time before. I settled beside her, flipping through the CDs to find some music to listen to. She unpacked the goodie bag, laying out turkey croissant sandwiches, potato chips, apple juice, and candy—a feast for only two. She leaned over me to grab the boom box and placed it between us.

I shook my head. As usual, she took control of the music, already humming along to the first few notes. Clearly unimpressed with the current song, she jabbed the button to skip to the next track. A smooth R&B groove filled the air, the familiar beat instantly recognizable.

"I tell him to kick off your shoes and relax," she sang along, swaying to the rhythm.

"Who sings this one?" I asked, cracking open the apple juice and leaning back. Summer gave me a pointed look. "Xscape," she replied, as if it was the most obvious thing in the world.

"Exactly. Let them sing it, then," I shot back, laughing so hard I nearly choked on my juice.

Her expression hardened, but the corner of her mouth twitched with amusement. Animatedly, she raised her middle finger, and whispered, "Fuck you," though her voice carried more mischief than malice.

"You love nineties music," I said, wiping my mouth after biting into the sandwich.

"Why do you say that?" she challenged.

"Because every time I'm in your room or hear you singing in the art center, it's always old-school Mariah Carey or Whitney Houston," I pointed out.

Summer let out a delighted breath, lighting up as she nodded in agreement. "The perks of having older siblings, I guess."

"How much older?" I asked, leaning forward slightly, genuinely curious.

"My brother is twenty-seven, and I have two sisters—twenty-three and twenty-one," she said, shrugging.

"Ah, so you're the baby. No surprise," I teased, a chuckle escaping as I saw her roll her eyes.

"Whatever." She playfully swatted at me. "What about you? Oldest, right?"

I nodded proudly. "Yep. Two sisters, two brothers—fifteen, thirteen, nine, and eight."

Summer let out a low whistle, shaking her head. "*Whew.* God bless your mom."

A warmth spread through me at the thought of my mother. "Yeah, my mum holds it down though."

Her head tilted slightly, curiosity flickering in her eyes. "Mum?" she repeated, her voice piqued with interest.

I nodded again, this time more thoughtfully. "My parents are from Nigeria. I was born there, but we moved to the States when I was just weeks old. In my family, it's tradition to call your mother *mum*. It's a sign of respect."

"That's sweet," she murmured, almost adoring, as if my words had touched her. The conversation faded, replaced by a hush that wasn't awkward but peaceful, like the stillness was a part of the agreement when at this place. We both leaned back, taking in the sky's expanse. I don't know why the quiet felt so easy with her, but I wasn't going to question it. Everything was moving so fast. Camp was going to be over before we knew it, but in this moment, everything was paused, and I didn't mind at all because the more time I had with Summer, the better.

"Do you have a boyfriend back home?" I blurted, breaking the quiet and immediately regretting it.

Summer's head snapped toward me, her brow arching in surprise. She shook her head. "Nope," she said simply, turning her focus back on the stars like I'd asked the dumbest question in the world.

My brow furrowed at her nonchalant tone. "Why'd you say it like that?"

"Like what?" she responded curtly, her voice calm but edged with something I couldn't quite place.

"Like that was a bad question," I replied, watching her closely. There was something in her posture, a discomfort she was trying to hide. "My bad. I didn't mean any harm. I'm just...surprised."

"Surprised? Why?" she asked dryly, almost daring me to say something stupid.

Because you are fucking gorgeous, I thought, but caught myself before the words slipped out. Instead, I shrugged. "Because you're dope. I'd think dudes would be all over you."

Her narrowed eyes darted my way, sharp and skeptical. I couldn't tell if she was amused or annoyed, but the moment was tense.

"Nope. That's not my story," she replied, bobbing her head to the music but looking more annoyed with every passing second.

"Sun, real talk," I said, leaning forward a little, hoping to break through her distraction. "Nobody likes you? No dudes trying to get with you?" The corner of my lip curved slightly in disbelief because whatever she was going to say couldn't be the truth.

She wrapped her arms around her legs, shrinking into herself in a way I hadn't seen before. "No," she snapped, her tone cold and clipped. "No dudes like me for real. No dudes are trying to get with me."

For real. I wondered what that meant. The words hit harder than expected because the way she said them stuck with me. It carried something heavier, but I momentarily held back from prying further. She was clearly pissed, uncomfortable even, and I probably should've let it go. But like the idiot I sometimes was, I just kept going. "I'on know, Sunshine," I said, shaking my head. "That sounds crazy to me. It's plenty dudes around here who try to get with you."

"Who?" Her pursed lips and creased forehead made it clear she was unimpressed with the flex. "And please don't say Kyle."

"Nah, not that corny dude," I replied, the thought alone making me mad because I'd heard the disrespectful way Kyle talked about girls. "What about Josh? He's always in your face."

Summer's face scrunched into a deep frown, like I'd just said the dumbest thing imaginable. "In the six or seven years I've known Josh, he's never asked me out—ever," she said. "He lives around the corner from me and goes to my school, so no, not even Josh," she said firmly. Her voice carried a sharp edge, tinged with impatience and finality, like she was daring me to say something else.

"Well, he's dumb as hell, man. If you weren't budding into my new best friend, I would be all over that," I said, biting the corner of my lip.

Tilting her head slightly, Summer studied me with caution, suspicion all over her face. "Boy, bye. Every girl at camp is '*Echo this*' and '*Echo that.*' You would never be checking for me."

"Nah, Sun, it's not even like that," I scoffed. "I'm just a friendly guy. I don't like any of these girls."

"Oh, really?" she challenged, her voice a bit lighter now. "So, what do you like in a girl, Echo?"

I spun my hat around before leaning back, thinking aloud. "*Hmm.* What do I like in a girl? I guess a crazy, sexy, cool type of chick."

Summer snorted, her lips quirking into a smile. "Soo, basically TLC."

I nodded, rubbing my hands together with exaggerated enthusiasm. "Exactly. You're not the only one who loves nineties R&B."

"Boy, please," she said, shaking her head. sOur chuckles were faint, floating off with the warm breeze. And for the first time in a while, an awkward lull settled between us. Summer tugged at her ear—a little nervous tic I'd noticed before—and then almost shyly, she whispered, "D–Do you think I'm crazy, cool…and, *um*, sexy?" Her voice was so soft I almost missed it, but I caught the way she avoided my stare, a blush creeping up her cheeks.

Hell yeah! Those eyes, that smile, those lips, damn, those thighs! Shit, she was all those things and more. But instead of telling her the truth, I played it off, laughing like a fool.

"Your ass is definitely crazy, Sunshine!" I nudged her shoulder, thinking that she'd share in the banter, maybe roll her eyes, or shove my shoulder back, but the smile I was waiting for never crossed her lips. Instead, her face stayed stoic, her eyes fixed somewhere in the distance. I thought I was breaking the tension, lightening the mood, but I'd fucked around and only managed to make it worse.

CHAPTER SEVEN

Echo
October 2019

PATIENCE WAS TRULY a virtue and never my strong suit, except when around Summer. The temperature was dropping by the second, yet my Sun seemed unfazed by the chill. She'd cried so much, I imagine she was probably numb to the chill. I glanced at my watch, then back at her, wondering how long we were going to stay out here. Caressing her, I realized how perfectly Summer's body still fit against mine. She wasn't the same girl I'd known at seventeen—she'd grown, evolved into someone more complex, yet, somehow, she was exactly the same. Soft but unyielding. Delicate yet unbreakable. Fearless, with that familiar trace of vulnerability lingering beneath the surface.

Summer lifted her face toward me, that subtle, closed-mouth smile doing what it always did—make my damn heart skip a beat. "E," she whispered, her voice the warmth I needed.

"*Hmm,*" I murmured, the sound barely audible.

"I'm glad you're here. I needed you more than you'll ever know."

"Me, too," I whispered back. I kept her close, holding her tighter, as restless thoughts of how we ended up here unraveled in my mind. My runaway-bride best friend. Here we were, at the spot that had always been ours. Our complicated friendship, riddled with so many twists and turns, and now this. Once again, it felt like we were teetering on the edge of something we could no longer ignore.

Her phone buzzed, and I glanced down to see Deshawn's name on the screen. He'd been calling nonstop for the past hour, and she sent him to voicemail...again. Pressing the voicemail button, she activated the speakerphone, and the anger and distress in her fiancé's voice couldn't be denied.

"You have ten new messages," the automated voice said.

"*Summer. Can you please call me? I'm not mad, baby, I'm worried about you. At least text me. Let me know you're okay. Summer? Baby? What the fuck happened? How could you just leave me like that—embarrass me, us, our families?*" Summer abruptly ended the message, tossing her phone to the side.

"Summer, you need to call him back," I said, my tone a bit stern. Although I didn't give a shit about Deshawn Towns, I wouldn't wish this kind of torment on my worst enemy. Not knowing where Summer was for even a couple hours nearly destroyed me. I couldn't imagine what he must be going through. "I'm sure your parents called him, but *you* need to call him. I don't know what happened, but you owe him at least that much."

She nodded, her trembling hands swiping away another round of tears. "I can't marry him, Echo. I just can't," Summer cried as she buried her head against my shoulder.

I allowed my hand to move gently up and down her back, trying to calm the storm inside of her. *I can't marry him.* Those were the main words she'd uttered for hours. I couldn't take it anymore—this endless dance with these cryptic-ass statements and silence. What's done is done, so it was time for her to cut the shit and talk.

"Summer, what happened?" I asked softly. "It's clear you can't marry him, or we wouldn't be here. Talk to me."

She swallowed hard as if the words were sticky in her throat. The piercing stare carried the same defiance I remembered from the hard-headed girl of yesteryear. The silence between us grew heavier by the second. I'd known Summer for almost half of my life, and if there was one thing I understood, she wouldn't be rushed—not into speaking. Shit, not into anything. She'd talk to me when she was ready…not a minute earlier.

"This isn't like you," I said, brushing my lips against her forehead. I cupped her chin with care, guiding her face upward until our gazes aligned. "You're not someone who makes rash decisions. You calculate and process—you don't just act on impulse. It's been a long time, but I still know you, Summer. And I refuse to believe you just woke up this morning and suddenly decided to walk away from the man you were supposed to spend your life with. When it's the love of your life, you don't just abandon everything you planned. Something happened. Something changed. Tell me I'm wrong." I pushed because this was how we worked. How we always had. Yes, she might be emotionally wrecked today, but she was strong—strong enough to handle whatever came next.

Summer shook her head, tears spilling freely, like a faucet that refused to shut off. She swiped at them with the back of her hand, agitated, almost angry at herself. She was sick and tired of crying. Her chest rose and fell unevenly, but then a dry, humorless chuckle slipped from her lips. It was hollow, tarnished with disbelief. It wasn't joy, wasn't amusement—just pain disguised as sound. "The love of my life, huh?" she whispered, her voice cracking under the weight of the words. Like saying them out loud would somehow make them real. Like maybe, if she repeated them enough, she'd finally believe them.

Echo
December 2018

"Yo," I answered the phone, lounging on the couch with a beer in hand while half-watching the basketball game. The cool December night in LA was perfect for a rare weekend to do nothing but chill.

"Yo." Seth's voice came through the line, brimming with energy. "A nigga's getting married," he blurted out. I shot upright on the couch, the game now the last thing on my mind.

Seth Daniels and I had met in grad school at Washington University. He'd come to St. Louis from Charlotte for school and a gig at Boeing. Over the years, we'd shared plenty of good times—partying and bullshitting hard, and dating more than our fair share of women. A wedding announcement from him of all people hit me like a curveball.

"What? For real?" I stammered, still trying to process. "Congrats, man. When do I get to meet the mystery lady?" Seth had been seeing someone—a woman he'd met online—for about six months. But he'd kept things unusually low-key—no social media posts or details shared. Still, an engagement this fast? That was unexpected.

"Brooke's not a mystery," Seth said, his tone defensive but proud. "We just wanted our shit to be our shit, you feel me?"

"I feel you, bro," I said, nodding to myself. "Congrats again, man. When it's time, it's time."

"We're not wasting time, either," Seth continued. "The ceremony's just family a couple of weeks from now, then we'll throw a big reception in May for our birthdays."

"Damn, that's quick," I said, nearly choking on my beer. "She pregnant or something?"

Seth laughed. "Hell no. She's just my heart, man. I can't wait to change her last name from Thompson to Daniels. Like, right fucking now."

"Thompson?" I asked, the name pulling at a thread in my memory. "Where's she from?"

"St. Louis," he replied, chuckling. "Crazy, right? Same city all along, and I had to find her through an app."

My chest constricted with something I couldn't name. *Brooke Thompson?* If she was the same Brooke I knew from Camp Quest—the one who was Summer's best friend—this was about to get real interesting.

"You good, E?" Seth's voice broke through my thoughts.

I cleared my throat. "Yeah. Yeah, I'm good," I managed, though my voice faltered. "I think I might know your fiancée." Without dragging Summer's name into the mix, I gave Seth just enough details to confirm it: His Brooke was *that* Brooke Thompson. *Damn.*

"So, you and Kourtni coming, right?" Seth asked, his tone light.

I masked my unease. "Yeah, man. I wouldn't miss it."

CHAPTER EIGHT

Echo
May 2019, Seth and Brooke's Wedding

"OH MY GOSH, babe. It's gorgeous," Kourtni exclaimed, her voice lifting with excitement as we stepped into the grand ballroom at the Drake Hotel for Seth and Brooke's reception and birthday celebration. The hashtag #DanielsbyDestiny shimmered in elegant script across a sparkling royal blue carpet as guests entered the dreamlike space. I watched as Kourtni's lips parted slightly, awestruck as she took in the room's grandeur.

"Yeah, it's nice," I muttered, doing my best to play it cool. But even I couldn't deny, it was breathtaking. Kourtni looped her arm around mine as we made our way to our assigned seats at table number eleven per the hostess's instructions.

Kourtni had been my on-again, off-again girlfriend for the past two years. We met shortly after I moved to LA at the Indie Film Festival. She and a friend were looking for a roommate, and I desperately needed a reasonably priced spot in a safe neighborhood. Although Kourtni was undeniably beautiful, back then, I wasn't in the market for a girlfriend. I had just arrived in a new city and was channeling my inner Akeem from *Coming to America*, ready to sow my royal oats. Kourtni was one of many I pursued during that phase, but we didn't start taking things seriously until much later.

Things between us were complicated. She wanted more than I could give right now—maybe more than I would ever be able to. I pulled out the golden chair, its back tied with a sheer ribbon and waited for Kourtni to sit before settling into my own seat. I surveyed the space with casual detachment, though my thoughts were far from calm. The tables glimmered beneath sequin-lined rose-gold linens, each adorned with vibrant floral arrangements in royal blue, blush rose, and bright sunflower yellow. Our names were written in intricate script on place cards, which were perched atop an elaborate place setting. My head swiveled, scanning the space for *her*. My chest tightened slightly at the thought of seeing her in person after almost fifteen years. I can't speak for Summer, but the distance? That was intentional on my part. At first, I was angry about how things ended. She left for school and built a life in Atlanta, and I was doing my thing in St. Louis. By the time I heard she'd moved back home, I had already left—first briefly returning to Chicago, then settling in LA. All these years, and somehow, the universe had never aligned our paths to cross. Not until today.

Seth and Brooke had called me on FaceTime weeks ago to let me know Summer knew I'd be here.

"I had to tell her, Echo," Brooke had said, her voice calm but edged with unease and understanding. "I didn't want her to be blindsided when she saw you. It's been so long since you two have connected." Her expression had been a mix of concern and compassion, the faint lines on her forehead deepening as she spoke. Brooke knew everything about what had gone down between Summer and me. Of course, she would worry about her friend. I'd assured her it wouldn't be an issue, though I wasn't sure who I was trying to convince—her or me.

The head table was a centerpiece of elegance in the room, adorned with lush roses and garlands spilling over its edges like a waterfall. Behind it, a floral wall of roses, sunflowers, and greenery framed Seth and Brooke's monogram, symbolizing their new beginning, even though they had already been married for several months. Guests began filing into the room, their chatter and laughter indicative of the love shared by the happy couple. But as I looked throughout the crowd, I still didn't see *her*.

"Echo Abara," a familiar raspy voice called from behind me. A bittersweet pull of nostalgia tugged at my heart. I'd recognize Teresa Knight's voice anywhere. I stood and turned to greet her, her sweet spirit bringing back a flood of memories.

"Ms. Teresa, it's so good to see you," I said, stepping into her open arms.

"*Mmm.* It's good to see you too, Echo," she replied warmly, holding me at arm's length to take a better look at me. Her hands stayed firmly on my arms, grounding me in her presence.

"Is Mr. Knight here?" I asked, though the question I truly wanted to ask burned on my tongue: *Where the hell is your daughter?*

She nodded. "Yes, honey. He just stepped away to the restroom. You know how it is when you get to our age."

"Yes, ma'am," I said

A sharp throat clear behind me jolted me into remembering my manners. I turned to find Kourtni glaring, her eyes wide, clearly waiting for an introduction. "Oh, my bad." I stumbled over my words. "Ms. Teresa, this is my girlfriend, Kourtni Lang." It felt strange saying the words out loud, almost like I was confessing a secret I'd been hiding.

"Nice to meet you, Kourtni. You look so pretty," Ms. Teresa said, her tone pleasant but tinged with a bit of nice-nasty, which she'd perfected. The deejay's voice boomed through the speakers, asking everyone to take their seats, signaling that the reception was about to begin. "Well, you two enjoy yourselves tonight," Ms. Teresa said with a slight smile. "I'll make sure Oliver says hello before the night is over." She gave a parting nod before gliding gracefully to her table.

The lights dimmed, and the bassline of Kanye West's "Clique" pulsed through the room, commanding attention. A spotlight swept to the ballroom entrance, casting a glow on the doors as they opened. Although Seth and Brooke chose a private wedding ceremony, there was no way they'd skip the fanfare of a traditional reception. Some guests rose to their feet, clapping and cheering as the wedding party began their grand entrance, one by one. When Trinity's name was called, followed by Hailee's, I already knew who was next. "And the third best friend to round out this best-friend trio, Miss Summer Knight!" the deejay announced with exuberance.

Damn. I blinked. *Damn.* Summer stepped out, moving to the beat with a natural sway that damn sure made me stand to attention. Her pouty lips were pursed as she danced down the pathway, laughing and flashing that pretty dimpled smile. The royal blue strapless bridesmaid dress clung to her body with a precision that felt unfair, showcasing every natural curve as though the dress had been custom designed just for her. The sequin bodice glimmered, hugging her full, bountiful breasts, something I remembered her once being self-conscious about. Her wavy hair was swept over one shoulder, leaving the graceful curve of her neck and shoulders bare, drawing even more attention to the slight shimmer of her amber skin.

The back of her dress dipped just low enough to tease, exposing a smooth expanse of skin and hinting at a sensuality that was equal parts timeless and electric. The fabric hugged her waist, hips, and ass in a way that demanded attention…my attention. The years had done her body good, and I couldn't help but notice how her curves had filled out perfectly. That ass in particular was its own masterpiece. The royal blue hue enhanced the radiance of her complexion, while the sequins reflected in the spotlight, making her every movement shimmer. She was magnetic, her presence so commanding, it was impossible to look away.

"Damn," I muttered under my breath, the word slipping out louder than I realized. Kourtni's sharp glare pierced me, pulling my focus just long enough to feel her disapproval, but it didn't matter. Summer was still the most beautiful girl in the world to me. That hadn't changed, and seeing her now only made it more undeniable.

Dinner had been served, and the champagne toasts were behind us. The room buzzed with excitement and conversation, but my focus had been singular: Summer. I watched her from the moment she sat down to eat, catching glimpses of her and the way she lit up the mic with her well wishes for Brooke. She wasn't doing a great job avoiding me, though she tried. Our connection had always been magnetic, even in a room full of people. It didn't matter how many years had passed. As the party shifted into full swing, I decided enough was enough—it was time to talk. But Summer wasn't making it easy. When I first approached her at the bar, she darted off before I could say a word. When she grabbed a slice of cake, I caught up to her.

"Can I have some?" I asked, my tone playful.

"Nope," she said, not even looking at me before slipping away again, barefoot, her heels abandoned hours ago.

I'd lost track of Kourtni in the crowd, and honestly, I wasn't looking for her. She wasn't the type to sit still at a party, so I could almost guarantee she was on the floor, picking up the latest line dance. My eyes, however, found the beauty in the royal blue dress seated next to a man she'd been with for most of the night. That had to be Summer's boyfriend, Deshawn. Seth had mentioned meeting him once at a gala Brooke had dragged him to, but I hadn't asked for details. Deshawn seemed more interested in his phone than anything happening around him, while Summer sat beside him, downing her drink like she was trying to wash away the night. She tapped his arm, murmured something, and gestured toward the bar. I moved slowly, weaving through the crowd until I reached it, cornering her before she could disappear again.

"Vodka and pineapple juice, please," she said to the bartender, her voice calm and steady.

"Light on the vodka. She's a mean drunk," I joked, making my presence known. Summer froze for a second, her shoulders rising as she inhaled deeply at the sound of my voice. "Hi, Summer," I said, taking in the graceful curve of her back before she turned to face me.

She spun around slowly, and despite herself, she blessed me with as soft, familiar smile. "Hi, Echo." My heart stilled, remembering the first time she had me at hello.

Echo
That One Summer in 2004

Rushing around my room, I hopped in the shower and set a personal record for speed, washing only the essentials. Minutes later, I threw on underwear, a clean pair of basketball shorts, a white T-shirt, and tall socks, mentally gearing up to call Summer. Camp had ended a week ago, and I'd been itching to call her, but I didn't want to look desperate. Before I could psych myself up any further, faint knocks interrupted my thoughts. I groaned because I knew that it was my little sister, Sadie. She'd been my shadow since I'd come home.

"Echo, whatcha doin'?" she sang as her little eyes peeked around the door, long, beaded braids swinging into her face.

I tried to fight it, but my mouth lifted, welcoming her in. "I'm a little busy, Didi. What's up?"

"Can we play the game?" she asked, her little pout forming as if she already knew I was going to say no.

"Not right now," I said, gently steering her toward the hallway. "Where's Eazy?"

"Napping with Dada," she replied, crossing her arms as if she was considering her next move.

"Well, why don't you take a nap, too? When you wake up, we can play whatever game you want," I offered, pinching her cheek before nudging her farther out of the room.

"You promise?" she asked skeptically, testing my sincerity.

"Pinkie swear," I said, holding up my finger. Sadie knew better than anyone that a pinkie swear from me was ironclad. Her face lit up as we joined fingers, and she took off full speed down the hallway. I couldn't help but chuckle as I closed the door, finally giving myself a moment of peace. I walked over to my bed, flopped onto it, and stared at the ceiling.

With the phone clutched in my hand, I just held it, my thumb hovering over the screen, ready to call Summer What if our conversations were different away from camp? The thought gnawed at me. What if she was different? My throat was dry, and I couldn't make sense of the nerves coursing through me. Summer had been the first person in a long time who I'd let my guard down with so easily. Talking to her had been natural. Uncomplicated. The fun we shared came unforced.

So why the hell are you nervous, dumbass? "Fuck it," I said, quickly dialing her number before I lost my nerve.

The phone rang, and then a deep voice broke through the silence. "Hello," her father said, snapping me out of my daze.

"*Um*, hello, sir. May I speak with Summer?" My voice cracked like I was ten years old.

"Who's calling?" he asked, his tone neutral but somehow intimidating.

"Echo, sir," I managed, clearing my throat to sound older, more confident. "A friend from summer camp."

A beat of silence stretched, feeling like an eternity before he finally yelled, "Summer! Phone!" His voice echoed through their house, then the line went eerily quiet. I glanced around my room, confused, wondering if he'd hung up.

"Hello?" I said lowly, checking the line to make sure we were still connected.

"I got it, Daddy," she shouted before speaking into the phone. "Hello. Who is this?" Her fiery tone burst through the receiver like a cannon, catching me off guard.

"Hey, Sunshine," I said, my lips curving into a smile as her familiar voice instantly washed over me. Lubrication returned to my lungs, and the tension in my chest dissolved as I leaned back into the pillows. "That's how you answer the phone?" I teased, already feeling like myself again.

"Hi, Echo."

Echo
May 2019, Seth and Brooke's Wedding

"You done running from me?" I asked, leaning casually against the bar. She took another deep breath, her eyes flitting over me for just a second too long. Her body language spoke volumes, although her words remained guarded.

"Running? I wasn't running," she said, feigning nonchalance. "Just busy making sure Brooke is having the time of her life." Her expression softened, watching her friend on the dance floor.

"Can we talk?" I asked, my voice softer, almost pleading.

She shook her head lightly. "About what?" she replied, her tone cool, though the way her fingers fidgeted with the glass told another story.

"Just to catch up," I said, rubbing my hands together as if steadying myself. "It's been a long time, Sunshine." The nickname rolled off my tongue effortlessly. She hesitated, her walls visibly wavering at the sound of the name I'd never given another.

For a moment, it felt like we were teenagers again, caught in that timeless push and pull that never seemed to fade. "Just a second, Sun, please," I begged, my voice barely above a whisper.

Our breaths synced, shallow and unsteady, as my finger barely skimmed her forearm. The contact was a spark—no, scratch that, a fucking inferno—rekindling something in me that had smoldered for fifteen years. And from the way her throat bobbed, the way her breath caught ever so slightly, I knew she felt it, too. Something ancient and burning flared back to life for us both. The same slow burn, the same fire that threatened to consume us all those years ago.

She swallowed hard, a tremor rippling down her neck, her body betraying what her mind hadn't yet given into—my tongue across my lips, as my thumb traced small, lazy circles against her skin, a whisper of a touch—deliberate, yet unconscious. A silent plea for just a moment with her. That's all I was asking. That's all we both deserved. But as the air between us thickened, one truth remained: This moment was dangerous, and neither of us was sure we should take it.

CHAPTER NINE

Summer
May 2019, Seth and Brooke's Wedding

FIVE THOUSAND, FOUR hundred seventy-five days. One hundred thirty-one thousand, four hundred hours. That's how long it had been. That's how long I had tried to forget him, to bury the weight of what we were beneath time and distance. *It wasn't meant to be*, I'd tell myself over and over, as if repetition could make it true. As if I could will myself to believe that whatever we had was child's play, a moment in time that had passed. And yet here I was, still caught in the pull of Echo Abara, powerless to resist. No matter how much I wanted to walk away, I found myself here—standing on the patio just outside the ballroom, drifting back into his orbit once again.

If someone asked me to define what Echo and I had, I'd borrow one of my favorite words from Shakespeare: *labyrinthine*—intricate, complex, impossible to navigate. A complicated word for a complicated situation. The perfect way to captured the maze of emotions, history, and unspoken truths lingering between us. Or maybe it was just confusion. Either way, it was a tangle I couldn't seem to unravel. Not then. Not now. And God help me, I wasn't sure I wanted to.

My eyes flickered between the St. Louis Arch glowing faintly in the distance and the string lights draped along the patio's edge, both casting a soft, golden glow over the night. The scene was set for something intimate. But we didn't need ambience. This wasn't a romantic moment between me and Echo.

"You dragged me out here, so talk," I snapped, my voice carrying more attitude than was necessary.

He exhaled, unfazed. "I don't recall you kicking and screaming," Echo shot back. "Not much has changed, I see."

I stiffened, crossing my arms, leaning on my feistiness as a protective shield. "Actually, a lot has changed. I'm not the same Summer you once knew."

"I can see that," he said quickly, the words slipping out before he could stop them. For a split second, regret flashed across his face, his gaze dragging over me like a reflex. It was clearly unintentional, but undeniable. I bit my bottom lip, trying to suppress the blush crawling up my cheeks.

"Real talk…it's really good to see you, Summer," he admitted, relaxing against the brick pillar. "What are the odds that my boy would end up with your best friend?"

I nodded, letting a bit of my defensiveness melt away. "That is kinda crazy," I said. "Brooke kept Seth a secret for a while. We're just now getting to know him—and the company he keeps."

"Seth's good people. Brooke's in good hands," Echo said with certainty.

I nodded again, glancing back into the ballroom. Earlier, I had been searching for Deshawn, but this time, I was simply admiring Brooke, glowing with happiness as she danced with Seth. "She deserves every bit of happiness," I said quietly.

Echo tilted his head slightly. "What about you, Sunshine?"

"What about me?" I asked, though I already knew what he was getting at.

"Are you getting all the happiness your heart can hold?" he asked, his voice softer now as he took a sip from his glass, his brow lifting in question. His words hit deeper than I expected, and I fell silent, lost in a swirl of thoughts I wasn't prepared to confront. No one had ever asked me that before. But of course, Echo saw me—he always had. Even after all these years, he still saw me.

"I'm engaged," I said flatly, the words settling heavily between us.

"Congratulations," Echo replied, his tone laced with a hint of sarcasm that didn't escape me.

"Thank you," I muttered, watching him warily. "You don't seem surprised. I guess I should've known Seth told you."

He shook his head. "I don't speak with Seth about you," he said. "But I was aware. Again, congratulations, Sunshine."

"Thanks," I whimpered, my voice faltering under the weight of his presence. Or maybe it was the way he called me *Sunshine*—smooth and easy, like the years between us never existed. Like we were still the same kids who once believed forever was ours.

Echo tilted his head slightly, studying me, as if searching for the girl he once knew. "So, does the excitement grow over time, or is this…it?" he said, punctuating the words with a nonchalant shrug.

His voice was casual, but the question sat heavier than it should have. The eye roll of old returned involuntary—a reflex I thought I'd outgrown. I hated how easily he could read me, how he still peeled back my layers like no time had passed.

"Stop acting like you know me. I'm excited. Elated, even," I added, pushing the words out too forcefully. But even as they left my lips, they felt hollow.

A quiet scoff slipped from him as he shook his head, his focus drifting upward toward the steel arch towering above us. "This was the scene of your happy day, right?" He gestured to the monument, its soft glow casting shadows against the St. Louis skyline.

I nodded, ready to ask how he knew Deshawn had proposed there, but Echo continued before I could speak. "Maybe things *have* changed because I don't remember the pomp and circumstance of it all being your style."

"What do you mean?" I asked, my voice softer now, drawn in, clinging to every syllable. Somehow, I felt both affirmed and exposed.

"The Summer I used to know hated attention," he said, turning to me, his stare composed and unflinching. "I always imagined your dream engagement would be something simple—a quiet dinner at home, cuddled up by the fireplace with your sketchbook, the ring tucked away somewhere in the folds, waiting for you to find it. That's the Summer I used to know."

I swallowed hard, but the lump in my throat refused to budge. He was right. That *was* me. I didn't like attention, and the memory of the day I got engaged played back with startling clarity.

When Deshawn told me he had plans for Valentine's Day, I'd groaned internally. I was drained from a business trip, and the icy February wind cut through me as I stepped out of the car. My cheeks ached from forcing a smile as I saw the crowd—family, friends, and a few folks I didn't know gathered under the Arch. Deshawn stood holding a bouquet of roses in front of oversized, illuminated letters spelling out *Marry Me*. I remembered the freezing cold biting at my skin and the exhaustion tugging at my limbs. But what stuck out most wasn't the cold or the crowd, it was the disconnect between the spectacle around me and the quiet simplicity I'd always dreamed of.

"I..." I began, but the words caught in my throat as I felt someone else's presence on the patio. Echo and I turned in unison, pulled from our moment by the sight of Deshawn and who I assumed was Kourtni standing in the doorway. Brooke told me that Echo had a plus-one for the reception. Deshawn's expression curious; hers accusatory.

"Summer, babe, what are you doing? I've been looking for you," Deshawn said, his tone matter of fact.

"Echo, where've you been?" Kourtni chimed in, her eyes darting between us, but pausing to slowly examine me as she waited for him to answer. Echo leaned casually against the patio railing, his hands clasped in front of him. His calm demeanor contrasted sharply with my racing pulse. I felt like a guilty party, though I had done nothing wrong—well, maybe except walk down the dangerous road called memory lane.

Clearing my throat, I forced myself to speak. "Shawn. Hey. I just needed some air," I said, my voice thin.

Kourtni's stare was unwavering, silently demanding Echo explain himself. He stayed quiet, briefly turning to me before shifting to our visitors. Desperate to diffuse the tension, I spoke again. "Oh, *um*, Deshawn, this is Echo."

Echo stepped forward, extending a hand toward Deshawn. "What's up, man? Echo Abara." His tone was smooth, practiced, like nothing about this moment was uncomfortable. "And this is Kourtni Lang," he added, finally acknowledging her presence.

"Deshawn Towns, Summer's fiancé," Deshawn announced, his chest puffing slightly. Then his brow furrowed, and he snapped his fingers as though he'd just pieced something together. "Wait. Didn't you two go to the same camp with Brooke one summer?"

Echo's lips curled into something that could hardly pass as a smile, his sneer barely concealed. If his dark eyes were fire, we would've all been incinerated. "Yeah," he said, his voice clipped. "Something like that."

Straightening from the railing, Echo strode past me, his movements unhurried and deliberate, like he had already decided this conversation was over. I turned just in time to watch his back as he moved toward Kourtni, the woman who, despite standing only a few feet away, her connection to him remained a mystery to me. He hadn't introduced her as a friend. Not as a girlfriend. Not as anything. Just there, existing in his space with no clear title. Her expression was caught somewhere between frustration and uncertainty, as if she couldn't decide whether to be mad at him or to ask him what the hell was going on. But Echo didn't stop. He barely even acknowledged her. Instead, just before disappearing back into the party, he tossed one last glance over his shoulder, his voice casual, his words anything but.

"Oh, and congratulations, man. On the engagement." A beat of silence followed. The kind that stretched just a little too long.

Deshawn nodded, his thanks clipped, maybe even cautious. Then, without hesitation, he stepped closer, his arm snaking around my waist, pulling me into him like a quiet claim. His lips pressed to my forehead, a soft, lingering kiss, but the warmth of it did nothing to ease the sudden chill settling in my bones.

The unspoken tension buzzed between Echo and me the rest of the night—electric and undeniable, fueled by the charged history we shared. No matter how crowded the room, Deshawn and Kourtni's awareness never strayed far. Their curiosity was palpable, relentless, yet silent scrutiny and muted accusations hung heavy in the air, teetering on jealousy. Maybe they were justified because they became glue, clinging to us all night.

I thought about how Deshawn described my connection to Echo. *Camp one summer.* For anyone else, it might have sounded harmless, just words spoken without substance, but for me and Echo? That one summer wasn't just a fleeting moment. It was everything—friendship that blurred into something deeper, love that simmered quietly beneath the surface, and a thousand what-ifs that still lingered between us…unexpressed and unexplored. And no one—not Deshawn, not Kourtni, not anyone—could ever fully understand what it meant.

CHAPTER TEN

Summer
That One Summer in 2004

"YOUR ASS IS *definitely crazy, Sunshine!*" Echo's words replayed over and over in my head, blaring like a song I couldn't turn off.

Unlike Ice Cube's iconic words, today was not a good day. It was one of those Gemini days for me—the kind where nothing felt right. Two days had passed since Echo and I had spent the evening at what we'd claimed as our hideaway, and his words still had me in a mood. A bad mood. He'd been trying to get my attention ever since he'd walked me to my lodge that night, but I'd basically ignored him. I didn't want to talk. I didn't want to deal. I just wanted to be left alone, though that was nearly impossible when we were responsible for about fifty campers every day.

My roommate and one of my best friends, Trinity, could always tell when I was in my feelings. She knew the second Mariah Carey's heartbreak anthems started blaring through the room, with me belting the lyrics from the depths of my soul, as if I actually knew what that kind of heartbreak felt like. Mario's "Let Me Love You" played, and I maxed out the volume. My conversation with Echo played on a relentless loop in my head, tangled up with the saddest love songs I could find.

"*Your ass is definitely crazy,*" I recalled him saying. He thought that shit was funny. Of course he did. I'm not sure why I was surprised. I'd always been the girl guys thought was cute enough to be their friend, little sister, or *baby girl*, but never sexy enough to be taken seriously as a girlfriend.

Skipping the night's festivities, I paced the small piece of floor available in my compact bedroom, dressed in pajama shorts and a tank top, my face dotted with skin cream. I stopped to glance at my reflection in the mirror, scrutinizing my body again. I guess the figure staring back at me wasn't what boys my age considered sexy. Why did I care what Echo thought anyway? He was just a friend, not a boy I wanted to like me. His opinion shouldn't have mattered, but it did.

"Summer, you have company!" Brooke's voice rang out from the common area, snapping me out of my spiraling thoughts.

Company? Who the hell? I sighed, already irritated. "Who, Brooke? I'm busy!" Before she could answer, Echo strolled into my room like he owned the place, hat turned backward, repping Chicago like always, basketball shorts hanging just low enough to test my resolve, and a jersey clinging to the muscles he was clearly working on. I crossed my arms, my irritation flaring.

"Yo, what's up, man? Why are you not talking to me?" His voice carried just enough bite to tell me he was annoyed, too.

Heat creeped up my face. "Brooke! Why would you let him back here?" She knew I was in a mood. She also knew I had skin cream smeared all over my damn face.

Brooke peeked down the hall, her expression torn. With a shrug, she threw her hands in the air and walked off, wanting no part of the brewing storm. I sighed, turning back to Echo, who was now standing in the middle of my space like he wasn't about to make my entire evening worse.

"What do you want, Echo? I am not in the mood for—"

"Sun, go wash your face, and bring your ass outside," he cut me off, his voice low and brimming with frustration.

"Echo, I'm not—"

"Summer!" His tone sharpened, a seriousness I'd never heard from him before.

"Fine," I grunted, stomping off to the bathroom.

After splashing water on my face and pulling on a pair of jean shorts over my pajamas, I trekked down the hall, throwing another pointed glare at Brooke on my way out. She just shrugged again, making sure I kept her out of whatever what going between me and *my friend*. Outside, Echo was already walking ahead, casting a glance over his shoulder with a scowl to ensure I was following. We didn't head to our usual spot by the stream. Instead, he led me toward the front of the campgrounds.

The stillness of the night amplified every sound and unvoiced word. A light breeze stirred the leaves, their faint rustle mingling with the persistent chirping of crickets and the occasional buzz of cicadas. The moon didn't appear to hang as low in the sky from this purview as it did at our spot. The silvery light it casted across the trees that faded in the darkness was still beautiful. But my mood was ugly. The swing we shared sat underneath an aging tree like our tree. Echo sat leaning forward, elbows resting on his knees. He removed his hat and rubbed a hand down the wavy carpet of hair on his head. His posture was tense and jaw tight as if he was holding back words he wasn't ready to say.

I sat back, arms crossed defensively over my chest, eyes cast downward. I tapped my foot incessantly as I bit my bare nails, irritation simmering. The air between us felt thick, not with anger, because I had no real reason to be upset, but with confusion and contained emotions that we were likely too immature to name.

In a voice softer than I expected, Echo finally broke the quiet. "What is wrong with you? What did I do?"

"Nothing," I replied curtly, but it was the truth. He hadn't done anything wrong. But the Gemini that lived in me wouldn't tell him that. Instead, I kept shaking my foot, refusing to give him my attention.

"Then why have you been ignoring me?" he pressed.

Because I think I like you. "No reason," I blurted instead. "I'm cool." My tone was flat as I continued to gnaw on my nails.

"Would you stop tapping your foot and biting those damn nails and just talk to me, Summer?" he snapped, his voice rising slightly.

"You have one more time to yell at me, Echo," I said sharply, my tone daring him to try again. My foot stilled, my entire posture shifting as if to demand an apology without uttering another word.

"I'm sorry, and I'm not yelling," he said, his voice rising slightly with exasperation. Then he threw his hands up, his eyebrows pulling together in frustration. "Why are we arguing?"

It was a great question; one I didn't have an easy answer for. The tension between us felt like an unwelcomed third wheel, sitting heavy in the middle of a conversation that had somehow grown far too intense for two people who had only known each other a few weeks.

"Echo, I've just been in a bad mood. Sometimes that happens. I didn't want to talk to anybody, so that includes you. I just needed a day to myself," I huffed, turning away from him, pouting like a toddler.

"Man, you've had *days* to yourself. Plural. You wouldn't even come to our spot with me to chill. What's up with that? Who pissed you off?" He pointed at himself like he thought he was the problem.

I shook my head, desperately wanting to end this. "Nobody pissed me off," I snapped. "Maybe I just need a break from 'chilling,'" I said, throwing air quotes around the word.

"Sunshine. Come on. Be real with me. What's going on?" Echo's baritone was tender.

I sat silently for a long moment, my thoughts churning. Did I really want to tell him what was on my mind? In just a few weeks, we'd already peeled back so many layers, sharing dreams, fears, and truths we hadn't spoken aloud to others. He'd told me how strict his father was, how his mother wanted to work but was essentially forced to stay home because of tradition.

I'd confessed my fear that my parents wouldn't have enough money for me to attend Spelman, and even if they did, I was terrified to go that far away from home. But this? Did I want to share this revelation with him?

"I'm tired of being the chill girl or the crazy, cool friend with the cute face and pretty smile," I said finally, my voice trembling as I stood abruptly. Feeling tears threaten, I whispered, "I'm sick of that shit, E."

The words stung more than I expected. My frustration wasn't just about Echo—it was much deeper than him. It was about every guy who'd crossed my path, slapping the same label on me like it was all I could ever be. But unfortunately for him, he stood directly in the path of my rage.

"What does that mean?" he asked, as he tried to understand. "You are chill. You are cool. You are the friend with the cute face and pretty smile," he said, his voice steady while searching my eyes for agreement.

My fingers toyed with my earlobe, twisting my stud earring between them, wishing I could press reset on this moment. Wishing I could rewrite it, reshape it, make him see. But he didn't understand. Maybe he couldn't. How could I explain that I wanted to be more than just the crazy, cool friend? That I needed him to see me differently—something more than comfortable and familiar. That I wanted him to see me as...sexy, too? As...*his*.

"What else do you want to be, Sunshine?" he asked, stepping closer, brushing his shoulder against mine. His voice was calm, but there was something deeper in his tone, something I couldn't place.

I want to be yours, I thought, the truth hitting me with an intensity that made my heart hurt. But I shook my head, trying to push it away. I couldn't let myself go there. Echo had made it clear that we were friends—only friends. Nothing more.

I was angry, emotional, and confused, but as I stood next to him, I couldn't ignore the warmth of his presence. Echo had this way of making me feel safe and comfortable to just be me. Even when I was treating him like crap, he came to find me, pushed me to open up, to talk to him. And as much as I'd lied to myself these past few days, convincing myself I needed distance, one truth burned brighter than all the lies: I didn't want to be away from him. Even if it meant I'd always be his forever friend.

Shaking my head, I finally answered his question. "Nothing. I'm good. I guess I just needed to talk." I went silent, swallowing hard to find my voice to continue. "I'm sorry," I whispered, my tone tinged with fragility, but my eyes stayed connected to his. My words hung in the air, raw and honest, carrying a burden I wasn't ready to face. Instinctively, I turned to walk away, needing space to sort through the whirlwind of emotions. But before I could step away, his hand gently caught my arm. The touch was light, barely there, but it was enough to make me pause. He held me tighter, and I hesitated, resisting the silent plea in his gesture, my back still to him. For a moment, I considered ignoring it, pretending I didn't feel the pull. But finally, with a deep breath, I turned to face him. At almost seventeen, I was used to being fierce, full of fire and defiance, my resolve clouded, my breath unsteady with unshed tears I couldn't hide.

Echo's face softened. Without a word, he draped his arms around my shoulders, pulling me into him. It was our first hug, and it felt like home. His touch was warm and steady, familiar in a way that made me want to fall apart and stay whole all at once. He towered over me, resting his chin gently against the top of my head, like a shield of protection. With the lightest touch, he nudged my chin upward, drawing me into something neither of us had words for. It was too deep, too overwhelming for hearts as young as ours to fully grasp. But we felt it anyway—wild and crazy and all-consuming.

"So, we're friends again?" he asked softly, his voice the calm to my storm.

I nodded, the lump in my throat making it impossible to speak. When the words finally came, they were barely above a whisper. "Yeah, E. Forever friends."

CHAPTER ELEVEN

Summer
That One Summer in 2004

IT WAS OFFICIALLY the first day of summer, though the weather in Brighton Falls had already been flirting with triple digits for weeks. The heat wasn't new, but today felt different... special. It was a Saturday, which meant I could stay in bed just a little longer than usual. I glanced over and saw Trinity still curled up under the covers, clearly taking full advantage of the lazy morning, too. Stretching through a relaxed sigh, I rolled onto my side and looked out the window. The sun was already high, its golden rays streaming in, brightening the room in a warm, happy glow. Everything about today felt brighter and lighter. Maybe that was because today wasn't just any day. It was my seventeenth birthday.

In the Knight family, birthdays weren't just days; they were events, practically holidays. When we were younger, Mama would go all out—big parties with balloons, cakes, and all our family and friends running wild in the backyard. But as we got older and decided we'd rather party with our friends instead of our parents, Mama came up with a new tradition. Every year, she hosted one massive Memorial Day party to celebrate all four of her kids since our birthdays were packed into the months of May and June. It was her way of keeping the tradition alive. And for me, the Memorial Day party had an added significance: It was the perfect sendoff before I'd leave for camp. So technically, I'd already celebrated my birthday back home, so I didn't want to make a big deal out of my actual birthday today. Still, I'd promised my parents I'd call around ten o'clock before the day got busy, so I needed to get moving.

"Okay. Stop daydreaming, Summer Sierra," I whispered to myself, mimicking my mama's voice perfectly.

"Happy birthday, best friend," Trinity mumbled groggily, wiping the sleep from her eyes.

"Thank you," I squealed.

Before I could say anything else, a knock at the door caught both of our attention. Trinity barely lifted her head before yelling, "Yeah."

In burst Brooke and Neveah, our roommates, carrying a boom box blasting the iconic hood birthday anthem—Uncle Luke's "It's Your Birthday."

Brooke grinned and shouted over the music, "So, what's that number one birthday month?"

I shot up in bed, already dancing to the beat. "June!" I yelled, throwing my hands in the air. Neveah followed with, "And what's that number one zodiac sign?"

"Gemini!" I screamed, shimmying out of bed.

The room erupted as I perched my lips, bent low with my booty in the air and my hands on my knees, dancing like I didn't have a care in the world. My girls joined in, chanting and hyping me up. "Go, Summer! It's ya birthday! Go, Summer! It's ya birthday!" We collapsed into a fit of laughter, the kind that left my cheeks aching and my stomach sore. My friends knew, even if I didn't say it out loud, that as much as I complained about my family, I missed them on my birthday every summer. The birthday chant was a tradition my sisters had always done with me, and while I missed them dearly, my girls at camp filled that void perfectly this year.

I rushed around the room, scrambling to get ready. We'd had way too much birthday fun, and now I was running late. Jumping in the shower, I lathered my thick curves in cucumber-scented body wash, the fresh, clean scent clinging to my skin as I hurried to rinse off. Today was swim day for the campers, so I pulled on the blue camp-issued swimsuit, threw on a pair of denim shorts, and slipped into my thong sandals. Rushing across the quad, I waved at campers and fellow counselors who shouted birthday wishes my way. My heart swelled with every well wish, even as I checked the time and realized it was already a few minutes after ten. I'd have to talk fast to make it to the lake in time for my shift.

"Hey, Daddy," I said, my tone brightening instantly as the sound of his voice filled my ear.

"Happy birthday to you, happy birthday to you. Happy birthday, my baby, happy birthday to you," he sang, completely offbeat but with so much love it didn't matter.

I giggled like a little girl. "Thank you, Daddy."

"Oli, give me the phone," I heard my mother fuss in the background. "Hey, baby girl. Blessed birthday wishes to you," Mama said.

"Thanks, Ma. How are you?" I asked, the sound of her voice soothing me.

"Good. I'm about to take your grandmother to the grocery store, so pray for me." She chuckled.

I could already imagine the chaos that would ensue. "Oh, have fun with that," I said, knowing full well how particular Granny could be.

"You have anything planned for today?" Mama asked.

I shook my head, forgetting for a moment that she couldn't see me. "Not really. The kids are at the lake today, so my friends and I will hang out there, but no big plans."

"Okay, well, I know you have to go. Happy birthday, Summer. We love you," Mama said.

"Love you, baby!" Daddy called out from the background.

"I love you, too," I said, ending the call, a brief wave of sadness coming over me. Dashing out of the main building, I caught up with my friends just as they were heading to the lake. The sun was shining, my heart was full, and everything felt perfect.

The campers were having the time of their lives at the lake. Activities had been planned for everyone, whether they wanted to swim in the cool water or stay on land. And with the heat so brutal, the lake was practically a necessity. Not much of a swimmer myself, I stuck to helping with the other activities. A couple of hours of volleyball and double Dutch later, I was both hot and completely exhausted. Grabbing an ice-cold water and chips from the lunch area, I made my way toward where the girls were. They were sprawled out on blankets like they were at some glamorous beach. Some of them were even wearing oversized sunglasses and shiny lip gloss, giving off major wannabe Hollywood vibes.

"Damn, he's fine," I heard Madison say, her tone dripping with admiration. I followed her gaze toward the lake, and of course, it landed right on Echo. There he was, water dripping down his chest, his shorts slung low on his hips. I hated how easy it was to agree with her.

"I thought you were checking for Maxell," Trinity said, as she sat up, clearly unimpressed by Madison's ever-changing interests.

I plopped down on Trinity's blanket, shooting her a knowing look, which she returned, equally irritated.

Madison Harvey was the camp hoe—there was no other way to say it. We'd been coming to camp together for years, and a few summers ago, her body had developed to match her quickly growing ego. Her light skin, hazel eyes, and easy-access demeanor had every boy at camp smitten. She didn't have to try; they flocked to her like dogs to bones. And as much as I hated to admit it, she was probably exactly the type of girl Echo would call sexy.

"Maxell is so last year, girl. There's new meat to be devoured," Madison said, her voice dripping with innuendo as she bit her bottom lip, never tearing her eyes from Echo. "You know what they say about tall, lanky boys." She shared a high five with her roommate, Iris, who was lounging next to her.

Confusion swirled in my head, but I wouldn't dare let it show on my face. *What do they say about tall, lanky boys?* I had no clue. My traitorous eyes wandered back to Echo despite my better judgment. He was shirtless, wearing only the camp-branded swim trunks. He was playing water basketball with some of the campers, and the grin that lit up his face when our favorite camper, David, made a basket sent a strange, unexpected surge through my center. I swallowed hard, suddenly aware of the sensation I hadn't paid much attention to before. Something hot simmered low in my stomach, my thighs pressing together instinctively. I took a long sip of water, desperate for any type of distraction, but it was useless. I clung to his every move like a magnet.

"No. What do they say?" Leah, another counselor, asked, her expression mirroring my own confusion. I was thankful her question interrupted where my mind had just wandered. A harmless daydream, right? The funny feeling in my panties said it was something a little less innocent.

Madison spun around so fast, like Leah had just asked the dumbest question imaginable. Leah, unfazed, cocked her head, clearly waiting for an answer.

Madison's voice lowered like she was sharing a scandalous secret. "Let's just say, their third leg is as long as they are tall."

Leah's brow furrowed. "Can you stop talking in riddles? What does that even mean?" she demanded, her voice sharp, cutting through the tension.

I watched, silently thankful for her curiosity and boldness because I wouldn't dare ask for clarity myself, even though I wanted to know more than anything.

"That their dicks are big, girl, damn," Iris whispered through gritted teeth.

My eyes ballooned, right along with Leah's and a few other girls. Our reactions were identical and almost comical. Against my better judgment, my gaze flicked back to Echo. And now I couldn't help it, I was staring...*down there*. Mama said curiosity kills the cat. And right now, I was dangerously close to understanding why.

Echo
That One Summer in 2004

"Yo, you see them?" Kyle asked, standing waist-deep in the water, his voice just low enough to sound like he thought he was slick.

"Yep," Maxell replied, tossing the basketball to a camper but not even pretending to look anywhere but toward the group of girl counselors.

I didn't need to follow their gaze to know who they were looking at—I'd already seen who I wanted to see. Summer wasn't originally with the crowd of girls lounging like they were on a beach vacation instead of working with campers, but now there she was. I'd peeped her walking across the quad earlier, effortlessly pretty, as usual. Lately, she had a way of making everything seem... easy.

I was stuck in my own thoughts, mindlessly tossing the ball, when Bryant's voice cut through my haze. "What's the plan for Summer's birthday?"

My head snapped around so fast I felt the water ripple around me. *Her birthday?* I must've misheard him. "Her birthday is today?" I asked, keeping my tone as neutral as possible while heat rose in my cheeks. *Why the hell didn't I know it was her birthday?*

Bryant nodded. "Yeah, man. You know Summer, though. She hates making a big deal, but we drag her out anyway."

"Ain't that your girl, E?" Kyle chimed in, his voice laced with that annoying tease he always used. "And you don't even know it's her birthday?"

"Whatever, man," I said, brushing off his comment while anger simmered just beneath the surface. *How the hell did I not know?* I thought. After all the time we'd spent together, this wasn't something I should've missed. Without another word, I waded out of the water.

"Watch them," I ordered, pointing to the group of kids playing. The annoyance was clear in my voice.

When I glanced back, I saw Maxell and Bryant trailing me. We walked toward the group of giggling girls, and it was obvious they were whispering about us—or more likely just me. Fingers pointed in my direction, and their cackles grew louder with every step I took. Madison rose from the blanket, tossing her hair over her shoulder, like she was getting ready to greet me, but she wasn't the one I was coming for. The moment I directed my greeting at Summer, Madison's face collapsed into a scowl. It was obvious she didn't appreciate being overlooked, but I didn't care. I needed to talk to Summer.

"What's up, Sunshine?" I said, standing directly in front of her.

She squinted up at me, lifting a hand to block the sun, but her gaze didn't stay on mine for long. It danced back and forth from my face to somewhere else, like she couldn't quite decide where to focus.

"Hey," she replied, her tone casual, but the slight flush creeping across her cheeks and the way she avoided me told a different story. I was affecting her, even if she wasn't ready to admit it. "Can you, *um,* sit down, please?" she blurted, the words coming out awkward and rushed, like she was fighting to sound more composed than she felt.

I dropped to a squat, joining her on the blanket. "It's your birthday, Sun," I blurted, my words coming out more forceful than I'd intended.

She nodded, completely unbothered. "Yep. First day of summer, hence my name," she said, as if I was supposed to have magically known that bit of info. "I know. My parents are corny."

I stared at her, caught between wanting to kiss her cute face and feeling frustrated that she thought this was no big deal. "Why didn't I know it was your birthday, Summer?" I asked, my tone laced with the frustration bubbling inside me.

"I don't know when your birthday is, Echo," she replied, dragging out my name like she was making a point.

Once again, this girl had me stumped. Out of all the questions we'd volleyed, birthdays had somehow never come up. And damn, she was right.

"You're right," I admitted reluctantly. "I guess I just thought you would've said something."

She shook her head, brushing it off like it didn't matter. "It's not that big of a deal. I celebrated with my family before I left, so I'm good," she said. I stared at her for a moment, hearing the words but seeing something different in her eyes—something she wasn't saying. I pushed myself up from the blanket, and without hesitation, snatched the bag of chips from her hand, popping a few in my mouth.

"Echo!" she yelped, springing to her feet and reaching for the bag. I held it over my head because she was short compared to me.

She tried her best to stay mad but couldn't stop her cheeks from reddening.

Leaning down, I pinched the tip of her nose gently and said, "Be ready at ten tonight, Sunshine."

"For what?" she shouted at my back as I walked away, refusing to answer. *Let her wonder.*

Summer
That One Summer in 2004

Ten o'clock couldn't get here fast enough. I had no clue what Echo had planned, but the anticipation buzzed in my belly. Apparently, it wasn't something for just me and him because Trinity and Brooke were already in the living room when I walked out, dressed and waiting.

"You look cute, birthday girl," Trinity said, approvingly.

I'd chosen a denim skirt, my favorite Tupac t-shirt, and sneakers, casual but hopefully just right for whatever Echo had planned. Half my hair was pulled into a ponytail; the rest falling straight to brush against my shoulders. Gold hoop earrings, a swipe of eyeliner, and a little lip gloss finished the look. Simple, but that's what worked for me. A rapid knock at the door startled me, sending a rush of energy surging through me.. Brooke jumped up to answer it, and there they were, the guys—Echo, Bryant, and Maxell—looking good. Bryant and Maxell were cool, but my attention immediately zeroed in on Echo.

"You ladies ready?" Echo asked, his deep voice commanding but easy as he surveyed the room before landing on me, traveling slowly from my head to my toes, a teasing curve threatening to form on his lips.

"We are. Let the birthday festivities begin," Brooke said dramatically, already making her way toward Bryant. Trinity and Brooke darted out of the suite, leaving Echo and me alone in the doorway. He didn't rush me. Instead, he offered his hand, making my pulse skip with that same delicate thrill. "Are you ready, birthday girl?" he asked.

I nodded, my words caught somewhere between my throat and my heart. Taking his hand, I let him lead the way for a change, a thrill running through me, anticipating how the night would unfold. We snuck through the quad, sticking to the shadows to avoid any other counselors. The path Echo led us down felt familiar, heading straight toward our spot. A flicker of unease rippled through me at the thought. I silently questioned if he was really about to reveal our hideaway. If he was, disappointment would've swallowed me where I stood. That place was ours, a secret corner of the world meant only for us. Echo must have felt my hesitation because he shook his head with an unspoken promise. Without releasing my hand, he gave it a gentle squeeze, reassuring me that our sanctuary would stay just that: ours.

The path curved, leading us to an open space carved into the hillside. My breath caught. Shit, this place was stunning, almost better than our hideaway, if that was even possible. The moonlight spilled through cracks in the rocky ceiling, casting soft beams across the ground, providing just enough light to see the jagged walls. The air was cooler here, a needed escape from the suffocating summer heat. A handful of counselors were already there, swaying to the music blaring. The vibe was relaxed but charged, a private escape just outside the campgrounds.

"What is this place?" I asked, turning to Echo, excitement lighting up my face.

"Lincoln told me about it," he replied casually.

"Lincoln? Director Lincoln?" My tone shifted to concern. "He knows we're here?"

Echo nodded, unconcerned. "He's cool. We're good. Come on."

Without waiting for my reaction, he tugged me into the crowd. Almost instantly, the group started chanting the opening lines of 50 Cent's "In da Club." A rush of joy slipped out before I could stop it, my face heating as their voices grew louder. The attention made my skin prickle, but something about this—about my friends—made it impossible to feel special.

"Come on, Summer," Trinity called out, encouraging me to join in.

Before I could react, a deep, bass-filled voice murmured against my ear, sending a shiver down my spine. "Go shawty, it's your birthday." I spun around to find Echo, his movements slow and measured, a smooth two-step making his shoulders bounce to the beat. He was magnetic, and for a moment, I felt like his.

I moved on instinct, swaying to the beat as if the music had taken control. Echo's hands slid delicately to my hips, pulling me closer until my body was flush against his. The soft graze of my booty against the front of his pants sent a wave of warmth through me, causing anyone outside this dance to disappear in my mind. This was the closest we'd ever been, and it felt…almost too good, too right. We stayed like that, moving together to the rhythm, for what felt like forever but was probably just an hour.

Later, I found myself in the middle of the open space chatting with Brooke and Trinity when the music abruptly cut off. I froze, glancing around, bracing myself for whatever was next. Then hands began to clap, and the crowd burst into their best rendition of Stevie Wonder's "Happy Birthday."

Amusement erupted from me uncontrollably as I brought a hand to my mouth, trying to hide my embarrassment. My cheeks burned, and my eyes glistened when I saw Echo break through the crowd. He was holding a single cupcake, a lone candle flickering on top. The way he looked at me…his gaze never wavering, even as he sang the words. It sent my heart into overdrive.

"Make a wish, Sunshine," he said softly, his voice almost drowned out by the clapping and cheering around us.

I bit the inside of my cheek, not needing even a second to decide what my wish would be. My eyes lingered on his, every private feeling reflected at me in his gaze. I leaned forward slightly and blew out the candle, sending my wish into the heavens. Maybe someday, the stars would align and grant me the one thing I wanted most.

Echo
That One Summer in 2004

"Echo," Sadie's voice rang out as she ran toward me, her little legs moving as fast as they could. I scooped her up effortlessly, and she wrapped her arms around my neck, holding on tight.

Her familiar hug was exactly what I needed. I was surprised to see my whole family here to pick me up. My dad was traveling for work, so my mom had braved the nearly two-hour drive alone, much to my father's dismay. She stood near the car, her presence calm but commanding as always as my other siblings spilled out of the SUV.

My fifteen-year-old sister Yekemi, nicknamed Kemi, stayed in the car, her expression screaming irritated, like she'd rather be anywhere but here. My brother, Samir, thirteen and curious about everything, hopped out of the car gawking at the girls who passed by. Ezla, better known as Eazy, was nine. His face lit up with excitement as he chased Sadie. Sadie, my little Sadie, only eight, clung to my side as though I'd been gone for years instead of weeks.

"Mum," I greeted my mother, my voice warm.

"Echo," she said with that soothing sing-song tone, cupping the curve of my face with both hands before she kissed my cheeks. "You've grown," she teased.

"Mum, it's only been eight weeks."

Mum leaned against the car's passenger door, her attention briefly shifting to fuss at Kemi, who still hadn't gotten out of the car. I reached around and gave Kemi a light push on the side of her head.

"Echo," she yelled, her face twisted in mock annoyance.

I laughed. "Good to see you too, sis."

The Abaras were a loud and rowdy bunch, but I'd missed them more than they knew.

"Samir, help me grab my stuff," I said, nudging my brother. He followed me, heading toward the lodge, his attention fixed on every girl who passed by.

"Who's that? And her?" he blurted before I could answer the first inquiry. His questions came rapid-fire as we walked, and I had to thump his ear to get him to calm down.

I hadn't seen Summer since last night at the closing ceremony, so I decided to stop by her lodge before heading to my room. Although we'd sorta said goodbye already, I didn't want to leave without seeing her. I knocked on the door to the suite, and Brooke answered.

"Hey, Echo," she greeted, leaning casually against the doorframe.

"What's up, Brooke?" I said, peeking over her shoulder, looking for my target.

She waved to Samir, who was lingering shyly behind me. "And who is this cutie?"

"This is my brother Samir," I answered, patting him on the shoulder.

"Hi, Samir," Brooke sang.

"Hi," he coyly mumbled, his face flushing as he looked down at his shoes.

"Is Summer in her room?" I asked, ready to walk in.

Brooke shook her head. "No. She's gone. Her parents picked her up early. They needed to get back for their family reunion trip."

Her words hit me harder than expected. I kept my expression neutral, even as disappointment tightened my throat.

"Ah, I see. That's what's up," I said, nodding and forcing a smile. "Well, it was nice meeting you this summer, Brooke. Good luck in your senior year."

"You, too, Echo." She extended her arms, and we shared a friendly hug.

I nodded, turning away as Samir and I headed to my lodge. My feet felt heavier, my stride slower as my mind replayed Brooke's words: *She's gone.*

After grabbing my bags, I stalked back to the SUV and loaded the trunk. Kemi was still pouting in the front seat, while Sadie and Eazy were already buckled in the third row, chattering away about a random toy.

"You want to drive?" my mother asked.

Normally, I would kill for the chance to drive, but today, I just wasn't in the mood. My mind was weighty, crowded with tangled thoughts.

"No, ma'am," I said, shaking my head. "I'm kinda tired."

She regarded me with a slow, assessing look, possibly sensing something was off. "Are you okay, son?"

I nodded quickly, not wanting to filter any more questions. "Yeah, Mum. We were up late, so I'm just gonna take a nap."

Her gaze lingered on me for a moment longer, as if trying to read between the lines. Finally, she nodded and slid into the driver's seat. Instead of fighting Kemi for the front seat like I usually did, I climbed into the middle row next to Samir. Even he looked a little surprised as I buckled in without a word. My mother raised a questioning brow at the unusual silence between Kemi and me but didn't say a word.

The drive was a blur because I slept through most of it. The familiar clamor of Sadie and Eazy in the back didn't even register. I'd grown used to their noise, so it was easy to block out once I slipped on my headphones and let my thoughts wander about Summer. I should've asked Brooke for Summer's number before I left, but that would've seemed too thirsty…desperate. Maybe I could ask Maxell since they knew some of the same people. A dull ache settled in stomach. I was going to drive myself crazy.

When we finally pulled into the garage, I blinked awake, stretching as the headlights illuminated our two-story colonial home in the northern suburb of St. Louis. I'd only been in this house a few weeks before I'd left for camp, but I didn't expect it to look so different. My mother's magical green thumb had been at work while I was gone. Vibrant flowers lined the front yard, and a new set of patio furniture was neatly arranged below the picture window. Seasonal decorative touches like a wreath on the door and an entry rug with the letter "A" on it gave the house warmth it didn't have before.

Stepping into the foyer, the changes were even more noticeable. The once sterile white walls were painted with warm hues of gray and peppered with family portraits and colorful paintings from Nigeria. *Maybe this place can feel like home.* I climbed the steps two at a time, eager to finally crash in my room. The moment I pushed open the door, the changes my mother had made were perfect. I eyed the fresh shade of blue paint on the walls, and framed posters of my favorite Chicago sports teams hung perfectly. New linens covered my queen-sized bed, and the faint scent of fresh laundry filled the air. To my delight, a sleek new computer was sitting on my desk.

I dropped my bag on the floor and sprawled across the bed, too tired to admire the details further. I'm sure I would admire the rest of the features later. Right now, I needed to draw, to lose myself in the lines and sketches, which always seemed to help me clear my head. I would play around with my new computer later. Reaching into my backpack, I pulled out the black spiral notebook that was practically bursting with sketches I'd filled it with over the past eight weeks. Our hideaway was the place I'd sketched the most. Most of my and Summer's time in our sacred spot was spent wrapped into quiet moments—only the sound of our pencils scratching against paper. She always sketched with ease, her talent effortless, while I preferred the precision of computer-aided design to bring my ideas to life. As I flipped through the pages, I let my mind drift between then and now, the moments I'd captured—trees stretching toward the sky, the waves on the lake on a windy day, campers discovering new things, and Summer. Every angle of her beauty was splattered on these pages.

As I turned another page, a white envelope slipped out and landed softly on the mattress. Frowning, I picked it up and turned it over. A single letter "E" was scrawled across the front in neat yet swirly handwriting. My breathing was sporadic as I ran my thumb over the ink, knowing it was her...praying it was her. The envelope wasn't sealed, so I opened the flap and pulled out a neatly folded piece of paper. Unfolding it, I scanned the words. It was her. For a second, I wondered how she'd pulled this off, then it hit me. Last night, she'd insisted that her sneakers needed to go in my backpack while we watched a movie in the amphitheater.

Echo-ho-ho! Ha!

I bet you're laughing. Anyway...I can't believe the summer is already over, and I'm back home—well, technically on a bus headed to Orlando for my family reunion! I am already missing the Creative Crew and the crazy fun we had. Thank you again for being an amazing partner in crime.

Honestly, I didn't expect—or even want—to make new friends my last year at camp, but I did...you. On those crazy days when I thought I would lose my shit, you always made me laugh... and reminded me to breathe. So, thank you for being you and for making this summer one I'll never forget.

Until we meet again!
Summer a.k.a. Sunshine a.k.a. Sun
P.S. Just in case you want to meet again, my number is 923-0001.

And just like that, she was here again, as if her voice whispered to me through every curve of the letters on the page.

"Yes," I shouted, pumping a fist in the air like I'd won a prize.

CHAPTER TWELVE

Summer
Senior Year, 2004

SUMMER BREAK WAS officially over, and my senior year was in full swing. While I was excited about everything that was ahead, I'd somehow managed to overload myself—again. Between student council, volunteer hours, and the endless assignments from my classes, I was barely keeping my head above water. But to my surprise and relief, Echo had become my steady calm in the chaos, the anchor I didn't know I needed.

He'd worked his way into my tiny circle of best friends, right alongside Hailee, Trinity, and Brooke. Our playful, flirtatious banter still lingered in the background, but we never crossed that line. Sometimes I wondered how I felt about adding another boy to my ever-growing list of "just friends." I'd always been the girl who could hang with the guys, talk smack during a game, and hold my own in any debate. Maybe that was the problem—since I acted like one of them, they treated me as such. Echo was no exception.

Although he didn't attend my school, he only lived about fifteen or twenty minutes away. We were practically inseparable, as my mother liked to remind me. *"You act like you can't go a single day without talking to that boy,"* she'd say, shaking her head with exasperation. And maybe she was right. If we weren't up talking until ridiculous hours, he was at my house under the pretense of helping me with homework, but he mostly just raiding the fridge like he lived there.

It wasn't hard for Echo to win my parents over. His charisma was like a magnet, drawing everyone in. My dad had no problem with our friendship; in fact, he'd gained a new buddy to watch football with on Sundays. My mom, however, wasn't as easily convinced. While she liked Echo, she didn't love how much time we spent together.

"Are you supposed to be liking this boy?" she'd fuss, arms crossed like she was ready to interrogate me.

My answer was always the same. "No, Mama! He's just my friend." But deep down, there were moments when I wasn't so sure myself.

Echo was *just* my friend. Okay, sure, we flirted now and then, but it was harmless—like how distant step-cousins might joke around at family reunions. It was the perfect setup for both of us. We got all the fun of a relationship—late-night talks, inside jokes, easy companionship—without the mess. No guessing games, no pressure, no wondering if a kiss was coming. And sex? Yeah, that was never part of the equation.

Not that I could deny it—Echo was cute. Borderline fine. The attraction from camp had dulled—at least, that's what I told myself. Friendship was easier to hold on to, less risky. Besides, it wasn't mutual. Echo had a type, and I wasn't it. He'd moved past the crazy, sexy, cool type and started gravitating toward the slim-thick, light-skinned girls who always looked perfectly put together. That *was not* me. Girls lined up for him—at school, in his neighborhood, and even mine. But with me? It was always something softer, something safe. Something rated G.

Echo saw me—the version of me that existed beyond perfection, beyond performance. Messy hair, old sweats, scarf tied up for the night—and I never felt self-conscious. With him, I was never too much or not enough. I didn't have to impress, didn't have to shrink myself down. He accepted me, no conditions, no judgment. And that feeling? It was a rare kind of freedom for a girl like me.

"Girl, where are you going now?" Mama's thunderous voice rolled down the hallway as I tried to slip out unnoticed. I sighed, already knowing where this was headed. "Did you finish your paper?" she asked, but didn't pause to give me time to respond. "I don't want to hear nothing about you being stressed because you didn't give yourself enough time, Summer," she continued, giving me that look that meant she wasn't playing.

This wasn't about the paper. This was about Echo. Mama liked him—*loved* him, actually, although she played tough. She was always talking about what a respectful young man he was, always piling extra food on his plate whenever he came over. But no amount of good manners or full plates changed the fact that, in her opinion, he was still a distraction. And maybe she had a point, but I wasn't about to pretend I hadn't been handling my responsibilities like I always had.

"Mama, why are you fussing?" I shot back, not really expecting an answer. "I'm going to hang with Echo. I already finished the paper. I just need to print it out, and that'll take like five minutes." I rolled my eyes, regretting it immediately.

"Well, you've got five minutes right now," she said, teasing but with an edge that warned me not to push it. "So go finish."

"But Mama—"

"*But Mama* nothing!" she interrupted, cutting her eyes at me. "Now...Summer Sierra. And roll your eyes one more time—you'll be sitting right here with me and your daddy for the rest of the night!"

I groaned under my breath but headed back to my room. Mama wasn't one to bluff, and I wasn't about to test her patience tonight. These were the moments when being the baby of the family was both a blessing and a curse. I stomped away like a six-year-old, hating that my mother knew me so well. She was right. The paper was mostly finished, but I still had to add the cover page and reference sheet. Not that I was going to admit that to her.

"*Ugh.* She gets on my nerves," I muttered under my breath, making sure my bedroom door was closed. I wasn't trying to be grounded at home *and* to get popped in the mouth.

With a few minutes to spare before Echo showed up, I reached for my sketchbook, hoping it would steady the restlessness humming beneath my skin. I told myself it was just another hangout, just another night of friendly, easy conversation. But the truth was, knowing he was on his way always did something to me—like I was waiting for something I couldn't name. The moment my pencil touched the page, my thoughts drifted—not to the lines I meant to draw, but to *him*. The way his presence carried an ease, a quiet warmth, like I never had to try too hard. Even the first day we met, when I hit him with all the attitude I could muster, I still sensed it—that pull, that undeniable way he filled a space. Making everything warmer, lighter. And I felt it every time. It was comfort. Familiarity. It was safe. Maybe *too* safe.

A heavy thud from outside my window yanked me from my thoughts. *Echo.* Jay-Z's voice blasted from his car speakers, rattling the air like a personal announcement of his arrival. I groaned, shaking my head because I already knew—without a doubt—he was handing my mother fresh ammunition. As if I wasn't already tiptoeing out of this house on borrowed grace, here he went, throwing gas on the fire. Right on cue, Mama's voice rang out from the kitchen.

"Is that Echo playing that loud music in front of my house?" she hollered, still carrying the edge of irritation from our earlier exchange.

"Oh, Lord," I heard Daddy grumbled from the family room, his tone resigned. "Yeah, that's him. *Knucklehead.*" He sighed long and knowing. I could picture him now, peeking out the window, shaking his head in mild amusement, fully aware that Teresa Knight was about to start firing verbal bullets.

I shot up from the bed and bolted toward the front door, determined to intercept Echo before my parents—especially Mama—could get to him. Throwing open the screen door, I stood in the doorway, waving my arms like a maniac, trying to warn him, mouthing for him to *turn the music down.* He, of course, was completely oblivious, still blasting Jay-Z. My mouthing turned into a sharp, desperate screech. "Turn the damn music down, E!"

Mama missed nothing. "Oh, so you curse in front of your mama now? That's what we're doing with your *new friend?*" she called, her voice laced with mockery.

Stepping onto the porch, I put my hands on my hips just as Echo stepped out of his car *clearly enjoying himself,* the slight tilt of his head and easy confidence making it clear that he was oblivious to the second of chaos he'd caused.

"What's up, Sunshine?" he said, flashing that wide, mischievous grin.

"Boy, are you crazy? Now you know my parents do not play that!" I hissed, my irritation bubbling over.

"What?" he asked, his face scrunched in genuine confusion.

"Your music was loud as hell," I said through gritted teeth.

"Oh, my bad," he whispered, looking sheepish now.

My tone dropped with a sharp warning. "Now, my daddy likes you, but keep playing, and he'll quickly label you a *li'l thug* and threaten to get his gun," I teased, but I was serious. "And Mama? She's still on the fence about you."

"Man, Ms. Teresa loves me. But real talk, I'm sorry, Sun. Let me come in and apologize," he said, raising his hands in surrender.

Before I could respond, the familiar squeak of the screen door behind me announced that someone had joined us. I turned to see Daddy standing there, his face serious in a way that caught me off guard.

"How're you doing, Echo?" Daddy asked, his voice calm but firm. "Now, that music was too loud, son."

"Yes, sir. I'm doing good. Sorry about the music. It won't happen again—"

Before he could finish, Mama appeared, practically nudging Daddy out of the way with her no-nonsense demeanor.

"Boy, don't come down my street with that boopidy-bop music that loud anymore. You understand me?" she said, her tone as colorful as her vocabulary.

"Yes, ma'am! I'm really sorry," Echo replied, and I could see the corners of his mouth twitching as he tried—and failed—to suppress his grin at Mama's choice of words.

I shot him a warning, but even I had to fight the twitch of my cheeks. Amusement flickered between us in a silent conversation.

"Yo, your mama don't play," Echo's raised brows mutedly communicated.

I arched my brow, with pursed lips, my expression doing all the talking. *"You think? Keep testing her, and you'll find out exactly how much she don't play,"* my face all but said.

Echo chuckled softly, shaking his head then nodded as if to say, *"Message received, Sunshine."*

"Where are you all going this time?" Mama asked, and I wanted to roll my eyes because I'd already told her this.

Just hanging out at the mall," Echo answered, his voice casual but his eyes darting to me for confirmation, like he was hoping he'd nailed the right answer.

I bit back a smirk. The mall was always the safe, parent-approved starting point, but we both knew it was just that—a starting point. From there, the night could lead us anywhere, and I never offered those details to my parents.

"And Sonic," we said in unison, our voices overlapping as we broke into laughter.

Mama nodded, her sharp focus fixated on the two of us with her arms crossed. She wasn't saying much, but the gears in her head were definitely turning as she inspected us, her silence louder than any question she could've asked.

"You ready to go, Sun…I mean, Summer?" Echo said as he reached out to pinch the tip of my nose like he always did.

I swatted his hand away, but the corner of my mouth lifted. It was so natural with him, this easy rhythm we had. Still, I could feel my mother's eyes burning into the back of my head, making me hesitate before heading back inside to grab my things. "*Um*, yeah. Let me grab my purse. I'll be right back."

When I returned with my purse slung over my shoulder, the scene hadn't shifted much. Daddy was leaning on the porch railing, chatting with Echo in that calm, easygoing way he always had. Meanwhile, Mama remained in the doorway, arms crossed, her expression hovering somewhere between curiosity and disapproval.

Echo straightened as I approached, his trademark grin lighting up his face. As I slipped by Mama, I felt her hand gently fix a stray curl that had fallen out of place. "You have your phone and keys?" she asked, her tone softer now, but still laced with authority.

"Yes, ma'am," I replied, turning to give her a quick hug. I kissed Daddy's cheek before stepping off the porch. "See y'all later. Love you."

"Have fun, baby girl," Daddy called out, his voice warm, "and remember what your mama said."

"Remember your curfew, Summer," Mama called after me in a tone that carried equal parts concern and warning.

"I always do," I replied, glancing back over my shoulder with a small, reassuring smile. It wasn't a lie—I'd never missed curfew, but her stern warning still made me feel like she thought I would chance it for my *new friend*.

Without thinking, Echo grabbed my hand, guiding me toward his car. I didn't resist. This was just us—easy, familiar, the kind of comfort that didn't require second-guessing. As we walked, we bumped into each other playfully, our normal carefree banter. But just as I reached for the passenger door, Mama's voice carried through the air, quiet but sharp enough to land.

"You see what I'm saying?" Her words were meant for Daddy's ears only.

I hesitated, my fingers brushing the door handle. Daddy sighed, his tone weary but firm. *"Tee, let it go,"* he said, already turning back toward the house.

I sighed, shaking my head as Echo waited for me to settle into the passenger seat before gently shutting the door behind me.

"What?" he asked, sliding into his seat and starting the car.

"Nothing," I said, securing my seatbelt. "Just my mama being my mama."

I brushed it off, but the truth sat somewhere deep in my heart, too heavy to ignore. Mama wasn't just fussing to fuss. She saw it. She saw the way Echo and I moved around each other, how we never quite crossed a line, but never really stayed in the lines either. She saw how I let him pull me along without hesitation, how he knew exactly what to do to make me smile. How he made himself at home in my world like he belonged there. Mama knew what that meant. She and Daddy were high school sweethearts, so she knew firsthand that friendships like this—the ones that felt effortless, the ones that made you forget where you ended and the other person began—those were the ones that could change everything. And not always in the ways you wanted.

Maybe she saw something forming the first time I introduced Echo to my parents. My sudden giddy and slightly ditzy demeanor wasn't lost on my parents. And Mama? She noticed... Because she noticed *everything*. She didn't always say much, but the way her lips pressed together, shaking her head the way mamas do when they know their daughters are about to get caught up in something they can't control. Since Daddy made it clear that he didn't want to hear it anymore, I was sure she was on the phone with my auntie right now. *"That boy got too much of your time, Summer. That kind of closeness? It don't stay innocent forever."*

And maybe she was right to be worried. Because I knew it, too—somewhere deep down, in a place I wasn't ready to face. Echo was special. And feelings like we had? They had a way of sneaking up on you when you least expected.

CHAPTER THIRTEEN

Echo
October 2019

SUMMER AND I left the park a little after nine. I practically had to coax her into my car after she stubbornly insisted on driving herself home. She'd calmed down some, but she was in no shape to make the nearly two-hour drive back to St. Louis. As I double-checked that her car doors were locked, I made a mental note to text Maxell later and see if he could pick up her car tomorrow. She sat quietly in the passenger seat, staring out the window. Her expression was distant, her gaze unfocused, though traces of anguish still lingered in the tension in her jaw and the faint tremble of her hands. Over the past couple of hours, I'd realized that her sadness wasn't entirely about the demise of her relationship. It wasn't the *what* that troubled her—it was the *how*. Summer was grappling with the gravity of what she'd done, not the reasons she'd done it.

The Summer I knew was a people pleaser and a meticulous planner. I was certain that she had her life all mapped out—married by now, with a kid and another one on the way. The imaginary biological clock probably fueled her need to please Deshawn and everyone else who saw them as the picture-perfect couple. But the

Summer I also knew was resolute once she made a decision, so when the dust finally settled, I was confident there'd be no regrets for her.

She leaned against the center console, her cheek resting in the palm of her hand. Tenderly, I reached out and swiped a finger across her brow, hopefully brushing away the tension etched there. My hand drifted to her nape, massaging softly, and the faint smile that graced her face told me that my actions were appreciated. But I could still see tears glistening as silence settled between us.

I reached for her hand, rubbing my thumb over her palm in slow, soothing circles. "You hungry?" I asked, breaking the quiet.

She shrugged, indecisive about everything. "I could eat."

"Yes or no, Summer. I'm sure you're hungry," I teased, nudging her out of her vagueness.

"Yes, Echo. I'm hungry," she said.

"What do you want?" I asked, glancing at her to see her brows furrowed as if I'd asked the dumbest question. We locked eyes for a beat before blurting out simultaneously,

"Sonic!" We burst out laughing.

"Sonic always comes through," I said, shaking my head.

"We ate so much damn Sonic back in the day, I should be tired of it. I had to stop eating those French toast sticks because my ass was spreading…wide." She stretched her last word exaggeratedly.

Don't say a word, Echo. Don't say shit about her ass. It wasn't easy, especially since her ass was looking better than ever. "Nah, Sun. You're good," I finally blurted. "Remember when you came back from winter vacation? You were gone forever it seemed, and I was sick. I didn't know what to do without my road dog." I pulled into the restaurant, parking in an available stall.

If my memory served me correctly, I already knew what she wanted to order. "Hey, sweetheart," I greeted the car hop. "Let me get one double cheeseburger meal with fries, a six-piece chicken tenders with tater tots, two large blueberry slushies, and French toast sticks."

"Extra ranch and barbecue sauce, please." She leaned over me, giving instructions as if I was going to miss those important details.

Summer glanced at me, her lips quirking. "Yeah, but I took care of you when I got back, remember?" she said, clutching my hand. The soft, delicate touch was a balm to my weary soul. For a moment, we weren't in the aftermath of her broken engagement—we were just us. Two friends reminiscing about a time when life felt simpler and happier.

As we waited for the food, my mind drifted to the past, pulled back by the quiet gravity of memory. My first winter in St. Louis was like springtime compared to Chicago. We were on break from school for the holidays, and Summer's family was spending Christmas at her brother's house in Nashville. I'd been counting down the days until she came back because I'd been miserable. Not only did I have a cold, but I was also missing her. I thought maybe I was high from the cold medicine when I heard a voice eerily similar to hers. But I wasn't dreaming. It was like she appeared out of nowhere. I remembered that night so vividly, it felt like yesterday. Her standing in the doorway, bags in hand, looking like she could sense that I needed her.

I heard her melodic voice before I saw her face. She had been chatting with my sister, the easy rhythm of their conversation carrying through the house. The sound of it alone made my chest tighten. I had missed her so much it hurt. And then, finally, she walked in. She was balancing two bags and a drink carrier, her Nike jogging pants hugging her curves just right—just enough to make it impossible to look away. She smiled that shy, knowing smile, and our eyes met. It was like she had never left. Without a word, she unpacked our food: double cheeseburger, fries, chicken tenders, tater tots, French toast sticks, and blueberry slushies. *All for us to share. Then, without needing to ask, she slid the barbecue and ranch sauce across the table because she just knew. She always knew.*

She settled onto the floor pillow beside me, nudging my shoulder, her voice low, soft, full of something unspoken. "Hey, E."

I turned to her. "What's up, Sunshine?"

The moment had been so simple, so small, and yet, it was one of my favorites because it reminded me of everything I loved about her. Because she knew me better than anyone ever could. And even though we'd been distant, she always would. I blinked, not fully realizing that we'd received our food and were now pulling in the driveway of my parents' house.

Summer's jaw tightened, her gaze sweeping over the familiar brick two-story house she'd once frequented with ease. Her angst was voiceless, but I could feel it anyway. This place held both joy and pain, memories tangled together in ways only she could fully understand.

"Are they home?" she asked, her voice measured, but the weight behind it unmistakable. She meant my parents.

I shook my head. "No. They're in Chicago, and Sadie's at a friend's house." We both stared at the tan garage door, the silence stretching between us. "You're good here, Summer," I said gently. "Get some rest. I'll take you wherever you want to go first thing in the morning."

She nodded but remained wordless.

Walking to the front door, I struggled to unlock it while carrying the food bag in the crook of my arm, while holding her hand. This behavior was instinctual, just as natural as breathing for me. My fingers found hers without thought, no conscious decisions or deliberate moves, just muscle memory. Shit, my heart remembered, too. It didn't matter that we hadn't seen each other in years. Since I'd stepped foot on that hill, there was no hesitation nor awkwardness between us.

I switched on the lights in the foyer, slowly moving farther into the house. Summer's fingers slipped from my grasp, and I turned to see her still standing by the door. The space hadn't changed in years, every detail frozen in time, and I knew what she was thinking: This was the scene of the crime.

"Sunshine," I called. With a tilt of my head, I motioned for her to follow me into the kitchen. She trailed, leaning against the counter as she sipped her slush.

I busied myself unbagging the food, then arranging it on a tray. When everything was ready, we climbed the stairs to my childhood bedroom. I loosened my tie, tossing it carelessly across the room, and unbuttoned the top button of my shirt. Summer perched on the bed, planting one knee before sitting crisscrossed. She leaned forward to slide the tray closer, her movements hurried because she had to be starving. With Sonic spread out between us and her sitting in that familiar position, it was like no time had passed at all. And damn, it felt good. I powered on the TV, but somehow, I was certain it would be watching us instead.

"How's California treating you?" she asked, dipping a chicken tender into the barbecue-and-ranch mixture we'd concocted as kids.

"Good. Good," I said, my mind briefly drifting to how much LA had become home. "I like the balance. It's fast-paced but somehow steady. The opportunities are endless…so much damn money to be made." I paused, mimicking her as I dipped my tender. "You'd kill it there with your design and marketing skills."

She sighed, momentarily drifting off to somewhere far away. "I can't even imagine leaving St. Louis. I stayed in Atlanta after college because I'd found my tribe, but California?" Her voice trailed off, a hint of hesitation threading through her words. "That would be a huge change."

I chose my next words carefully. "Your world has already changed, Summer. When the church altar stayed empty today, *everything* changed." My voice softened. "You made a big decision." I brushed my thumb lightly along her forearm. "I'm proud of you."

The words hung in the air, raw and honest, surprising both of us. She was caught off guard by the admission, but I meant every word. What she did today was nothing but faith and hella brave. Yeah, her future might be uncertain, but it was completely hers to define, free from doubt or hesitation. "Maybe," I started, "maybe the universe is hinting at other shifts in your future."

Summer didn't respond right away, but a quiet ease settled over her face, and for the first time that night, chaos was replaced with curiosity—a glimmer of hope for what might come next. She stretched out on my bed, resting her head on her arm, and a deep sigh escaped her lips. I watched her quietly, taking in the familiar curve of her face and the way her lips naturally puckered when she was sleepy. The even rhythm of her breathing, soft and unhurried, seemed to settle something restless inside me.

There were times I thought I'd never see her again—thought she was lost to me for good. But now, here she was, just an arm's length away, her presence grounding me in a way I hadn't felt in years. Summer burrowed deeper into the pillow, surrendering to her exhaustion. A soft exhale escaped her, the last traces of tension fading from her pretty face before her eyelids fluttered closed. A moment of peace and serenity settled over her.

I felt a sense of relief watching her finally rest, but in the silence, the questions I'd buried for so long started to rise. What could come next for us? Would this fragile moment of connection be enough to bridge the years between us? Or would we fall back into the gaps life had carved? For now, I didn't have the answers, and while I wanted to stop myself from hoping, I couldn't.

Summer
October 2019

I stirred awake as Echo gently caressed my foot, the weight of sleep heavy in my limbs. He was standing at the end of the bed, looking like slumber was in his near future, too.

"Sun. Baby girl, come on, let's get you in bed," he murmured, his voice dripping with fatigue.

I stretched, blinking to bring my surroundings into focus, confusion fogging my brain. "I am in the bed, right?" I said groggily, because I honestly didn't know. It felt like I was floating in the clouds.

"You're fully dressed and laying on top of the comforter," he said, a hint of exasperation hardening his tone. "Come on. I'm sleepy." The gruffness in his voice reminded me how cranky he would get when he was tired. Reluctantly, I slowly lifted upright, stretching through a squeal as I stood next to the bed watching him pull back the comforter.

"How long was I out?" I mumbled, sliding off my socks before leaning my head against the wall. Every part of me felt clunky and weighed down by the whirlwind of the day. Being a runaway bride was nothing short of draining.

"Not long," he replied, pausing mid-motion, concern apparent on his handsome face. "You, okay?" he asked, crossing the room. His worried eyes searched mine as he reached out, pressing the back of his hand gently against my forehead.

"I'm not sick, E. I guess the day is finally getting to me. I can barely stay awake," I murmured, leaning into him and resting my head in the center of his chest. For a moment, it felt like the turmoil of the day had momentarily quieted.

"I got you, Sun," he said, his voice a low rumble against my ear.

Echo dipped his face into my hair, allowing me to rest in the comfort of his embrace. For a few long minutes, we stood there, the quiet between us more restorative than any words. Then, delicately, he lifted my chin, his fingers brushing against my skin as he eased the sweatshirt over my head, revealing the fitted white tank top beneath. The sparkling *Bride* script shimmered under the dim light, a cruel reminder of the day's reality. I was nobody's bride. He must have noticed my brief moment of unease because without hesitation, he tossed the sweatshirt into the closet, tucking it out of sight. I felt his eyes on me, lingering—not just looking, but truly seeing. Mapping the way the thin fabric clung to me, tracing my curves as if committing my soft places to memory.

Heat rushed to my cheeks as I felt the undeniable tightness of my nipples against the cool cotton material. Oh God, this was not the time for my breasts to reveal all my secrets. I prayed he wouldn't notice, but his subtle, yet deep breaths told me otherwise. Still, he didn't say a word as my headlights beamed in his face. He stepped away, grabbing a t-shirt for me then moved back in front of me with an unreadable expression.

"Thank you, E," I whispered.

Echo didn't say anything, and it was probably for the best. The magnetic energy that always defined us was never in grand gestures or significant, defining moments. It was the little things. Like the way he kissed the top of my head, swiped a knuckle down my cheek, or offered a private smile only visible to me. Or like right now, the way he just simply took care of me.

"Jogging pants staying on or off?" he asked, an unintentional tease playing in his tone.

I softly pushed him back. "Are you trying to get me naked, Echo Honor Abara?"

He shook his head. "Don't play with me, Sun. It's not like I haven't seen you before." He lifted a knowing brow. "I just know you'll be burning up in the middle of the night. So, on or off?"

"Off," I whispered, damn near coyly.

Without hesitation, he slid them off, folding the pants and placing them neatly over the chair. I didn't make a move immediately, just watched him. His movements were careful and deliberate as he gathered our trash, brushed his teeth, and changed into basketball shorts and a t-shirt. Damn. Echo looked good. He never lacked confidence or a commanding presence, but time and maturity had carved a physique etched with broad shoulders, a solid chest, strong jawline, and sharpened features that made him strikingly handsome. But the curve of his smile and dark, attentive eyes offered a glimpse of the boy I used to know.

The adorable boy who'd grown into a fully grown, ridiculously fine man had me feeling all kinds of mental and physical sensitives I would not dare admit out loud. My god, my pussy had no business reacting this way, but it was. Just hours ago, I had been moments away from marrying one man, and now, my body was betraying me for another. Not just any man. The one who used to be my best friend. The one who knew me before the pressure of expectations and the noise of life pulled us apart. And yet, here I was, heart pounding, pulse racing, not for the man I almost vowed forever to, but for the one I had never truly let go of. My mama would've said, *"Now that's just hoe shit, Summer Sierra."*

But no matter how much I tried to deny it, I couldn't ignore the tender spark that always surged when Echo was around. Even after all these years, we were still so lovingly hazardous to one another. I immediately felt it at Brooke's wedding, and I felt it now…more intensely than ever, with the pulsing throb in my center refusing to let me forget.

Echo had this way of just making everything feel safe, even when my world was crumbling. Sitting on the edge of the bed in just my tank top and panties, I reached for my phone, trying to refocus. A notification lit the screen—another voice message from Deshawn. For a second, I stalled because I was certain that by now, he'd talked to my family and likely knew that I was with Echo.

"*I talked to your dad. He told me that you called.*" Deshawn's voice crackled through the message, then came a bitter snicker. "*But you couldn't call me. That's fucked up, Summer. I'm sitting her wracking my brain, trying to figure out what the fuck happened. I thought we were good. I thought that the past few weeks were just nerves. But this shit...*" His voice broke, and I could hear anger and pain resonating through the phone. "*This shit is unforgivable, Summer.*" The line didn't cut off immediately. Instead, heavy breathing filled the silence for an extended heartbeat until the message finally ended.

He was right. This was an absolutely unforgivable offense. And while I wanted his forgiveness, it wouldn't change the life I was chasing, the one I refused to compromise. I was no longer interested in a relationship built on conditions, timelines, and rules—love that came with expectations instead of exhilaration. What I wanted was simpler, yet somehow more complicated at the same time. I just wanted to feel...butterflies.

My tears seemed to have a mind of their own, refusing to stop, no matter how many times I swiped them away. Giving up, I climbed into the bed, desperate to find my peace from earlier. I peered over at Echo lying on his back, one arm lifted as if instinctively knowing what I wanted. Shit, what I needed: him.

I nestled right in as if I was always supposed to be there. *Am I supposed to be here?* My thoughts were a mangled mess, but his arm tightened around me, holding me like I was something precious, something fragile. The heat of his body radiated against mine, the balanced beat of his heart calming my broken soul.

Even in our slumber, I could feel his presence—his protective hold and steady breathing. When I shifted slightly, his hands moved instinctively, pulling me closer to stroke the curve of my face. He wouldn't allow sleep to fully claim him until I was settled. The moment felt perfect—almost too perfect—but I knew it couldn't last. Tomorrow, I'd have to let go—of Deshawn, of Echo, of the dream of escaping the mess I'd made. And even though I already knew which one would be harder to lose, I wasn't sure I was strong enough to face it.

CHAPTER FOURTEEN

Summer
October 2019, The Day After the Wedding that Wasn't
2:34 a.m.

THE FLICKERING LIGHT from the TV stirred me from my sleep, but Echo's arms were still wrapped tightly around me. Carefully, I slipped free from his grasp, trying not to wake him, and padded across the room to the bathroom. As I sat on the toilet, my gaze roamed the small space, reminiscing on the time I'd spent at the Abara home. Most of them were good, filled with fun and amazing food, but one memory stood out, engrained so deeply in my mind, it would never fade.

After washing my hands, I caught my reflection in the mirror and paused, momentarily seeing the teenage girl I used to be. My tears had dried hours ago, but my face still bore evidence of a long, grueling day. I looked like hell. Leaning against the sink, I shook my head, mutely questioning, *How the hell did I end up here?*

Not being honest with yourself, that's how, I silently scolded.

I splashed cold water on my face, hoping it would somehow wash away the heaviness clinging to me. I was in for a long day, but right now, I wanted nothing more than to fall back to sleep and pretend none of this had happened.

Before I flicked off the light, I hovered in the doorway watching Echo. His body was relaxed, but there was something about the wrinkle between his brows even while asleep that made me wonder what was going on in his head. Did he see me differently now, after what I'd done today? His cocoa-brown skin glowed faintly in the dim light, his chest rose and fell to the same rhythm of his soft snores. My gaze traveled down the slope of his chest past the ripples of his stomach to be greeted by the slight bulge in his basketball shorts. I caught myself biting the corner of my bottom lip before I yanked it free, as if that alone could stop the dangerous direction of my thoughts. I had no right to be thinking like this—not now, not after the day I'd just had.

I cannot be this reckless. Lord, I gotta get the hell out of here.

Echo shifted, extending his arm, reaching for me. "Sun?" he mumbled, his voice thick with sleep. "You good?"

"Yeah. Go back to sleep, Echo Honor Abara," I said, turning off the bathroom light before stepping back into the room.

"Damn, you're using my whole government." He rubbed his eyes, exhaling deeply. "If you're up, I'm up." He patted the empty space beside him and motioned for me to come closer.

I didn't want to feel this—this kind of simplicity. Deshawn's was safe. But Echo's? His simplicity came wrapped in roses and butterflies.

"I'm not up," I teased, walking back to the bed and pulling my hair loose from its tie. Sliding back under the cover, I found that perfect spot again. He reached out to take my glasses off, but I playfully swatted his hand away.

"You still can't see shit, huh, Sunshine? Take off your glasses if you're going back to sleep," he said.

Without a word, I handed them over, the silence between us filled with the familiar ease of his presence, the recognizable comfort of being around him. But as I settled back in, my hand unconsciously moved to my ear, tugging at my lobe, and I cleared my throat—telltale signs of my anxiety.

"What's wrong?" he asked in a soft tone. "Why are you nervous?"

"I'm not nervous," I lied, knowing damn well I was. My heart was pounding, and I could feel the heat between us, but it wasn't just the unresolved feelings—it was everything. Deshawn. The future. The terrifying reality of what this moment might mean. And yes, the way Echo's body was pressed against me, his hardness impossible to ignore, didn't help.

"So, you're just gonna pull your ear off for no reason?" he teased. "You forget, I know you better than anybody."

"Shut up, E. Stop acting like you know me," I snapped, even though we both knew better. He did. He always had. And despite my words, despite the weak protest I tried to put between us, my body gave me away, leaning into him, drawn to the comfort I swore I didn't need. His voice grew gentle, his tone laced with something softer, but I could feel it—the tension simmering just out of reach, the restraint in the way he held himself back, like he was fighting a battle just as hard as I was.

"Sun, I know these are messed-up circumstances, but I have to admit, I'm really glad to see you—to have you here," he said, pausing briefly before continuing. "I've missed you."

I turned to look at him, his face partially illuminated by the light from the TV. His expression was vulnerable in a way I hadn't seen in years.

"I've missed you too, E," I murmured, the truth slipping out before I could overthink it. The air was thick with things felt but not spoken…unfulfilled longing. He cradled my chin, his thumb grazing my earlobe with a tenderness that sent a wave of heat through my core. Then, softly, timidly, he kissed me on the lips. A featherlight peck, fleeting, yet electrifying, reigniting a spark deep inside, sending a current through me that I wasn't prepared for.

"Sweet dreams, Summer Sierra Knight," he whispered against my lips, my full name rolling from his tongue like perfection.

"Oh, so we're using government names now?" I teased, as our foreheads pressed together.

For a moment, the world outside ceased to exist, and everything felt right. There was only us, cocooned in something nostalgic yet dangerously new. Then, before I realized what was happening, before I could second-guess, his lips were on mine again. This kiss was different—it wasn't brief or unsure and far from friendly. It was charged with urgency, longing, something ardent that had been simmering for years. I thought I'd pull away, stop this before we crossed a line we couldn't come back from, but I didn't.

Echo faltered, his eyes intense as they searched mine, as if waiting for me to change my mind. Instead, I reached for him, my fingers curling into his shirt as I pulled him closer, my hands finding their way to the chest I'd been curious about as the kiss deepened. His hands roamed everywhere with an intentional gentleness, tracing the delicate lines of my face, sliding down my throat, and navigating the contours of my body, which he seemed to have memorized long ago.

"I missed you so much, Sun," he murmured against my lips, his breath hot against my skin, his voice raw with yearning.

His words melted into me, soothing the storm of confusion and the ache swirling in my mind like a healing balm. His touch was careful yet insistent, not a luxury, but a necessity, one I hadn't allowed myself to crave until now. His lips found my neck, pressing soft, reverent kisses along my skin. A shiver ran down my spine as his mouth trailed lower, his thick lips leaving behind a heat that threated to unravel me completely. Every rational thought clawed at me, screaming for me to stop him—to stop us, but I couldn't. Not tonight. Not when I needed this. Not when I needed him.

But then, like a sudden gust of cold air, reality struck me. My reckless choices, my entangled emotions, the heaviness of everything I'd just done, everything I was about to do flashed before me. I couldn't be a runaway bride *and* a woman who crossed this line on the same night. The words tumbled from my lips, breaking the spell we were caught in before we lost ourselves completely.

"E. E, I–I'm scared," I whispered, my voice trembling under the strain of my emotions.

His lips hovered near my cheek, brushing against my skin as he whispered, "Scared of what, Sunshine?" The tenderness in the gesture was almost too much to bear.

"Everything. This. *Us*. Again," I croaked as a lone tear slipped down the side of my face. "I don't know what this means for us," I admitted. And that was the truth. I didn't know if we were reopening an old wound or healing it—if this was fate or just another mistake waiting to be made. But I knew one thing for certain: I had never stopped feeling this way about him—feeling the butterflies. As I stared into his eyes, searching for answers I didn't have, unchecked tears began to flow, narrating a silent conversation between us. Words were unnecessary because the gravity of his touch said it all as his thumb caught my tears, wiping them away with the care only Echo could give.

Echo
October 2019, The Day After the Wedding that Wasn't

I stilled instantly, my grip loosening as I leaned back, giving her space and taking a little for myself to absorb the burden of her pain. Concern must have been written all over my face. It was never my intent to put her in this predicament. "Sun, I'm so sorry,"

I said quietly. "We don't have to do this. We probably *shouldn't* do this."

Her chest rose and fell rapidly, her breathing uneven, and I could see the conflict swirling inside her. Her heart was racing—I could feel it—and more tears threatened to spill over. The sight twisted something deep in me, making me wish I could erase her doubts, her pain, her fear.

I cupped her face gently, my thumbs brushing against the damp trails of her tears as I tried to calm the storm brewing in her.

"Sunshine," I said, "we don't have to figure it out right now. Not tonight." I leaned in closer, hoping my words would sink past her fear. "You don't have to be scared. Not with me."

The way she looked at me, like she was torn between running away and leaning into me, made a heavy knot form right in my gut. I could see the struggle, the fear tangled with something deeper—something I hoped was trust. I held my breath, silently willing her to believe me, to let herself feel what she was so clearly trying to resist.

"Talk to me," I urged, brushing my thumb against her cheek, careful not to push her further than she was ready to go. "What do you need right now, Summer?" In that moment, nothing else mattered but her. If it took patience, time, I'd give her both.

"I shouldn't have let it go this far, but..." She tensed, her voice fading into the uncertain space she always seemed to retreat to, the one that reminded me of when we were kids.

"But what, Summer? Talk to me, please." I cradled her face gently in my hands.

I pressed soft, comforting kisses across her cheeks and forehead, hoping to soothe the angst radiating from her. I'd seen this movie before—*The Unsettling of Summer*—and I knew how the story usually ended. But this time, I wasn't letting her go. Not without a fight. Because for the first time in years, it felt like we were having a breakthrough, teetering on the brink of rediscovering something we'd lost long ago: us. I wasn't ready to let it slip through my fingers again. I tightened my arms around her, silently daring her to pull away, to say my name and tell me to stop. But the words didn't come.

"But what?" I repeated, my lips lingering against her ear, desperate for her to meet me halfway. I should've been the one pulling back. She was engaged—meant to marry someone else today, for God's sake. But I couldn't. Logic begged me to step away, to let her go, but my heart wouldn't listen.

"I think I want this, but it's not the right time," she said finally, her voice barely audible, as if speaking any louder might break her completely.

"Just like last time," I murmured.

Summer
Senior Year, 2004

Yesterday marked the last day of school before holiday break, and my parents and I were already packed and ready for our trip to Nashville. We'd be spending the holidays with my brother and his family, staying through the New Year. Normally, I'd be thrilled at the thought of weeks with my new niece and endless opportunities to bother my siblings, but this year, the excitement was dulled by one glaring fact: I wouldn't get to see Echo.

Knowing it was my last day in town before vacation, I'd promised him we'd spend some time together, and I'd made good on that promise. Echo whisked me away for a full day that included the mall, the arcade, and dinner. Now, our last stop brought us to Maxell's house—the unofficial hangout spot, thanks to his always out-of-town parents. I'd only been here once before but agreed to come tonight since some of our old camp friends were supposed to be there.

The moment we stepped into the basement, I realized this wasn't the low-key gathering I'd imagined. The space was packed, bodies pressing against each other as music pounded from the speakers. Laughter and shouts blended with the unmistakable clink of red plastic cups. I glanced at Echo, my wide-eyed expression betraying my surprise.

"This wasn't what I expected," I said, leaning closer so he could hear me over the noise.

"We don't have to stay long," he said, his voice reassuring as he leaned in closer so that I could hear him.

"I'm good."

Before we could move farther into the room, a familiar squeal pierced through the noise. "Summer!"

I turned just in time to see my friends, Trinity and Brooke, weaving their way through the crowd toward me. Their excitement was infectious as they pulled me into a group hug.

"Hey, boo!" they chimed in unison.

"Hey, hey!" I sang back.

Brooke's eyes flicked toward Echo, standing a few steps behind me. "Can we steal her for a minute?" she asked, already tugging me toward the far side of the room before Echo could even respond. He gave me a small knowing nod before leaning back against the wall to survey the room. Even in a crowded party, Echo was my anchor, and I felt lighter knowing he was nearby.

Maxell's house was beautiful, and the basement was like its own private apartment, complete with plush couches, a mini kitchen, and even a built-in bar area. Brooke and Trinity dragged me toward the bar, where red plastic cups were stacked next to a haphazard collection of bottles filled with clear and dark liquids.

"Are y'all drinking?" I asked, my tone teetering on motherly concern.

"Just a sip," Brooke said. Her flushed cheeks told that it was likely much more than that.

"Here, I'll make you something," Trinity offered confidently, grabbing a cobalt-blue bottle and pouring a clear liquid into one of the cups. I watched her movements in disbelief.

"How do you even know how to do that?" I asked.

Trinity shrugged, a sly grin playing on her lips. "Trial and error," she said as she reached for a bottle of pineapple juice and poured it in after the clear liquid.

"As long as it's sweet, you'll be fine," Brooke assured me, nudging the cup closer.

I hesitated, staring at the cup like it might explode. The most alcohol I'd ever had was champagne and wine during New Year's Eve toasts, and even then, just a few sips. "What is this, anyway?" I asked, taking a cautious sniff.

"Vodka," Brooke replied nonchalantly.

I wrinkled my nose. "Well, if you want me to even try this, it needs way more juice," I insisted, pushing the cup back toward Trinity. They laughed as Trinity obliged, adding more pineapple juice before handing it back to me. Folding under the pressure, I took a tentative sip. To my surprise, it wasn't bad, so I took another sip. And then another. Before long, I was swaying along with Brooke and Trinity on the makeshift dance floor in the center of the basement. I noticed Echo approaching. He slipped the cup out of my hand and brought it to his nose, his brow lifting in mock disapproval.

"You sure you can handle this?" he asked.

I nodded. "It's not too bad," I said as the room seemed to spin ever so slightly.

"Dance with me," he said, taking a sip of my drink before setting it aside on a nearby table. He draped my arms across his shoulders, pulling me closer.

His six-foot frame towered over me as he guided us into a slow rhythm that matched the music's beat. The warmth of his hands on my waist sent a soothing steadiness through me. Echo had a way of balancing his adventurous side with an unwavering instinct to protect. Even now, he was ensuring I didn't drink too much while still letting me enjoy the moment. I tilted my head back to look at him, our movements synced effortlessly. For a few minutes, it felt like we were the only ones in the crowded, noisy basement, swaying together under the dim glow of string lights.

We stayed at the party for about another hour before heading home. As Echo pulled into my driveway, he parked the car but didn't turn off the engine. He leaned over, pressing the release on my seat belt so I could shift and get more comfortable. It was still well before my curfew, but we always dragged out the night. For us, the end of an evening wasn't just a drop-off; it was a continuation of whatever conversation we'd left hanging.

"Thank you for another great night," I said, tucking one leg under the other as I turned to face him. "Next time, dinner's on me."

"Next time is, what, like two weeks?" he replied, his tone unintentionally laced with annoyance.

I nodded with an exaggerated pout. "Yep. Something like that. You'll survive. Plenty of basketball to play, and lots of girls to…*play*, too," I teased, raising an eyebrow.

"Man…" he started, trailing off as he ran his hand along his freshly grown stubble. "I told you before, I'm not tripping off these girls."

"Oh, really? Then who? A guy? Are you tripping off a guy, E?" I asked in mock shock, my voice dripping with mischief.

He playfully nudged the side of my head. "Man, fuck you, Sun."

I nudged him back. "Okay, okay, so who are you tripping off of?"

He shook his head, his lips pressing into a tight line. "Nobody," he said, though the faint tension in his voice told a different story.

"*Mm-hmm.*" My curiosity was piqued. Before I could press further, he shifted the conversation. "You sober yet?" he asked, his brow raised.

"I wasn't drunk," I shot back, but as I leaned my head against the window, I winced slightly. "But my head is starting to hurt."

Without hesitation, he reached over, gently turning my face toward him. "Come here," he said, pulling me closer. He gently placed his hands on either side of my head, his fingertips grazing my temples. His touch was warm, sending a wave of comfort through my throbbing skull.

"I'm never drinking again." I groaned, leaning into his hands as he began to circle his thumbs across my temples, tracing down the sides of my nose with practiced ease.

"You will. Trinity and Brooke didn't know what they were doing." He chuckled. "Tell me if this helps." His voice dipped to something softer, something that lingered dangerously close to my ear. A shiver ran down my spine, but it wasn't from the December chill. It was the way his voice wrapped around me, a sweet, subtle caress I couldn't escape.

"It's perfect," I whispered as my body melted under his touch, and I let out a soft, unintentional sigh.

I didn't miss the flicker of satisfaction across his face. Tilting my head back, his hands moved with a gentle yet purposeful rhythm, cradling my head like it was something fragile and precious. Our faces were barely an inch apart now, as we leaned over the middle console.

"Better?" he asked. I nodded, licking my lips.

My throat was suddenly dry, and I knew it wasn't from the heat of the car. It was him—his proximity, his touch. My breath hitched as one of his fingers brushed across my bottom lip. *What the hell, Summer?*

I had to fight the wild, crazy urge to pull that finger into my mouth. What was happening to me?

"Much better. Th–Thank you," I stammered.

His grin was crooked and warm. "Anytime, Sunshine," he said, his touch still lingering on my lips for just a second longer than necessary before he finally pulled away. But even after the touch was gone, the heat of it lingered, making it nearly impossible to think of anything else.

The five seconds of awkward silence between us felt like an eternity before Echo placed a gentle hand on my neck, his other hand cupping the curve of my face. His touch was so soft, yet deliberate, as he pulled me in for the sweetest, most unexpected kiss. His lips lingered on mine, warm and unhurried, his tongue delicately tracing the outline but never fully entering my mouth.

My hands rested against the curve of his chest, unmoved as if trying to anchor myself against the pull of whatever this moment was turning into. But then, his kiss deepened, growing stronger. One hand slid up the back of my neck, cradling my head, while the other wandered down my back with a confidence that sent shockwaves through me. Before I knew it, I was nearly in his lap, my body molding into his like it was second nature. And I didn't stop him.

What the hell was I doing? I was in my driveway—my parents' driveway. My mama—my crazy-ass mama—was mere steps away. Panic crept in, but it couldn't compete with the heat rising between us. My body was betraying me, aching with a need I'd been trying to suppress. Then, out of the corner of my eye, I stole a glance at the house. The lights were still off. But just as quickly as I thought I was safe, I felt it—him. The rise and strength of his firm, insistent arousal pressed against me, and suddenly, reality crashed in like a tidal wave.

Honk!

The car horn blared, piercing the intimate bubble we'd created. I don't know if it was heaven or hell, but my heart leapt to my throat as if struck by lightning. And instantly, all the passion building inside me expelled, like an exorcism. I lifted my head to verify that the house was still dark.

"Echo, stop!" I shouted, pulling away from him as if I'd been burned. I straightened my sweater and reclaimed my place in the passenger seat, trembling with a mix of overwhelming desire and sheer panic.

Echo was gasping for air like he'd just run a marathon. "I'm sorry," he mumbled, wiping my lip gloss from his mouth.

I struggled to calm my pounding heart. My eyes flicked downward to his lap, where his arousal still stood defiantly, and I exhaled sharply. "What the hell was that?"

He cleared his throat. "A kiss," he said, as if that explanation would make everything better.

"That was more than a kiss, E! Why would you do that? We don't…we don't do that!" My voice was shaky, caught somewhere between fear and anger and desire.

He didn't respond at first, just stared blankly at the steering wheel, his breaths still uneven. Then, almost as if snapping out of a trance, he turned to me, frustration and something unspoken clouding his face.

"Echo!" My voice cracked with a mass of unsteady emotions. "Why did you kiss me?"

His irritation broke through. "I guess for the same reason you didn't stop me, Summer!" he shouted, the words hanging in the air like a challenge. I froze, his words hitting harder than I cared to admit. My breath came in short, shallow bursts as I tried to reconcile the emotions clawing at me. Echo ran a hand down his face, his breathing beginning to steady. The lines of tension on his face faded, and he reached to pinch the tip of my nose, a familiar gesture that only made the moment more confusing.

"I'm sorry," he whispered, his tone quieter now. "I guess I got caught up in the moment."

I turned my head away, fixated on the dashboard. A glaze of unshed tears clouded my vision. My voice was thick with conflicted feelings. "I can't do this. Not like this. Not here."

The tension between us hung heavy, suffocating the air in the car. For a moment, neither of us spoke. We just sat there, two hearts beating loudly in the silence, two friends unsure of what had just changed forever. I practically yanked my ear off I tugged so hard, the nervousness and anxiety clawing at my chest. Even when the moment didn't merit it, tears were often my uninvited guest, a release I couldn't control.

I reached for the door handle, desperate to escape the heat still lingering between us. My purse was forgotten in the rush, but before I could make it more than a step, Echo was out of the car and chasing after me.

"Sun, wait. Don't leave," he pleaded, his voice was raw as he caught my arm, gently pulling me to face him. Before I could react, he pressed me against the wall of my house. I quivered under his scrutiny, and I held my breath as his forehead dipped to rest against mine. For a second, I thought he might kiss me again.

"Don't leave like this, Sunshine. Please," he whispered, his voice breaking just enough to make my heart clench. "I'm sorry. Okay? I'm sorry."

I nodded, swallowing hard. "Me, too."

"Are we good—me and you?" he asked, lifting my chin so our eyes could meet. His gaze was soft, yet intense, searching mine for reassurance.

I nodded again, my trembling fingers swiping at a stray tear. "Always," I whispered, the word as much a promise to myself as it was to him.

Echo walked me to the door, standing so close that the heat of him seemed to follow me. He waited as I slid the key into the lock, watching intently as though he couldn't bear to turn away just yet. When the door finally opened, he gently nudged it wider, ensuring I stepped inside safely before offering a quiet, "Good night, Sunshine."

I closed the door behind me, locking it with a forceful click before leaning back against its solid surface. My chest rose and fell in quick, weak breaths as I rubbed a hand across my face, my lips tingling with the ghost of his kiss. No matter how hard I tried, I couldn't erase the memory of the passion—shit, confusion—he'd left behind.

Darting down the hall, I kept my head low, hoping to make it to my room unnoticed. But, as if she could sense something in the air, my mother peeked out of her bedroom door, her robe draped loosely around her shoulders.

"Summer," she called, her tone carrying relief and a hint of curiosity.

I paused mid-step, schooling my face into nonchalance. "Hey, Ma."

She inspected me as she always did. "You have fun with your *friend?*" she asked, her voice calm but probing.

I nodded. "Yeah, Ma. It was cool."

Her gaze lingered for a moment longer, but she said nothing else, retreating into her room. As soon as her door clicked shut, I exhaled, finally releasing the breath I didn't realize I'd been holding. Once in the safety of my room, I dropped my purse on the floor and collapsed onto my bed, tracing the edges of my lips. Echo's words, his touch, his kiss... They replayed over and over in my head, and no amount of rubbing or distraction could erase the way they made me feel.

CHAPTER FIFTEEN

Echo
October 2019, The Day After the Wedding that Wasn't
7:17 a.m.

SUMMER FINALLY FELL back to sleep, her breathing soft, but laden. I stared at her, any hope of comfort escaping me. The room was still covered in darkness, except for the sliver of light casting from the sun. It illuminated her pretty face, highlighting my favorite features, but the weariness in her body was undeniable. Exhaustion had left her disoriented; muddling her words and thoughts after we kissed. She said she wanted me, but it wasn't the right time. I released a bitter laugh because it never seemed to be the right time for me and Summer. She said she had her reasons for calling off her wedding, but she didn't share them with me. After living fifteen years in a fog of confusion when it came to Summer Knight, I needed answers.

"Summer. Wake up," I said, my voice indicating the early hour.

She glanced around the room, slowly focusing on her surroundings. "What time is it?" she murmured.

"A little after seven. Wake up. I need to talk to you," I replied, leaving no room for argument.

Her features clouded with thought, her blank expression momentarily darkening as she searched for the right words. Her face shifted into a knowing scowl, the kind that told me she realized her time for vague answers and conflicting behavior had run out. It was time for her to come clean.

She sat up slowly, reaching to grab a bottle of water from the nightstand before leaning against the headboard. She tossed the water back with a few gulps. "What's up, E?"

I snickered, though shit wasn't funny. "Talk, Summer. Now. And I'm not playing." Her scowl deepened, and I didn't give a damn. I continued to stare unflinching because I didn't care about her irritation; I cared about the truth.

"I met Deshawn at homecoming a few years ago," she began. "He was handsome and sweet and smart. He checked every box on my 'list'." She lifted her hands, making air quotes when she said *list*, before continuing. "It was a whirlwind. I went from dating myself for almost two years after a nasty break-up to suddenly traveling with a man who loved food, wine, and culture just as much as I did. He was climbing the corporate ladder, just like I thought I wanted to, but…" Her words faltered. She slightly shook her head. "When the honeymoon phase ended, and the dust settled, it became obvious we didn't have much in common beyond traveling, food, and wine. My heart never skipped a beat when I was with him… There were no butterflies."

"So why agree to marry him?" I asked, keeping my tone even as I leaned slightly closer.

She shrugged, her teeth catching the corner of her bottom lip as tears brimmed in her eyes. "Because I want a husband. I want a family. And being in love wasn't at the top of that list I mentioned," she admitted, swiping quickly at the tears spilling onto her cheeks. "I thought that giddy, delightful, bubbly feeling would come with time. But life moved so fast, and one day, I looked up, and I was engaged. I was planning a wedding, but I was caught up in the frills of it all, not the love."

"*Hmm,*" I said, joining her against the headboard, giving her space but staying close enough for her to know I was there.

"I thought about ending it. God, I wanted to end it so many times, but then I woke up, and it was my wedding day. And I felt sick to my stomach." She paused, her voice trembling as she stared down at her hands. "I thought about going to Shawn, telling him everything. I thought maybe we could tell everyone together. Or Trin and Brooke—they'd help me. But nothing felt right yesterday morning. Nothing except going to our spot."

Her words lingered in the room like a confession, raw and unpolished. I didn't say anything right away, allowing the heft of it all to settle. When I finally looked at her, I saw the vulnerability in her eyes—the fear, the relief, the guilt—all beautifully woven together in a way only Summer could carry.

"When did things change?" I asked, trying to keep my voice steady, but the need to know hammered like rain pelting the pavement.

"Some months ago," she admitted. "But I guess, if I'm being honest, I always knew that I shouldn't have accepted his proposal." Her gaze dropped to her lap.

Her admission hit me harder than I expected, and my interest piqued at the timing. Some months ago? Could it have been five months ago at Brooke and Seth's wedding? Something shifted on that patio. I felt it then, and I had a gut feeling now... Summer called off her wedding for the same reasons I broke up with Kourtni. Because deep down, we both knew we were supposed to be together.

"Did you have dreams about what your wedding would be like?" I asked.

She nodded, her expression pensive. "Of course. I think every girl dreams about her wedding day."

"And what did you see?"

Summer leaned her head back against the headboard, closing her eyes as she let the vision wash over her. "An outdoor wedding, right as the sun is setting, surrounded by large trees and colorful roses. Maybe seventy-five guests—only the closet family and friends. Great food, lots of wine, and good music."

"And who do you see, Summer?" I asked, my tenor soft yet probing.

Her mouth parted, confusion flickering across her face. "What do you mean?"

"Who's standing there, waiting to receive you as his wife?" I clarified.

Her eyes widened, like I'd reached into the most intimate, private corners of her mind and unveiled something she'd been hiding, even from herself. I trailed my eyes over her face, down the slope of her neck, watching as her breaths grew shallow and labored. The truth—her reality—hovered on her lips, but she fought to let it out.

"Close your eyes," I urged, "and tell me who you see."

Her voice broke when it finally came, a shaky exhale slipped from her lips. "I didn't see Shawn's face," she whispered, her words trembling under the enormity of her confession.

I nodded knowingly, though she couldn't see me since her eyes were still shut tightly as if that would protect her from what she'd already divulged. "Who, Sunshine?" I pressed gently, leaning in closer, my heart pounding as I waited for her to say it. To name what we both already knew.

Summer shot up from the bed, her movements frantic as she shook her head vigorously. "No. No. I can't do this," she cried, pacing the short length of the room like a caged bird trying to escape.

I stood quickly, closing the gap between us in a few strides. "You can't do what? Tell me the truth? Tell yourself the truth," I demanded, stepping into her space.

Her face was a battlefield of emotions—anger and reassurance colliding like opposing storms. Angered by the truth, yet there was a quiet solace in it, too, as if acknowledging it might finally set her free. But she remained hushed.

My patience snapped, a mix of angst and fierce admiration for this woman seething through me. I nudged her back against the wall, my taller frame towering over her as I pinned her with my stare. "Say it," I growled through gritted teeth, my hands braced against the wall on either side of her. "Whose face did you see?" The eerie silence stretched loud, scoring the music of the moment. My face was so close that I could feel her shaky breaths against my skin. I could've easily sucked her tongue into my mouth with no effort. Her lips trembled, her eyes piercing mine as several long, agonizing heartbeats thudded before she finally broke.

"You," she cried, her voice cracking and body limp. "Echo, I saw you."

Relief—shit, redemption—surged through me because I was gaining back what I'd lost. I released a heavy breath I hadn't realized I was holding, a tide of emotions washing over me. "It's always been you, Summer," I murmured, my forehead pressed to hers. "Always."

Summer
Post-Graduation, Summer 2005

This year, my birthday felt lonelier than ever. And it was my eighteenth—if any year deserved to be celebrated, it was this one. I should've been kicking it with my friends, soaking up the milestone with laughter and fun. Instead, I was at camp, surrounded by the sounds of nature but feeling miles away from the people I cared about most.

As usual, I celebrated with my family at my family's annual Memorial Day celebration before I left, and my friends who would normally be at camp with me even threw me a party, complete with cake and hugs that lingered too long. But on the actual day? It was just another rotation of busy camp activities, and I couldn't shake the emptiness gnawing at my chest.

I hadn't planned on returning to camp this summer—at least, not until I found out my scholarship wouldn't cover all of my housing at Spelman. I had other options, full-ride offers that would've made things easier. But they weren't Spelman, so I made the choice. The money I'd earn here, along with the scholarship funded by the founding family of Camp Quest, would secure my future at the school of my dreams. And for that, I was willing to spend one more summer in a place that had shaped so much of who I was.

Since I was no longer a high school counselor, I held the position of assistant director, which included counselor responsibilities, among other things—coordinating schedules, training new counselors, and managing the chaos. It was great for my résumé, and I always loved it here, but this summer, something was missing—or maybe someone.

I didn't need to think long to figure it out. I missed Echo. His face—the way his brow furrowed in disappointment when I told him I'd be working at the camp—replayed in my head more times than I wanted to admit. His college plans were set and fully funded, which meant returning to Camp Quest wasn't on his radar. And we hadn't made any official plans for the summer, but we didn't have to. It was understood. This was supposed to be *our* summer. And I'd broken those unspoken plans without so much as a second thought.

The sky was always a masterpiece at this time of the day, painting streaks of orange and violet as the sun slept for the night. The moon was pale, yet luminous as it began to awaken, casting a faint glow over the campgrounds. It was a perfect first evening of summer. The cool breeze rustled through the leaves, and the chirps of birds and bugs blended into a soothing melody. Even the air felt lighter, a reprieve from the stifling heat of the day.

I was relieved that the day was finally winding down and my shift was over. The campers were nestled in the amphitheater, enjoying dinner and a movie, their chatter fading into the background as I finished my rounds. After double-checking that everyone was accounted for and fed, I made my way back to my room. Thankfully, assistant directors had the privilege of their own space, and tonight, I was more than ready to sink into the solitude. The promise of quiet felt like a much-needed gift at the close of this lonely birthday.

My steps slowed, navigating the gravel road from memory while I marveled in the beauty of my surroundings. Staring into the night, I willed the first stars to show their light. And then, there it was, a faint twinkle streaking across the sky. I paused, closing my eyes as I made a wish. But this time, I whispered the words aloud, letting the stillness of the night carry them away. The path was empty, its hush amplified by the faint rustling of leaves in the evening breeze.

So, when a soft, almost imperceptible sound broke the quiet, it seemed to echo louder than it should have. My ears perked instinctively, straining to catch what might not have been there at all. I shook my head, telling myself it was just my imagination playing tricks. But as I took a few more steps, the sound came again, stopping me in my tracks.

"*Psst.*" The whisper was sharp, cutting through the serene night like a blade. I scanned the shadows, my pulse quickening.

"Hello?" I called out, my voice urgent yet low, laced with restrained authority. "If you're supposed to be watching a movie, you better get there…now," I said firmly, assuming some campers were sneaking where they shouldn't be.

"Don't hurt me, Sunshine," the familiar voice murmured from the shadows, the teasing edge instantly unraveling my tension.

I froze, my heart pounding as the figure stepped into the moonlight. The glow illuminated the curve of his jaw, the warmth of his smile, and the easy confidence in his stride. Recognition hit me like a wave, and my breath caught.

"Echo," I screeched, my voice ringing through the trees. He lifted a finger to his lips, his playful expression urging me to be quiet.

"What are you doing here?" I asked, my tone a mix of surprise and joy.

"Happy birthday," he said. Without thinking, I closed the distance, falling into his arms as if it was the most natural thing in the world. His embrace was firm and familiar, and just like that, the loneliness that had weighed down my day lifted. What had been gray and dull was now bursting with color—vibrant, brilliant, and calm all at once.

Echo
Post-Graduation, Summer 2005

"Summer solstice is here, giving us the longest day of the year and plenty of sunshine to soak up. Whether you're planning a trip to the amusement park, a barbecue in the backyard, or just enjoying the warmth of the season, today is the perfect time to celebrate everything summer has to offer. Stay hydrated, don't forget the sunscreen, and let's make the most of this sunny start to summer!"

The television's glow faded as I turned it off, not wanting to be reminded what day it was. Today wasn't the first day of summer, but it was Summer's birthday. And I wanted to see her…bad. She'd had been gone a few weeks, but it felt like an eternity. Her absence left a hole where all the hours we used to spend together used to be. Don't get me wrong, my summer wasn't empty. Between volunteering and the internship my dad had secured for me at the university's School of Art, I had plenty to do. But no matter how busy I was, in every quiet moment, Summer filled my thoughts. She was like a drug I couldn't quit, and on her birthday, the craving hit harder than ever.

I glanced at the clock, realizing I was running late. The fellas were already waiting at the basketball court. I threw on some shorts, a tank, and sneakers before darting out of my room and bounding down the stairs.

"Echo," my mother called out, halting my momentum.

"Yeah, Mum?" I responded over my shoulder, stopping mid-step.

"Come here, please," she requested. Peeking into the kitchen, I noticed Sadie and Eazy at the table eating lunch. It struck me as odd. Meals in the Abara household were almost always shared as a family.

"Where is everybody?" I asked, stepping fully into the room.

"Kemi's at a friend's house, and Samir just left for his Boy Scouts weekend," she said, reminding me of my little brother's first overnight trip with his troop.

I nodded. "I'm heading to the court to play basketball. Did you need something?"

"I was going to ask if you wanted to join us for a movie," she said, gesturing toward Sadie and Eazy whose faces lit up with excitement.

"We're going to see *The Adventures of Sharkboy and Lavagirl*," Eazy blurted, practically bouncing in his chair.

"And then Mum is taking us to the arcade," Sadie added, beaming.

I remembered how much I used to enjoy these kinds of outings with my mum when I was younger. With Dad away for the weekend with Samir, she was making the most of her time with the youngest two.

"I'll pass. You three have fun," I said, kissing my mum on the cheek and giving Sadie and Eazy quick tickles that left them giggling. As I turned to leave, an idea sparked in my mind like a lightbulb flickering on. "Mum, can I stay at Maxell's tonight?" I asked.

She tilted her head, considering for a moment, then nodded. "As long as it's okay with his parents. Are they traveling?"

"I don't think so, but you know they're always cool with it. Donte might be there too," I added, laying the groundwork for my plan.

"Okay. Be careful, Echo," she said, her tone warm but laced with the usual motherly concern.

"Always," I replied, already halfway out the door. By the time I reached the basketball court, my plan was fully formed.

"What up, E? You're late!" Donte called, wiping sweat from his forehead as he grabbed a water bottle.

"My bad," I said, noting that they'd just wrapped up a three-on-three game and were taking a break.

"Yo, Max, can I stay at your crib tonight?" I asked, raising an eyebrow with just enough mischief to make him suspicious.

Maxell leaned against the fence, squinting at me. "Yeah. My parents are out of town, but they won't care. Why are you looking like you're up to something?"

I was unable to hide my excitement. "Because I am."

"Care to share?" Maxell prompted, crossing his arms.

I hesitated, glancing at Donte, then back at Maxell. Finally, I spilled, "I'm going to see Summer."

"At camp? In Brighton?" Maxell barked, his disbelief loud enough to make the other guys glance over.

"Yeah," I said, grinning like a kid who'd just gotten away with something. "Today's her birthday."

"I know," Maxell said, looking at me like I was insane.

"It's less than two hours," I continued to plead my case.

Maxell rubbed his temple like my plan was giving him a headache. "You realize this is a terrible idea, right? Less than two hours away or not, what if you get caught? Mr. Abara is going to whoop your ass, dog."

"I know," I admitted, shrugging, "but it's worth it."

Maxell sighed, glancing at Donte for backup. "And how do you plan to get onto the campgrounds? You know they lock the gate at night."

"I've got someone on the inside," I said with a grin, feeling my excitement build. "I'll sneak in right as it's getting dark and be out before morning." Donte nodded in approval, while Maxell, who followed rules only when it was convenient for him, wasn't convinced.

"Just tell your parents I'm staying just in case my mum calls your mom," I said, patting his shoulder. "Call my cell phone if some shit pops off," I continued, sounding all too confident.

Maxell shook his head, muttering under his breath, "This dude," as we jogged to the court. My plan wasn't perfect, but as far as I was concerned, nothing would stop me from seeing Summer tonight. After a few intense games of basketball, I went home to shower and pack a bag before heading to Maxell's place.

Walking into his house, I couldn't help but shake my head at the scene in his basement. For someone who always gave me grief about following rules, Max clearly didn't follow them all. He, Donte, and a few other guys were chilling with a group of girls I recognized from school, music blasting as they sipped from colored cups. The vibe was pure *Home Alone*, and they were clearly enjoying it. Before heading out, I ran down my plan one last time for the guys, just in case things went sideways, and they needed to cover for me. Max nodded begrudgingly, agreeing to play lookout if needed.

Sliding into my car, I said a quick prayer, even though I was pretty sure God wasn't thrilled about me sneaking around. I made a few stops to grab a few essentials for my surprise, including the bribe that would get me past the gates of Camp Quest. The sun was sinking lower, painting the sky in deep purples about an hour into my drive. Another forty minutes, and it'd be completely dark—but by then, I'd be at Quest. I had no idea how Summer would react to me showing up unannounced, but I hoped she missed me as much as I missed her.

When I pulled up to the oversized gate marking the camp's entrance, a wave of relief hit me as I spotted Lincoln in the security booth. Last year, he'd been my partner in crime when it came to pulling off Summer's birthday surprise, and he'd come through for me again. My text earlier with the details of my plan had been met with a single request: shrimp fried rice and grape Vess soda. I parked in one of the security spots and stepped out, backpack slung over my shoulder and greasy paper bag in hand. Lincoln's face lit up as I approached, the scent of takeout already putting him in a trance. We exchanged a quick dap before he snatched the bag from me, holding it up like a prized trophy.

"Man, you gotta be outta here by six at the latest," Lincoln warned, his tone serious despite the grin. "If your ass gets caught, I don't know shit."

"I got you. Thanks, dog," I said, grateful as I followed him through the gate. He pointed me in the direction of the assistant director's lodge, though I didn't really need it. The layout was burned into my memory from last summer.

To stay low-key, I wore my camp shirt and pulled my hat low over my face. Lincoln had told me most of the campers were at the amphitheater, which explained the quiet walkways. Still, I leaned against a tree near the lodge, waiting for the coast to be clear. A few campers lingered nearby, but they quickly ran off toward the theater. I exhaled, silently questioning how I'd get Summer's attention without drawing a crowd. As if the universe heard my plea, she appeared, walking slowly down the path. My breath caught as I took her in—her hair tied back, her soft features illuminated by the glow of the lanterns lining the walkway. She was as pretty as ever, but I noticed a hint of sadness on her face.

I couldn't help but smile, even as my pulse pounded at the sight of her like this. She didn't see me at first, so I stayed still, watching her, waiting for the right moment to call out. Maybe this was crazy, but seeing her made every mile of the drive and every ounce of sneaking around worth it. I stood frozen, watching as the moonlight bathed her face in a soft glow. Her gaze was fixed on the stars above, a look of quiet wonder sparkling in her eyes. Then, as if sharing a secret with the universe, she slammed her eyes shut. My eyes darted upward, catching the streak of light racing across the dark sky—a shooting star. She was making a wish.

I could've stayed rooted there for hours, soaking in her presence, her peace. But she was too close not to touch. The ache in my chest won. *"Psst,"* I whispered, low but clear. Wide and alert, she scanned the path like a hawk searching for prey.

"Hello?" she called out, her voice sharper than usual, laced with the kind of authority only an assistant director could master. "If you're supposed to be watching a movie, you better get there…

now," she fussed at imaginary campers, and I couldn't help but be amused as I stepped out of the shadows.

Her head whipped toward me, and when her eyes met mine, the squeal of my name echoed through the night air. The pure joy lighting up her face was all the confirmation I needed—I'd made the right choice. I was probably going to be grounded for life for this stunt, but in that moment, her smile made it all worth it. Before I could say a word, she closed the gap between us, leaping into my arms like she'd been waiting for this exact moment. I held her tight, feeling her warmth melt into mine.

"What are you doing here?" she asked breathlessly, her voice trembling with joy and disbelief.

I rested my chin gently atop her head. "Did you really think I'd miss your birthday, Sunshine?" I said, the nickname falling from my lips like a promise. We slipped quietly into her suite, moving quickly to avoid any curious eyes. Once the door clicked shut behind us, I finally exhaled, leaning against the wall. But I couldn't stop staring at her—the way her shy confidence lit up her face, a perfect balance of playful curiosity and disbelief. It was one of the things I loved most about her.

"How…How'd you do this?" she asked, her voice a mix of wonder and amusement.

"What do you mean?" I replied as I leaned forward. "I'm spending the night at Max's house, remember? You haven't seen me." I winked.

"Echo Abara," she said, her voice dripping with sarcastic disbelief, "you lied to your mum."

I nodded with zero shame. "I did."

She lowered her head and asked softly, "Was it worth it?"

Her question carried more weight than she realized, but I didn't hesitate. "Most definitely," I said, stepping closer, lowering my voice. "Now, get dressed. We have to celebrate."

CHAPTER SIXTEEN

Summer
Post-Graduation, Summer 2005

I HURRIED INTO the bathroom, eager to let the hot water wash away the whirlwind of emotions swirling inside me. Meanwhile, Echo remained in the bedroom of my suite, his presence quiet but undeniable. I still couldn't believe he was here. As the water pounded against my skin, I pictured him moving around the room, his curious fingers tracing the edges of the pictures and posters tacked to the walls.

Knowing him, he was analyzing every little detail, piecing together parts of my life. If he looked closely, he would see that he was a part of my life. The photo from prom night—the one where he crashed the evening I had carefully planned with Devin—hung within the collage. I imagined his smirk, the knowing gleam in his eyes as he took in the moment we'd frozen in time. He was probably feeling pretty damn proud of himself for that one.

I was prancing through the house singing my best rendition of Mariah Carey's "Emotions." A clear indication that I was in a good mood—correction, a great mood. It was prom night. The night I'd been waiting for since I'd stepped foot into high school.

My mom had my dress steamed, and it was hanging on her bedroom door. My sparkly silver pumps with the matching clutch were still in the box on my dresser right next to my jewelry. Raqi had just applied the final touches of my makeup, and I was ecstatic by the reveal. I felt pretty.

I was nervously getting dressed, praying that the look I was envisioning was going to be to Devin's liking. I heard my mother in the family room chuckling on the phone. "Boy, you are crazy. Let me see if she can come to the phone."

I was sure it was nobody but Echo. I rolled my eyes as soon as my mother peeked in my room handing me the phone. "E, I'm getting dressed. Shouldn't you be doing the same?" I said, irritation lacing my tone.

"You know it don't take me long to get ready. I'm about to go pick up Aliya but wanted to catch you before you leave. I just wanted to tell you I know you look beautiful, Sun, and have a good time tonight."

I paused, staring at my shocked face in the mirror. A smile sweetened my voice when I said, "Thank you, Echo. I'm sure you're pretty handsome yourself right now."

"Well, you know how I do." He chuckled, and I could only imagine that bright Colgate smile on his face. "Y'all at the Drake Hotel, right?" he randomly asked.

"Yep! Trinity's cousin already checked into our room and took our bags," I said.

"Alright, Sunshine. Let me get out of here." He paused with another sigh. "Oh, Sun, don't be letting Devin kiss all over you. I don't know dude, but that nigga is not treasure worthy."

My eyes bulged at him referring to my lady parts as treasure like my mother. I shook my head, realizing I might have shared too much with him.

"You are a mess." I giggled. "Goodbye, Echo Abara!"

He laughed, too. "Bye, Sun."

As much time as Echo and I spent together, people often thought we were boyfriend and girlfriend, but that was far from the truth. I'd had other boys who were friends with some kissing benefits, but Echo...he'd had at least three girlfriends that I knew about. He'd quickly planted his feet in the new city. But no matter what either of us had going on, it never interrupted our friendship flow. We'd even made a pact to go to each other's proms because our relationship didn't come with the pressure of expectations.

"Sun, you know we'll kick it at prom, and I promise not to touch your booty," he'd teased one night on the phone.

Leave it to Echo to make a girl feel special. But unfortunately, our proms were scheduled for the same night, just like our graduations. Echo was going to prom with a girl named Aliya from his school. He claimed she wasn't his girlfriend, but I could tell he liked her the couple times I'd met her. We'd known for weeks that we couldn't fulfill our pact, but somehow the thought of him going to prom with someone else stung a little every time I thought about it. Devin, my friend since middle school, had asked me to prom. He was cute and sweet, so it made sense to say yes. So, it was settled. Two separate proms on one night. We wouldn't see each other. And I told myself it didn't matter. But honestly, it did, more than I wanted to admit. And as much as I tried to ignore it, the thought of not being with Echo that night made my heart pound in a way I couldn't quite explain.

Prom was amazing. The night felt like a dream, and I looked the part—the soft yellow dress with a beaded bodice sparkled under the lights, its empire waist cinching just right, and the tulle overskirt added a touch of whimsy. Every step I took, I felt like I was floating. A crowd of students were hanging out in the lobby, still riding the high of prom night—the flashing lights, the thumping bass of the last song, the thrill of dressing up, and the memories. Some were still buzzing with excitement, retelling moments from the dance floor, while others were already slipping into exhaustion. My crew was hungry after the dry hotel chicken and scoop of potatoes. Picking at a slice of pizza, my phone buzzed inside my clutch. Flipping it open, I barely had time to say hello before a deep and slightly impatient voice rang out.

"Where you at?"

Echo. I blinked, sitting up straighter. "Um, eating in the lobby at the hotel," I replied, confused by the question.

"What are you eating?"

I glanced at the table. "Imo's." There was a brief pause before I heard it—his unmistakable scoff.

"That shit nasty. Where's the Chicago-style?" he teased. But this time, his voice wasn't just in my ear. It was behind me. I spun around, my mouth dropping open as Echo and Aliya pushed through the crowd of prom-goers, walking straight toward me.

"What in the world are you doing here?"

He grinned, eyes sweeping over me slowly, lingering in a way that wasn't exactly...friendly. "Sun...you are stunning."

I swallowed, suddenly hyperaware of the stray curl slipping from my intricate updo. My cheeks had already been dusted with blush, thanks to my sister, but now, my whole body was heating, causing me to clench my thighs. And damn. Echo looked good. The weight training for basketball had done him justice, filling out the once-lanky frame. He had always carried himself with a maturity beyond his years, but the white tuxedo jacket trimmed in black, the tailored pants, and fresh haircut were giving me...dare I say, sexy.

My lips parted before I could stop myself. "E, oh my god, you are so handsome." A bit too much excitement coated my words, and I knew it the second they left my mouth. He knew it, too, but didn't have to say a word. I could see it in the way his features shifted. Nervously, I switched my attention to Aliya, and her deep, unimpressed scowl told me everything I needed to know.

I cleared my throat. "Aliya, hey. You look gorgeous. I love your dress."

Her smile was tight, her brows still pinched together. "Thank you," she said dryly.

I turned back to Echo, searching for an answer. "How was your prom? What are you doing here?" I asked again.

Echo's lips curled slightly, like he was amused by the question. "We were at the Clayton, not far from here." He shrugged. "Did you really think I wasn't gonna lay eyes on you on prom night?"

I lost my breath because…yes, that's exactly what I thought. I chose not to say that aloud. Instead, I glanced at Devin, who had been completely silent this whole time. His expression matched Aliya's now—confused, slightly irritated, but mostly trying to figure out what the hell was happening here. Realizing I had been staring at Echo too long, I quickly turned back to Devin.

"Oh, I'm sorry." I cleared my throat, suddenly remembering my manners. "Um, Devin, this is my friend, Echo. E, this is Devin."

They exchanged the driest head nods I had ever seen. "What's up, man?" they muttered in unison.

Wanting to break the awkward tension, I gestured toward the pizza. "You guys want some?"

Echo's lip curled in disgust. "Now you know I don't eat that shit." He shook his head. "It's cardboard. A cracker."

"Boy, you have one more time to argue with me about Chicago-style pizza versus Imo's."

"I'm just saying, there's no comparison."

It never took us long to block out the world when we were together. We joked and laughed like there weren't other people standing right there waiting for our attention. We swapped prom stories, our conversation slipping into an easy rhythm. I should have noticed the way Aliya's arms tightened across her chest or how Devin checked his phone twice, exhaling sharply. But I didn't. Not until Aliya finally snapped.

"Echo, how long are we staying?" she said, irritation dripping from every syllable.

Her stance was rigid, bordering on possessive, and it made my stomach twist because she was right. I had no business monopolizing her date's time on prom night. If the roles were reversed, I'd be furious. I forced myself to look at Devin, expecting the same frustration. I wasn't wrong. His creased brows matched Aliya's.

And suddenly, it clicked. Echo and I were more than close. We had become so inseparable that even on a night meant for other people, other dates, other memories, we still found our way to each other. It was like breathing. And yet, as I glanced at Aliya's crossed arms and Devin's clenched jaw, an unsettling thought crept in. This wasn't normal… right? It couldn't be. This was dysfunctional, right?

I swiped a hand down my face to disrupt the memory before I joined Echo. "Hey," I said, my voice soft. I'd slipped into black cotton shorts and a cropped tank with *Birthday Girl* painted across the front in glittery letters. The shirt revealed just enough of my navel to play peek-a-boo, and as I turned back toward Echo, I caught the slight curve of his lips as his eyes lingered on the words across my chest.

"The Creative Crew?" he asked, tilting his head slightly, clearly curious about the origin of the shirt.

I nodded. "How'd you guess?"

His eyes traveled over me, starting from my long tresses hanging loose but pushed back with a decorative scarf, down to the silver hoops dangling from my ears. I could feel the weight of his gaze, not in a way that made me self-conscious, but in a way that made me hyper-aware. Over the past year, my style had definitely shifted.

Baggy clothes were now a distant memory, replaced by outfits that were a little more appealing—or maybe just a little more revealing. I'd grown, changed, and maybe even glowed a little. I wasn't just the witty and outspoken girl I used to be. I was finding confidence in myself, piece by piece, and I could tell he noticed.

"You think the coast is clear out there?" he asked, nodding toward the window.

"It should be," I said, stepping closer. "But where are we going?"

His lips quirked mischievously as he held up the mystery bag he'd brought with him. "It's a surprise," he said, his voice smooth and playful.

Adrenaline and excitement coursed through us as we weaved our way through the woods, sneaking to our spot. By the time we arrived, the familiar clearing brought an instant calm over me. I hadn't been back since returning to camp. It just hadn't felt right to visit without Echo. Yet here we were again, and it felt perfect.

The skyline hadn't changed. Stars scattered across the blackness like diamonds, with the occasional streak of a shooting star zipping by above us. I stood still, staring into the vastness, getting lost in the night's beauty. It was so mesmerizing that I didn't even notice Echo moving around behind me, laying out a blanket, positioning his old boom box, and retrieving food from his bag.

"E, what is this?" I finally asked, turning to find him sitting cross-legged, grinning.

"A birthday picnic," he replied, matter-of-factly, like it was the most obvious thing in the world.

He patted the space next to him, and I immediately joined him on the blanket. I couldn't help but smile. The food was cold, but it didn't matter. We dug into our favorite meal from Sonic. The silence between us was comfortable; I didn't have words for how I was feeling, but my grin spoke volumes. It stretched wide, brighter than the stars above, as gratitude and warmth swelled in my chest. I was simply happy to be with him, honored that he thought enough of me to plan something so thoughtful.

But then, I lost my breath when I spotted a greeting card and a small box sitting on the edge of the blanket. The box was burgundy, tied with a neat yellow bow. I reached for it immediately, my curiosity getting the best of me. "Be patient, Sunshine," he teased, his voice light but firm. "Open the card first."

I reluctantly set the box aside and picked up the card. It was blue and pink with gold foil print. The front reading, *To my very best friend on your birthday.*

As I read, my heart squeezed. Every word inside perfectly described our whirlwind friendship—the debates, the endless laughter, the way we'd effortlessly fallen into each other's lives. By the time I closed the card, my cheeks hurt from smiling so much.

"Okay. Now you can open the box," he said. "I know you're dying to...impatient ass."

I did a little celebratory wiggle before finally untying the yellow bow. Inside the box was a delicate, unique butterfly charm made of white and yellow gold, its center lined with six tiny pearls. It was so pretty. I stared at it, speechless. Words failed me. Instead, I looked up at Echo, grateful for his presence. He must've noticed my inability to speak because he leaned in, filling the silence.

"I saw it when I was in Chicago last week. I thought it'd be a nice addition to your charm bracelet," he said, "something to make sure you always think about your boy." He pointed a finger dramatically at himself.

He closed the distance between us. My fingers tightened around the box when his forehead gently pressed against mine.

"Happy birthday, Sunshine," he said. "I hope I was able to make your day a little brighter."

I nodded, my breath shallow, too nervous to break the moment. He cupped my face with a tenderness that sent shivers down my spine. So many unvoiced thoughts hung in the space between us, thick and charged, as the stars bore witness.

The world around us faded as Echo whispered, "I–I think I love you, Summer." His voice trembled with a vulnerability I'd never heard. Before I could react, he pressed a soft kiss to my forehead, the warmth lingering long after his lips moved away.

I sat there, still clutching the box, trying to steady my breathing and my racing thoughts. The words I'd held back for weeks suddenly slipped out in a hushed whisper. "I think I love you, too, E. Thank you…for everything. It's really beautiful."

"You're really beautiful," he said, his voice barely audible but powerful enough to send a shiver through me.

Feeling the intensity of the moment, I nervously tugged at my earlobe. Echo noticed, and with a loving affection, he cupped my chin with one hand while his other moved to rub the earlobe I was fidgeting with, calming my anxiety. His gaze locked on to mine, searching for something I wasn't sure I was ready to give, yet couldn't seem to withhold.

"Can I kiss you?" he asked, his voice thick with anticipation.

"You always kiss me, E," I said, trying to lighten the weight of the moment.

And it was true. Echo never left my company without a forehead kiss, a peck on the cheek, or a playful press of his lips to my hair. They were gestures of comfort, of friendship. But this… this was different. This was intimate.

Echo's expression remained serious. "Nah, Sun. Not that kinda kiss."

Before I could ask what kind of kiss he wanted, he silenced my words with the softest, gentlest kiss I'd ever experienced. His lips molded to mine, tentative at first, testing the boundaries of what we'd always been. Air escaped my lungs as I grabbed his forearms instinctively, my fingers clinging to him with a silent plea to continue. And he did.

Echo deepened the kiss, parting my lips with his tongue as he pulled me closer. His hands were everywhere—one cupping the back of my head, his fingers massaging my scalp; the other sliding down my neck, over the swell of my breast, and grazing my navel. The sensations were overwhelming, each touch sending a wave of heat coursing through me. I gasped, my body reacting in ways I didn't fully understand.

A sound escaped me, startling me as much as it seemed to embolden him.

"Mmm," I murmured, the deep, guttural noise surprising me with its intensity.

I didn't even know I was capable of making a sound like that. Was this really happening? My thoughts raced as his touch continued, gentle but assured, each movement unraveling parts of me I hadn't even realized were tightly wound.

Echo kissed me with a hunger that felt desperate, as if he was afraid this would be the first and last time he'd have the chance. My thoughts warred with my emotions. *This is my best friend. My boy. This will change everything. This must stop.* But I couldn't stop. I didn't want to stop. Every fiber of my being screamed for more, for *him*.

Somehow, I found myself in his lap, my legs draped over his thighs as his hands continued to roam. One slid down my leg, his palm grazing my thigh before creeping higher. I trembled, my body betraying every ounce of caution my mind tried to hold on to.

"Open your eyes, Sunshine," he commanded, his voice rough, and I obeyed, my lashes fluttering open to meet his gaze.

His eyes searched mine, looking for something—understanding, permission, maybe both. My breath hitched as he trailed kisses along my neck, his lips soft but searing. I felt exposed under his gaze, yet completely safe in his arms, caught in a moment that was both terrifying and exhilarating. Fondling the seam of my shorts, he fingered the fabric of my panties.

"*Your treasure is your most valuable, precious gem from God, Summer. The Bible says, 'for where your treasure is, there your heart will be also.' He must be special and worthy—someone who will respect you completely and cherish that sacred moment and your heart, baby girl.*" My mother's words echoed in my mind, soft and discerning: *Your body is your treasure.*

Was Echo deserving of my treasure? As his hands explored me with a tenderness that left me breathless, it sure felt like he was. My breathing was ragged, the haze of the moment pulling me under. But even as I surrendered to the intensity of his touch, a small, clear voice inside begged me to pause. I needed to ground myself, to find clarity in the only place I knew I could—*his eyes.*

"Echo," I whispered, my voice trembling as I tried to guide his face toward mine.

My fingers lightly cupped his jaw, coaxing him to look at me. I needed to see him, to know that this was more than just the heat of the moment. I needed my Echo, my friend, the boy who had always been my safe space. When his eyes finally met mine, they held a storm of emotions—desire, affection, and things I couldn't quite name. But within that storm, I saw the boy who had always been there for me, who had been my anchor when I felt unmoored. In that moment, I realized that if I searched his eyes long enough, I'd find my answer. Echo would help me make the right decision, because that's what he'd always done.

Still snuggled in my neck, he pulled my thighs forward, his erection piercing my center. My breath hitched—hell, I almost choked from the sensation. Echo was teasing me, slowly grinding his body against mine. The air between us was electric, charged with something I felt deep in my core. The rise and fall of my chest came in uneven waves as I clung to him, burrowed against the solid warmth of his body. My heart raced, and every nerve ending sparked as he slowly trailed his finger against my essence, a touch that was both tender and deliberate. I gasped softly, the sensation wet, sticky, and utterly consuming. My body trembled under his care, a mix of vulnerability and trust swirling in the space we shared.

"Look at me," he requested, his voice steady yet gentle, locking me in the now. His lips brushed against mine in a delicate kiss, pulling me from my haze.

When our eyes connected, the potency of his gaze unraveled me. It was more than just desire; it was adoration, favor, and an unspoken promise. His finger moved in slow, purposeful circles, massaging the crown of my jewel with an expertise that left me spent. I knew that Echo wasn't a virgin, but I had no dream he would be a skilled puppeteer, commanding my mind, body, and soul. I was lost in a moment I never wanted to end.

"Oh my God!" I moaned while he continued to drive me insane. "Where... Why do you know how to do this?"

Echo snickered, gliding one finger in then out and in then out of my wetness.

"*Mmm*," I hummed, my body moving to the rhythm he controlled.

Echo plunged deeper, harder, and I was losing all sense of taste, smell, and control. My body was behaving in a way that I didn't recognize. With a broken whisper, I said, "Oh, shit, E. What are you doing...Wh–What are *we* doing?"

Not breaking the rhythmic stride of his fingers, his only response was, "Please, Sunshine. Please." I didn't know what he needed. But I knew, without hesitation, I was willing to give it.

Goosebumps surfaced as I started to shake and tremble, ears popping and eyes cloudy, with tears streaming down my face. What the hell was happening? My first orgasm, that's what was happening, and it scared the shit out of me. I was trembling, every part of me quaking from the crown of my head to the soles of my feet. It was as though an icy winter breeze had swept through me, leaving a shiver in its wake, though the air around us was anything but cold.

In that instant, our entire friendship flashed before me—every laugh, every tear, every moment that had cemented our bond. It all came rushing back like lightning splitting the sky on a stormy night. Echo's gaze held a quiet plea, begging me not to stop, not to pull away. But those same eyes—protective, supportive, full of the warmth that had carried me through so much—also told me this was safe, this was us. This felt right. This felt *real*.

I reached up, cradling his face, my fingertips tracing the sharp, familiar lines of his jaw. His skin was warm, velvet-soft beneath my touch, and yet under that smoothness was strength, a quiet power that had always made me feel safe. He didn't move—barely breathed, as if he was afraid this moment might slip through his fingers if he so much as blinked. I let my thumbs glide over his cheekbones, memorizing him, anchoring myself to this reality as my pulse pounded in my throat. This was real. He was real. And I wanted this...wanted him. My breath shuddered as I exhaled, but my voice remained composed, despite the tremble in my body.

"Grant me my wish, E," I said, my lips just inches from his.

His Adam's apple bobbed as he swallowed hard. I felt his hesitation, the way his fingers hovered over my waist, asking without words if I was sure.

I was. I lifted my chin, letting my lips graze his, just enough to send a slow shiver down my spine.

"Make this moment special for me," I said.

For a long, intoxicating second, he just stared at me. Then, like someone who had just been given permission to breathe, he kissed me. Slow, almost worshipping. Like I was something sacred, something fragile, and powerful all at once. And as he finally pulled me closer, pressing me against the heat of his body, I knew this wasn't just a moment, it was the beginning of everything.

He stilled, his eyes searching mine as if he was grasping for certainty, trying to find the ground beneath his feet. Because this moment? It wasn't small or a casual fling. It was monumental. And he knew it. He knew how important it was to me.

"Summer." His voice was thick, gravelly with emotion.

That's how I knew he was serious because he rarely called me by my name. His fingers twitched at his sides, like he wanted to reach for me, to hold me but didn't trust himself to move just yet.

"Are you sure?" His voice was low, a quiet battle between hope and restraint. Like he wanted to believe me so badly but was terrified to fall...*to fail*. I swallowed, feeling my pulse drum against my ribs, an anxious beat of anticipation. Then, I nodded. And in that moment, I felt my certainty wrap around me like a protective shield.

"I've never been more certain of anything in my life." The words left my lips like a vow, a promise etched in something deeper.

His shoulders relaxed—just barely—like the tension gripping his body was finally loosening its hold. Then—finally, *finally*—his hands found me, his fingers sliding gently to my waist, his touch sending a slow burn through my skin. That's when I knew he believed me, and he was all in.

CHAPTER SEVENTEEN

Echo
Post-Graduation, Summer 2005

I BLINKED RAPIDLY, replaying her words over in my head. I stared at her for what felt like forever, almost waiting to wake up from this dream. Since the first day I'd stepped foot on these grounds, Summer Knight had been everything I wanted—everything I dreamed of having. And now, here she was, looking at me with a raw vulnerability that shook me to my core. She wanted this. She wanted me.

I kissed her lips softly, savoring the moment, but I couldn't tear my eyes away from her. She was still panting, her chest rising and falling in unsteady waves from the aftermath of her orgasm. I gently laid her down on the blanket, shifting her effortlessly as if she weighed nothing at all. Refusing to let even an inch of space grow between us, I nestled against her, burying my nose into the curve of her neck. But then I noticed how still she was—too still. My heart clenched with an unfamiliar panic as fear began to creep in.

"You don't have to do this, Sun," I said, my voice a mix of reassurance and quiet pleading. "We can wait. We have time." Even as I said the words, I knew I was hoping for the opposite. I wanted her to want this—*want me*—even just a fraction of how much I desired her.

"I want to," she whimpered, her voice a trembling blend of doubt and desire that made my chest constrict.

"Touch me," I urged, needing her to reassure me, to make this feel like this was ours, not just mine. I needed to feel like we were in this together.

"Where? How?" she asked, her innocence shining through, sending a jolt straight to my heart.

"However. Wherever," I rasped, my voice thick with emotion.

The moment was heavy with the kind of tension that was both exhilarating and terrifying. Her touch was timid and tender. My breath hitched as her hesitant fingers brushed against my skin, her touch igniting a flame burning deep within me. It was simple but immediately caused my erection to swell, pressing against the zipper of my shorts, transmitting both pain and pleasure.

Our kisses began soft and sweet, an innocent dance that made me fall in love with every sway. But then I parted her lips with my tongue, and everything seemed to tilt. She responded with a rhythm that caught me off guard, a skillfulness that made my pulse quicken.

She's a good kisser, I thought, surprised by the realization. Summer always carried this quiet innocence, a kind of effortless grace that made me wonder if she'd ever even kissed a boy. There was a softness to her, a resistance when it came to certain things. Not out of fear, but out of choice. Like she was always holding something back, waiting for the right moment, the right person. And I wanted to be that person. Hell, I *needed* to be.

My hands moved over her body, exploring with a tenderness that was barely held together by my control. She was so soft beneath my touch, so inviting. My lips trailed down to the curve of her neck, kissing, tasting, and lingering. The delicate scent of her skin filled my senses. Summer always smelled fresh and floral, like the first day of spring. I stayed there for a moment longer than I intended, nuzzling into the folds of her neck. This…*she* was becoming my favorite place to be.

I lifted her tank top, and a sharp inhale filled my lungs. Chocolate-brown perky breasts wrapped in a black bra covered with tiny bumblebees greeted me. I brushed my lips against the satiny fabric before reaching behind her to unhook the fastener. The anticipation was killing me. Her plump, round breasts spilled from the bra—big, brown, and perfect. Summer's eyes followed mine, her expression shifting as the fabric slipped from her skin. It held something—uncertainty, maybe even vulnerability. I saw the flicker of doubt in her eyes, and a rush of anxiety prickled my skin. Did she think I wouldn't find her beautiful? Did she not know she was already the most breathtaking thing I'd ever seen?

I slipped my tongue between the deep split of her cleavage, trailing it over the arc of her fullness. I kissed around the smooth edges of the more defined fudge-colored flesh before sucking in a gumdrop nipple.

"Oh my…oh," she stuttered as I gave the same attention to the left.

I moved with patience and care, fully aware of how important this moment was for her. I wanted to honor it, to ensure it was everything she'd dreamed of and more. Every touch, every kiss was intentional, as if I was memorizing her—every curve, every reaction. My lips continued down the soft, curvy path of her body, my hands gliding gently as I slid her shorts over thick, goose bump–covered thighs. She trembled beneath my fingertips, her body reacting to each touch in ways that made me shiver. I pressed a kiss to her navel, and a soft giggle escaped her lips.

"Silly girl," I said against her skin, my lips curving into a smile. I kissed her there again, this time lingering. With each breath, her body rose and fell beneath my lips. From there, I trailed tender kisses, one at a time, down the slope of her stomach, my lips sweeping over against the delicate expanse of her skin until I landed just above her center. The wispy hairs were short and tamed. She tensed beneath me, clutching the blanket tightly, as if anticipating what was to come. She was nervous, and that was okay. This moment was enormous, monumental, and I understood that, but I didn't want her to be afraid, not with me because I would never rush her, never be anything but exactly what she needed me to be. I paused, lifting my gaze to meet hers, looking for a change, searching her face for any reservations.

"You're safe, Sunshine," I murmured. "I promise, I won't hurt you." The words weren't just spoken; they were a truth she could hold on to. She met my gaze, something tender and trusting lingering in her eyes. Then, finally, she nodded.

Seconds later, I pressed a kiss to the treasure she had guarded so carefully, and in that instant, I understood why. It was soft, warm, and so impossibly wet that it felt like it was made for me to explore. I moved slowly, savoring every lick, every taste, letting my lips and tongue move in sync with the rhythm of the music playing faintly in the background. She responded to every touch, every gentle stroke, and it was intoxicating. I took my time, letting the connection between us deepen, making sure she felt every ounce of care and love I had for her. This wasn't just physical—it was something more, something profound. And I wanted her to feel that with every kiss.

"E, wait, wait. Oh my God. Don't st…don't stop," she panted. Her voice was a beautiful chorus, blending seamlessly with the symphony of the night. I peeled off my shirt and shorts, the warm night air brushing against my skin as I climbed back up the length of her trembling body. My lips traced a path along her silky skin, enjoying every shiver I felt, her taste still lingering on my mouth.

I kissed her slowly until we were face-to-face again. She didn't speak; the only sound between us was the unsteady rhythm of her breathing, her chest rising and falling in rapid waves. Her eyes held mine, filled with trust and just a hint of fear.

"Can I have you, Summer?" I asked, my heart pounding.

Her lips parted, and her voice came out serious, carrying the heaviness of the moment. "Echo, please be gentle."

I tenderly kissed her forehead. "Always," I said, my words a promise as I let myself fall completely into her.

As the night grew long, the darkness was deep, making it almost impossible to see. Leaning back on my knees, I patted around for my shorts, which I'd tossed to the side, to retrieve a condom from my wallet. I looked down at her. She was beautiful. The moonlight brushed against her silhouette, highlighting a shoulder here, a breast there, but it wasn't necessary for me to navigate her body. Summer surveyed me. She didn't need to see me clearly to know that I was there.

I hovered over her again, our eyes fixed on each other for what seemed like forever. I kissed her forehead, nose, then lips. "You ready?" I asked, eagerness causing my voice to quiver. Her nods were brief and brisk. "Don't take your eyes off me, baby, okay?"

She let out a soft, breathy whimper, her lashes fluttering as she nodded again. "Okay."

I drew in a deep breath before gliding my penis against her folds before piercing her treasure with gentle, measured strokes. Her body bucked, her nails grasping my skin. My gaze never left hers as I mumbled through my own moans, "Are you okay? Look at me, baby."

Pain and pleasure wove together in the delicate creases of her face, her expression a mix of desire and disbelief. I moved carefully, feeling the resistance as her body slowly adjusted to me, stretching reluctantly to meet my size. Every sensation was heightened, every moment etched into my memory. She clutched tightly at the nape of my neck, grounding us both as her eyes batted open to meet mine.

She nodded faintly, her lips parting as she said, "It hurts, but I'm okay."

Her words carried a strength that steadied me.

"Tell me if it's too much," I said, securing a kiss against her temple, vowing to move at her pace.

This was about us, about her, about making this moment as tender and meaningful as it deserved to be. My hands moved softly over her, caressing every quiver, soothing every chill, and kissing away each tear that slipped from the corners of her eyes.

"It'll get better, I promise," I offered, trying to settle her amid a storm of sensations. "But we can stop if it's too much."

Her response wasn't in words but in action. Summer lifted her head, her lips finding mine in a kiss that carried all her affections—trust, love, fear, and a muted but unmistakable plea to keep going. Her breathing was uneven, each exhale blending with the quiet hum of the night, and her body trembled beneath mine, quivering as she began to surrender to the feeling. I silently reassured her, letting her know I was with her every step of the way.

"Breathe, baby," I spoke against her skin, my lips pressing tender kisses along her neck. Each kiss was laced with as much love and adoration as she poured into me.

I was completely lost in the moment, every sense heightened, yet a part of me remained focused, ensuring I was gentle, careful, and attuned to her every need. I'd been with a handful of girls since I was fifteen, but this—*she*—was different. Summer—my Sunshine—was giving herself to me, and it felt like everything. But what she didn't realize was that I was surrendering to her, too, because *she* was everything—the sun that warmed me, the moon that kept me steady, the stars that made me believe every wish I'd made was meant to come true. And right now, under this sky, in our sacred place, she was mine—and I was hers.

"Shit, Sun," I moaned, my voice raw and heavy as I buried my face in the strands of her hair, inhaling her scent like it was the only thing keeping me sane.

"Echo. Echo, E." She practically sang my name, her voice breathless and sweet, wrapping around me like a melody I never wanted to end.

That was it. I couldn't hold back anymore. I claimed her mouth with mine, devouring her lips with a passion that had been building for what felt like forever. Each kiss was full of silent confessions, every stroke of my tongue a declaration of everything I felt for her. Carefully, I moved with her, every motion calculated, as if time itself had slowed just for us. Our bodies found a rhythm, a language of looks and touches that spoke louder than words as the tension built and our breaths quickened.

"You are so fucking pretty," I said as my body jerked, my voice raspy with emotion because she was the only thing that mattered in the universe. And in that instant, she was. My body was rigid, locked in place, every muscle coiled so tightly it felt like my member would shatter under the pressure.

"Echo," she crooned, her voice a melody that looped my name, wrapping me in heat. *Fuck.* She had to stop saying it like that. "Echo," she murmured again, this time breathier, almost pleading, and I lost it. Completely.

"Sunshine. Shit." I groaned, my voice strained, the words dragging through gritted teeth.

When we were done, I held her close, my arms wrapped securely around her until her breath found its rhythm again. Slowly, she melted into me, the tension fading bit by bit. When she finally settled, I pressed a kiss to her hair and said, "Let's head back." I helped her dress, moving with care, wrapping her in a blanket before instructing her to sit on the stoop. She was quiet. Too quiet. And as I watched her, something worried me.

I gathered our things quickly, then wrapped an arm around her, guiding us down the moonlit gravel path back to the lodge. The camp was silent, only the faint shuffle of our feet and the harmonic rhythm of our breathing breaking the tranquility. It was nearly two in the morning, but I wasn't going anywhere—not yet. We stepped into the dim bedroom, and the warmth of the space embraced us. Summer hadn't said a word the entire walk. Her silence fucked with me. Did she regret this? Did I push her too far? Too fast?

"Sun," I said, breaking the quiet.

She lifted her head, and the faint, closed-mouth smile she gave me chased away a fraction of my doubt.

"I'm fine, E. I promise," she said, her voice calm and reassuring, as if she could read my unspoken fears. "Do you have to leave?"

I shook my head. "Not right now. I need to be out by six, though, or Lincoln might actually kill me," I joked, trying to lighten the mood.

She was exhausted and maybe even in a little pain, judging by the slight limp in her step. Without a word, she disappeared into the bathroom. I waited. When she returned, her movements were unhurried, careful as she climbed into bed with a quiet sigh. I wanted to ask if she was okay, but she'd just say that she was fine. Instead, I slid in behind her, encasing her in my arms, holding her close…like she was mine.

Her warmth against me felt like home. I burrowed my face into her nape, pressing a kiss to my favorite spot, the place that always seemed to smell like spring. I knew I'd face hell if all of my plan didn't work once I got home, but it didn't matter. Summer was finally mine.

"Echo," she said, so quiet I almost missed it.

"Yeah," I answered, brushing my lips against her shoulder.

"You were worth the wait," she said, glancing back at me, her eyes glassy but filled with joy—satisfaction.

I cupped her face and kissed her, letting the emotions I couldn't put into words flow between us. Pulling back, I smiled and whispered, "Happy birthday, baby."

CHAPTER EIGHTEEN

Echo
October 2019, The Day After the Wedding that Wasn't

THE MEMORY OF our first time quietly danced between us as our foreheads kissed. It had always been a distinct honor to know that I was Summer's first, that she trusted me with something so precious—her treasure. That night, I knew. I knew that I loved Summer Knight. It was the way she could gaze at the endless sky for hours without a word and how she painted the soft blues of the clouds drifting lazily above us. I loved how only the two of us shared a place tucked deep in the heart of the woods where time slowed, worries faded, and the quiet magic of the earth waited for us to admire it together.

And all these years later, no matter how hard I tried, the shit wouldn't go away. Yeah, I tried. I tried fucking it away in college, burying the ache beneath meaningless bodies, running up in just about any girl with a pulse and half a brain, hoping one of them would make me forget. The cycle repeated when I moved to LA. It was a new city, new distractions, but the same damn ghost of that one summer haunting me.

Then Kourtni came along, and for a moment, I thought she was the cure—that her pull was strong enough to erase Summer from the deepest parts of me. But after Brooke and Seth's wedding, I realized that the amnesia had only ever been temporary because the second I saw Summer's face, the moment I heard her voice, every buried memory was resurrected, ripping through me like the pages from a torn diary—*our diary*—filled with recollections I had no business holding on to. And yet, there they were. She was still there.

Summer was caged between my arms, her back pressed against the wall in my bedroom as we focused on each other. But it wasn't restraint, it was gravity pulling us closer. We dallied there, in a space between her fears and our undeniable truth. Her admission and my confession of love still hung heavy in the room. An unspoken question lingered in the worried crease in her brow. *Where do we go from here?* While my breathless panting answered without words: *"We go, and we find forever."*

Unhurriedly, I stroked her face, still moist from tears. I tenderly kissed her lips, allowing them to dwell there as I brushed away a stray curl from her gorgeous face. She looked up at me, her eyes shaded with dread, yet burning with desire, a war waging between what she wanted and what she thought was right. I pressed my lips to hers again, teasing, savoring because while every part of me was eager to devour her—to make her mine in every way—I knew. I knew that if I took her now, if I let my hunger overtake me, I'd only be adding another layer to her mess...becoming another complication. So, I held back, just barely.

Summer was always in her head, always overthinking, her mind a maze of doubts and what-ifs. I knew I had to go slow with her, had to be patient—careful with every word, every touch. If I pushed too hard, she'd retreat. If I moved too fast, she'd convince herself this wasn't real.

"I missed you," I said, still holding her against the wall. "I missed you so much, Sun." I said it again, then again, like a mantra, like a promise, hoping my words could drown out whatever storm she was caught in.

She exhaled in a quiet surrender, but I knew she was still fighting, still trying to reconcile the pull between her heart and her head. So, I just held her, let my hands speak where words might fail. Somewhere deep down, I believe she missed me, too.

Soft kisses grew deeper, more urgent. Their gentle rhythm shifting into something more desperate. Our tongues became reacquainted, rediscovering each other with familiarity because their favorite lover had returned. I tasted her, savoring the way she melted into me. My lips sealed around her tongue, sucking it in and out of my mouth, enjoying the quiet moans vibrating between us. I halted, just for a moment, just long enough to catch my breath. Slowly, I pulled away from her mouth, guiding my lips over the curve of her chin before slipping lower down the smooth column of her neck. Her sweet, nostalgic scent was intoxicating. I breathed her in, pressing open-mouthed kisses against her skin, letting my lips map the places they once knew by heart.

My mind and body were at war, urging me to stop. I had to remind her—shit, remind myself—that she wasn't reckless. She wasn't the type to be a defiant bride or a cheater. That wasn't my Sun. But damn it, I couldn't resist her. I couldn't resist *this*. The soft curves of the girl had transformed into the graceful, shapely allure of a woman. Every dip, every line of her body was etched into my memory. My hands knew her without thought, without hesitation. So familiar, they knew exactly where to go. Although I wanted her ass bad, something deeper, something stronger held me back. I needed her, yes, but more than that, I needed us to mean something again.

My body roared with need, my dick screaming at me to keep going, to experience her again in the most intimate way. Every inch of me throbbed to bury myself so deeply inside her that the years apart would fade to nothingness. The girl Summer had been the sweetest indulgence for my eighteen-year-old mind, but the woman before me now—this Summer—she was an extravagant smorgasbord of decadence, a feast I had no business craving, yet one I was helplessly drawn to.

I traced the path I'd taken before years ago. My hand traveled the familiar slope of her back, the other sliding across the curve of her ass—kneading, claiming, remembering. Nothing had changed about my Sunshine. She was still just as soft, just as warm, just as perfect as before. She trembled under my touch, her body responding in ways that had me teetering on the border of control. My fingers explored, coaxing her back to me, back to this moment. I needed her to feel it the way I did, without reservations, without fear.

"I love you. I never stopped," I said, my voice raw and unguarded. The words fell like a confession, heavy with longing, regret, and an unshakable truth that had never wavered.

Her breath hitched. Wide eyes met mine, searching for doubt, maybe even hesitance. But she wouldn't find any. I meant every word. I always had.

"Echo," she said, voice wobbly. "I love you, too."

She was just as beautiful, just as intoxicating as she'd been that first night. And this time, I wasn't letting her go. Not again.

Summer

October 2019, The Day After the Wedding that Wasn't

"Are you okay, sis?" my sister Raqi asked.

I had called her to get a read on the mood at home before walking into it. I needed to know what category of storm I was about to face.

"That's a loaded question," I said, wiping my mouth after brushing my teeth. I was still in Echo's childhood bedroom, slowly pulling myself together to face the day.

"Have you talked to him?" she continued to probe.

I didn't have to ask who *him* was. I shook my head as if she could see me.

"No, not yet." I sighed, smoothing lotion over my face. "I need to see Mama and Daddy first, then I'll call him."

"Okay. See you soon. Love you, Pooh," Raqi said.

"I love you, too."

I wrapped myself in a towel and sat on the bed, stilling for a moment. The smell of bacon curled through the air, teasing my stomach. Echo insisted on making breakfast before driving me to my parents' house, and the thought made my chest tighten. I still couldn't believe I'd spent the night in this house—or that I was walking around this room half-naked like I had a right to. The twenty unread texts and countless missed calls told me it was time. No more delaying. No more pretending. And if the waters weren't already muddy enough, I had confessed my love for Echo. I told him. I admitted that it had always been him—the man I saw beside me in my dreams, the one I had never quite let go of.

After Brooke's wedding, I couldn't shake the feeling of Echo, couldn't ignore how easily he still slipped under my skin. Our exchange had been brief, but once again, he'd left a lasting impression, the way only he ever had. I'd had my fair share of relationships, but none of them ever compared to Echo. He was my first everything. All those years ago, that boy had planted something in my heart that I'd never allowed to bloom with another man—until Deshawn. Or so I thought. Deshawn was a good man at an okay time, and I had let my biological clock make a decision my heart should have controlled. It was an awful excuse, but it was my ugly truth—and today, I would finally be honest with him.

"Hey." The sound of Echo's voice pulled me from my thoughts. He stood in the doorway, hands in his pockets, watching me the way he always had—like he saw everything.

I zipped up the hoodie he'd given me to wear, offering a closed-mouth smile. "Hey."

"You good?" he asked.

I shrugged because I wasn't good or bad. I was just eager to get through this day and the next one without too much damage.

"I hear you." He nodded, smiling softly, like he could read every emotion I hadn't voiced.

Echo extended his hand, palm up, ready to receive me. I exhaled, grateful that in the middle of this storm, I had at least one anchor. I grabbed my purse and then his hand. He pulled me into his frame, warm and solid, supporting me without words. Pressing his lips to my temple, he murmured, "I got you, Summer. You hear me?" His fingers tilted my chin, urging my eyes to his. I swallowed hard, nodding.

I stared blankly at the muted gray sky as I rode in the passenger seat of Echo's rental car. The rich reds, burnt oranges, and deep yellows of the trees should've appeared vibrant, but today, they were dull, empty—just like my mood. The Abaras' house was only about twenty minutes from my parents' home, yet time dragged, stretching unbearably, as if we were driving to Mars. My stomach twisted when we pulled up in front of the familiar brick ranch-style house. Everything looked normal, but I knew better. Behind those walls, chaos waited.

My heart stalled at the sight of the sleek black Mercedes-Benz coupe parked ahead of us. *Deshawn. Raqi failed to mention that detail,* I thought, swallowing hard. Echo reached for the door handle, but I grabbed his arm before he could step out.

"You should go," I said, though my voice lacked conviction.

He looked at me like I'd just grown ten heads. "Summer," he said, his tone patient but firm, "I'm not trying to make things harder for you. I'm walking you to that door, and I won't leave until I know you're okay."

I exhaled slowly, watching as he climbed out of the car and rounded to my side. When he opened my door, he hesitated, reaching slightly for my hand before pulling back at the last second. I was grateful—his restraint was an act of respect...understanding. Before we could reach the first step of the porch, the front door swung open. My father stepped out, his expression tangled with emotions I couldn't unravel, but the strongest was relief.

"Daddy," I choked, stepping forward, tears blurring my vision, "I'm so sorry."

He didn't need to speak words. He just wrapped me in his arms, rocking us side to side, pressing kisses into my hair the way he had when I was a little girl.

"*Shh*," he soothed, his voice thick with emotion. "*Shh*, baby. It's okay."

"Summer." My mother's voice trembled, raw and aching, pulling me from my father.

Our eyes met, hers flooded with worry and a hint of knowing. I couldn't speak. I just fell into her embrace. Somewhere behind me, I heard my father's hushed voice ask Echo, "Is she alright?"

"No," Echo answered honestly, "but I think she will be."

Mama ushered me into the house. I didn't lift my head, even when two more sets of arms wrapped around me—my sisters. And then, a quiet voice, one that never carried unnecessary softness said, "We love you, baby girl." *My brother.* The safety of their arms steadied me, and after what felt like forever, I finally pulled back to meet my mother's gaze.

"I'm so sorry, Mama," I whispered, my voice thick, "but I couldn't do it. I couldn't marry him." Silence stretched for a beat then struck like a lightning bolt, shattering the moment.

"Why not?"

The voice wasn't Mama's. The load it carried was heavy and restrained, sending a cold shiver down my spine. I swallowed hard, my eyes shifting over my mother's shoulder. Deshawn stood at the entrance of the kitchen, hands shoved deep into his pockets, his dark eyes locked onto mine. Dressed in a black Nike tracksuit, his posture was tense, his expression unreadable—but beneath the hardened lines of his face, anger simmered, coiling tight. He deserved an explanation.

I inhaled sharply. "Shawn," I started, keeping my voice even, "let's go out back."

He let out a humorless laugh, shaking his head. "No, Summer. What is going on?" His gaze traveled past me, landing on Echo. He stiffened. "Why are you with him?"

Behind me, Echo's voice was fixed. "Sun." I didn't turn around. I couldn't. He stepped forward, close enough that I could feel him, but not so close that it would push this into something worse. A warm hand settled lightly on my shoulder. "I'll be back with your car," he said, voice calm, laced with something I couldn't quite name.

Deshawn's patience snapped. "What the hell is going on?" he repeated, his voice rising, his body tensing as he took a sudden step forward, his finger pointing aggressively toward Echo. "I'll ask again: Why is he here?"

Before he could get any closer, my brother moved, stepping in his path.

"Deshawn." My father's voice was firm, a quiet command. "Step outside." His next words were for Echo. "And you should go."

My attention bounced between the four men in the room, each imposing in their own way, but the common thread was me. They all loved me. I silently begged Echo to leave, to trust that we'd talk later. He gave a small nod, acknowledging my unspoken plea. I kept my back straight and chin high when I turned to face the fire—*Deshawn*—because that's just what Echo had instilled in me. Bravery. But when I heard the front door click shut behind me, a bit of that moxie wavered. *Here we go.*

A sharp inhale cut through the room. Deshawn's stare abandoned the door and locked onto me, his face unexpressive, but his eyes—penetrating and pained—those gave him away. Without a word, he turned on his heels and strode through the kitchen, heading toward the four-season sunroom attached to the back of my parents' home. I paused before following. The space had been a retirement gift to my parents from me and my siblings—a sanctuary meant to bring them peace. Floor-to-ceiling windows framed the backyard, allowing natural light to spill in, seamlessly connecting the indoors and the beauty of the chilled autumn afternoon outside. On any other day, it would've felt open, airy, free. But right now, as I stepped in, the walls were closing in on me. The space was too small. The air too thick. The looming hurt in the room too much.

Deshawn stood by the window, arms crossed tautly over his chest, his back impossibly straight. He didn't move, didn't turn, but the tension rolling off him was suffocating. I sank onto the plush ivory couch, perched on the edge like a bird ready to fly away at any second. Guilt and anxiety pressed down so heavily, I swore I might topple over. No turning back now. This was really happening.

Shaking his head, Deshawn turned to face me, though his stance remained rigid. "You said we'd talk," he said, voice flat, "so talk. The floor is yours."

I swallowed hard. "I know I owe you the truth, and—"

"Oh, you owe me a hell of a lot more than that, Summer," he interrupted, jaw clenched so tight I swore I heard his teeth grind. "You fucking humiliated me." His voice was raw and cutting, slicing through the space between us.

"People were running around, worried about your ass, thinking you were in an accident or some shit, and you were…" He dragged a hand down his face, exhaling sharply. "God only knows where."

I stayed quiet, letting him get this out. If the roles were reversed, I'd probably have been upside his head by now.

"I was waiting for you. In my tuxedo. Ready to say 'I do', and you humiliate me like I ain't shit. Like we ain't been shit." His bitter laugh was eerie. "And you chose to do this in front of my family, my friends, my business partners—" He shook his head. "The damn mayor was there, Summer."

If I weren't the guilty party, I might've cocked my head in confusion. What the hell did the mayor have to do with anything? But I didn't interrupt. I just swallowed hard, nodding as I let him vent.

"I know," I said, "and I'm so sorry, Shawn. I never meant to hurt you."

His eyes snapped to mine, burning with disbelief. "Then why, Summer?" His voice was quieter now, but the anger hadn't faded, it had only sharpened. "You said out there that you couldn't marry me. Why?" Slowly, he stepped closer. The room shrank to the size of a chickpea. His voice dropped lower; each word weighted with barely restrained fury. "And I swear to God, if you say cold feet or that you need more time or any other Hallmark bullshit, I might lose it."

For the first time, I felt something I had never felt with Deshawn before: fear. Not for my safety, but for the flood of unrestrained emotions cracking through his exterior. The heartbreak, the betrayal was palpable. This was a side of him I'd never seen, an imbalanced side...a rageful side. I promised to be honest. To tell him the whole truth. So here it was.

"I'm not scared of marriage." I paused, calming my breath. "I'm afraid of marrying you." The words left my lips like an exhale, like a truth I had been holding in so long my lungs had grown tired of carrying it. And yet, despite the guilt suffocating me, I couldn't ignore the relief settling deep in my bones.

Deshawn, on the other hand...his expression was a collision of devastation and downright outrage. "Wow." He breathed as if I had knocked the wind out of him. He ran a hand over his face before sinking into the chair beside the couch, close but still keeping a deliberate distance.

"Is that supposed to make it all better?"

I shook my head. "No," I admitted, "but it's my truth." His attention shifted to the ceiling, to the floor, anywhere but on me. I pressed on before my courage failed. "I kept telling myself that love would come."

At that, his head lifted slightly. "So, you don't love me, Summer." His voice was quieter now, ragged. "Since when?"

"I love you, Deshawn. I do." I swallowed against the lump in my throat. "But I'd be lying if I said I was *in* love with you. As much as I wanted to be..." I exhaled shakily. "I thought I was just overthinking things again, that if I leaned into the life we were building...the butterflies would come." My voice trailed off, as if the wind had carried my last words away.

But I couldn't stop now. "The truth is..." I delayed, then forced the words out. "I never felt it the way I should have. Not the way you deserve."

Slowly, I moved from my seat, lowering myself to kneel in front of him. He didn't look at me. I reached for his hands, fingers curling over his, holding on even though I could feel his resistance, his grief. "You are an amazing man, Deshawn," I said, "and you've been an even better friend to me." Finally, he lifted his eyes to mine. "And I am so sorry."

He stood abruptly, practically stepping over me to get away. "And when did you figure this out?" His voice was quiet, but the weight of his pain was undeniable. "That you didn't love me?"

He turned toward the window as if searching for an answer in the autumn sky. I stood, too, instinctively seeking my own window, needing something to ground me before I spoke.

Before I could find the words, a butterfly landed on the windowsill. Its vivid orange wings traced with bold black veins fluttered against the cool glass. A quiet smile ghosted my lips as a memory surfaced: Echo sitting on a tree stump at camp, his sketchbook in hand, capturing the delicate creatures that danced around us in our secret place.

"These are monarchs, Sunshine," he had said, eyes bright with wonder. *"Their wings may be fragile, but they're stronger than they seem. They are known for their resilience and endurance, even in their delicacy. Monarchs migrate thousands of miles every year, no matter what. I sometimes wonder what kind of remarkable journeys they've been on."*

His voice was warm like the summer air. Echo's creativity was almost lyrical, flowing like a song that only he could compose. He was always teaching me something new; his words a melody I never wanted to end. *"That's how I see you, Summer. Fragile, yet feisty as hell. Captivating…and I hope I get to have a glimpse into the places you'll go."*

I *was* like that butterfly. Delicate yet unbreakable. Strong enough to make the hardest choices, even now. The butterfly dallied for a moment, its wings trembling against the breeze. And then, as if sensing its purpose had been fulfilled, it took flight, disappearing into the sky. I blinked, returning to the present. Deshawn was still waiting.

"Deep down, I think I always knew," I admitted, my voice softer than I intended, "but I wanted a husband. A family. I didn't want to disappoint you. Or our families. Shit, myself." I swallowed hard. "I thought I wanted the future we planned, but every time I dreamed about the wedding…about my life…you weren't in it. Not in that way."

I heard a pointed exhale from across the room. "Damn," he murmured, his head tilting back slightly, as if absorbing the final blow. He pushed out an exaggerated breath before he spoke again. "So, all this time…I was loving a woman who was just convincing herself to love me?"

I said nothing because he wasn't wrong. But I had a question of my own. I turned, facing him for the first time since I'd shattered his world. "Was it truly love for you, Shawn?"

He stiffened the moment the words left my lips. The quiet was suffocating, like dust settling in an abandoned building. His jaw tightened, his Adam's apple bobbing as he swallowed hard, but the sharp outburst I was bracing for never came. Instead, when I searched his pained brown eyes, I found it—his truth, his acceptance. Deep down, he already knew, but just didn't want to be the one to say it first. Moments from the wedding planning phase flashed through my mind. The countless times I'd ask for his opinion, only to hear the same indifferent response: *"Whatever you want is fine with me."*

At the time, I had convinced myself it was just his easygoing nature, that he trusted me to make the right decisions, but now, standing here in the thick of our unraveling, I realized the truth. It wasn't trust. It wasn't compromise. Deshawn would've married me, built a stable life, and made a home filled with warmth and routine, even if he never once felt butterflies. That was just who he was. He took what was given to him and made the best of it, always turning lemons into lemonade.

But me? I needed more. More than comfort, more than predictability. I wasn't content with just making lemonade. I wanted an entire recipe of flavors, layers of something richer, deeper. I craved something that made my heart race, something that set my soul on fire. And that was the difference between us. He was willing to settle into a love that was unchanging and simple—something you built over time. But simple wasn't enough for me. I wanted extraordinary—that dizzying, breathtaking, instant love that didn't just spark once and fade, but an undeniable pull that lingered, even after a decade and then some.

He ran a hand over his face, exhaling curtly. "Damn," he muttered, shaking his head. "I should've seen this coming."

I opened my mouth to respond, but he lifted a hand, stopping me, not out of anger, but as if he just needed a second to gather himself. When he finally spoke again, his voice was low, almost tired.

"I guess…I guess I just kept telling myself that what we had was enough." His lips pressed together, his eyes searching mine. "That maybe love—at least the kind that makes your heart race and your stomach flip—wasn't as important as stability. As timing. As building a life together." A long pause stretched between us, the revelation I'd already grappled with now taking over him. "But we were doing everything right, weren't we? Right jobs, right plan, right time…"

"But not the right person," I whispered, my voice barely there. "We were building a future, but we were never building *forever*." I blinked rapidly, but the tears I'd been holding back finally released. Hurtful, yet healing. Even amid this unfolding, I felt like a coward. Guilt pressed against my ribs, making it hard to breathe because for so long, I knew the truth but ignored it.

"So, what now?" he asked, slowly walking toward me. His voice wasn't cold. It wasn't even accusatory. It was just…sad. Not because he was losing me—losing *us*—but because maybe he was ready to accept that he—we—deserved more than just safe. We deserved something real.

I sighed, stepping forward to meet him in the middle of the room. Unspoken words and quiet acceptance were like boulders clinging to our feet, overwhelming every step. Deshawn grasped my hands; his warmth caressed my skin. His touch had always been comforting, but tonight, it was a burdensome goodbye.

"So now…" My voice trailed off, barely making a sound, "we don't choose love, we let love choose us."

His eyes softened, filled with something I couldn't quite name—understanding, sadness, maybe even relief. He lifted our joined hands to his lips, pressing a dallying kiss against my knuckles. Then, with a tenderness that made my heart hurt, he reached up and swiped away a lone tear rolling down my cheek. One last touch. One last moment. He leaned in, pressing a soft, almost absentminded kiss against the corner of my mouth. And then, just like that, Deshawn was gone.

CHAPTER NINETEEN

Echo
October 2019, The Day After the Wedding that Wasn't

Maxell and I pulled into my parents' driveway a little after six o'clock in the evening. After leaving Summer earlier, I'd picked him up to ride with me to the camp so I could get her car. He had a lot of questions, and I wasn't in the mood to answer a single one.

"Okay, this is my last question, and hopefully, your grumpy ass will answer it," Max said, just as he was about to slip into the driver's seat of my car while I climbed into Summer's. I raised an irritated brow, silently urging him to hurry the hell up.

"Are you gonna give her space, or are you all in?" he asked.

I eyed him warily because, damn, that was a good question. The logical part of me knew she needed space after what could only be described as the most catastrophic event in her life to date. She had a lot of things to figure out, to fix, and giving her time made sense. But I also knew me. And I knew that I couldn't walk away.

"I'm all in," I said, nodding as my eyes wandered toward our hidden place behind the trees. "I can't go another ten-plus years... shit, ten days without her."

Maxell's grin stretched wide. "My nigga. That's what I wanted to hear."

The quiet drive back alone was the reprieve I needed. I had no clue what was in store for us. I was leaving for LA in a few days, and God knows I wanted Summer with me. But I knew Summer all too well. She was probably lying in that tiny yellow bedroom, letting guilt swallow her whole. Guilt for ending her relationship. Guilt for choosing herself. And if I knew anything about Summer, that guilt would cloud every decision she needed to make, including being with me. After Maxell picked up his car, I sent Summer a text.

Me: Hey.

Sun: Hey.

Me: You good?

Sun: Taking a nap.

Me: Ok. I'll bring your car in about an hour. That cool?

Sun: Yeah. Thanks, E.

Me: Anytime. You need anything?

Sun: No. See you later.

I walked into what I thought was an empty house, until Sadie bounced out of the kitchen, a bowl of popcorn in her hands.

"Hey, brother," she greeted, all smiles until she caught sight of my expression. Her face dropped. "What's wrong?"

I moved toward her slowly, reaching into the bowl for a handful of popcorn. "Summer," I muttered before heading to the kitchen.

Sadie let out an exaggerated sigh. "Get over it, brother. She's married now."

Leaning on the kitchen island, I dragged a hand down my face. "But she's not."

Sadie paused mid-chew, staring at me like I'd lost my damn mind. I didn't even give her time to voice the obvious question written all over her face.

"Summer called off her wedding," I said, nodding as I lifted a brow, mirroring her shock. "Before I even got to the church, Brooke called me. Summer never showed up to her hair appointment. She wasn't at her condo. Wasn't answering calls."

Sadie's eyes widened. "Wow." She dragged out the word, her mouth falling open in exaggerated shock. "I bet Ms. Teresa was losing her mind."

I nodded. "Low-key…I was too. I just didn't think she'd do something like that. There had to be something wrong." I exhaled, remembering the weight in my chest, the gnawing feeling that something bigger was happening. "But then I asked myself: Where would she go to clear her head?"

At the same time, Sadie and I said, "Quest." I nodded.

"You went to get her," she said, more a statement than a question.

I nodded. "I was the only one who could." My voice was quieter now, the memories of last night and this morning replaying in my mind.

Sadie's hands shot up, motioning for me to hurry up and reveal the rest of the story. "And? What happened?"

"And…I brought her here," I said, shrugging. "Since the house was empty, it was the best place for her to continue to hide. I called her parents. I assume they called him. And I just…" I sighed, rubbing the back of my neck. "Took care of her."

Sadie's brows lifted with suspicion, then she squinted. "Echo Honor Abara…" she started slowly. I already knew where this was going. "Y'all didn't have pity sex, did you?"

I coughed, nearly choking on the popcorn. "No, girl! But damn, I wanted to." I shook my head, exhaling as the taste of

Summer's kiss, soft and warm, and sweet as sin simmered on my lips. "But I told her."

"Told her what? The condensed version or—"

"I told her everything," I cut in before she could finish. "That I love her. That seeing her a few months ago sealed it for me. That she's it for me. The only one." I dropped my head, forehead resting on my arms, the quiet tension of it all pressing down. "I don't even know what I'm doing anymore, Didi."

"Yes, you do," she said without hesitation. I lifted my head just enough to see her determined expression. "You've spent so many years convincing yourself that the two of you were just an unfinished chapter that would never be complete." She leaned forward. "But now you have a chance to finish the book."

I laughed, shaking my head. "That was corny as hell."

Sadie smirked, popping another piece of popcorn into her mouth. "Yeah, but you felt that, though."

I laughed, but my thoughts were a tangled web of hope and the ache of impending heartbreak. "What if we mess up again? What if we're just not meant to be…holding on to a past we can't change?"

Sadie didn't rush to answer. She let me sit in the mess of my own doubt. Then, she said, "Then at least you finally tried." I exhaled, rubbing a hand over my jaw as my thoughts raced. "Look, you've loved that girl since you were kids. And yeah, maybe timing was never on your side. Maybe people got in the way. But now? The only thing standing between you and Summer…is *you and Summer.*"

I let her words sink in, the truth of them settling somewhere deep. Shaking my head, I kissed her temple. "When did you grow up on me?"

She smirked. "According to Mum? I've always been grown." We both chuckled, but her eyes turned serious again. "But, for real,

Echo…love isn't easy. It takes work, it takes risk. But deciding if she's worth it? That part shouldn't be hard."

I sighed, the pressure in my chest shifting, lighter now. "I love you, Didi. And thank you." I lifted a fist. She bumped it, then licked her tongue out at me.

Sadie smiled. "I love you, too. And I'm proud of you, brother." She pulled me in for a hug, and for a moment, I let myself lean into it, into the comfort only a sister could offer. When she pulled back, her expression turned expectant. "So…now what?"

I shrugged, exhaling a slow breath because that question had been haunting me for the past twenty-four hours. Then, finally, I gave the only answer that ever made sense. "Now, I go get my Sunshine."

I decided to enjoy dinner with my sister before taking Summer her car. By the time I pulled into the Knights' driveway, the house was dark except for a dim glow from the living room. Summer probably hadn't moved much since our last text exchange, either deep in sleep, lost in thought—or both. I could only imagine the emotional toll her conversation with Deshawn had taken. He looked like he was ready to spit bullets when he saw her, but when his eyes landed on me? That man was murderous. And honestly, I couldn't blame him.

I stepped out of the car, nerves creeping in like this was my first time meeting her family. Back in high school, I spent so much time at this house that Ms. Teresa would set a plate for me on Sunday nights without even asking. Now? I felt like the guy who'd messed with their daughter's head…again. I opted to knock instead of ringing the doorbell. A few seconds later, the door swung open, revealing Summer's brother, OJ. I didn't know him as well as her sisters. By the time I met Summer, he was already out of the house, living in another city. Still, I knew enough to recognize that defensive expression on his face—the same one his father wore when he wasn't giving much away.

"She's still asleep," OJ said flatly, making it clear that this was my cue to hand over the car keys and be on my way.

I nodded, pocketing my hands. He must have thought that meant I was leaving. He had no idea. I would sit on the edge of her bed and watch her sleep until she woke up, just like I used to.

"Come on in, Echo," Mr. Knight called from the couch.

OJ hesitated for a second before stepping aside to let me in. Both Knight men studied me as I entered. They were not angry, exactly, just…uncertain. Like they were questioning my motives as they tried to piece together what the hell was going on. This was about to be interesting.

"Summer should be up soon," Mr. Knight said, pushing up from his seat on the couch, "but until then, let's talk." He turned off the television and started toward the four-season sunroom before stopping at the fridge. "You want a beer?" He grabbed one for himself and handed another to his son.

"Yes, sir. Thank you." I trailed them into the room as he flicked on the light and queued up the same basketball game on the mounted TV.

They sat on the couch. I took the chair. And just like that, I found myself in another situation I wasn't entirely prepared for.

"Who you going for?" OJ asked, staring at the TV.

I followed his sightline, only now realizing who was playing—the Celtics against the Bulls. "The Bulls," I said easily. "Chicago was the first place I could call home."

OJ scoffed. "What? You're not rooting for the hometown kid?" He was, of course, talking about Jayson Tatum.

I laughed, shaking my head. "Yeah, when they're not playing the Bulls." I took a sip of my beer.

"Figured you'd be a Lakers fan with how long you've been in LA," Mr. Knight said.

"Nah, never that." A brief silence settled over the room, the kind that made me wonder if this was just casual conversation or a quiet warning.

Then, without looking away from the game, OJ said, "Baby girl is hurting." The words were calm, but they hit like a punch. "What happened yesterday was a clear sign that she hasn't been happy."

Mr. Knight sighed, shaking his head. "Just settling."

A slow breath pushed through my nose as I nodded, knowing that was true. OJ finally turned toward me, not attempting to hide the sharp lines in his face. "I know y'all's history is complicated, but if you're here to add more to her plate, this conversation is about to go real different." His words hung between us, the tension thickening.

"That's not why I'm here at all," I said, my voice even with sincerity. "I came to St. Louis knowing my heart would be broken. I came to see her get married, to support my friend." I shook my head. "I ain't on no bullshit when it comes to Summer." I glanced at Mr. Knight, catching myself. "Excuse me, sir. No disrespect."

Mr. Knight offered an understanding nod. "None taken," he simply stated.

OJ didn't blink. "Summer is vulnerable right now. Don't confuse this situation by letting her run to you just because she doesn't know where else to go."

I leaned forward slightly, my elbows resting on my knees. "Summer and I haven't really known each other as adults. But the Summer I remember? She doesn't run unless she knows exactly where she wants to land."

They didn't know what I knew. While they saw yesterday as a hasty decision, I knew it wasn't. Yeah, Summer was hurting, but she wasn't lost. She wasn't looking for a distraction. What they didn't realize was that we had finally stopped lying to ourselves.

OJ was still watching me, still measuring my words. "Again... your past is complicated. I don't think she ever recovered from that." A beat of silence stretched between us. Peeling back the layers of our past meant exposing wounds. Some still healing, some still raw.

"I don't believe either of us will ever recover alone," I said, my voice firm but calm. "We have to face it—the good, the bad, the ugly. All of it." I shrugged. "It's really as simple as that." Then I met both of their gazes, my voice dropping lower. "But real talk, man to man?" I let the words settle. "I'm not losing her again."

OJ continued to watch me carefully, searching for cracks in my resolve. Mr. Knight examined me, too, but something in his face shifted, softened—just slightly. Finally, he spoke. "Echo, can I ask you a question?"

I nodded. "Yes, sir."

"How did you know where she was?" he asked, lifting a curious brow.

"Because I know my Sunshine, Mr. Knight." I let the words sink in before adding, "Even after all these years, I'll always find her when she needs me."

A moment passed. Then, synchronous nods from both men spoke volumes without them saying a single word. *"You have my blessing, but tread lightly."* I returned the respectful nod, silently acknowledging that their message was received loud and clear.

"Hey," a serene voice called from the doorway.

I turned, but the other eyes in the room stayed on me, measuring my reaction to *her*. I smiled because *damn*, there she was. A crown of curls framed her face, a little wild from sleep.

The redness in her eyes from crying had faded after getting some much-needed rest. She was wrapped in an oversized hoodie—my hoodie—and leggings; tall, fluffy socks swallowed her feet. She looked so damn pretty.

"Hey," I said, standing to greet her.

Mr. Knight shifted in his seat then stood. "It's getting chilly out here. Junior, let's finish watching the game downstairs."

He pressed a gentle kiss to her temple before stepping away, her brother following suit—but not without playfully nudging the side of her head. They loved her. They just wanted her to be okay, which meant we had something in common.

Once they were gone, my attention was back on her. "How are you feeling?"

She shrugged, her voice laced with exhaustion. "Tired, but I'm okay."

"Come here." I didn't stammer because it wasn't a request.

She didn't unfold her arms from around her body as she plowed into me, curling into my embrace. She needed this hug just as much as I did. The potency of it was riddled with unspoken turmoil, remorse, and love. But above all that, the weight of what came next hung the heaviest in the room. I guided her to the couch, careful not to overstep or push, letting her move at her own pace.

"You wanna talk about it?"

She wrapped her arms tight around her knees, staring into nothingness. "I'm such a fucked-up person," she said, voice hollow. "How could I do that to someone I claimed to love?"

I didn't answer right away. She wasn't looking for an answer—just a space to say the things clawing at her insides. I ran my hand slowly down her arm, grounding her. "You did what you needed to do, Sun. For you. For your sanity." I exhaled, rubbing my thumb against the inside of her wrist. "I know it was hard, and I know he was angry—hell, I don't blame him—but do you regret it?"

She rubbed her forehead, thinking. A long pause passed before she said, "I regret the way I did it, but I don't regret what I said."

I nodded, but I wanted to hear her say it. "And what was that?"

She lifted her head, finally meeting my eyes. "That I wasn't in love with him. That I was forcing something that was never really there." She swallowed, her voice soft but sure. "That I want butterflies." She uttered the last words breathlessly.

Something in me shifted. A warm, undeniable realization spread through me, my body tensing with memory. She didn't have to say my name. She didn't have to confess what I already knew, what I could feel humming in the space between us, because I knew. *I* was butterflies. Heat rising to my face caused me to blush like a damn lovesick fool, but I didn't care. Our eyes locked, cloaked in the same wordless knowing.

Gently, I reached for her legs, uncurling them from her body and draping them over mine. I traced slow circles on her knee. "So…where do we go from here?" I lifted a brow, voice teasing, but I wasn't playing.

Summer sighed, voice strained, like she hated what she was about to say. "E…" I knew what was coming. I felt it. "I don't know. I don't know what I'm supposed to do next."

And just like that, frustration coiled in my gut because, *What the fuck, Summer?* That wasn't the answer I wanted to hear.

CHAPTER TWENTY

Summer
October 2019, The Day After the Wedding that Wasn't

I EXPECTED ECHO to toss my legs off him after my statement, to shake his head, maybe even call me out for the mess I had made. What did he expect me to do? Flake on my wedding and jump right into his bed? Well…that is kind of what I did. I swallowed hard, but he didn't move. He didn't push me away. Instead, he just watched me, his gaze penetrating, his touch merciless.

"Echo," I started, vulnerability straining my voice. "I just walked away from my wedding—from a life I spent years building. A life I thought I wanted." My throat tightened, and I blinked rapidly, willing the emotions away. "I just told a man I care about that I never really loved him."

The truth sat heavy on my heart, suffocating me. I shook my head, trying to make sense of it all. "And now I'm here, with you, and I—" I faltered, running a hand down my face. "I don't even know where to start."

Echo's voice was resolute when he spoke. His tenor low and rich, like an anchor pulling me back from the storm. "Breathe, Sunshine," he said. His thumb brushed against my knee in slow, soothing circles. "You start by breathing…and then you start over."

I let out a weak, breathy laugh. "You make it sound so simple."

"Because it is." He paused, reaching out to gently nudge my chin, tilting my face toward his. His touch was featherlight, his eyes searching mine with something recognizable, something I missed. "You've been holding your breath for years, Summer, trying to force yourself into a life that didn't fit. You start by letting yourself breathe again, baby."

The corner of his mouth lifted into a small, teasing smile. Just enough to soften the corners of my doubt. I offered him the faintest one in return, though I still wasn't convinced that it would ever be as easy as he made it sound.

"Yesterday, you thought you wouldn't make it through today," he said.

I inhaled sharply. "I almost didn't."

"But you did," he countered, his voice firm, "and you'll make it through tomorrow. And the next day. And the next."

A deep, shaky exhale pushed through my lips as I sank further into the couch. I hated that he was right. Yesterday, I thought my life was over. I thought my truth would wreck everything—Deshawn, myself, our families. And yet we were all still here. Hurting, yes, but alive. Still standing to face another day to heal the wounds. Echo reached out, tucking a stray curl behind my ear. His fingers lingered at my jaw, faintly tracing up and down.

"I'm not saying it's not going to be tough," he said, "because it will be. People are going to whisper. They're going to ask questions you may not have answers for, but you keep pushing. Keep fighting for what you want, Sun."

I swallowed the lump in my throat, staring at my hands, at the way my fingers trembled against my lap. "I don't want to make another mistake," I said. "I don't want to hurt anybody else."

I don't want to hurt you. I didn't say it, but I felt it.

Echo studied me, a fleeting emotion danced with something unreadable before his grip on my knee tightened just slightly. His response was simple, assured. "Then don't."

Like a morning alarm cutting through REM sleep, his words hit me, forcing me to acknowledge what I had been avoiding: My dream—my everything—was right here. And I was right on the edge of taking that leap, of finally saying yes to the love I'd spent a lifetime running from. But then…the past reared its head. We had so much unsettled history, so many wounds still lingering between us, and suddenly, I wasn't sure if I was ready to open Pandora's box again. Because what if this time we couldn't put the pieces back together?

"But what—" I started.

"But what?" Echo cut in, his voice keen with frustration. "What will people think? What if this doesn't work? What if we fuck it up?" He closed his eyes briefly, inhaling deeply, as if trying to shoo away the same concerns burdening me. Then, his gaze snapped back to mine, unshakeable and determined.

"Summer, we've spent fifteen years pretending we didn't feel this. Pretending we could just move on and forget what we meant to each other. And look where that got us: You standing at an altar you didn't want to be at. Me in a relationship that was never going to last."

His words squeezed at something fragile inside me. "I don't want to hurt you, E. I don't want to be hurt," I said, my voice cracking, on the brink of a cry.

Shaking his head, he said, "Too late. We did that already."

Then, with a gentleness that made my breath stutter, he took my hand, bringing it to his lips, kissing my palm. I smiled despite myself, tracing the familiar curves and lines of his face with my eyes, memorizing him all over again.

"Today Max asked me if I was going to give you space...or if I was all in." He massaged small circles into the back of my hand, lulling away my cares. "I told him I was all in, but that's not fair to you."

"E..." I practically whined, his words causing pressure to build and build, threatening to spill over.

Without hesitation, Echo reached out, sliding his hand to the back of my head, pulling me closer. With his other hand, he pressed two fingers against my lips, silencing me. His touch was like a song I'd never heard before yet somehow knew by heart.

"You've been the only thing I've ever wanted." Emotion clung to his voice. "And I know this is messy. I know you need time." Then, his forehead met mine, the warmth of his breath mingling with mine, his caress unyielding and necessary.

"I'm going to give you the space you need, Summer, but please understand, I'm going to be pressure. I'm not letting up until you tell me to."

The thump in my heart had moved lower, deeper, pounding between my thighs. I should not crave this man the way that I did. But when he looked at me like that, searching my face for doubt, for the hesitation that had defined us for years, I knew there was no use fighting it. His grip tightened ever so slightly, his fingers threading into my hair.

"I'm not giving up unless you're telling me you don't feel this. If you're going to act like what we just admitted doesn't mean something, then say it now because I'm done pretending, Summer."

A trembly breath escaped me every time he called me Summer. It wasn't just the way his rich baritone wrapped around the syllables like a caress. It was the undeniable truth in his voice. When he said Summer, that meant that he wasn't being casual—it wasn't just a habit or a nickname. It was a promise, a claim that he meant every time. Lost in the way he said my name, I almost forgot his question. But my body knew the answer before my lips could form it. And then, barely above a whisper, I said, "I can't say that."

Something in his gaze eased just enough for me to know he believed me. His thumb brushed against my cheek, lingering there, as if memorizing the way I felt beneath his touch. His voice carried the responsibility of something heavy. "Then don't run. Not this time."

I closed my eyes, pulling in a slow breath. When I opened them again, Echo was still there. Waiting. Watching. Wanting. "I won't."

And for the first time since we were teenagers, I closed the space between us and kissed him. It was slow and steady. No rush. No urgency. Just the raw, aching sweetness of something we had both lost and found again. I'd kissed my fair share of men since high school, but none of them—not one—ever tasted like this. Because Echo's thick, smooth lips and his even thicker tongue were always imprinted in my mind. And if I was being honest, I wanted them imprinted all over me.

"Summer, do you want—" The sound of the screen door creaking open followed by my sister's screeching voice didn't deter us from the kiss.

"*Oohh,* pay up, Nette." Raqi's voice was smug, layered with satisfaction, and when I finally opened my eyes, I saw her standing there with Annette, both peeking around the doorway like nosy little kids.

"Oh, shit." Annette snorted, eyes wide before she folded her arms casually. "Well…I guess it's about time."

Echo and I finally pulled away. "What are y'all doing?" I demanded, still breathless.

"Uh, no, baby sis. What are *you* doing?" Raqi chuckled, nudging Annette playfully. "I told you, Nette. Echo was gonna get his girl. I didn't think you'd move this fast, though, li'l E," she teased, winking his way.

Echo didn't say a word, but when I turned to look at him, a cute, shrewd smirk was already curving his lips, all confidence and quiet victory. I rolled my eyes, but the way his fingertips traced tender, deliberate strokes across my exposed skin had me melting instead of fuming. My sisters' cackling faded as they meandered out of the sunroom, but I barely registered their retreat because the second we were alone again, Echo captured my lips, urgently pulling me back into the moment—into us.

He wrapped his arms around me, lifting me effortlessly until my legs straddled him. An intense, leisurely exhale passed between us as he pressed his forehead to mine, our breaths mingling, our hearts pounding in sync. We sat there, consumed by each other, saying nothing. The only sound was the love and longing woven into the light, tender pecks. The truth was out. And no matter what came next, we were finally facing it together.

Echo swept his lips over my cheek, his voice a rough, reverent whisper against my skin. "I always wanted us, Summer. I wanted our family."

Family. The word hung between us, like an elephant in the room, an obvious but ignored reality. His eyes, heavy and laden, swirled with emotions too big, too agonizing to be spoken outright. Memories, division, and unbalanced regrets still blurred the lines between us, full of things we never dared to say out loud.

A shudder ran through me, a gasp catching in my throat because I knew exactly what he meant. I felt it, too. I always had. My chest rose and fell at a rapid pace, the swell of tears burned. There were plenty of things from our past we could ignore. Several mistakes we could pretend never happened. But this? This was a truth we couldn't outrun. A truth that still lived and breathed in the recesses of our hearts, refusing to perish. And if we weren't careful, if we let it consume us without knowing where it would lead, it would either bring us back together…or break us completely.

Summer
Summer 2005, A Few Weeks Before SpelHouse

Since coming home from camp, life had been a whirlwind of preparation and anticipation. College was only weeks away, and my excitement bubbled over. I'd already connected with my roommate and a couple of girls from school who'd also be attending Spelman. What made it all even sweeter was knowing that Echo had been accepted to Morehouse. The SpelHouse dream we'd talked about was finally coming true, and it felt like the stars were aligning.

Echo and I had fallen back into our rhythm—*our inseparable shit*, as we liked to call it. The kind of bond we had was unnatural and sometimes scary. We could finish each other's thoughts and spend hours together without realizing how much time had passed. Only now, things were different. After my birthday, after the night I had given him the most intimate parts of me, everything changed. Something between us had shifted, deepened, twisted into something neither of us could untangle, even if we wanted to.

When I got home from camp, it took him less than an hour to show up at my door. And when I opened it, there he was. The tingly blissful feeling between my thighs quickly returned at the sight of him. I wanted to experience him again, but his expression was a storm of concern and curiosity, like he wasn't sure where we stood. Like he feared I might regret what we'd shared. Seeing him had been like opening the floodgates—memories of his touch, his kiss, the way he made me feel rushed in all at once. I couldn't stop thinking about it—about him. But alongside the exhilaration, there was fear of what this new territory meant for us, for our friendship.

We hadn't crossed that line again, but we danced around it, teetering on the edge. Our hugs lasted a little longer, our kisses were a bit hungrier. It was undeniable we weren't just friends anymore. Echo was mine, and I was his. Today, though, he'd been tied up with his parents, running errands for school, which gave me the perfect excuse to catch up with Trinity and Brooke. They'd been on my case for weeks about hanging out, and I knew I owed them some time before we all went our separate ways. Our friendship had withstood so much over the years, and even though life was pulling us in different directions, I knew we'd find a way to stay connected. Tonight was a chance to celebrate us before everything changed.

"Summer, you want some of this?" Trinity asked, extending a red plastic cup filled with something mysterious.

We were camped out at her sister's apartment, the perfect setting for a long-overdue girls night. Her sister, just a few years older, had given us free reign with only one rule: no drinking and driving. It was the ultimate slumber party—comfort food, drinks, and an endless playlist of Black love movies to feed our souls.

"Trin, why do you think you're a bartender?" I teased. "The last time you made me a drink, I got pissy drunk."

"Yeah," Brooke interjected, "and tongued down your other best friend!"

Trinity gasped theatrically. "Exactly! She needs this drink after *fucking* her best friend. Here you go," she said, her grin wide as she thrust the cup at me.

I groaned but grabbed the cup, taking a hesitant gulp. The sweetness hit my tongue, cutting the potency just enough to make it tolerable.

"Shut up. I hate I even told y'all," I said, though the warmth of my smile contradicted my words. I took another sip and raised my eyebrows, nodding as I gave Trinity a thumbs-up. "Alright,

alright. You might be on to something, Trin. You're getting good at this."

"Hey," she screeched, adding a body roll. "That's what I like to hear." She winked before grabbing her own cup.

"I'm just glad y'all finally figured it out," Trinity said, her tone playful but full of relief. "All that friendly flirting was getting old."

"Whatever. We were—are—friends," I replied, feeling the heat creep up my neck as I stumbled over my words. "We're just... attracted to each other, too." My bashful smile only made Trinity and Brooke exchange skeptical looks.

Before they could say anything, a wave of nausea hit me like a Mack truck. Gagging, I spit out the chicken I'd been enjoying just seconds before. "Brooke, are you sure this chicken is done?" I asked, holding up the half-eaten wing like it was the culprit of my sudden discomfort.

"*Um*, yes. Don't insult me. You know damn well I can fry some chicken."

"Well, it's making me sick. I feel like I gotta throw up," I said, my face twisted in disgust.

I reached for the Sprite Trinity had used to mix the drinks, hoping to settle my stomach, but the second the fizzy sweetness hit my tongue, I knew that was a bad idea. Without another word, I bolted for the bathroom, barely making it before I vomited up everything I'd eaten that night. Collapsing to the floor, I leaned against the cabinet, my head spinning like a carousel. Every slight movement made my stomach churn.

"Come in," I said, groaning when I heard a knock at the door.

Trinity peeked in, her face a mix of worry and amusement, with Brooke hovering just behind her. "Are you okay, boo?" she asked.

I nodded weakly. "I said I was never drinking again, and now, one sip, and I'm hugging the toilet."

Brooke narrowed her eyes as she crossed her arms. "Are you sure that's all?" she asked, her tone laced with suspicion.

"Brooke!" Trinity yelped, smacking her on the arm.

Brooke shrugged, but her doubtful expression lingered. I glared at her, wishing I had the energy to come up with a comeback. Instead, I just stared at her, the sting of her words making my blood boil.

"Why would you even think that?" I demanded, my voice unsteady as I stumbled to my feet.

Trinity quickly extended a hand to help me, and I leaned over the sink to rinse my mouth out. My gaze flickered to Brooke's reflection in the mirror, pointed yet full of compassion.

"I'm just saying..." She shrugged. "You've been eating everything in sight since you got here, and didn't you say your stomach was hurting the other day?" Her tone carried a hint of sympathy, but her words got on my nerves.

"Yes, that's because my period is going to start in a few days," I snapped, glaring at her like I could set her on fire with my stare.

Brooke raised her hands in surrender. "Okay. Okay. Look, I hope that's all it is."

I straightened, turning away from the sink but still feeling the weight of her words hanging in the air.

"We used a condom, and it was only once," I said defensively, the doubt in my voice negating my confidence. Was I trying to convince her—or myself?

"She's right, Brooke. Don't act like you've practiced safe sex every time," Trinity chimed in, her voice firm as she came to my defense.

Brooke's brows shot up, and her lips pressed together in a knowing expression that said, *Fair point.* I knew both Trinity and Brooke had far more experience in this area than I did. They'd had their own moments of recklessness—things I could barely imagine with my one-time-ever self. Trinity handed me a bottle of water she'd brought into the bathroom, and I accepted it gratefully. The cool liquid eased my throat and, thankfully, stayed down without any issue.

The tension began to lift as the night carried on. I found myself back on the couch with my friends, grazing on snacks and laughing at scenes from our favorite love stories. For the rest of the night, I pushed Brooke's words to the back of my mind, deciding to enjoy the comfort of my girls and the fact that, at least for now, my nausea was gone.

Echo
Summer 2005, A Few Weeks Before SpelHouse

I glanced around my room, trying to organize the chaos of boxes and shopping bags from the endless trips my mum and I had taken to prepare for school. In two weeks, I'd be packing everything up for Morehouse. Summer was leaving even earlier, heading to Atlanta for a special program tied to one of her scholarships. The thought of her being there without me for even a few days was troubling, but I shook it off. I shoved some things out of the way, clearing space because Summer was on her way over. Normally, we didn't hang out in my room when my dad was home—he had strict rules about that. But with him on campus with my brothers, my mum had loosened the reins. She'd given the green light, as long as the door stayed wide open.

The house was unusually quiet. My sisters were visiting my aunt in Chicago, and Mum was taking full advantage of the peace with a day of self-care. I'd called her earlier to make sure she was cool with Summer coming over, and of course, she'd given me her standard lecture about behaving. I nodded and agreed, promising like the obedient son I was. Misbehaving wasn't really an option, anyway. Summer wouldn't let it be. Yeah, we'd kissed and touched here and there—mostly in the basement when we were "watching TV"—but we hadn't gone all the way since her birthday. Eight weeks, four days, and about nine hours ago. Not that I was counting or anything. I wanted to—damn, did I want to—but I wasn't about to push her. That night had been everything to me, and I'd wait as long as it took for her to be ready again.

The doorbell rang, and I practically floated down the stairs. My excitement to see Summer was ridiculous, but I couldn't help it. It had only been a few days, but my pussy-whipped self missed her like crazy. When I opened the door, there she was…just so damn cute. She had on this simple blue T-shirt dress that fell just right, her thong sandals showing off freshly polished toes, and her braids were tied into a messy bun that somehow looked perfect. No makeup, just her fresh, natural beauty shining through.

"Hey, Sunshine," I greeted, pulling her into a hug.

My lips found hers in a soft kiss because, honestly, I couldn't resist. The fact that this girl—Summer Knight—was mine still felt unreal.

"Hey," she replied, her tone flat, holding a bag that I hoped had Sonic in it. I grabbed her hand, leading her upstairs, but she hesitated at the bottom of the staircase, giving me a look like I'd lost my damn mind.

"I thought your mom wasn't here," she said.

"She's not," I reassured her with a grin. "She said it's cool. I just want to show you the stuff I got for my dorm room."

She nodded but still looked skeptical, like we were sneaking around. Once we made it upstairs, I kissed her temple. "We're good. I promise."

Sitting on the edge of the bed, I reached and pulled her to stand between my legs, wrapping my arms around her waist.

"What's wrong, grumpy?" I teased, nuzzling my face into her stomach. "Did you bring me something good?"

Instead of cracking one of her usual jokes, Summer stayed quiet. Too quiet. I pulled back, focused on the contents of the bag, which she'd silently dumped onto the bed. My grin vanished. Lying there, scattered across my neatly made bed, were three different pregnancy tests. My throat went dry, my heart drumming as I stared at the boxes. When I looked up, Summer was already watching me, her jaw tight from fear and tension.

"Sun…" I croaked. "What…?"

Her lips parted, but no words came out. The silence between us stretched, heavy and stagnant.

"Summer, what is this?" I asked, the thud in my heart beating like a chorus of bass drums.

She shook her head with a slight shrug, uncertainty written all over her. "My period hasn't come," she finally said.

"I–I thought you said you were cramping. That's why I couldn't come over the other day," I said, confusion and concern thick in my voice. I studied her, searching for any understanding, but she refused to meet my eyes.

"I lied," she blurted, her voice trembling. "I was hoping… praying for cramps. Praying that it would come, but it didn't. It–It hasn't. Echo, what am I going to do?" Her words came out in a rush, uneasy and unfiltered, her eyes finally locking onto mine. A storm of dismay swirled in them, threatening to drown us both.

Panting roughly, she was on the brink of a panic attack. I didn't think; I just reacted. Closing the gap between us, I wrapped her tightly in my arms, pulling her into my chest.

"Baby," I whispered, stroking the back of her head, "you're not in this by yourself, okay?" I tilted her chin gently, needing her to understand. "You're not alone, Summer," I repeated over and over until she gave me a shaky nod.

I glanced at the tests spread out on the bed, staring back at me like ticking time bombs. The unopened boxes sat silently, their presence loud and rambunctious, like they were waiting to detonate. She wanted to do this together, that much was clear.

Swallowing hard, I looked at Summer. Her hands fidgeted with the hem of her t-shirt dress. Her shoulders were stiff, her eyes darting anywhere but at me. It was rare to see her like this—so unsure, so vulnerable. It made me want to wrap her in my arms again and shield her from whatever truth we were about to uncover.

Taking a deep breath, I said, "It's probably nothing, but we have to find out." My voice was steadier than I felt, the calm tone surprising even me.

Clasping her hand in mine, I led her to the Jack and Jill bathroom that my brother and I shared. The air in the room felt heavier than we'd ever experienced together. The mundane, boyish details of this space felt at odds with the gravity of the moment. Samir's Iron Man toothbrush and a slightly damp towel hanging on the hook. My own razor sat in its holder, a tool I'd only started using a few months ago when the faintest stubble had shown up.

Summer wouldn't let me leave. She peed on all three tests, right there in front of me, the tension between us as evident as the tile beneath our feet. After cleaning herself and washing her hands, we sat on the bathroom floor, leaning against the tub. I held her close, my knuckle brushing gently along her cheek in a rhythm meant to calm her—and maybe me. Those four minutes stretched into an eternity, each second laden with instability.

In that span of brutal silence, my mind played tricks on me. Instead of despair, I started building an imaginary life with my Sunshine—attending the same college, renting a small apartment, and raising our baby side by side. The load of it wasn't light, but the idea of it didn't terrify me. It felt almost…possible. Then, the timer on my watch jolted me out of my daze, as if telling me to wake the hell up and get real.

Summer's face told a completely different story. She wasn't constructing mythical futures in her head. She looked utterly wrecked—terrified, as if her world had already crumbled. Her knees were drawn tightly to her chest, her body rocking faintly like a leaf caught in a relentless wind. Peeling her off my chest, my body stammered a little before standing. Her gaze stayed fixed on some invisible point, refusing to follow me as I turned to the tests. I swallowed, but the mountain building in my throat wouldn't move. It was a visceral punch to my gut, stealing the air from my lungs. Two pink lines. On all three tests.

Summer was pregnant.

"Summer..." I croaked, the scratchy tone of my voice frayed with remnants of the boy on the verge of becoming a man. I reached for her. She didn't move. I bent, scooping her up like I could somehow carry both her and this crushing new reality. Her petite frame folded into me, trembling, her tears soaking my shirt. Together, we stared at the tests, hoping for a miracle that wasn't coming. The lines remained as bright and clear as the new truth we were being forced to accept.

"Hey, look at me," I whispered, cupping her face. "Summer, look at me." She lifted her tear-streaked face reluctantly, her eyes glassy with despair. "Everything is going to be okay. I promise."

She shook her head, tears falling harder now, her voice broken. "No, E. It's not."

Her sob hit me like a wrecking ball, and I couldn't hold back my own tears. We stood there, locked in this debilitating bubble of grief and angst like a boulder crushing us both.

"Echo! What is going on?" My mother's voice cut through the air like a blade, pulling us violently back to the moment. Her footsteps stopped abruptly in the doorway. Her sharp, questioning eyes darted from the tests on the counter to Summer, then to me.

"Is she pregnant?" she asked, her voice rising into an almost shrill pitch.

I swallowed hard, the lump in my throat making it almost impossible to speak. I held Summer tighter, as if shielding her from the monsoon that was yet to come. "Yes, Mum," I said, my voice wavering, taking on that awkward pubescent crack.

Her reaction was immediate. "Echo. No!"

The anguish in her voice echoed through the small space, a siren marking the magnitude of the moment. Summer buried her face deeper into my neck, trying her best to hide in me. I tightened my hold on her, bracing us both for what came next.

CHAPTER TWENTY-ONE

Summer
Summer 2005, Two Weeks Before SpelHouse

I CRINGED WHEN THE DOORBELL rang at exactly seven o'clock as scheduled. From my room, I peeked out of my window, my breathing stalled when I saw the familiar SUV parked in front of the house. The streetlights cast a dull glow over the pavement, stretching shadows beneath the figures standing at our doorstep. Even from here, I could see Echo's tall frame, his posture rigid beside his mother and father. The Abara family was here to discuss the fate of my and Echo's future. As if one conversation could undo the mess we had made.

I was pregnant. Seven weeks. My first time having sex had resulted in a passion I still couldn't fully comprehend…and a baby. Echo and I shared something rare that night—something tender, something that felt larger than both of us. We were careful at first, but by morning, as he prepared to leave, we were swept away by the moment. Caution fell by the wayside. We were impulsive. Reckless. And now, the consequences had arrived, knocking at the door like an unwanted guest. It had been nearly a week since we'd found out. Five days of pure hell. After Mrs. Abara's urgency-riddled tone screeched through my parents' phone, rapidly spilling Nigerian lingo they couldn't translate, only two words required comprehension—*Summer* and *pregnant*.

My mother cried for three days straight. My father drank through hell week, spending sleepless nights pacing the house, his movements restless, his silence loud. Neither of them could look at me. Not that I gave them much of a chance. I had barely left my room since walking out of Echo's house that day. Under normal circumstances, I would have told my mother everything—how Echo was worthy of my treasure, how he had treated me like something sacred, a prized possession. How it wasn't just sex, but an awakening, a moment that changed me. But my mother didn't want to hear any of that. She didn't care that Echo made me feel cherished, that his touch wasn't selfish or rushed, that what we shared wasn't some meaningless teenage mistake. She didn't care that it had been the most beautiful, exhilarating experience of my life.

My sisters, though, they listened. Because they knew me. They knew I hadn't reached this decision lightly—that I hadn't just fallen into Echo's arms on a whim. That I had chosen him. That I loved him. They tried to assure me that everything would be okay. My brother, on the other hand, had threatened to fly to St. Louis and kill Echo himself.

None of it mattered now. Because in two weeks, I was supposed to leave for Spelman. How was I supposed to do that with a baby in my belly? No one was more disappointed in me than me. I knew better. God knows my mother had given me *the talk* more times than I could count, ever since my first period in middle school. And yet, here I was. Trapped in a moment that was about to change my life forever.

Mama was a teenage mother, and she often blamed it on my granny's inability—or maybe just lack of desire—to have real conversations with her children about sex. The only sex talk they ever got was a blunt: Don't do it.

But Teresa Knight? She was determined to break the generational curse. She shared her own experiences and regrets openly, especially with us girls, never shying away from the hard truths. Mama was adamant that not only her daughters, but my brother, OJ, too, would have a different path, come hell or high water.

My mother was traditional about arbitrary things like wearing skirts and pantyhose to church, but when it came to life lessons? No topic was off the table, especially sex. Because in the Knight household, getting pregnant wasn't an option. Period. I remembered the night I overheard my parents talking about Echo—about the time I spent with him, about whether it was becoming too much. Our house was small and cozy, but the walls, they were paper-thin. Even though they were trying to whisper, I could hear everything from my bedroom.

"I think that girl is spending too much time with that boy. I think we need to—"

"Tee," my father interrupted, his tone soothing. *"That boy is harmless. He seems like a good kid. Now, Summer says he's just her friend, so I believe her."*

Mama let out a frustrated huff, her voice sharp. *"You would let that li'l girl do whatever she wants. She's got you tied up and wrapped around her little finger."* A pause. Then came her final warning, each word stressed like she was laying down the law. *"Let her come up in here with a baby, and you're gonna be the pappy babysitting because I am not."*

Daddy just chuckled, his voice light, completely unbothered. *"Now you sound like your mama."* I could hear the tease in his tone, the easygoing way he tried to diffuse her frustration. *"And besides, Summer wouldn't disappoint me like that."*

Silence. Then, Mama's begrudging sigh. "Whatever you say, pappy." Her footsteps faded as she walked out of the room.

I stared at myself in the mirror, my father's words echoing in my head, looping like a quiet warning. *"Summer wouldn't disappoint me..."* He was right. At least, I didn't want to disappoint him—them. I had spent my entire life making sure of that. Good grades. Honest. Following the rules—well, most of them. Going to church. Praying. Being the daughter they could trust. It was all part of the unspoken agreement I had made with myself—the silent promise to never be the reason my parents lost faith in me. I had never been the kind of kid to risk a whooping just to prove a point. But the truth was, it wasn't punishment that scared me. It was the look in their eyes. That quiet, heavy weight of disappointment, of knowing I had somehow let them down. That feeling cut deeper than any scolding, any lecture, any grounding ever could.

To me, their approval wasn't just about staying out of trouble. It was about the love and respect I had for them. Making them proud had always been my way of showing I cared, of proving that their sacrifices, their lessons, their expectations weren't in vain. The thought of losing that, even for a moment, sent a sharp ache through my chest. A lump formed in my throat, my vision blurring as tears threatened to spill. Because disappointment didn't just sting—it lingered. It changed things. And I wasn't sure if I was strong enough to face that kind of shift.

I startled, even though the tapping at my bedroom door was light. Closing my eyes, I inhaled deeply, calming myself before finally looking in the mirror one last time. I wasn't ready. I wasn't ready to face the dismay, the disappointment that had settled over the house like a dark cloud, thick and smothering. But when I opened the door, my daddy stood there, his pained, forced smile a clear indication that he wasn't ready either. He nodded a silent question, asking if I was prepared. I wasn't. But I nodded back anyway.

I was grateful that the first face I saw when I stepped into the hallway was Echo's. He was seated on the edge of the couch, fingers intertwined, his head hanging low. At the creak of the floorboard, he lifted his head, his eyes finding mine instantly. He tried to mask it, to brighten his expression, but I could see through it. His week had been just as hellish as mine. We hadn't talked. At all. And that made everything ten times worse. Every time I called his house, his mother said he was busy. His father flat-out refused to let me speak to him. Echo hadn't called me either, and I wouldn't have been surprised if his father had stripped his room of every means of communication and banned him from leaving the house altogether. But if he could have gotten to me, I knew he would have.

I smiled when our eyes met, needing that one sliver of comfort, but it quickly faltered when I noticed his parents' scowls. His mother's expression was softer than his father's but still creased with worry and disappointment. My mother, whose fair skin was slowly turning beet red, did not look happy. And I wasn't sure if her frustration was directed at me, at Echo, at his parents, or just the entire situation unraveling in front of us.

Choosing not to speak to anyone, I moved to the chair on the opposite side of the living room from Echo. His mother sat beside him on the couch. My mother perched stiffly on the arm of my chair. And the fathers? They stood on separate sides of the room, arms crossed, each looking like they wanted to be anywhere but here. The tension in the air was pungent enough to choke on. Then, Mr. Abara's voice cut through it, harsh like the blade of a dull knife.

"This is exactly what we were afraid of." His words sent a jolt of ice down my spine. "Our son has worked his ass off to get into college. He has a full ride, a future. And now this? This could ruin everything."

I stole a glance to my left, watching my father push off the wall, his entire posture shifting. Then, I darted my gaze right, watching my mother sit up straighter, her spine stiff, her expression unreadable, but her silence deadly.

"You think our daughter doesn't have a future?" my father challenged. His eyes were narrowed, burning into Mr. Abara.

My mother's tone was cool, but beneath it lay the cutting edge of her infamous nice-nastiness. "Our daughter has a scholarship to Spelman College. She, *too*, has a future."

The room felt like a battlefield, the strain between our parents like an invisible tug-of-war. Then, Mrs. Abara spoke, her exhaustion bleeding through her voice.

"That is not what my husband is saying at all." Her tone was measured, tired, like she'd spent the last few days having this same conversation behind closed doors. "We're not happy about this either. But what's done is done. Now, we need to figure out what comes next—for both of them."

Echo and I stole a glance at each other, something unspoken but understood passing between us. While our parents sat there talking over us, debating our futures as if we weren't even in the room, neither of us had been given the chance to say what we really wanted. Mr. Abara looked at his wife incredulously, shaking his head, his frustration boiling over.

"What comes next? What comes next is our son losing everything he's worked for. This girl—*your daughter*—has completely derailed his life," he scoffed, tossing his hands up in exasperation.

A stunned silence filled the room for all of half a second before my parents' voices erupted in unison. "*Excuse* me?"

My body went rigid, my narrowed eyes locking on to him. How dare he put this all on me? I shot a glance at Echo, hoping, needing him to say something, and sure enough, he was already glowering at his father.

"Wait just one damn minute." My father's tone was edgy, unwavering. "You are going to respect my daughter in my house. And let's be clear, our daughter didn't get here on her own. Your son holds some responsibility here, too." His voice held no room for argument, and from the way his fists clenched, I knew that if he weren't trying to remain civil, he'd have already escorted Mr. Abara to the door.

"Yeah, Dad. Chill," Echo muttered.

Mr. Abara shot daggers at his son, and for a second, I thought he was going to smack Echo upside the head. His glare turned venomous.

"I knew they were more than just friends. This—" Mr. Abara gestured wildly at both of us. "This so-called friendship has been unhealthy since day one."

My parents didn't even argue with him on that point.

Echo turned to me, and when our gazes met, we both had the same tear-filled eyes, the same silent, aching question: How did we get here?

And then suddenly, all hell broke loose. Both sets of parents were on their feet, arguing over what was best for *their* child. Mr. Abara was practically ready to have me burned at the stake. Mrs. Abara kept talking about adoption.

My father wouldn't even consider keeping the baby. Abortion was the only answer for him.

And my mother? She was the only one who wanted the decision to be ours. Helpless. Hopeless. That's what we were. Until Echo snapped.

"That's enough!" His voice boomed, commanding the room, making all four parents freeze. He stood to his full height, taller than both our fathers, his chest rising and falling in deep, sporadic breaths. His jaw was tight, his nostrils flaring, but his voice was clear when he spoke again. "Do Summer and I get to say anything? This is our doing—our baby."

My father's glare turned cold. "You've said and done enough, young man."

And just like that, he and Mr. Abara, two men who hadn't agreed on anything today, were suddenly on the same team. But Echo didn't care. He ignored them, his long strides closing the space between us in seconds before kneeling in front of me. His hands found mine, cradling them, his grip warm. He kissed my fingers, one by one, his lips lingering just enough to make my breath hiccup. I felt his thumb swipe away the tears I hadn't even realized had started falling. The world—our parents—blurred into nothing. For a fleeting second, it was just us. Like we were back in our sacred place.

His voice, when he finally spoke, was soft but sure, full of a certainty that I didn't expect from him—maybe not even from myself.

"Summer, I love you." He halted, scanning my eyes to ensure his message was received. For good measure, he said it again. "I love you, and I'm sorry. I'm sorry that this happened like this, but I think...I think we can do this. We can have this."

I froze. *We can have this.* His words sat heavy between us, full of meaning I couldn't yet process. My eyes widened, my throat closing around all the words I wanted to say but couldn't. Because what was he saying, really? We could have what? A baby? With no money, no education, no plan? That wasn't the future I had envisioned for myself. I was supposed to go to Spelman, major in marketing, become student council president, pledge a sorority, go to parties, live my life, graduate on the dean's list in four years. A baby with Echo's tawny brown skin, his full lips, my bright eyes, full cheeks, and dimples wasn't a part of that plan.

"E," I whispered, placing both hands on his cheeks, my thumbs brushing away the tears that neither of us could stop.

His eyes, full of hope, fear, love, and desperation, searched mine. "We can do this," he repeated, his voice barely above a breath. Then, he pressed a soft, sweet kiss against my lips, sealing us inside our own fragile bubble.

Our parents watched in agonizing silence, their presence barely registering, though I caught Mr. Abara shifting as if he was about to say something. But before he could, my mother raised her hand, silently commanding him to let us figure this out.

"Echo...we're only eighteen. We can't raise a whole human." My voice trembled, my words laced with a heart-wrenching mix of guilt and finality.

His brows drew together, realization dawning as my words veered in a direction he hadn't expected. "People do it all the time. We're the smartest people I know. We can do anything, Sun." His optimism, his belief in us, ripped me wide open.

I shook my head, lips pinched tight. His hopefulness was endearing, but it did nothing to change my mind. "And people fail, E," I whispered, my throat raspy. "We had a plan, remember? SpelHouse connection." The weight of my gaze didn't just remind him, it called out to him, begging him to remember. To remember who we were just a week ago before this. To remember the future we were supposed to have.

I saw the exact moment it hit him. The subtle swing in his expression, the way his shoulders sagged just a little. Echo knew me better than anyone, and I could feel it. He already knew my decision. I did not want this baby. I had made a mistake, and I would carry it with me for the rest of my life, but I wasn't ready to sacrifice my future. Our foreheads met, our lips hovered, each conjoined breath the only air we had left to breathe. And then, I said the words that shattered him.

"I love you, Echo. I am so sorry, but I–I can't do this. I can't have this baby."

He went completely still, his fingers tightening around my waist. His grip was firm, almost desperate, as if holding on to me could somehow stop the ground from shifting beneath him. His gaze locked onto mine—frantic, searching—like he was trying to wake up from a nightmare he didn't know how to escape. But I didn't waver. I was firm. Resolute. And when the finality of my words hit him, I felt his entire body break. His head collapsed into my lap, his arms clenched around me as he sobbed, raw and heart-wrenching tears. I bent over him, resting my cheek atop his, folding my arms around his shoulders. And together, we cried, our sobs blending into the most devastating, harmonic melody, a sorrowful lullaby that only we would ever sing.

CHAPTER TWENTY-TWO

Echo
Summer 2005, The Life-Changing Decision

THE CLINIC LOOKED like any other doctor's office—neutral-colored walls and sterile white floors. Soft, impersonal décor attempted to mask the gravity of why most of the women here had come. Photos of smiling families lined the walls, their joy a stark contrast to the reality of this place. Women of all ages sat quietly in stiff chairs, waiting for their name to be called. Some carried the unmistakable glow of anticipation, their hands protectively cradling their growing bellies, their eyes bright with the promise of new life. Others, though... Their faces were drawn, heavy with quiet sorrow, women weighed down by the life-changing decision they were making.

When I walked through the clinic doors, her eyes found mine instantly. Surprise flickered across Summer's face, but more than that, solace. She hadn't expected me to come. She knew my father had forbidden it. But Maxell covered for me, saying he just wanted to get me out of the house. I dropped him off at his girlfriend's place and drove here instead, gripping the steering wheel like my life depended on it. She studied me, and I studied her. She wore the same dispirited expression that hung in the air of this stuffy, emotion-charged room. Ms. Teresa sat beside her, holding her hand, mumbling what looked like a silent prayer. When her focus settled on me, she nodded, motioning for me to sit. I swallowed, my throat tight and dry, then lowered myself into the seat beside them. I looked at Summer, and she quickly turned away, as if the lines of dejection were written too clearly across my face.

"Quest Knight," the nurse called. Summer rose to her feet, and my brows knitted together, confused by the name she was responding to.

Then I remembered the small crowd of protestors in the parking lot, their voices chanting over one another: "My body, my choice." "Your baby has a heartbeat." I now understood the need for anonymity. *Quest.* She had used the name of our sacred place. That realization nearly stole the breath from my lungs. It was the name of the place where we became more than just best friends, we fell in love. The place where we made this baby.

"Echo, you go with her," Ms. Teresa said, pulling me from my thoughts.

I snapped my gaze to her, surprised. She knew how my parents felt about this. She knew I wasn't supposed to be here. And yet, she wanted me to go with Summer. I nodded, rising to my feet, though my legs felt weak and wobbly beneath me. Summer didn't look at me as we followed the nurse through the door. The moment we stepped inside the exam room, a faint, unfamiliar scent filled my nostrils. Something sterile, but also sharp—burnt rubber and disinfectant. I swallowed the nausea threatening to rise. The room was cold, unnervingly quiet. We still hadn't spoken a word to each other.

Summer undressed in silence, draping the thin paper gown over her trembling body before lying on the exam table. I sat beside her, my fingers clenching into tight fists against my thighs. My eyes wandered, landing on the poster hanging on the wall. *The Phases of Pregnancy*. It was brightly colored, offering an oversimplification of something so impossibly complex. On the section marked *Week Seven*, our baby was no bigger than a blueberry. Too small for Summer to feel movement. I squinted, reading the fine print beneath the image. *Facial features begin to take shape, with dark spots forming where the eyes and nostrils will be, and tiny buds appearing for the ears.*

A debilitating pang lodged in my chest. Since finding out Summer was pregnant, I had dreamed of a baby girl. I had imagined her with Summer's round face, almond-shaped eyes, and deep dimples that made everything brighter. But now... My dream morphed into a nightmare. This was real, and there was nothing I could do to stop it.

"Hello. I'm Dr. Moss. I'll be performing the procedure today." The voice was light, almost too cheerful for this moment.

I turned to see a short woman with chin-length blond hair, looking no older than us. She extended her hand to Summer first, then to me. Summer barely lifted her fingers, her grip weak, her entire body drained of emotion.

Dr. Moss glanced at the clipboard in her hands, her voice calm and routine, like this was just another day. "I see that you've chosen a vacuum aspiration. Is that correct?"

Summer's nod was small and hesitant. "Yes. Yes, that's correct," she said breathily. I watched her closely, searching for any sign that she might change her mind. She didn't.

"Okay. It's a simple procedure," Dr. Moss said.

My head snapped back. *Simple? There's nothing simple about this shit.* I wanted to yell it, wanted to grab her clipboard and throw it across the room, but instead, I quietly choked on the rage burning its way up my throat and turned my eyes back to the poster on the wall. *The Phases of Pregnancy*. The one I'd been staring at for the past ten minutes, memorizing details I never thought I'd need to know. Our baby—our blueberry—the one I would never get to know.

Dr. Moss kept talking. Her voice was pleasant, but still professional and detached. "A local anesthetic will be inserted into your cervix. You may feel a little pressure from the vacuum, but the procedure should only take about ten minutes. As long as you're feeling okay after an hour, you can go home."

I felt my fists clench involuntarily. Home. Like it was that simple. Like we would just walk out of here and pretend none of this had ever happened.

"The nurse will give you post-op care information, but you should be good to go."

Summer's voice was soft but laced with fear when she finally spoke. "Will there be a lot of pain after?"

Dr. Moss shook her head, smiling a little too easily. "Nothing a Tylenol can't handle." She gave Summer's shoulder a light tap, a gesture that was probably meant to be reassuring, then walked toward the door. "The nurse will be in to get you prepped, and I'll be back in a few."

Summer gave a small, polite smile, the kind that didn't reach her eyes, then shifted her stare to the ceiling, crossing her arms over her stomach protectively. Her expression was unreadable. And if my mind was this fucked up right now, I couldn't begin to imagine what was happening inside hers.

"Are you scared?" I asked the question lowly, though I already knew the answer.

She nodded immediately, blowing out a chilling breath. "Yeah."

Silence. I exhaled, rubbing a hand down my face before I looked at her again. "You want to think about it some more? This pamphlet says you still have time." I fidgeted with the edges of the tri-fold paper, my last, desperate attempt to change the course of this moment.

Summer didn't move. Didn't react. She just kept breathing, slow and steady, as if she were convincing herself to stay in this body, to see this through. "No," she finally answered, her voice blank, emotionless.

I turned away, jaw pinched tight as I took in a deep breath, trying...failing to stop myself from pushing, but my heart had other plans. "What if you regret it?"

Her breath hitched. Her hands curled into tight fists, the paper sheet crinkling beneath her grip. Then she turned to me, and my chest caved in at the single tear that spilled down her cheek. Her voice was so soft, so devastatingly final when she spoke.

"I *will* regret it. Probably every day for the rest of my life." An aching sigh left her lips. Her gaze drifted back to the ceiling, her fingers curling into her stomach, as if she were mourning something she hadn't even fully grasped yet. "But I'd regret resenting this baby... resenting you more."

And just like that, everything inside me shattered. I nodded, reluctantly absorbing the reality in front of me. A chalky dryness coated my throat, making it hard to breathe; each swallow felt like sandpaper scratching my insides. There was a hammering in my chest, a silent, desperate plea lingering on my tongue. But I wouldn't say it because I believed it was her body, her choice. Even if it shattered me. Even if every fiber of my being wanted to beg her to reconsider. Instead, I reached out, sliding my hand on top of hers, then slowly lowered my head to rest there. She convulsed, veiled grief rippling through her body. I knew she was holding that sob hostage, trying to keep it in. But under my touch, it broke free. We sat like that for what felt like an eternity, locked in a sorrow that neither of us knew how to escape.

I blinked. And somehow, it was over. Ms. Teresa entered the room as Summer was being observed post-procedure. Everything moved in a dazed blur. An hour later, she was free to go, sent off with instructions to rest for the next day or two. We stepped outside into the thick, humid air. The crowd of protestors had mostly thinned. Some signs were still scattered along the pavement. Ms. Teresa slid into the driver's seat of the car, giving us a moment. I stuffed my hands into my pockets, knowing I would melt if I touched Summer right now. She wrapped her arms around herself, as if she were cold, but the air was stifling, thick with heat and grief. Neither of us knew what to say or do. Until she spoke.

"I love you." Her voice was fragile, yet sure.

"I love you." I didn't hesitate. I swallowed hard, then exhaled. "I'm still on lockdown, but I can sneak away if you need me to."

Amusement curved her lips, and she nodded. I lifted my hand, brushing my fingers along her jaw, then stroking her cheek with my thumb. I memorized her face, committing this moment to memory because I wanted to remember her just like this—strong and brave and broken. She melted into me as I wrapped my arms around her, holding her like I could somehow keep her from slipping through my fingers. Her face pressed into my chest, her fingertips gripping the fabric of my t-shirt, a silent request to stay a little longer. We didn't speak. We didn't need to because our bodies spoke for us. The slight tremble in her hands. The lingering touch before pulling away. The way we stalled, standing only a mere inch apart, just enough to feel the air between us again. Neither of us looked at each other right away. Because looking would mean acknowledging the turning point we were facing, but I couldn't leave without one last thing.

I bent, pressing a soft, reverent kiss to her forehead, then let my lips glide over the curve of her nose before finding her mouth. I didn't care that her mother was in the car watching us. I kissed her slow, unhurried, my hands cradling her face like she was the most precious thing I had ever held. I tasted her tears, absorbing them like medicine, as if they could heal me. She traced over my chest, then down my stomach, resting at my waist. I parted her lips with my tongue, and she moaned softly, breathlessly. Our mouths moved in perfect sync, tongues dancing to a flawless melody. This wasn't a heated, reckless kiss. This was devotion. By the time we pulled apart, I was gasping for air, but breathing for her. Our foreheads touched, and we exchanged one last embrace, holding each other a little tighter, knowing that when we let go, we would never be the same again.

Echo
October 2019, The Day After the Wedding that Wasn't

Summer wouldn't let me go. Or maybe I wouldn't let her go. I wasn't sure. All I knew was that it was midnight, and we were still tangled together on the couch in the sunroom. The Knights' house had long since fallen into silence, the soft chirps of crickets outside the only thing breaking the stillness. After her sisters' funny interruption, no one else had bothered to check on us, as if they already knew we weren't ready to leave whatever moment we had found ourselves in.

Summer was burrowed under my arm, her head resting on my shoulder, and I let myself sink into the peace of it. The peace of her. The disclosures we'd shared tonight had unearthed old bones, skeletons of emotions I had buried deep, only to realize they had never really stayed dead. Every year, around the first week of August, my mood would shift, a restless, unnamed ache burdening me, like something missing. For years, I hadn't understood why. Then I'd remember. That last kiss. The way Summer had felt in my arms. The way she had slipped through my fingers before I ever had the chance to hold on. I kissed her forehead softly, and she stirred, mumbling something incoherent before curling in closer.

"Are you asleep? I should go," I said, though I didn't move.

A sleepy, stubborn whine answered me. "No."

I chuckled as she tightened her grip on me, her arms locked around my waist as if she could physically keep me from leaving. "It's late, Sun." The words dragged, my reluctance thick—I didn't want to leave. "I don't want your parents waking up to find me still here. Besides, I promised mine I'd have breakfast with them in the morning."

That made her pause. Slowly, she shifted, tilting her head to look at me in the dim light. "What do you think they're going to say?" she asked. "About us."

The question shouldn't have surprised me. But still, I stiffened. I'd been asking myself the same thing. Summer had always been welcomed in the Abara house. My siblings adored her, my mother had once treated her like she was part of the family. But my father...he had never seen it that way. He had never been shy about his opinion, never hesitated to remind me that we were too much, too fast, too young. I exhaled slowly, my fingers trailing lazily down her arm as I gave myself a second to answer.

"I don't know. But it doesn't matter. I'm grown. I make my own decisions, and my choice is you."

The tense lines of her face mellowed, but something flickered in her eyes—unease, doubt, guilt.

"They wouldn't be wrong to be concerned, you know," she said, her fingers tracing unhurried, absentminded circles against my chest. "What kind of woman plans a wedding just to not show up, then in the same day tells her first love he's been her only love all along?"

I should have been angry at the self-blame in her voice, but I wasn't. Instead, a quiet warmth came over me, because she was finally saying the words I had always known to be true. "The kind of woman who needed time," I said simply, brushing my thumb over her cheek. She shrugged, doubt lingering in her expression. She wasn't convinced. Worry was etched across her face, her lip caught between her teeth as if she were bracing for words she didn't want to speak. Her fingers found her ear, tugging lightly—her silent confession of angst.

"I don't really give a damn what they think, Sun. Or what anybody thinks, for that matter," I said firmly, cutting off whatever argument she was about to make before she could even voice it. "We've been through too much, wasted too much time to start worrying about other people's opinions now." She halted. The hesitation was in every breath, every small shift of her body.

"But they were right back then," she said, the weight of the past pressing into her words "Your parents weren't wrong, E. We were really deep really fast."

I let out a short, humorless laugh, shaking my head. "They weren't right either, Summer. They were scared. And yeah, we made mistakes, but damn, we were just kids—kids who didn't know better, who never even got the chance to figure it out."

My chest felt tight, the old frustration creeping in—the years we'd lost, the choices we didn't get to make. We had been too young, but we hadn't been wrong. Summer ran a gentle hand across my face, her touch grounding me.

"Maybe he was just protecting you," she said, her gaze drifting into the darkness, like she wasn't really speaking to me but to something…someone who would listen to her muted thoughts.

An unsettling riddled my stomach. I reached for her chin, tilting her face back up to me. "Summer, what are you not saying?"

Her lips parted, but no words released, only uneven breaths, as if caught between what she could say or what she shouldn't say.

Aimlessly, she swiped her fingertips up and down my stomach, but she remained silent. I raised a brow, urging her to talk to me.

"I came to your house before I left for Atlanta," she said finally.

My brows drew together in confusion, then tightened with something heavier—anger, dread—because I already sensed this was heading somewhere I wouldn't be able to shake. I sat up on the couch, bringing her with me.

"What?"

"The night before I left for Spelman. We hadn't talked since the clinic, and I couldn't leave like that. I needed to see you. To talk. To say goodbye." Her breathing was labored as she spoke, her legs instinctively tucking over mine. "But I never got the chance."

A bitter, acidic burn settled in my gut. My voice came out sharp. "Why?" But I already knew. *My fucking father.*

"Mr. Abara…your father wouldn't let me."

I went still, my breath escaping in ragged intervals. All this time, I thought Summer just left. Just said fuck me and went off to live her life without looking back. All this time, I thought I hadn't meant enough to her to say goodbye. And it was him.

"My father," I said, the words hollow as they left my mouth.

Summer swallowed, the memory dancing just beneath the surface of her expression.

"He answered the door. And before I could even say anything, he stepped out onto the porch." She paused, her lips pressing together before she forced herself to continue. "I don't know if you were there or not, but he told me to stay away from you—that you had your whole future ahead of you, and I would only hold you back."

The words sliced through me like the sharpest blade. I sat back, stunned. Speechless. Barely holding on to my sanity.

"What else did he say?" My voice was controlled, but rage churned beneath my skin. My father was the smartest man I knew and a great provider, but he could be a heartless son of a bitch.

Summer debated, shaking her head. "Nothing."

But I knew that was a lie. I leaned forward, my jaw tense. "Tell me, Summer."

Her gaze faltered, as if she was searching for a way to soften the truth. Then, her voice came quiet, strained. "He said that you deserved better than a girl who..." She left the rest unsaid, but I already knew how it ended. It hit me like a punch straight to the ribs, knocking the air from my lungs. I already knew the ending to that sentence. My family was traditional. Strict and sometimes unforgiving. My father, especially. Marriage preceded pregnancy under any circumstance. In our village, an unmarried, pregnant girl would have been disowned, sent away, a walking disgrace. A stain on the family's honor.

"My fucking father." The words were guttural, bitter, filled with something between nausea and fury. I needed air. Needed to move. I quickly shifted her legs off me and stood.

"Echo, it doesn't matter now." She tried to convince me, but it wasn't enough to cool the fire spreading through me.

"The hell it doesn't, Sunshine." I was pacing now, dragging a rough hand over my face. "I spent years wondering why you left without a word. Years thinking I didn't mean enough for you to even say goodbye."

She reached for me then, wrapping a hand around my arm, halting my erratic pursuit of relief. "E, I would never do that. I wanted to... God, I tried, but he looked me in the eye and told me you didn't need me anymore." Her voice cracked, breaking me open. "I felt so dirty...like a cancer poisoning you." The way she said it, like she believed it, nearly crippled me. "He said the best thing was for us to go our separate ways."

"And after everything we'd gone through, you just listened?" The bitter words left my mouth, and I immediately wished I could swallow them down because this wasn't her fault. Summer's arms dropped to her sides. She exhaled shakily, taking a step back.

"Echo, I was eighteen." Her voice was biting and pained. "My world had already fallen apart. I thought...maybe he was right. Maybe I had done enough damage. Maybe walking away was the best thing to do. For you. For both of us." She turned away from me.

"Sunshine," I said, unable to quell the rawness in my voice. "Summer, look at me."

She stood at the window, motionless, focus fixed on the night, as if searching for answers neither of us could grasp.

I couldn't take it. The distance, the ghosts of everything we'd lost pressing between us. I closed the space, wrapping an arm around her waist, drawing her back to me. She didn't resist.

"You were never something I needed to be protected from," I said, my lips brushing against the shell of her ear. "You were the only thing I ever wanted, Sun."

She exhaled, her head tipping back to rest against my shoulder. "Every day, I thought about marching to Morehouse, banging on every dorm room door to find you. Wishing that maybe we'd just run into each other at an event or homecoming."

I let out a bitter snicker, but not a damn thing was funny. "He took Morehouse away from me, too."

Her head snapped up, those wide, pretty brown eyes locking onto mine. Confusion. Concern. The beginning of something breaking open inside her. "What?"

I clenched my jaw. The anger simmering beneath my skin was old, but it still burned like fresh embers. "He didn't trust me to stay away from you, so he tightened the leash. Made me stay home. Forced me to go to WashU."

A sharp, quiet inhale slipped through parted lips, regret threading through the space between us. "E...I'm so sorry," she whimpered. "I didn't know. I chose not to chase after details. I knew enough to know that you were okay."

I shook my head. "It's cool, Sunshine. I had the experience I was supposed to have, but like you said, it doesn't matter now." It was a lie. It did matter. The years, the choices, the love stolen from us under the guise of protection. I kissed her temple, my grip constricting like I could make up for the time we had lost. "We lost years because of them. Because of him. Because they thought they knew what was best for us."

Summer nodded her silent agreement. I ran my thumb along her cheek, guiding her gaze back to mine. I needed her to see me—to hear me. "But I'm telling you right now, nobody decides for us anymore. You hear me?"

Her lips trembled for a moment, but when she spoke, her voice was stable, certain. "Nobody."

CHAPTER TWENTY-THREE

Summer
October 2019, The Calm After the Storm

THESE HAD BEEN the longest three days of my life. Only two days had passed since I had called off my wedding, but it felt like I had been drifting through time, caught between what was and what could have been. I still hadn't gone back to my house, instead finding comfort in the familiarity of my old tiny bedroom. The same four walls that had once held my teenage dreams and whispered secrets now held the woman I was trying to rediscover. And with my siblings still here, it felt like old times. I needed them more than they knew. Our mother, overjoyed to have all her babies under one roof, had taken it upon herself to feed us three times a day. If I stayed any longer, I was sure to leave at least ten pounds heavier—but I wasn't complaining. There was something healing about home-cooked meals and the kind of love that didn't require explanation.

I still hadn't checked my emails or social media. Didn't have the energy to. I could only imagine the speculation, the whispers, the carefully worded posts that weren't so carefully disguised. Thank God I worked for myself. My clients were already squared away, and I had planned to be offline for three weeks after the wedding anyway. The original plan was to spend that time basking in newlywed bliss. Instead, I would spend it figuring out my next steps without the weight of an almost marriage pressing on me.

Hailee, Brooke, and Trinity had come over multiple times demanding that we find somewhere—anywhere—to wear their bridesmaids' dresses. I had laughed, like truly laughed for the first time in days. They were a reminder that life moved on, even when I felt stuck. And finally, a full day turned to a night without me crying. I hadn't expected Deshawn to respond when I finally gathered the courage to check on him, but he did. A short, civil response. We still needed to settle some things—namely, the outstanding wedding expenses—but I was giving him space. I was prepared to cover the remaining costs and reimburse my parents for everything they had lost because, no matter the cost, I had to clean up what I had messed up.

And then there was Echo. He was leaving tomorrow. He wanted to change his flight—offered to, even. But he had a client waiting, and I insisted that he go. Not because I didn't want to spend more time getting to know the man Echo had become, but because I needed time to get to know the woman I was becoming. His disappointment was fleeting, but unmistakable, the silent question lingering between us. Was I planning to run away from him, too? I wasn't. I couldn't. Not anymore. But I needed time, and for the first time in my life, I was giving myself permission to take it.

I'd never been a morning person, but today, I was awake before the sun. Instead of lying in bed drowning in thoughts I couldn't organize, I got up and grabbed my sketchbook before heading to the kitchen. A cup of coffee and a doughnut was just what I needed. Sitting at the table allowed my feelings to run free in my art. I was so focused on drawing that I hadn't noticed the moment when the dark gave way to the light. The house was still quiet, but outside, the sun was beginning to rise, casting a golden haze over the backyard. I took a slow sip of my coffee, letting it warm my insides. This moment—this stillness—belonged to me. Soon, my siblings and their families would be up, filling the house with noise and laughter and chaos. But for now, for just a little while longer, I allowed myself to sit in the quiet and exist.

The sound of footsteps interrupted my haze. I turned toward the kitchen entrance and saw my mother standing in the threshold, the silk of her floral-print robe just grazing the floor, her hair still wrapped tight in a scarf. Even this early in the morning, she was a beauty.

I smiled. "Good morning, Mama."

"Good morning, baby girl," she said around a yawn. "You hungry? I'm going to cook after I have my tea and say my prayers."

I shook my head. "Not only am I unwed, but you're going to make me fat, too," I quipped, but Mama did not share my amusement.

Her lips pressed into a firm line as she prepared her morning cup of tea. "Summer Sierra, don't say things like that," she fussed.

I sighed, looking at my shero. After days of crying, my mind was finally clear enough to see it—the quiet hurt lingering beneath her expression. My smile faded. "I'm sorry, Mama."

She turned, her brown eyes already brimming with emotion. Closing our distance, she sat across from me, placing her cup on the table. Swiping away a tear, Mama leaned back in the chair before folding her arms across her body protectively. "You should have talked to me, Summer." Her voice was soft, but firm. "When have you ever not been able to talk to me?"

I shook my head, struggling to suppress the sudden thickness in my throat. "I honestly thought I could go through with it—that everything in my head was just nerves, my mind playing tricks on me." I looked away as the morning of my wedding replayed in sharp, agonizing detail. "But that morning, I woke up in a cold sweat, like something bad had happened. And then I remembered my dream…" I waited, inhaling shakily. "A vivid depiction of my wedding day… but Shawn wasn't in it. He wasn't there."

Mama held her teacup in one hand while the other gently caressed the top of mine. "Let me guess," she said knowingly. "It was Echo."

I nodded.

"I figured." A small smirk tugged at her lips before she took a sip of tea. "That boy's name has always had a way of lingering in your heart."

I sighed, a quiet delight warmed my cheeks. "He told me he loves me…still."

Mama didn't react—not in shock, not in judgment. She simply watched me, letting me find my own words. "And the crazy thing is, it was so easy for me to tell him I loved him, too. On the day I should have been destroyed." I shook my head, still reeling. "But I don't know what to do with that now. Everything feels so complicated."

Mama arched a brow. "Complicated how? Seems pretty straightforward to me."

I rubbed my temples. "You sound like Echo."

She shrugged, as if that wasn't surprising. "So, what's the real issue?"

I sighed, pressing my lips together before the words tumbled out. "Oh, I don't know… Maybe because I just left a man at the altar? Because I've spent a good part of my adult life pretending I was over Echo? Or maybe because I'm afraid." My voice faltered, my fears spilling out of me faster than I could stop them. "Afraid to open that door again. We were fast and furious back then, but we're not kids anymore."

Mama hummed, the calculated kind that always made me brace myself, then she leaned back, studying me. "Let me ask you something, baby girl." Her voice was gentle but pointed, like she already knew the answer. "If there were no past, no expectations, no opinions but your own, what would you want?"

I stammered because I was completely caught off guard by the simplicity of the question. But when I closed my eyes, the answer came too easily, almost painfully so. Barely above a whisper, I exhaled the only truth I knew: "Him."

Mama nodded, taking another sip of tea. "You know, I often think about that day we met with Echo's parents," she started, her voice present but distant, as if she was looking through time itself.

She never said it outright. Never could. My pregnancy. The clinic. The choice that changed everything. It was always wrapped up in the phrase *that day*.

"I didn't think love between two kids could be so potent," she said, "but I saw it in that living room. I saw it at the clinic. And I see it now." She paused, brushing a gentle finger down the side of my face, her touch warm and supportive. "You've been looking for everything Echo gave you in just one summer in other people, but it's time for you to accept that nobody can fill those shoes but him." She lifted an affirming brow, as if daring me to deny it.

I swallowed hard. "What if it's not as simple as you and Echo seem to think?" I asked.

"*Tuh.*" Mama made a small *tsk*, the sound laced with amusement and warning. "Baby, love ain't supposed to be perfect. It ain't always neat and convenient. But real love?" She leaned in, her voice dipping. "Real love has a way of making you face yourself. Face your fears. And I think Echo has been doing that to you since the moment you laid eyes on him."

A blush crept up my neck, warming my face. She wasn't wrong. Mama gave me a moment, letting her words settle, then reached across the table and tilted my chin up gently, forcing our eyes to meet. "Love, when it's real, has a way of finding you no matter how far or fast you run. If you want him, then fight for him, Summer. But if you walk away…" She exhaled, holding my gaze with quiet certainty. "Don't do it because you're scared. Do it because you're sure."

The words settled in my soul like an undeniable truth. Deep down, I already knew. I had never been sure of anything the way I was sure of Echo. For a moment, relief washed over me, light and intoxicating, the salvation of truth wrapping around me like the scent of fresh roses, but Mama didn't let me float in it for long.

"Now, what you did, Summer Sierra, was wrong—dead wrong." Her sharp tone jolted me, ripping me from my gleeful disposition like a record scratch. "You had ample opportunity to talk to Deshawn and end whatever you two had before it came to this. If I weren't so worried about your li'l ass, I would've popped you in your mouth myself." I winced. The mushiness? Completely gone. "I didn't raise my daughter to hurt people."

I let every shot land, blinking through the sting because I deserved this. My fingers found my earlobe, grasping onto something—anything—to hold myself together. Mama sighed, shaking her head. "Honestly, Deshawn wasn't my first pick, but that doesn't give you the right to hurt him." My head jerked up, caught off guard by her words. She noticed right away, her expression thoughtful, measured. "I just always felt like you were settling for what was safe instead of what was meant for you."

Settling. Ouch. The word stung.

"Deshawn is a good man—everything a mother would want for her daughter," she admitted, "but I knew you wouldn't be happy long-term with him."

"You never said anything."

"It wasn't my place," Mama said, a light shrug lifting her shoulders. "You were moving forward, building a life with him, and I thought maybe I was wrong. Maybe you saw something I didn't. But I also knew I'd be there to help you pick up the pieces if necessary." She gave me a long, pointed look. "And I hope and pray that one day he can forgive you…but none of us will forget anytime soon, including you."

The words landed like a boulder dropping right in the center of my chest.

She sighed, shaking her head as she leaned back in her chair. "But I understand one thing, baby girl. The heart leads the way, even when our mind tells us to take another path."

I sucked back the tears, my eyes stinging. The truth was I had been following my mind for years. And now, my heart was begging me to listen. I smiled, feeling lighter, as if Mama's words had stitched together something inside me that had been torn for years. This was exactly what I needed—a come-to-Jesus conversation that only a mother could provide.

Standing, I squatted in front of her, grabbing her hands, holding on to her like she was my lifeline. "I love you, Mama. Thank you."

I barely got the words out before I fell into her embrace, burying myself in the warmth that had always been my refuge. Mama's arms always felt like home—a place where I was safe, protected, no matter how lost or broken I felt. It wasn't just an embrace. It was certainty. Comfort so pure and unconditional, it wasn't something you could see or touch. It was a feeling. She held me tight, stroking my back in soothing circles, just like she had done when I was a little girl. Then, with perfect timing, she pulled away, tilted my chin up with that familiar mischievous glint in her eye, and smirked.

"Now, I have to find somewhere for your daddy to take me so I can wear my dress. I looked good yesterday, girl," she teased.

We burst into laughter, the sound filling the kitchen, wrapping around us like the sweetest kind of relief. For the first time in days, I let myself feel light, without hesitation. Without guilt. Because if there was one thing Mama had just reminded me of, it was that love—real love— always finds a way.

CHAPTER TWENTY-FOUR

Echo
October 2019, The Calm After the Storm

I STEPPED INTO the kitchen where my parents sat having their morning coffee. I hadn't seen moments like this often growing up. My father worked so much. Always moving, always providing. But now that he was retired—well, semi-retired, since he still dabbled in teacher training—they spent mornings like this together more often. Mum lifted her eyes to look at me, apology and sympathy woven into her gaze. Her sweet spirit was unchanging, unwavering, and I knew she had only ever followed my father's lead. Followed tradition. So the blame wasn't on her.

"I'm headed to the airport," I said, crossing the room to place a kiss on my mother's cheek. She stood, and I bent to wrap her in a hug, savoring the warmth of her embrace.

"I can drive you," my father offered.

I had every intention of ignoring him until Mum spoke up. "So soon?" she asked. "I thought your flight doesn't leave until three."

I nodded. "I don't need a ride. Summer is picking me up for breakfast, then taking me to the airport."

He nodded, eyeing me carefully. A sigh escaped him. I wasn't ready to make this long-overdue talk easy for him. After Summer told me what happened between her and my father—what he said to her, how he sent her away like she was nothing—I had to have a man-to-man conversation with him. Yeah, he'd apologized in his own way, but it was nothing more than a string of excuses tied together with the threadbare justification of tradition. While my hurt from the abortion was a wound that would never fully heal, I had come to terms with that reality. What I couldn't wrap my head around—what I wasn't sure I would ever be able to forgive—was him removing her from my life. He knew—shit, everybody knew—how I felt about Summer, so for him to look her in the eye and tell her to disappear…to deliberately drive the dagger farther into my chest. That was something else entirely. He'd watched me walk around numb, drowning in grief and depression, and he had never uttered a word about his exchange with her. Never told me she had come for me. And that realization? Forgiving that was going to take time.

I watched as my father stood, crossed the room with his coffee cup in hand, and placed it in the sink. He didn't say a word, just grabbed his book and walked out of the kitchen like any other day. I knew where he was going: the front porch. He had been reading there before he took a walk for years, always in that same worn chair, always with that same quiet presence. Mum watched him leave, too. She lingered at the doorway, thirty years of love, of knowing, of understanding. Then she turned her attention back to me. My mother was a gentle soul, always knowing how to calm me, how to correct me without saying much at all. She squeezed my hand, her thumb gliding over my skin in quiet reassurance.

"We…he did the best he knew how, Echo." Her voice was gentle, but there was something else in it, too. A quiet pain. Regret, maybe. "I didn't know she came looking for you until months later," she admitted. "I gave him a lashing when I found out." She chuckled, but it was a sad sound. "But I kept my husband's secret."

I nodded because I understood. "I get it, Mum." She searched my face, as if trying to see just how much I truly meant those words. "I said what I needed to say to him. I accept his apology, but it's just going to take some time."

She nodded, placing a soft kiss on my cheek. "I prayed that if your hearts carried even a fragment of what you two once meant to each other, that God would bring you back together." I braced myself for the scripture that would certainly follow.

"Matthew, chapter seven, verses seven and eight," she recited, her voice full of conviction. *"Ask, and it will be given to you; seek, and you will find; knock, and the door will be opened to you. For everyone who asks receives, the one who seeks finds, and the one who knocks, the door will be opened."* She lifted a discerning brow, as if she already knew exactly what I was seeking.

I pressed a kiss to her forehead, thankful for the prayers of my mother. "Thanks, Mum. I'm giving her space, so I hope your prayers are being answered."

No matter how certain I was about her, I still wasn't sure if Summer was ready for what I was seeking.

A chime sounded from my phone, pulling me from my thoughts. I glanced at the screen. It was Summer. She was outside. "I gotta go, Mum. I love you."

"I love you, too, son," she said, settling back into her chair.

I grabbed my backpack and started toward the door, but before I could step out, her voice called me back. "Oh, Echo."

I turned. "Ma'am?"

She smiled, eyes full of something I couldn't name. "Proverbs, chapter eighteen, verse twenty-two."

Together, we recited, *"He who finds a wife finds a good thing, and obtains favor from the Lord."*

Mama winked, satisfaction glowing in her features as, amused, she walked out of the kitchen. But the moment I opened the front door, the ease disappeared. Expecting to see my father on the porch, I picked up my suitcase and stepped outside, only to find Summer standing next to her car talking to my father. I slowed my pace as I took in the scene. At the sound of the front door closing, my father turned, his usual stoic expression unreadable. I tensed instantly, my grip tightening around the suitcase handle. *What the hell is he saying to her?*

My gaze snapped to Summer, ready to step in and shut this shit down if necessary, but she wasn't tense. Her lips curved a bit, a faint trace of a smile—small, barely there, but unmistakable. Then, she shook her head ever so slightly. Just enough for me to notice. Silently signaling for me to stand down. I exhaled sharply but obeyed. Dragging my luggage down the walkway, I reached my father but then halted. What was I supposed to do here? He wasn't the hugging type, and after everything that had gone down between us, I wasn't sure if I even wanted his embrace. But then, without hesitation, he lifted his hand and patted my shoulder then a simple nod.

"I'm about to take my walk. Have a safe flight, son." His voice was even, carrying its usual firmness.

I nodded, trying to decipher what had shifted. Older. Maybe wiser. But still the same. A man of few words, of firm decisions, of burdens he'd carry but never confess. Mum had said he did the best he knew how. And maybe...maybe that had to be enough. I returned his gesture, clapping a hand against his back before stepping away. No extra words. No forced reconciliation. Just an understanding that it would take time. I watched as he started his slow stroll down the sidewalk, hands tucked behind his back, posture straight despite the years resting on his shoulders, then I exhaled and turned toward the car.

Summer eyed me with a sweet smile painted on her face. I winked, then placed my bags in the trunk. I rounded the car and slid into the passenger seat, closing the door behind me. I turned to her immediately, waiting for her to explain to me what the hell had just happened. But she was hushed. Not giving me anything. Deciding not to waste our time inquiring about my father, I studied her instead, taking in her features. She looked good. Rested. Something about her was lighter. That alone made my shoulders loosen.

"You good, Sunshine?" I asked, then gently pinched the tip of her nose.

She turned to me, her lips twitching at the nickname. "Yeah, I'm good."

I wanted to ask her when she was planning to leave her parents' house—to resume her routine. Hell, I wanted to beg her to get on this plane with me. But instead, I just sat back and enjoyed the ride, letting Jill Scott croon through the speakers about being put back together again. I wondered if that's how my Sun felt about us. We pulled into the parking lot of First Watch, and before we even stepped inside, I could tell this was her spot. As soon as we walked in, one of the waitresses greeted her like they were old friends.

"You come here often?"

"Mm-hmm." She slid into the booth across from me. "Sometimes I come here to work when I can't focus at home."

I nodded, filing that piece of information away, then placed my order after she placed hers. The waitress returned a moment later with our coffee and water before scurrying off, giving us space, but I didn't waste time.

"Have you talked to him?" I asked, cutting straight to it.

She exhaled, stirring a sugar packet into her coffee. "I texted him, but we haven't talked."

"Did he respond?"

She gave me a small nod. "Yeah, surprisingly. While this is hard, I think we both know it was for the best. Saved us on attorney fees in the long run, I guess." Her words were light, but I saw the seriousness behind them.

I let a beat pass, then leaned forward. "When am I going to be able to see you, Summer?"

She lifted a brow, looking away as if searching for the right answer. "I don't know," she admitted. "I still have a lot to figure out—clean up my shit, as my daddy told me yesterday."

She laughed, shaking her head, and I had to laugh too because Mr. Knight was like my father, a straight-shooting man of few words but unquestionable truths.

I sighed, leaning in. "This is going to sound crazy, but I want you to take the time you need…" I reached across the table, taking her hands in mine. "I just don't want you to take too long."

She didn't pull away, but she didn't meet my eyes either. Instead, she changed the subject. "What did you say to your dad?"

I drew in a slow breath, steadying myself. "What did my dad say to you?" I shot back, unwilling to let her deflect so easily.

She paused for a beat, fingers tightening slightly around her coffee cup. "He…apologized…I think."

My brows pulled together. "You think?"

Shrugging, she fiddled with her hoop earring. "In his own way, I guess. But yeah, I'm pretty sure it was an apology." A short pause followed, then, "He even asked about my parents."

I relaxed in my seat, rolling my shoulders as I processed that. My father? Asking about her family? I snickered, rubbing a hand over my jaw. "Well, damn."

Summer then tilted her head to the side. "Now your turn."

I shrugged, my thumb absentmindedly tracing circles over the back of her hand. "I spent my whole life following my dad's rules—trying to be who he wanted me to be. It was a life that looked good on paper but never felt right." Her eyes lifted to meet mine. She knew all too well the pursuit of false perfection. "I told him I don't want to live like that anymore," I said steadily and with certainty. "I want a life that looks *and* feels perfect, and I told him that was you."

Her mouth opened slightly, as if she had something to say, but the words never came. I let the moment settle between us before reaching into my bag.

"I have something for you." I pulled out a box I had grabbed when we got out of the car.

She didn't say a word as I slid it across the table. But the coy blush in her eyes? That said everything. She untied the bow, peeling back the wrapping paper with careful fingers before lifting the lid of the box. A sharp gasp escaped her, and her eyes misted instantly at the sight inside.

"E," she whispered. That one letter, my name on her lips, never failed to send a shiver through me.

I bit the corner of my lip, watching her take it in. "I found my sketchbook buried in a box in my closet," I admitted. "I drew so many pictures that summer, I didn't even remember this one. But when I saw it again…it just felt right."

Reaching into the box, I lifted the framed sketch, turning it toward her so she could see it fully. It was her. Crisscrossed legs on the tree stump draped with a blanket, sketchpad on her lap, lost in her own world. I shaded the curve of her face, the way her lashes cast delicate shadows against her cheeks, how her bottom lip jutted out just slightly when she concentrated. The moment was captured just as a cluster of butterflies surrounded her, drawn to her like they belonged there. She was art. She always had been.

She brushed over the edge of the frame. "It's beautiful, Echo," she said.

But I wasn't looking at the drawing. I was looking at her. I searched her face, trying to unscramble the thoughts running through her mind. And when her gaze lifted to mine, I saw it... reverence, care, something deeper, something adoring. Then, she smiled. That dimpled, breathtaking smile that had owned me since we were kids.

"I prayed last night," she whispered. "I prayed that this thing...this love between us...doesn't just exist in memories or in the curiosity of 'what if.'" Her words rested deep in the cavernous corners of my heart. "I prayed for a second chance to get it right... when the time is right."

I appreciated her honesty, her vulnerability, and I needed her to hear mine.

"I'm not asking for this to be easy." I reached across the table, my fingers skimming over hers again. "I'm just asking for you to be mine."

The moment of silence was charged with something bigger than both of us.

"Here we go!" The waitress's cheerful voice broke the spell, snapping us back to reality.

Leaning back, I waited as the waitress placed our plates in front of us. I needed Summer to say she was ready to be mine, but I wouldn't push her—not now. So, just like that, I let our loaded past settle into the background, choosing instead to simply enjoy her in this moment. We shifted into easy conversation, normal banter, something light because the past three days had been heavy enough. I clung to every word of the woman Summer, just as I had the girl.

We arrived at the airport about an hour and a half before my flight. I insisted she pull into the garage instead of the drop-off lane. I needed a moment with her without the blaring horns or the rent-a-cop security waving us along like we were just another passing car. This moment wasn't fleeting. It meant something. I smirked, glancing ahead toward the terminal before leaning toward her.

"Damn. I want to pack you in my suitcase."

She blushed, but before she could respond, I kissed her. She didn't resist. Didn't hesitate. She kissed me back, hungry and urgent, her fingers tangling into my hoodie, pulling me closer. Fuck. I had to pull away before I walked through this airport with a damn problem in my pants. My dick was so damn hard. I rested my forehead against hers, my restraint was slipping by the second.

"Can I trust you, Sunshine..." My fingers found her chin, tilting her face up, brushing my lips there, savoring the moment, "to come to me when you're ready?"

Her eyes stayed closed, her body still lost in the moment—in me. "Yes. You can trust me."

I nodded, knowing this was me putting my heart on the line for her. "Check your email," I blurted out suddenly. Her brows furrowed. "Just do it."

That damn eye roll—it grounded me in the past and present all at once. A piece of our history that I wouldn't dare change. She grabbed her phone, unlocking the screen before tapping into her inbox. A second later, her breath hitched. "E," she said, questioningly.

Sitting there, clear as day, was a confirmation email for a one-way ticket to LA. Sent to her an hour ago. I had known I was going to buy it. I just waited for the perfect moment.

"If you haven't figured it out yet, this is me...being pressure." I winked.

She bit her bottom lip, but I didn't let her keep it for long. I captured it between my own, stealing back the control—taking what was mine. This kiss wasn't slow. It wasn't careful. It was needy. Burning. Wild. I tangled my fingers in her hair, gripping tight, desperate and consumed as we pressed harder against each other. I was ready to pull her across this center console and fuck her right here in the car. And judging by the way she gripped the back of my head, the way she moaned greedily into my mouth, so was she. Fuck. Fuck. Fuck. I forced myself to break the kiss, my breaths coming hard and unsteady. "Sun. Sunshine." My voice was rough, weighted with restraint. "Baby, I gotta go."

Her swollen lips grazed mine before she pulled away, easing back against the driver's seat, rubbing her mouth like she could still feel me there. I reached for the door handle, needing to get the hell out of this car before I missed this flight.

"I can drive you around," she offered, her fingertips skirting against my arm, as if she wasn't ready to let me go just yet.

I shook my head, forcing myself to be stronger than I felt. "If I don't walk away now, I won't let you leave."

She smiled. It was tender, delicate, and devastatingly exquisite. It shot straight through my damn heart. I kissed her hand, letting my lips rest there for just a second longer than necessary, then I forced myself out of the car. Retrieving my bags, I rounded the car, stopping at her window. I bent, taking her face in my hands, kissing her one last time. Not hesitant. Not hurried. Just enough. Enough to make sure she felt me long after I was gone. I pulled away, my lips barely brushing against hers as I whispered, "I love you."

She didn't stall. Didn't avoid me. "I love you back."

CHAPTER TWENTY-FIVE

Echo
December 2019

SINCE MOVING TO California, one thing I'd always missed about the Midwest was winter. Maybe I was one of the few who actually loved the crisp, biting air filling my lungs; the way the chill clung to my skin long after stepping inside, especially in December, when every home and storefront glowed with festive lights and decorations, turning the city into something almost magical. But the real treat? Snow. Whenever we were lucky enough to get it, the whole world changed. A fresh, quiet blanket covered the streets, rooftops, and trees, softening the edges of everything. And for a little while, the city slowed down, wrapped in a peaceful kind of stillness.

Winter in Los Angeles was a complete contradiction. The sun shone boldly, the sky a brilliant blue. The air carried a hint of crispness—just enough to remind you it was December, but never enough to bite. The city hummed with the energy of the holidays, palm trees wrapped in twinkling lights, fake snow dusting storefronts. And then there was the scent—a mix of ocean breeze and cinnamon spilling from local bakeries and coffee shops. A strange blend, but somehow it worked.

It was the middle of December, one of those days where I was out before the sun rose and didn't get back until it dipped behind the moon. A long-ass day. One of those chilly evenings where a jacket was necessary, but my friends and business partner still insisted on sitting outside for dinner. I declined. I wanted to go home. It had been over a week since I'd heard from Summer, and her absence was pissing me off. Since I'd left St. Louis, we'd been like a *90 Day Fiancé* trial run—getting to know each other all over again through FaceTime calls, sharing lovey-dovey Instagram messages, late-night texts of *I miss you*. Then suddenly, it stopped. Actually, no. I knew exactly why it stopped. A couple of weeks ago, I'd asked her to spend Christmas and New Year's with me. And instead of an answer, she just went silent. She had promised me she'd come to me when she was ready. Maybe she wasn't ready. And that terrified me. Because I was—I had been. And I couldn't keep waiting, couldn't keep standing still while she decided if she'd ever meet me there. The uncertainty gnawed at me, hollowing me out in ways I didn't want to admit. I told myself I was done waiting, but that was a lie. If I could have truly moved on, I wouldn't be here. Wouldn't still be waiting for her like she was the only thing that had ever made sense.

I pulled into my garage a little after seven, too drained to even stop for food. Tonight would be a delivery night. Stripping out of my clothes, I stepped into the shower, letting the steam clear my head. Craving didn't even begin to describe what I felt for Summer. I yearned for her. Not just sexually, though don't get me wrong, I was more than ready to bury myself inside of her. But it was more than that. I needed her touch. The sound of her voice. I hadn't realized how much she calmed me until she was gone. Tonight, my plan was simple: eat, then call Summer. And if she didn't answer? I had a voice text ready to go, demanding answers. *Who am I kidding?* If I were being honest, the message wasn't about closure, it was about holding on. About forcing a response, anything to keep this thing between us from slipping further into the silence. I wanted answers, but more than that, I wanted proof that she was still on the other side of this, still tethered to me in some way. And if she wasn't? If she let the call ring out, ignored my words, made it clear that I was the only one still trying, then I'd have no choice but to walk away. I'd done it before—lived without her, moved on, survived—so I could do it again, right?

Lying ass nigga. Hell no, you can't do it again. Even the thought of sending the message made my stomach churn. I wasn't ready for what came next if she didn't respond.

My phone chimed. For half a second, I let myself hope it was her, but I knew better. It was just the app letting me know that Marco was two minutes away with my food. I ran a hand over my jaw before sliding into gray sweatpants and a black t-shirt. I poured myself a glass of whiskey, the ice clinking as I walked over to the living room, rapping softly along to Kendrick Lamar playing through the surround sound. I could already taste the mushroom chicken and vegetable lo mein from my favorite Chinese spot, and after the day I'd had, I needed something warm and familiar. But Marco needed to hurry the hell up because I was starving.

Grabbing a bottle of water from the fridge, I downed it in a few gulps as I headed to the front door. I was going to need hydration because I planned to have a few glasses of whiskey tonight. Peeking through the frosted window, I saw the glow of headlights pull into the driveway. Finally. I didn't even wait for him to knock, I walked out to meet him, handed him a tip, thanked him, and was about to head inside when a blue car with an Uber sign in the windshield made a U-turn and pulled up in front of my house. I frowned.

Who the hell is that in an Uber?

For a second, I was ready to curse out whoever thought now was the time to play games coming to my house unannounced. But then, my expression eased, my breath hitched. I blinked—once, then again—making sure my imagination wasn't fucking with me. Because it was *her*.

A brown peep-toe boot hit the pavement, followed by a long leg wrapped in fitted jeans. Then came the deep orange sweater, a plaid cape draped over her shoulders, tortoiseshell glasses sitting high on her nose. The streetlight hit the wavy tresses of the new bobbed haircut as she pushed a few stray hairs behind her ear. And suddenly the food in my hands was forgotten. She smiled at the driver as he pulled two large suitcases from the trunk. I couldn't move. I was too busy taking her in. And she looked exactly as I remembered. Exactly as I'd dreamed about every damn night since I'd boarded that plane.

Then, her gaze lifted, landing on me. She froze, realization dawning as I stood there. And in that moment, I saw it—the slight catch in her breath, the way her lips parted just so, the hesitation laced with something that felt like hope. I leaned against the doorframe, ignoring the mouthwatering scent of food teasing my nose. My focus stayed on her, my voice smooth but tinged with something else.

"You lost, Sunshine? You sure you're in the right place?" I asked, fighting the urge to run and scoop her into my arms.

She smirked, but there was something beneath it—an edge of nervous energy she couldn't quite mask.

"You've always enjoyed getting on my nerves," she teased, but she still hadn't moved.

She stood at the end of the driveway, her purse hanging from her shoulder, hands gripping the suitcase handles. Waiting. Waiting for me to say something. To invite her in, I guessed. But she required no invitation. As far as I was concerned, she was already home. I moved toward her slowly, deliberately, dissolving the space between us. Hopefully putting her at ease.

"You traveled all this way just to talk shit? Or do you actually have something to say to me?" I bit my lip, stepping right into her space.

She shrugged, her confidence faltering just a little. Then, shyly she said, "It's been a minute. I didn't know if you'd still want me here."

Shaking my head, I briefly shifted my focus down the street then back to her. "*Hmm.* Considering I told you exactly where I'd be when you were ready—where I've wanted you to be all along—you shouldn't have any doubts." I moved in closer, desiring to mesh our bodies into one. "Have I given you reason to doubt me, Sun?" I said against her lips.

She quivered, wanting me, but she held back. Instead, she shrugged again, tossing up her hands like she was surrendering. *Here I am. Take me or leave me.* I was ready to take her. Forever. I swallowed hard, trying to ground myself, but my voice came out rough anyway.

"Are the loose ends tied?" She nodded. "What took you so long?"

She looked past me—almost through me—before her focus returned.

"I needed to be sure. I didn't want to come to you broken, full of regrets and second thoughts. I didn't want to bring you a half-hearted version of myself, Echo. I wanted to be ready…for you. For this."

I bit my lip, fighting like hell to keep my emotions in check. She leaned into me, desperate, pulled by something unseen. We were still outside. Neighbors coming home. Dogs being walked. The world continued moving around us. But in this moment? Nothing existed. I wanted to cradle her in my arms. Devour her.

But I wouldn't. Not yet. She'd taken her time to make sure she was ready—for me, for this. So I couldn't rush it. Wouldn't. I needed to move with the same patience, the same thoughtfulness. Summer brushed her lips against mine. Just barely. Just enough. Then, she wrapped me in an embrace so warm, so full of love, it was as if she had read my heart before I even spoke.

"If you haven't figured it out yet, this is me...being pressure," she teased, and my damn dick lurched. She was using my words, and I loved that shit. Then she said, "E, I'm here, and I'm ready."

The world tilted, and my fucking lungs stopped working. I gripped her face firmly, my free hand clutching her jaw as I searched her eyes, needing to be sure, needing to see if there was any apprehension—any trace of indecision. There was none. A slow burn settled in my chest, heavy with the weight of everything it had taken for us to get here. I fought against the lump in my throat, telling myself I wasn't about to cry. But damn, it was close. Summer Sierra Knight. My Sun. She was standing in front of me asking to be mine. I didn't know if I should kiss her senseless or make her say it again just so I could hear the words over and over. Instead, I needed reassurance.

"You sure about that, Sunshine?"

Her dimples sank into her cheeks as she wrapped her arms around me again. Those pretty brown eyes carried a smoldering fire, glowing with certainty and intent. "I've never been more sure of anything in my life."

Fuck it. My self-control was non-existent after hearing her confession. I cupped her face, nearly dropping the damn food in my hand. Without a second thought, I tossed the bag onto her suitcase, my fingers tracing over her cheeks, memorizing every curve, every detail. This was the face I wanted etched into my memory forever. The one stricken with love and happiness. And then, I crashed my mouth into hers. A slow, deep, and consuming connection. A kiss full of everything said and unsaid. Weeks—shit, years—of wondering, longing, anticipating, all of it was wrapped up in the way our mouths moved, in the way our tongues tangled. Our bodies melted into each other—grasping, squeezing, holding on like letting go wasn't an option. Right there, in front of my house, for the whole damn world to see.

And Summer clung to me like she needed proof I was real. Like she needed to be claimed. Reluctantly, we pulled back, but barely. Our foreheads stayed pressed together, breaths mingled, lips hovering in that charged space between restraint and surrender.

"So…does this mean I'm staying?" she asked.

A slow, leisurely smirk pulled at my lips. If I didn't have to grab her suitcases, I would've scooped her up right then. Instead, I clutched her ass, pulling her flush against me, burying my face into the curve of her neck. I dragged my lips up to her ear, kissing there before speaking.

"Do you really have to ask? The real question is how long are you staying?"

We held each other's attention, knowing her answer would set the course for whatever came next. "For as long as you'll have me," she said.

I bit my lip. "That's what I thought…. You're staying forever."

She didn't let go, refusing to release me, just as I refused to release her. With one arm still wrapped around her, I grabbed the luggage handles while she secured the food. We walked inside clumsily, bumping into each other as if it were the most natural thing in the world. Because it was. This was who we had always been. Who we were. I kicked the door closed behind us, and just like that, she was home.

CHAPTER TWENTY-SIX

Summer
December 2019

WALKING INTO ECHO'S place felt surreal. I'd spent years wondering what his life looked like now, stitching together scraps of his life—secondhand stories, social media snapshots, and the one run-in with his sister. When I asked the simple question—how is he? Her answer was simple: He's good. But now, I was here, in his space, in his world, for an undetermined amount of time. It felt both insane and inevitable at the same time.

"Are you hungry? I was about to eat," Echo said, pulling me from my daze.

I nodded. "Yeah. I could eat."

He licked his lips, sending a shiver down my spine. My steps were slow, unsure, because...what now?

"Come in, Sunshine. I don't bite. Make yourself at home." He winked. "I'll get your bags and show you around after we eat."

I settled at the kitchen island, replying to text messages from my mother, my sisters, my friends—all checking to make sure I'd arrived safely. When Echo left St. Louis for LA a few months ago, I felt lost. Those few days together after my wedding disaster had changed everything, made it impossible to return to the life I had built with Deshawn. I'd had half a mind to hop on the next flight after Echo, but I promised him that I would tie up my loose ends before stepping into this new beginning.

And I had. I took the weeks I would've been off for my honeymoon and spent them doing some deep, painful soul-searching. Then, I did the hardest thing: I faced Deshawn. Our final meeting had been awkward, yet oddly peaceful. We hadn't spoken since that night in the sunroom, and now we were two people standing at the end of something that had never quite had a real beginning.

When I told him I was considering moving to LA, he wasn't surprised. *"You're going after what you've always wanted,"* he'd said, his voice calm but knowing.

And I knew exactly what he meant: *Echo*. When I slid the engagement ring across the table, he studied it for a long moment before pushing it back toward me. *"Keep it,"* he'd murmured, but I'd refused. I didn't want any part of my past tethering me to a life I no longer belonged to.

I took a sip of the deep red wine Echo had poured me, watching him move effortlessly in his space—the way he plated our food, the way his broad shoulders flexed, the casual confidence in every movement. This was his world, and I was finally stepping into it. He carried the plates to the dining table and motioned for me to join him. He didn't ask about Deshawn. Didn't press for answers about what came next. We simply existed together, enjoying each other.

After dinner, Echo gave me a tour of his condo. It was stunning. The floor-to-ceiling windows framed a breathtaking view of the city. The color palette was dark and sophisticated, a balance of deep blues, rustic tones, and ivory—undeniably masculine but with a refined, homey touch. The kind of space that felt lived in, but not lonely. When he pulled me into his bedroom, I took in grown-man Echo.

"Your place is beautiful, E," I said.

"Thank you." He scanned the room as if seeing it through my eyes. "Kemi did her thing."

My brows lifted. "Kemi decorated?"

He laughed. "Yeah. My sister's got skills. Taxed the hell outta me for it, too."

"Damn. She's good."

"Yeah. She's killing it. Already got a few celebrity clients under her belt." He paused, eyes tracing my face. "You wanna change, get cleaned up?"

I nodded, and he directed me to the bathroom. "I'll be in the living room. I want to show you something when you're done."

Fresh from the shower, wrapped in his robe, smelling like him, I moved down the hallway, drawn toward the soft glow of the city beyond his windows. Echo stood there, glass of wine in hand, the skyline reflecting in the window. He didn't turn when he spoke.

"You good?" he asked, reaching for me to come to him. I obliged, quickly diminishing the space between us. He lifted his glass to his lips then pressed a slow kiss to my temple.

I melted against him. *"Mm-hmm,"* I hummed. "I'd be even better if I had another glass of wine."

"I got you. Come on." He slid open the patio door, leading me outside, then up a winding staircase.

When I reached the top, I lost my breath. The rooftop was magnificent. The view stretched wide and endless, city lights flickering below, casting a soft glow. A pergola draped in soft lights framed an oversized couch and two lounge chairs. A stone pathway led to a small heated pool and Jacuzzi, its surface reflecting the moonlight. A fire pit flickered nearby, warmth combating the crisp night air. And on the couch sat a tray with an open bottle of wine and an empty glass waiting for me.

"I turned to him, awestruck. "E…this is amazing."

"I thought you'd like it." He moved behind me, pressing his body into mine, his warmth chasing away the night's chill.

His lips found the curve of my neck, soft, unhurried and deliberate kisses. His hands traced the familiar path of my body, exploring me, remembering me, claiming me. When he untied the robe and realized I was bare beneath it, his breath faltered.

He groaned, his voice raw, wrecked.

I tilted my head back, capturing his lips in mine. The kiss was messy, needy, hungry. Damn, I wanted him to fuck me. But I wanted to be made love to, too. If anyone could satisfy my need, it was him. I couldn't ignore the bulge pressing into my ass when he pressed his body into me. Given the soft breeze, he didn't remove the robe completely, just opened it slightly. Tiny bites to my neck and shoulders made me moan.

"Echo," I said as his hands roamed, grasping everywhere—sliding up my body and grabbing my breasts. They were so swollen and heavy, the touch of his cool hands dispatched a sensation that almost made me climax.

"Baby," he said before swallowing my tongue.

He gently brushed his hands down my stomach, sweeping his fingers over my smooth mound. Two fingers split open my folds, revealing my clit. He nipped and tugged at it, causing my knees to weaken.

"Echo, shit. Baby, that feels too good," I said.

"Nothing is too good for my Sunshine," he said.

He repeated that motion slowly, over and over, before slipping one finger, then two into my pussy.

"Oh my god," I yelped into the wind. I felt his face lift into a teasing grin against my cheek. He remembered that spot.

I refused to be the only one partaking in pleasure. I reached behind me, finding the waist of his joggers. My light scratches and tickles caused him to quiver. I slowly dipped into his pants, partially pulling them down, causing the inches of his dick to fall out. Pushing the bottom of the robe to the side, I arched my back a little so that his dick could nestle in the crease of my ass. I swayed up and down, massaging and stroking his girth with my round, plump backside.

"Sunshine, shit. That feels so fucking good," he said, grunting.

His fingers were still bound within my lush, wet walls, coated with my syrup. I'd lost control, and given his erratic motion, he had, too.

"E, please," I said.

"Please what, baby?" he said.

"Please fuck love to me," I said, my words making absolutely no sense.

He chuckled. "You want me to fuck you and make love to you, Sun?" he asked.

"Yes, Echo. Yes."

Echo
December 2019

"Please fuck love to me." The words tumbled from her lips, half moan, half plea. Damn, she was flustered, but I knew exactly what she desired and *why* she desired it. We'd only shared one sexual experience, so while this moment called for lovemaking, Summer wanted to be fucked—gently cherished while being wrecked and put back together. And I was more than willing to give her both. She trembled, on the brink of undoing when I released my fingers

from her wet center. Spinning her around in one swift motion, I hoisted her up, guiding her legs to wrap around my waist.

She nestled her face into the crook of my neck as I grazed my teeth along the delicate shell of her ear, her body trembling beneath my touch. I silently thanked my sister, Kemi, for convincing me to buy this expensive-ass reclining chaise because right now, it was the perfect place to *fuck-love* my Sunshine.

"E…" Her breathless, shaky voice shattered the haze wrapping around us.

Damn. Was she in her head again? I was ready to solicit, plead, conjure, and pray for Summer to let me lose myself in her, to explore every inch of her soft, soaked essence.

I exhaled slowly, steadying my voice. "What's wrong, baby?"

She shook her head. "Why am I so nervous?"

I kissed her forehead, sweeping my lips across her skin in lazy, featherlight strokes, then captured her mouth in mine.

"Because it's déjà vu." I smiled against her lips, pulling back just enough to study the misty depth of her gaze. "Under the stars. In our private oasis," I said, tracing the memory between us with my fingertips. "And because this is a turning point for us…just like last time. Just like our first time together."

Her eyes locked onto mine, heavy with muted certainty. "Because this changes everything…again," she said.

Instinctively, we nodded because we both knew there was no turning back.

A smile danced across her lips as she lifted her head to greet my mine. I didn't say a word, just covered her mouth with languid, dreamy kisses. I drew her in, closing the microscopic crevice, allowing our kindred heartbeats to unite as one. My careful kisses grew hungry, clinging to her pouty lips with a desperation I couldn't tame.

"Damn, Summer, I've missed you," I said, and I meant every word.

Summer's tears fell, their salty trace mixing with the sweetness of her lips against mine.

"Why are you crying, baby?" I asked, swiping the moisture from her face.

"I don't know...because I'm happy. Because I missed you. Because it's you. Because it's always been you."

My lips brushed her forehead before kissing down the length of her body. I paid special attention to the swollen chocolate-brown areolas, which I had envisioned in my dreams. Summer's impassioned murmur lodged in her throat as I continued my perusal. She gasped when my lips breezily brushed against her pulsating clit. The tip of my tongue casually fondled her, savoring the plump folds of her pretty pussy. My blunt fingertips regained entry as I mercilessly feasted on her treasure, guzzling her sweet juices like a deserted man whose thirst desperately needed to be quenched.

"Shit, Summer! You taste better than...*shit*, everything," I said, warming places that quickly became reacquainted with my touch.

It didn't register that Summer wasn't breathing until I spoke. "Breathe, baby. Breathe," I said, granting her license to exhale.

"E, please," she begged as an uninhibited hunger surged, jolting through her body. She rubbed and nibbled and pleaded like she'd been craving this beautiful battering.

I trailed my tongue up the beautiful bumps and smooth layers of her velvety skin. I wanted to take my time surveying her, beholding her, fucking revering *her*. My Summer Sun, my best damn friend—the love of my life.

"Summer, I love you," I said, my eyes were wet with emotions as I kissed her. "I will spend the rest of my days loving you, baby."

She cradled my face in her palms, holding me like I was something sacred. Something irreplaceable. Coveting me. Loving me. We dallied for a moment, the fifteen years racing in our minds. So much lost time, so many words left unsaid. But none of it mattered now because we were always meant to be. Yoked. Bound in ways deeper than flesh. Our bodies moved toward each other with instinctive trust, free of hesitancy, free of doubt. I let my gaze travel over her, drinking her in, memorizing the way her curves caught the moonlight, the way her breath hitched as I traced a path along her skin. To me, she was a masterpiece—my Mona Lisa. Timeless. Priceless.

Hypnotized by plump breasts, thick thighs, and the irresistible heat of her center, I groaned because I could no longer resist the unyielding desire to sink every inch of me into her ocean. Upon immediate entry, we zealously uttered, "Damn."

My strokes were unhurried and languid. I wanted to explore her, searching the deepest depths of her perfection. In and out, and back and forth, we entwined in the most delightful coupling. Tenderly, yet eagerly, I tossed her legs over both my shoulders, biting against her inner thighs, plummeting deeper, harder, faster.

"*Aah!* Oh my God. E. E," Summer moaned, unable to fully catch her breath.

"Summer Sierra Knight! Shit. You feel amazing." Calling her by her government name? I meant that shit. I could feel her begin to shudder against my skin. She was there, and I was ready to guide her through this climax.

"Let it go, baby. I know you want to," I teased, drawing my dick out to the tip before slowly easing back in. "You're safe with me, beautiful. You ready to come for me, Sunshine?"

"*Aaahh!*" she said. "Echo. *Mm-hmm.* Yes. Yes."

"*Mm-hmm.* That's it. That's my girl." I groaned, feeling my dick stiffen, on the brink of an explosion.

She was beautiful in the throes of an intense, spellbinding orgasm. I'd been her best-kept secret for far too long, but with every slow grind, I reminded Summer who the fuck I was. The pleasure and the pain of the moment felt so good and was long overdue. I glanced at her, shifting my weight before resting my head against her breasts. Our bodies melded as if we were one—no recognition of where she began and I ended.

I nestled my face in the folds of her dampened neck. "I love you," spilled weakly from my mouth.

The room was still and quiet other than our faint, labored breathing until she murmured, "I love you back."

A satisfied grin spread across my face. Because at last, I held the key, the one that unlocked the intricate, complicated masterpiece known as Summer. The girl who had tormented and captivated me since I was seventeen. The woman who had shaped my every want, my every defined longing. And now that I had it—had her—I wasn't giving that shit back.

CHAPTER TWENTY-SEVEN

Summer
March 2020

MARCH IN LOS Angeles had a way of being effortlessly beautiful. Mornings carried a crisp coolness, only to be softened by the warmth of spring by midday. The days stretched longer, bathed in a hazy light that made everything feel just a little more alive. I blinked, and somehow, three months had passed since I'd arrived in LA, and I was loving every minute of it. Maybe it was the city's easygoing yet electric energy. Or maybe it was the neighborhood—a perfect mix of city convenience and quiet, suburban charm. Or maybe, it was simply *him*. We'd certainly made up for lost time with weekly dates in the city, long walks in the park, Food Truck Fridays where we sampled everything in sight, and endless coastal drives for weekend getaways. Whatever this was between us, I loved it. There was no rush to define things, no pressure to put a label on it. Just the quiet understanding that I was his, and he was mine.

We never had to say it. Our actions said it for us. I moved forward with leasing my townhouse back in St. Louis, slowly shifting more of my life to California. Echo had even renovated the third bedroom into an office just for me, pulling me deeper into his world in ways neither of us could put into words. I let my gaze drift across the bedroom, landing on Echo, still fast asleep. A rare sight. It was Saturday morning, and for once, he actually planned to sleep in, which, for him, meant waking up at nine-thirty instead of six. That was one place where we were wildly different. He thrived in the early mornings; I wasn't my best self until well after ten. But this morning, sleep had escaped me, replaced by a craving for coffee and a warm pastry from the local bakery.

Instead of waking him, I sent a quick text, letting him know I was taking a walk. I slipped into a baby blue jogger set, laced up my sneakers, and tossed on a hat. Echo's neighborhood was thriving, an up-and-coming community filled with middle-aged professionals and growing families. Tree-lined streets wove between modern townhomes and sleek condos. Stepping onto the patio, I smiled and waved at joggers, dog walkers, and parents pushing strollers. The fifteen-minute walk to Main Street was exactly what I needed to clear my head. And let's be real, the caramel latte and apple fritter were calling my name. In the short time I'd been here, I'd already found my rhythm—the barista, Callie, who had perfected my order; the friendly woman who managed the small farmers market; and the corner store that always stocked my favorite snacks. I'd sometimes forget that the electric pulse of the city was just minutes away until nightfall, when it shimmered in the distance.

After grabbing some fresh fruit and veggies to juice later, I made a quick stop at the corner store before picking up my coffee order. An hour later, I walked back into the house, and like clockwork, Echo was up, lounging on the couch in nothing but his boxers, watching predictions for the day's college basketball games.

"Hey, bae," I greeted.

"Good morning, Sunshine," he said, tilting his head back on the couch to look at me.

He puckered his lips expectantly, and I couldn't fight my smile. I set the bags on the counter before walking toward him, leaning down to press my lips to his. His morning kiss was my favorite part of the day.

"You said you were grabbing coffee. Looks like you went shopping." His voice was still laced with sleep.

"Just picked up a few things for our juice and these." I handed him his coffee and a small brown paper bag, watching as his lips curl in appreciation.

"French toast sticks." He groaned playfully, tearing into the bag like he hadn't enjoyed the sweet deliciousness at least once a week.

I watched him, amused, until his wide grin slowly faded into something indescribable at the sight of the contents in the bag. A flicker of bewilderment, anticipation…joy.

"Summer, are you…?" His voice trailed off, as if he needed a moment to find the words.

I shrugged, staring at my bouncing leg. "I don't know. My period's late."

Echo reached up, his fingertips brushing against my chin, nudging me to meet his gaze.

"How late?" His voice was calm but still unreadable.

"Almost two weeks."

My eyes searched his, trying to decipher what he was feeling, but his expression gave nothing away. Without a word, he grabbed my hand and lifted me to my feet, then with quiet determination, he led me down the hall, straight to his bedroom, then into the bathroom. I swallowed, heart racing as I pulled down my pants and sat on the toilet. Too many reincarnated moments crowded the space. Too many times we'd stood on the edge of the unknown, waiting.

"E, I'm—" I started, but he lifted his hand, stopping me.

Shaking his head, he said, "Don't do that, Summer. Don't you dare apologize." His eyes softened. "For what?" Then, raising a questioning brow, his tone turned absolute.

"Whatever happens in the next few minutes, I'll tell you the same thing I told you last time... I got you, Sunshine."

The weight I hadn't realized I was carrying dissolved just a little. Oddly, this time, I didn't feel like my world was falling apart.

Echo—October 2020

"I don't think you're making it to the end of November, Sunshine," I teased, following Summer as she waddled up the steps to the rooftop. "We're gonna need a crane to get you up here."

She shot me a glare over her shoulder, chewing on a bite of French toast. "It's not funny, E. I already feel like the Michelin Man," she whined.

I shook my head, biting back a smile. It was October, and my Sunshine was eight months pregnant. After three positive pregnancy tests, we wasted no time scheduling a doctor's appointment to confirm. Summer cried, but this time, they were happy tears. She was five weeks along, and though the baby was technically the size of a pea, I liked blueberry better. After weeks of brutal morning sickness, we flew to St. Louis for her dad's birthday and surprised the family with the news. We were nervous, but the second they saw the pure joy on our faces, her parents were ecstatic. In true Obi Abara fashion, my father wasn't thrilled about another pregnancy before marriage, but he wished us well. My mother, on the other hand, couldn't contain her excitement and immediately started planning our baby's traditional Nigerian baptism gown.

I often thought back to that day in the clinic all those years ago, wishing I could've seen the stages of our baby's growth. That wasn't our time then. But now? I never missed an appointment. Never missed a chance to bond with our little blueberry. At almost seven pounds, the baby was already a chunkster. They loved rap music during the day and the sound of rain at night. And my Sunshine? She was a masterpiece—a breathtaking force of strength and beauty. Her belly was round and full, a rich, deep chocolate hue that seemed to glow. That delicate line running down the center was my favorite. It marked the journey her body had taken to bring our little soul into this world.

Well...maybe her hips and ass were my favorites, too. Because, *damn*. Pregnancy had given her curves an elegance, a soft, full confidence I couldn't take my eyes off of.

Sometimes, when she thought I wasn't watching, she'd rest a hand on her belly, in awe at the tiny kicks, or whispering softly, introducing herself as "Mommy" to the tiny person inside. Summer had always been a stunner. But pregnant? She was luminous—even with her swollen nose and puffy lips, I couldn't stay away from her.

"What are you writing in your journal tonight?" I asked, settling behind her on the chaise longue.

We'd spent so many nights out here just being together—our new sacred place. Summer adjusted, opening her pregnancy journal, a little tradition she kept most nights, unless she fell asleep mid-sentence.

"I'm writing about how your baby kicked my ass today," she grumbled.

I shook my head. "Hey now, don't talk about my blueberry like that."

She shot me a look, but I didn't miss the soft smile tugging at her lips.

"What would you call heartburn all day and a burning feeling in your butt? Sounds like an ass kicking to me." She chuckled.

I winced, mouthing, "*Ouch.*"

She laughed, shaking her head as she continued pouring her thoughts onto paper. Meanwhile, I sat back, sipping my wine while she drank her sparkling grape juice. Watching her like this had become one of my most cherished pastimes. There was something about the way she lost herself in her thoughts, the way her lips would purse in concentration, the way her fingers glided over the pages as if they carried something sacred. Summer flipped to the next page but then paused. Her brow pinched in confusion before softening as she began to read.

Hey Sunshine,

I've been sitting here for hours, staring at this blank page, trying to find the right words to ask the most important question of my life. But the truth is, there's nothing I could write that would ever capture how much I love you—how much I love us.

I remember the moment we found out that we were pregnant. Your eyes were filled with fear and wonder, searching mine to see if angst or panic would show up first. I'm not going to lie, my ass was definitely panicking, but honestly, all I felt was awe. All I imagined was you carrying the best parts of us.

These past months, I've watched your body change, watched you create life with a quiet strength that humbles me. I've memorized every moment—your sleepy smile in the mornings, the way your hands instinctively cradle your belly when you're lost in thought, the way you whisper to our baby when you think I'm not listening.

And one night, while I was lying next to you, whispering to our blueberry about how much I loved their mama, it hit me: I never want to spend another night, another morning, another lifetime without you.

I love you, Summer. I love this life we're building. Yeah, it's a little fast and furious and maybe even a little crazy, but this is us.

So, I decided to commemorate this moment in your journal because this isn't just a proposal. It's a promise to you and our baby.

I promise to love you with every part of me. To be the man who holds your hand through the hard days and the one who laughs with you on the best days. I promise to be the husband to always give you butterflies. I promise to be the father our child deserves.

I don't need anything extravagant. No grand gestures, no audience. Just you and me and the little blueberry between us.

So, what do you say, Sunshine? Will you marry me?

Yours truly,
Summer's Echo

EPILOGUE

Almost a Year Later

"HAS ANYBODY SEEN Summer?" Trinity asked, rushing into the hotel suite.

"What do you mean, 'Has anybody seen Summer?' She was in your room this morning," Brooke said, her face pinched with worry.

Trinity's gaze darted around the room. "You think she ran again?"

"Oh my God." Hailee's voice dropped to a whisper, her eyes nearly popping out of their sockets. "She wouldn't, would she?"

A tight, nerve-wracking silence gripped the room, each second stretching unbearably long, pounding like an unrelenting drumbeat. It was eerily reminiscent of the feeling that had gripped them almost two years ago—the same suffocating fear, the same chilling uncertainty.

"Wouldn't what?" Summer strolled in with effortless confidence, completely unbothered, the picture of calm. She took a slow sip from her bedazzled coffee cup, the word *Bride* elegantly scripted across the front.

Trinity yelped, "Gotcha." But nobody else thought it was funny.

"You really get on my nerves," Brooke said, rolling her eyes.

"What? What's wrong?" Summer asked, her brows knitting at their uneasy expressions.

Hailee plastered on a bright smile and nudged her toward the chair. "Nothing," she sang a little too sweetly. "Just...it's a beautiful day for a wedding, right?"

Summer scanned the room with suspicion. Something felt off. But instead of pressing, she took a slow breath and let it go. Today was her wedding day. And nothing—not lingering stares, not hesitant smiles—was going to ruin that. Her mind drifted to the love of her life.

Last night, when she and Echo were supposed to go their separate ways after the rehearsal dinner, he somehow found his way to her suite around one in the morning. They kissed and cuddled and simply reveled in the magic of the night before they committed forever until sleep finally stole them away. Echo slipped out before dawn, before the sun had even stretched across the sky, leaving her with a few extra hours of rest and the lingering warmth of him. And today? The only thing Summer felt was elation. She wouldn't dare compare today to the day she was supposed to marry Deshawn because there was no comparison. This time, everything was right. Echo was the right man in the right place at exactly the right time. He was...*butterflies*. The sun shone bright over Brighton Falls, the air was a perfect seventy-eight degrees, and the day ahead felt like it had been written just for them.

"Summer, make sure you eat something," Raqi ordered, lips pursed as a makeup artist carefully applied her lipstick.

Summer blinked, startled back into the present. "Yes, Mom," she teased, throwing her sister a playful look.

"Is Raqi bossing people around again?" At the sound of her mother's voice, the whole room erupted into excited squeals, completely ignoring the question. But Summer's eyes locked on the real reason for her joy.

"*Awww,* come here, my little blueberry." She reached out, heart full, arms wide, as her growing baby girl was carried into the room.

Quest Wynter Abara had arrived just one week after Echo proposed on the rooftop. Summer, in fact, did not make it to the end of November. Their baby girl came three weeks early, weighing just shy of eight pounds. She had Summer's round face, deep dimples, and million-dollar smile and Echo's dark eyes, tawny skin, and full lips. She was a gorgeous baby. And today, she was Mommy and Daddy's little wedding angel dressed in an all-white dress. The crystals woven into the tulle of her skirt glistened against her tiny sequin shoes. And her thick, curly hair was tamed beneath a sparkling headband. Quest was the most perfect piece of the life Summer and Echo had built together.

Summer's sisters, sisters-in law, and closest friends filled the bridal suite with laughter and love. The afternoon was spent sipping Bellinis, playing with Quest as she ran around the room on wobbly legs, and basking in the glow of the day. Dressed in floor-length gold gowns, their matching jewelry and nude-toned makeup highlighted their beauty effortlessly. The bridesmaids were stunning, but to Summer, nothing compared to the feeling of joy and excitement in the room. As she took it all in, her heart swelled with gratitude.

Walking away from her last wedding had been the hardest decision she'd ever made, but she would do it all over again for this. For *this future*, one where she was surrounded by the people who loved her and walking toward a man who would move mountains to make her happy.

In the groom's suite, Echo and the guys were the picture of Black excellence and elegance. They were dressed in meticulously tailored tan suits, accented with deep green silk ties and matching pocket squares. Bottles of bourbon and boxes of cigars lined the table, adding to the day's festivities. Lively banter mixed with the occasional clink of glasses filled the air as the photographer captured each moment.

But Echo? He could barely sit still. He paced the floor, his nerves wrapped in anticipation, his mind only on two things: his bride and his blueberry.

"Yo, E. You good, man? Calm down." Maxell gave his shoulder a firm pat.

He took a sip from his glass. "I'm good," he said, though the restless energy in his stance said otherwise. "I'm just ready."

One of the wedding coordinators walked in, carefully pinning boutonnieres onto their lapels. "The ladies need about fifteen more minutes," she informed them, glancing at her phone, "then we'll head down for the first look."

Just then, Mr. Abara and Mr. Knight stepped inside, arriving just in time to see the guys tossing back another pre-wedding toast. Mr. Abara shook his head, but there was a rare playful glint in his eyes. Mr. Knight's expression was warm—equal parts fatherly pride and gentle warning.

Extending his hand, Mr. Knight met Echo's gaze. "I trusted you with my daughter years ago," he said, his voice steady, "and I trust you now. Take care of her, son. Take care of your family."

Echo swallowed past the tightness in his throat, gripping his father-in-law's hand. "Yes, sir. They're safe with me. You have my word."

Mr. Abara stood back, allowing his son this moment with Mr. Knight. But as soon as their exchange was over, he stepped forward, closing the space between them.

"You ready?" his father asked, extending his hand.

Echo clasped it firmly, locking onto his father with the same unwavering intensity he'd inherited. "More than ready."

They held the moment between them, a silent acknowledgment of everything they'd been through. Over the years, they had worked diligently to mend the fractures in their relationship. Mr. Abara was still a man of few words, but he had learned to respect his son's choices.

"I'm very proud of you, Echo." His father's voice wavered, thick with emotion he rarely allowed himself to show. "Very proud." He swallowed hard, quickly pulling himself together.

Echo, however, let a single tear fall, unashamed. He nodded, his voice raw with gratitude. "Thank you."

Fifteen minutes felt like fifteen years as Echo stood waiting, his heart pounding with anticipation. He was finally about to see his two favorite girls. They had planned a first look before the ceremony—an intimate moment just for them before the whirlwind of the day swept them up. Camp Quest had been transformed into a breathtaking outdoor oasis, yet it still held the same magic as when they were kids. The quad where they'd first met was now framed by a canopy draped in cascading wisteria and lush greenery, the wooden beams entwined with soft ivory roses. Towering oaks and whispering willows stood silently guarding the space, their branches swaying lightly as sunlight filtered through the leaves. The fresh scent of florals filled the air, mingling with the excited whispers of arriving guests.

Echo watched the goings-on from the top of the hill where he waited at their sacred place. Raqi carried Baby Quest while Brooke steadied the train of the bride's gown, carefully guiding Summer toward her groom. The photographer stood off to the side, ready to capture the moment. The gentle rustling of the leaves signaled her arrival, but Echo felt her presence before he even turned. His shoulders tensed, his lips parted, an exhale slipping out like he'd been holding it for years. His hands flexed, longing to touch her as a pressure built deep inside him, too big to contain. She was everything. Summer was a vision. A timeless beauty. Her mermaid-style gown hugged every curve, the delicate lace molding to her body before flowing into a graceful, sweeping train. Her sheer cathedral-length veil, adorned with tiny pearls and diamonds, framed her radiant face. But it wasn't just the dress. It was her. The way she carried herself with a quiet confidence. Their eyes locked—bright, alive with nervous excitement and unwavering certainty. This moment—this day—belonged to them.

"Sunshine," he whispered, his voice barely holding together.

She smiled, warmth laced in her teasing tone. "Hi, bae."

He reached for her immediately, cupping her chin before pressing the sweetest kiss to her lips. Slow, thoughtful, full of everything unspoken between them. Then, with the kind of pride only a father holds for his little girl, his expression filled with pure admiration when he turned to retrieve their baby.

"Blueberry, you are beautiful," he said, his voice raw with feeling.

Quest practically burst with excitement, wriggling in Raqi's arms at the sight of her daddy. He covered her chubby cheeks in kisses, making her giggle wildly before reluctantly handing her back. As their families stepped away to give them a moment alone, Echo pulled Summer into his arms.

"Hi, Mrs. Abara," he said against her ear with an amused, knowing tilt of his mouth.

Her lips parted in silent amusement, fingers twisting into the lapels of his suit, anchoring herself in the secret only they knew.

October 2020
Two Days After the Proposal

"I can't believe this baby has grown another two ounces since last week," Summer mused from the passenger seat, scrolling through the ultrasound images on her phone. They had just left the doctor's office, and she was still reeling from the magic of hearing their baby's heartbeat.

"I think I'm going to start calling them Watermelon instead of Blueberry." She rested her hand over her belly.

Echo smiled, but his usual easy banter was missing. His grip on the steering wheel tightened, his focus locked on the road ahead. Summer noticed immediately.

"E?" She turned to look at him glancing out the window as the streets blurred past. They weren't headed toward her favorite burger spot like they usually did after appointments. Instead, they were going in the opposite direction.

"Where are we going?" she asked, curiosity creeping into her voice.

"I just need to make a stop," Echo said, his tone unreadable.

Summer furrowed her brows. "Me and your baby are way too hungry for stops, Daddy," she teased, rubbing her belly for emphasis.

"Keep calling me Daddy if you want to," he said, throwing her a wink that sent a shiver down her spine.

Shaking her head, her curiosity deepened as they drove another five minutes in silence, then Echo pulled up in front of the Los Angeles Courthouse.

Summer's breath caught, her eyes darting from him to the building. "Echo?" she said. "What's going on?"

He shifted in his seat, turning toward her fully. His hands found hers, his touch easy and assured.

"I realized something," he started, his voice deep, laced with conviction. "Tradition isn't just about rules and protocols—it's about building something real, something lasting. I may not be traditional *like my father in most ways, but when it comes to us?"* His thumb traced gentle circles over her palm. *"The one thing I am traditional about is making sure our foundation is solid before our baby ever takes their first breath."*

Summer's lips parted, her pulse thudding like a drum against her ribs. The baby must have felt it, too, because a flurry of tiny kicks fluttered against her belly, as if expressing happiness for their parents.

Echo held her gaze, his own glistening with surety. *"I want to bring Baby Abara into this world as Mr. and Mrs. Abara."*

And just like that, the dam shattered. Tears streaked down her face before his words were even fully spoken. Her breathing turned uneven, chest rising in deep, trembling waves. One hand clutched his, the other pressed instinctively to her belly—cradling the life growing inside her.

"Summer," Echo said, his voice rough and raw with love. *"Will you marry me—right here, right now, today?"*

A watery laugh bubbled from her puffy lips as she gripped his face between her hands, memorizing the moment. *"Yes,"* she said. *"Yes, Echo Abara. I will marry you anytime, anywhere, anyplace."*

The tension drained from his body as he melted into her, his broad frame extended over the car's console, pressing against hers. Echo's fingers tangled in her hair, his other hand cradling the gentle curve of her belly. He pressed soft, lingering kisses across her face, as if marking her with his love, with his promise. Somehow, without him even realizing it, their future had already begun.

As the sun dipped low in the sky, casting a golden haze over Camp Quest, Summer and Echo stood together, hands clasped, hearts open, in the place where their story first began. This was their sacred sanctuary. The place that had held their secrets, where their love had been whispered into the wind, where they had lost and found each other all over again. Now, it would bear witness to their forever. Summer's eyes misted as she looked up at Echo—the boy who had been her best friend, her first love; the man who had become her home.

"This place has always been ours," she said. "Where we met, where *I* broke, and where we found our way back to each other. It's only right that we promise forever here."

Echo sighed, his grip tightening around hers. His thumb traced slow, deliberate circles over her skin, a silent reminder that he was here, and he wasn't going anywhere.

"I prayed we'd find our way back to each other," he admitted. "For a minute, I thought I'd lost you, but God had a different plan." He curled his lips into a small, knowing smile. "I will always find you, Sunshine, and I'll spend the rest of my life fighting for us."

Just like their love, their vows were fast and furious—no grand speeches, no rehearsed words, just real and unfiltered. Echo lifted her hand to his lips, kissing her palm, while his head rested against hers. When they were teenagers, it was a promise. Today, it was a vow.

"Come here, Sun," he whispered, pulling her into him, pressing his lips to hers in a kiss that held everything—the past, the present, and every moment yet to come.

The intimate crowd of family and friends erupted in cheers and happy tears, knowing they were witnessing a love reborn, a second chance written in the stars. As the guests transitioned to the reception space, the newly minted Abara family stayed behind, sharing a quiet moment beneath the vast evening sky. They sat one of the old wooden swings facing the lake, watching as the first stars peeked through the dusky haze. The same stars that had witnessed their first love.

Quest slept soundly against her daddy's chest, his rhythmic heartbeat lulling her into peaceful dreams. Summer sighed, burrowing deeper into his side, her head tucked against his shoulder, wrapped in *him*. Echo pressed a kiss to their daughter's tiny forehead, then let his lips linger against Summer's temple. His smile curved against her skin, memories flickering behind his eyes—splashing in the lake, sneaking snacks under the old oak tree, wordless dreams whispered beneath the stars. She sighed softly, and he knew she was remembering, too.

"You good, Sunshine?" Echo asked.

She tilted her chin, meeting his gaze, her eyes filled with something adoring, something unbreakable, something that would last forever.

"*Mm-hmm.*" She nestled even closer. "I'm happy to be home."

THE END

WWW.BLACKODYSSEY.NET

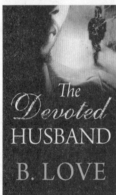
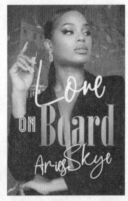